Oaken of the Winds

(The Sword for the Sky)

Robin John Morgan

First published (Paperback) in the UK in 2025 by Violet Circle Publishing.
Manchester, England, UK.

Print ISBN: 978-1-910299-48-7
Digital ISBN: 978-1-910299-49-4

British Library Cataloguing in Publication Data.
A catalogue record for this book is available from the British Library.
All paper used in the production of this book are sourced only from wood grown in
sustainable forests.

Human Authored. No A.I. Written Content contained within this book

www.violetcirclepublishing.co.uk

Most people do not really understand the true depth of what evil is.

They know that it is evil, but they cannot really see the full potential of that. Evil is not dark Ria, because people can look into the darkness.

True evil is brighter than the sun, and because of that, no one can look into it and see its full depth, and so people underestimate evil, and think they can overcome it, but they cannot.

(Evander of Animatre)

Chapter One

Andarla

Some wounds never heal. Some anger smoulders slowly. All hatred grows.

Undine... A race divided from all others, on the opposite side of a vast desert terrain. In legends of old, it was said they were the undying race, who were given an extended life by the powers of the earth (Elohim) on which they lived. In truth, for them, there is no death, for all they do, and all they achieve is made from the land that surrounds them. They see themselves as a part of it, nothing more, and so what we call death, they see as a return to their spirit, to once again become at one with everything, and they are absorbed back into all things.

They choose peace, and yet have learned over the ages to be aggressive fighters in defence of their race. Their appearance is not like most of the other races, and within that, they have at times had their moments where they were forced to protect their lands and people. They are slender, with a white skin, that holds a blueish translucence to it, which is the strongest in the light of a full moon. Their eyes are white or the palest of grey, which can be disturbing to those who have never encountered them, and yet, there is a kindness to their glance, a compassion to their demeanour. As the Leyarken discovered when they shared the land of the jungle terrains, they have a deep generosity, and an ease to share in all things.

They are a spiritual people, not in so much as they praise a god or deity, because they have none, their belief is within the land which sustains them. They met often with the Andalan, the philosophers and deep thinkers of the high mountains, and established good trade with them, as they bartered for the things they made, for access to some of the powerful healing herbs of the mountain passes.

They understand the land below their feet, in ways many others never would, and treat it with reverence, for they believe their life is part of the earth they tread. When the Summanu rose up, and attacked the Leyarken Jungle, slaughtering many of the towns and villages on the border, Shengara gathered the Undine. He divided his people, as half walked new paths over the mountains of Andalan, and into the Heliospan Desert, in search of a new land, then Shengara led a gorilla war in the jungles of their land, to push back the Summanu.

The war lasted forty eight years, and only ended when Shengara snuck into their camp in the night, found the Summanu leader, Balalaran, and cut off his head in front of his young son Balathral. The shock of the death of the Summanu leader, who was seen as a god on the earth, living as the voice of the god of the night thunder, Bharl, set back the Summanu. They withdrew, but swore to avenge the murder of their living god, and not rest until the Undine were wiped away forever.

Shengara knew his people were doomed, for the Summanu were a mighty people, who outnumbered the Undine a thousand to one. His only choice was to follow his instincts, and he gathered the rest of his clans, and with the blessings of Andalan, he led them across the Heliospan Desert, into the new lands of his people, and established the new land of, Undinalashka. In the common tongue, it was known as the land of the living dead.

The other tribes of the Leyarken race moved to the centre of the dense jungle, where there were steep hills and valleys, and built new dwellings. They then planted up all of the roads and tracks to hinder any who would try to conquer their lands again, sealing themselves into the heart of their lands. In a bid to help them, the Andalan spread rumours of spirits with animals' souls that stalked strangers who wandered into the jungles, catching them, so they were never seen again. Such was the fear created, when Balathral was proclaimed a new living god by the Summanu, his thoughts turned to seeking out the Undine, leaving the jungles of the Leyarken in peace. Balathral chose to send two armies, one to the lands of Keytan, east of the jungle, and one to Shodalt, west of the jungle, ensuring Andalan could not be aided, and interfere, as they had in the past.

Balathral had only one mission, to convert all the lands to the praise and wonder of Bharl, the god of the night time thunder, and those who refused were enslaved or slaughtered. Any Undine that was caught, were taken to Salanula the capital of the lands of Sumanula, and in front of all of the citizens, they were disembowelled in praise and sacrifice to Bharl.

Andalan, was the home of those who sought peace and knowledge. The Andalan were a race that took great time in contemplation, and looked to the sky and the gifts of their spiritual deity Nuada, ruler of the sky, and the four winds of wisdom and truth.

All of the chaos and war was watched over by the Andalan, as from their land, they looked out across the four corners of the wide plains, that contained the regions of Shodalt in the west, Keytan in the east, and across the Heliospan Desert to Undinalashka in the north. To the south, below them lay Leyarken, a wide land of dense green jungle, and beyond that, a barren expanse of hostile terrain, that led to the fertile lands of Sumanula, and a walled off land paved with gold, and rich in metals.

Andalan was a mountainous range of stone steps, that rose almost to the clouds A coarse region of soft rock, which had been carved out to create lavish temples and dwellings for what had once been race of mighty warriors, who sought knowledge and kept peace and stability across most of the continent. For the thirty years since the Summanu had been stopped by the Undine, the leader of the Andalan's, Andalyn, had managed to keep his people safe and at peace, but as he stood on the high cliffs and looked south, he could see the smoke rising to the west and the east, and he knew, soon, the peace would end.

Death was everywhere, across Keytan and Shodalt those slaughtered were left to rot, the streams were filled with the stench of death. In the last year, sickness and more death had touched every land, as the burial grounds of old, had filled and spilled over into the surrounding lands, such was the increase of those who had died in misery alone. The numbers had become so great, it had become habit, to burn them where they fell, as the gravediggers had become overwhelmed.

Andalyn stood alone, the lowering sun on his face, and the soft breeze flowing softly over the stones, and swirling the dust at his feet, his sharp hazel eyes fixed on the scene across the whole of the continent of Pangela, and he felt concern in his heart, as he spoke softly to himself.

"So like your father, filled with your own myths and lack of wisdom. You have it all Balathral, fertile lands, and the earth filled with minerals and precious metals, and yet, just like your father, your greed far outweighs your senses. How many have to die or be enslaved before you understand that no matter how much you slaughter, rape, torture, and sacrifice, that false god you worship, will never be sated?"

He gave a long sad sigh, and felt the warm arm come around him from behind, and looked down from his shoulder. Sarka stood and looked out from his side, her voice soft and caring.

"Watching will not halt him, smoke rises east and west, the day is drawing closer. Oatin is sleeping, he missed his father tonight, you know of what day this is?" Andalyn gave another long sigh.

"I do, I placed herbs on her marker, and asked Nuada to maintain a watch over her, for she resides in the lands of the winds now. I miss her too, and felt the need to be alone in remembrance of her, which is why I am here." She smiled a soft smile, knowing of the deep love of his mother, and her eyes lifted up to watch the side of his face as he watched out across the lands below.

"They will be here soon; the smoke of the burning draws closer. I know how you hate to leave her here without us, but my husband, since the Undine left and the illness came back, you must know, we have not enough left to defeat him?" Andalyn blinked as if coming out of his thoughts, his voice was quiet.

"The books of the sky and four winds speak of this time, and the one who will rise to finally end the lust of Balathral. I have dedicated my life to the study of all things surrounding the books, as did your parents, and even though the Summanu swarm like the seed bugs across the land devouring everything, in my heart there is hope. I feel that this land will remain held in the care of Nuada. I gave the order this morn to block all the paths down to the base of the mount." She was surprised.

"You have?" He gave a nod.

"It was not a decision taken lightly, for there are still many who flee the evil of Balathral, but he is closer. Now is the time to act, otherwise, within weeks, he will flow like a dust storm up the high passes, and everything will be lost. The landslides we have caused will block all the roads and make his job harder, it will not stop him, but it gives us time to prepare."

She took a deep breath, leaving the mountains had been spoken of many times over the years, and yet there was a part of her that had always hoped it would never happen.

"What about those who have fled here to us, they live below us in the basin, and have established themselves on the mixed lands of Ranblate, will we desert them?"

"We have spoken to their chieftains, and they have the same choice we have, but they fear the desert, and do not wish to try and cross it. They also fear the Undine, for they refused to help them, when the Undine reached out to them for support. I am afraid the curse of Shengara still holds a grip on the hearts of those who lead. It is up to them, and is their fate now, my place is to lead our people to safety and protect what the ancients bestowed to us, for we can never allow the Summanu to hold the power that was granted to us."

The mountains of Andalan ran around in a large arc shape, and nestled below, protected on three sides was the wide lands of Ranblate. It was not the best land, it was rocky and the soil was poor, but faced with the vast desert that stretched out to the north, it had become a mixed land of races, all gathered in one cause, seeking peace and protection, away from the Summanu.

In the last thirty years there had been many mixings of races, as people met and had children, which to a degree had united them as a race of mixtures. They had struggled and strived to create a new home, a place to belong, which to a degree had evolved from the melting pot of mixed thoughts and ideas into a new identity. It was a place outcasts found a home, and whilst it could be unruly, together they had found a new form of unity. The name came from many sources, linking those words meaning to "run" and those meaning "anger", and as the mix of the other languages merged. It helped create a new sense, built for those who fled in anger, and found sanctuary around the water that was abundant in the region, as it seeped from the high mountains behind them.

It was out of Andalyn's hands, he had consulted with many leaders, and they were determined to stay, and three months later Andalyn was right. The forces of Balathral used alchemy, and blew their way through the road blocks, and the first surge of forces approached the summit. It was a sad day, as the Andalan fled, leaving their homes and places of study and worship behind them. Led by an Undine guide named Pallum, they headed down the northern passes out of their lands towards the Heliospan Desert, their number dwindled after some fierce fighting to just six hundred survivors.

The wars over the years to support the Undine and the Leyarken, plus the illnesses that followed had taken its toll, and so with the last of the population of a once proud and intellectual race, the Andalan fled. It was their only chance for survival, as they now faced the same fate as the Undine, flee to safer lands, or be wiped out forever.

As the old and the young huddled together, and were shepherded down the pass, Andalyn and his best fighters held off the Summanu raiding party. Once the people arrived at the base, and several Undine stepped out of the dunes to greet them, Andalyn retreated slowly, giving Pallum the time to get his people out. The pass was narrow and not easy to navigate, which was why he had chosen it, as it slowed down the raiding party, and as he reached the base, he saw his wife with his son.

"Why are you still here? Go.... Go now and get away to safety." He slipped the bag off his back, and swung it towards her, on which a large wrapped bundle of cloth stuck out.

"Take these, now hurry... Go... I will be there soon, take our people to safety, Pallum will guide you. Sarka, you must protect Oatin, this is his tenth summer, soon we will know if he is marked with the signs of our ancestors. Now leave, take him to safety, for the Undine have sworn to protect us. Take my son, for in him is the love I hold in my heart, protect him Sarka, he is our future." With tears in her eyes, she threw herself onto him and held him tight.

"Hurry back to us, they will not follow us into the sands, so do not risk yourself, we need you, as you are light from the sky as sent by Nuada. Do not waste your life to hold a place that is no longer ours." She released him, and he gave her a nod, as behind him, his men took up defensive positions.

"Go... You are wasting time, you must take our son to safety, Nuada will watch over you."

As Sarka took the bag, which she knew contained the four books of the sky and four winds, as well as the ancient sword, she knew in her heart, it was the last time she would see him. Holding her son Oatin tight, she was the last of their people to leave accompanied by Pallum, he reached out his arm, his white eyes filled with a calmness, and nodded.

"He has his master to aid him, the voice from the sky will watch him. Now hurry, we must make up lost ground, your son must live, he is your future."

She understood, she knew the Undine were deeply instinctive, and like her, she knew that even though he had not said the words, Pallum knew Andalyn was now lost to them. It choked in the back of her throat as she ran, holding her son close with tears in her eyes, as her hatred of Balathral intensified tenfold.

The fear of the desert was justified, and the heat was overbearing, after several hours within the large dunes, they were exhausted and overheated. The Undine made shelters to shade them, and dug holes in certain parts of the sands to find water, as they wanted to save as much of the water they had brought with them, because they knew, hard times would come when water was scarce. When they were far enough away, they made their camp, and Pallum suggested they travel at night, as it would be cooler for them, and so began fifteen days of walking by night, and sheltering by day. Six hundred and twenty nine packed to leave, and when Sarka finally made it out of the desert, up through the rocks, onto green lands with rivers and trees, only four hundred and fifty seven had made it.

Their journey had taken them into the unknown, illness, exhaustion, lethal snakes and insects had taken many. Their progress had been slower than it should have been, as the elderly and the young struggled, and as many fell ill, they had to be carried, extending the journey and increasing the toll of the people of Andalan. They were led inland a little way, to a place that when spoken in the common tongue meant 'serenity,' and it was a beautiful oasis, filled with life. There was a large cool lake, with a river running into and out of it, lush green pastures, and an abundance of fruit, and fish to eat. It took another two weeks before the last soldiers of Andalyn arrived back, and much to the heartbreak of Sarka, her husband was carried into the open pasture on a stretcher by two Undine, he was dead.

Andalyn was struck in the final moments of their defence of the pass with a poisoned tipped arrow. He had made it into the desert, but under the growing heat, the poison acted quickly, and five days before making it through, he died, and was carried with honour out of the desert with his four surviving warriors.

As Balathral arrived believing all of the Andalan's were dead, and took over the temples of the Andalan, and set up alters to his god Bharl, the dawn rose, and the first light flooded out over Undinalashka. Sarka, with her ten year old son Oatin, held a burning torch to the wood, and ignited the pyre of Andalyn. She spoke her last words of grief, and honoured the man who had sacrificed everything for his people, and as all of them gathered, and wept on their knees, the Undine paid homage to a great man, as they chanted the walk of one world, into another.

Several days later, the Undine led Sarka and her people up the mountain side, to where a wide gorge divided the land. Pallum turned to her, as she looked out over the vast drop of a thousand feet, that was spanned with a wide wooden bridge.

"This was your husbands request of us. Across the gap, is a land made of similar rock, and is very much the same as your homeland. This land is separate from ours, and there are only two ways to reach it, this bridge, and on the far side, the sea. The bridge can be raised so no one can cross, your people will be safe here, this is your land, a gift from my grandfather and his people, to yours. Your husband is a man of high honour here, as he has done many acts of kindness for our people, and we will be kin to each other always because of it. The great lord of the Undine, Shengara, wishes this, and we have with his command created this for you. At the top of the rock, there is a place of worship, built by those long before us, with similar markings to those of your land, the dust of Andalyn already resides there, for he named this place Andarla." It was hard to speak, as her eyes filled with tears, Pallum nodded, he understood, and placed his hand on her arm.

"The little Oatin will thrive here, for this will also be the land of his father."

It was miraculous as they journeyed over the bridge and into the land, which had a wide plain of fertile soil, buildings made of wood, and some carved from the stone. High up above, Sarka placed the four books of the sky and winds into the ancient carved temple, and laid the old cloth wrapped sword beside the polished container of her husband's ashes, as the elders, which were now few in number, gave their thanks to Nuada. It was a time to recover, a time of rest for the Andalan people, and a time to settle in a new land now given the name of Andarla.

Pallum lived with many of his people amongst them, and taught them much of the plants and trees. Oatin grew strong and thrived, as he was taught by the elders and also by the Undine. Sarka settled with Pallum always at her side, and as the years past, they grew close, and two years after their arrival, Sarka joined with Pallum and gave birth to a daughter, who Pallum named Yandalla. In the common tongue, it carried the meaning of white flowers of the pasture.

Yandalla was pale, yet did not have the blueish tinge to her skin as her father did, she had bright green eyes, but like her father, her hair was as black at the darkness. She was a happy child, and very clever, and Oatin doted on her as they grew close, spending every waking moment together. For Sarka, it brought a joy to her heart that she had thought she would never feel again.

The Undine were a caring race, and had a calmness to them which Sarka felt had influenced her children. It was normal for Oatin to sit on the rocks and stare out to sea, as he contemplated his studies and lived a calm life. Yandalla was similar, she was very loving, quick to smile, and always on hand to help her mother. She had a natural instinct that sensed others feeling, and often in his times alone, she would come to Oatin, sit at his side, and hold his hand. Everyone else was unaware, but she sensed it and understood it, she knew of the pain hidden within him, as he remembered those final moments in the sand, as he left his father to fight. Yandalla sensed this, and would squeeze his hand, and with a soft voice, she would tell him.

"Oaken... Study hard, a day will come, when you will take us all back to your father's home. I know this, you have the winds inside you."

Across the sands, the storm clouds were gathering. Across the plains of Keytan, and the once green fertile lands of Shodalt, the large army of the Summanu were gathering. Fires burned, as swords and arrows were crafted, timber had been gathered, as long lines of carts with cages were being prepared. Balathral was once again preparing, and this time his mind was set firmly north, he had studied and planned for years, and he was almost ready to make his move. The thunder of Bharl would roar from the mountains, and call out doom to the Undine, as he stood alone on the top of the mount, and smiled.

"The time is almost here, I want those books and that sword, and when the Undine and Andalan are wiped away forever, I alone will hold all the power, Pangela will be all mine to rule as I and Bharl deem fit. The sky will soon light up to the screams and pleas of those vile freaks and abominations, and their blood will quench the thirst of the night sky forever."

Chapter Two

The Gift of Nuada

Oatin pulled up the boat, onto the beach, as he laughed with Shaylil and Penjin, they had caught a lot of fish, and were celebrating, when he heard his name called, and looked up. Yandalla was running down the beach from the rock face ladder, her eyes sparkling green, and she was wearing a big smile, as her long black hair flowed behind her.

"Oaken... Oaken!" She waved, and he smirked.

Yandalla had grown up, she was now fifteen summers, and soon approaching her sixteenth, and was clearly becoming a woman of great beauty. She came up smiling, her breathing in short bursts, and before he could speak, she burst with happiness.

"Oaken, Anna Pa has told me I can go with he and Anna Ma to the celebration, I am so happy, it has been long I have waited."

He smiled; he knew how much she had wanted to go last year, and he pulled her close and hugged her, as she snuggled into him, and he looked down at her, as she looked up, her pale face filled with happiness.

The celebration was a special ritual done by the Undine; to mark the moment they arrived in the new lands. It was in many ways a feast to mark the passing of another year of peace, and the Undine would travel from all across the region, to gather in front of the large meeting hall, to hear the address of their now quite old leader, Shengara. More importantly, for the young Undine, it was an important turning point of their lives, for attendance meant that they were all passing into adulthood. Yandalla would be regarded from that point onwards, a woman in the eyes of everyone.

There would be dancing and feasting, and a few tears from those old enough to remember the hard times they faced when they first arrived, having been forced from their lands. Oatin smiled, as he held her close, hugging her, as her happiness and excitement bubbled inside her.

"I am pleased for you Yandy," She looked up at him, he was much taller and wider these days, her face wore a frown, and her eyes furrowed.

"Yandalla!" He gave a chuckle, as he glanced down at her.

"Really, and yet Yandy is easy, it slips off my tongue." She pulled back with a giggle, and pointed at her mouth.

"You make funny, my tonk not always say your way." He smirked, and pointed inside her mouth.

"Not tonk, tongue, and I am Oatin, not Oaken." She smiled.

"I am Undine and Andalan, and yet some of your words form hard in my tonk, you knowing this Oaken."

She looked serious and he smiled, in all honesty, he loved the way she spoke, and her bright disposition. She was special to him, she had been at his side for most of his life, and at times when his thoughts grew dark, she had always come to him and sat quietly with him, holding his hand. It meant a great deal to him, she slipped out of his embrace and looked at the boat, Oatin turned, and lifted five large fish joined by a hook through their mouths.

"Here, take these to mother, we will be some time, as we have to return the boat and deliver the fish we caught." She took them, and lifted them up.

"You good, shame no wife yet."

With a high pitched screech, she spun around, and ran up the beach as the other two Undine laughed. He understood, the men of the Undine married young, he was twenty seven summers and had still not taken a wife. Few understood him, but he did not mind that, his mother had told him often that his father had been the same, he had waited until he was sure he was ready, and Oatin felt the same.

He said goodbye to the others, as he lifted his net bag of fish, and headed up the wooden ladder that led up to the first road of his compound. The other two pushed out the boat, they would sail around to their part of the island and take their share of the fish to the market. Oatin watched as he winched up the ladder, leaving the beach below, and ensuring no one could gain access to the island up the sheer cliff. He had fish to deliver, and no time to waste, so turned and walked onto the dusty worn path up the side of the rock.

Oatin stopped after a long walk up the steep paths towards the temple, where a row of huts had been built, and saw the old figure of Bettle sat in her chair, he smiled as he opened his net bag, slipped out, and handed her a large fresh fish.

"It was a good day to fish, and Nuada rewarded me." She took the fish with a smile.

"I watched as the winds guided you to the right place, I feel the sky noticed you and assisted you. Eliaston wishes to see you, I hope you have one for him too?" Oatin nodded.

"I have one for all of you, it is a thanks from my family to bless the elders." Bettle gave a low bow and smiled.

"It pleases me to see one so young embrace our customs, I feel your father would be very proud of you." He hoped so. He lifted the largest fish out of the bag, and then handed the bag to Bettle.

"I will take this large one to Master Eliaston, would you mind ensuring the others get theirs for me, I feel, I should not keep the master waiting?" She took it with a smile.

"You go, the master has waited for your return, fear not, all will be fed this night."

It took a little time to make his way up to the Master's House, which was cut from the soft rock face. To get there, he had to walk the whole length of the road, and then turn sharp right, and up the short incline to the opening of the temple space, where the master had his home. Oatin stopped just before the temple, and looked out across the sea, had Bettle been joking about the winds guiding him?

The sea was calm at the moment, reflecting the sun, it glistened as it headed towards the horizon, a vast expanse of shimmering blue, he had no idea why. He felt something stir within him whenever he thought of it, was it the peace and vast openness of space, he really did not know? Maybe it was just being at ease, rocked gently by the water as it had today when they entered the calm waters, no sound for miles, no children playing, or women talking as they worked, or men chiselling.

It was probably just that, with no others to break the silence, just like when he meditated in the caves for the master. He took a breath of sea air and turned, Master Eliaston was stood at his door watching, he lifted the fish, and walked towards him.

"Master, the catch was good, see the bounty I brought to share with all of you." The old man nodded, his smile partially lost below his white beard, and flapping white long hair.

"Come... Did I not say the sky would bless you if you honoured it?"

Oatin entered, and placed the fish in a large wooden bowl, as Eliaston brewed his usual tea of strong herbs, and walked them into the large room, where there were mats all over the floor for them to sit on. He was surprisingly nimble for his age, and had no problems sitting cross legged, as he held his beaker with both hands and sipped at his tea. Oatin sat sipping, he knew the old man like to calm things down and bring peace before speaking, and so waited patiently, and the old man nodded to himself, then looked up, and straight at Oatin.

"Did you do as I suggested today in the boat?" Oatin gave a nod.

"I did. We sailed to where no winds blew, and once the sheet was still on the poles, and closed my eyes and concentrated." The old master nodded, his voice almost a whisper.

"Then what happened?" Oatin gave a sigh.

"I felt at peace, it was quiet, and I could feel something within me, but I cannot explain what it was. Master, it was calming, and yet violent, I have not the right words for it."

"Tell me what happened, both inside and out." Oatin frowned.

"How do you mean? I told you, I felt something stir in me, and then I thought of the boat, and when I opened my eyes, the wind had lifted, the sheet was flapping, and we were moving again. I did not have long enough to focus. Master, we had to get the net out." The old man sipped his tea, and his eyes twinkled.

"What do you mean focus on it, the deed was done, you had no need to focus?" Oatin put his beaker down.

"What.... That makes no sense at all?" The old man gave a chuckle, and got up on his feet. He turned, and walked towards the oil dish, and the flickering wick within it.

"It makes far more sense than you realise, I was right, you truly are your father's son."

He lifted a taper, and began to walk slowly around the room. With the taper he had lit, he began to light more oil dishes. The light in the dim room began to brighten, as Oatin watched on puzzled, not really understanding the old master at all.

When all the oil dishes were lit, Oatin could see that he was surrounded by light, all them with a steady flame, the old master pulled the door too, and turned to Oatin.

"Stand in the centre of the room, and I want you to do exactly as you did in the boat today." It made little sense, but Oatin arose with a sigh, and stood still, closing his eyes. The soft voice of the master echoed in the sealed room.

"Think as you did, there is no wind here, and the sheets are still. Calm your mind, and bring up that feeling once again, but this time, focus on it so you understand its true feeling and true power."

Oatin took a deep breath, and held it as he calmed himself down, and tried to relax. It was harder stood on his feet; the boat had been more comfortable lay on the nets. His breathing slowed as he drifted inside his mind, and he began to feel the surge, almost as he had today. He felt his breath flow past his lips slowly, and the quiet voice of the old master spoke softly.

"Good, I feel it, now my young Andalan, I want you to place your hand slowly on your heart."

It felt like an odd request, as Oatin lifted his hand, and felt the warm skin of his hand, as it touched his chest through the open sleeveless long coat he wore. The voice spoke quietly.

"When I say so, I want you to push your arm quickly away from your chest, and as you do, open your eyes." Oatin nodded, and took a deep breath in, he was far more interested in the strong sensation growing within him, and the old master smiled to himself.

"Alright Oatin.... NOW!"

Oatin flung out his arm as his eyes snapped open, and just for a second in the light he saw a swirl of dust, and then almost all of the room went completely dark, as all the oil dishes blew out. The old master roared with laughter, lit from behind by a large glass lamp in which a single flame still flickered. Oatin was confused as he looked around in the darkness, smelling the smoke from the snuffed out wicks.

"What just happened?" The old man gave a chuckle; his face was still dark as he was stood in front of the lamp.

"That my boy, is why you are your father's son."

He had no understanding of what that meant. The old man turned, lifted a taper and lit it from the lamp, and then walked around the sealed room relighting all the oil dishes.

"Oatin, your father was blessed by Nuada, it is why he was the keeper of the four books. Many in his line have held the gifts bestowed on this race by the ancients many long years past. Sit, for we shall talk more."

With the room lit, Oatin sat feeling confused, as the old man sat down in front of him, and stroked his soft white beard as he spoke.

"Your father used the powers of the four winds in many battles, had it not been for him, all of the Undine would have been lost to all the lands. It is why they gave us a safe haven. Without him, there would be no land for them, or I will add your sister, who I see you have bonded deeply with. Tell me, what have you learned in your studies with the teachers of the temple about the four winds?"

Oatin lifted his beaker, his tea was almost cold, but he needed a moment as his mind spun, and he tried to make sense of what he was hearing. He looked down at the beaker in his hand and tried to focus his thoughts, because to be honest, he was so confused about what had happened, it was hard to find the right words.

"The four winds never meet, they flow around each other, over and through each other, for it is said on the few times they met head on, it brought devastation." The old master nodded.

"Which is true, unless of course the owner who wields the sword for the sky is present." Oatin sat back.

"How, how can a sword in the hand of man control the winds, it is not possible?" The old man chuckled, and his eyes sparkled brightly.

"My boy, you are both right and wrong at the same time." That made even less sense, and he gave a long sigh.

"How?" The old man leaned in, and patted his leg.

"If an ordinary man stood with a sword, and held it aloft, the odds are, he would die when the four winds met. But... If that man was not ordinary, and held up the sword for the sky, he would hold the wind together, and then, he could use it as he wished."

"Do you mean my father, because I have never seen him as an ordinary man? He was a giant in my eyes." Master Eliaston gave a soft smile below his white beard, and nodded softly. His voice was low and soft, and filled with reflection.

"He was, he was the most honourable man I have ever met, and a treasured friend. I have missed him dearly, and have no idea of how all this must have felt for you all these years. I cannot deny, I have watched you often, and I will admit, you remind me greatly of him. It is clear to me, that you have all his quality, including his gift of the four winds, sent down from the sky by Nuada. I will also add, you also lack in confidence as he did, for he doubted himself for many years." It took a moment for that to sink in, as the old man smiled at him.

"Are you saying, this man who was not ordinary was my father, and he had a gift to control the winds, and now I have it?" Eliaston leaned forward, and patted his leg again.

"That is exactly what I am saying, and I will add, that sword that lies at his side in the temple, now belongs to you, because my boy, in your hands it is a mighty powerful weapon. Your gifts have come just in time, for if the sky is right, storms are coming, and we will have need of it." Oatin let out a long breath, and dropped his head, and stared at the swept stone floor, and the old man chuckled quietly.

There was much to think about as darkness approached, and Oatin left the home of Master Eliaston. He walked slowly down the road, his mind filled, and something occurred to him and he stopped. To the side of the road was a rock, he thought of what the master had told him, was he right, did this naturally flow from him without him knowing? He was quite sure he was just plain and ordinary as every other Andalan was, he certainly did not feel gifted or powerful as his father had been.

Oatin looked at the stone, and pondered the idea, in a way it felt stupid, and he shook his head and smiled, it could not be that obvious. He lifted his hand and flicked his wrist.

"Get out of my way rock."

Oatin's heart almost stopped, as he watched the rock shudder, and then it rolled off the road and into the bushes. He felt his breath caught in his throat, how was that even possible? He looked at his hand, and then thought of the rock, and gently reached out his hand as if cupping the large rock in his mind, and flicked his wrist.

To his utter surprise, the leaves of the bush shook, and out from under it rolled the rock, he gasped, the master was right, and he was a little shaken. Blowing out wicks on oil dishes was one thing, but that was a pretty heavy rock. He swallowed hard, and decided to get home quickly, he needed to think about this, this was not at all normal.

He took the path onto the lower shelf above the meadows, where carved into the back of the rock face, under a wide overhang was his home. Yandalla was cooking with her mother on the fire when he entered, which was into a long room, carved from the rock face, with large sections removed to allow the light to flood in. Each large open space, which was well below the overhang, had shutters of thick strong woven split grass canes, some of which his mother had already closed.

The meal was boisterous, Yandalla was happy and very excited as she ate and talked none stop. For her, this was a huge deal, because for the first time in her life, she would be allowed to wear pants, like all the other women of the Undine. They were woven from a fine silken fabric, which had been bought by Pallum and stitched in secret by her mother. Oatin watched her, and then looked at his mother, they were so alike and yet different, both their eyes were green, and their skin pale, but his mother had long golden hair like his, and Yandalla's was black. Both had kind and gentle hearts, and were both loving and caring, something often noted to him by others, and he smiled, his mother was strong, he knew that.

Sarka had in the first days of arrival filled her husband's shoes, and carried all the responsibility of the people on her shoulders, the elders had been weakened, and even they looked to her for guidance. His mother had carried all of them, until the Andalan had grown strong enough to share the responsibility, and Oatin admired and respected her deeply, equally as much as he did his father. He had asked himself many times if Yandalla was as strong, and yet in many ways he did not want to find out. He had seen how his mother suffered under the strain, and his love for his sister was such, he never wanted her to suffer a similar fate.

When the meal was done, he was so lost in his thoughts, he walked outside and leaned against the wall. Watching the darkness, his mind filled with his conversation with Master Eliaston, and his strange moment with the rock. He was lost to his thoughts when he became aware of movement at his side, he blinked out of his thoughts as she smiled at him, and handed him a cup of tea.

"I saw the book on your bed, it is the first book of the winds, I am assuming the master has finally told you?" Oatin nodded, turned slightly, and faced his mother.

"So, it is all true, he was a master of the winds?" Sarka smiled.

"It is, and he was powerful, I saw him use it a few times, and he used it for great things." Oatin nodded.

"The master said the gift has been given to me, and yet I feel nothing, and have no idea how I would really use it if I felt it." Sarka walked towards a low wooden bench in front of him, and sat down holding her cup.

"I remember his mother telling me how much he doubted himself, and like you just now, at first, he had no understanding of how it worked or what it felt like. He once told me his father described it as just a flick of the mind, and it could be there, and would serve its purpose. Then in the blink of an eye, it would be gone, not unlike the wind." Oatin sipped his tea, it was hot.

"The master told me I should take his sword, and that does not feel right to me. It is his, he always had it in the bundle of his pack."

She understood how he felt, she had been glad when it was taken to the temple, for in the early days, it had been a bitter reminder of the loss she felt.

"Oatin, the last thing he did, and the last words he spoke, were to tell me to take the books and the sword, for one day you would need them. I understand it is hard to see that sword and not think of him, but I also feel that maybe you need to. One day my son the winds like with him, will flow to you. I saw him do great things to protect many with that sword, and a day may come when you also may be called upon to do something similar." Oatin nodded, and took a deep breath.

"You say great things; what did he do with it?" Sarka smiled, and he could see by the look in her eyes, it was a deep memory attached with some powerful emotions. Her voice was soft, caring and gentle.

"When the Undine fought the Summanu on the plains of Keytan, they were struggling, as more and more of the Summanu fighters poured onto the field. The Summanu greatly outnumber all of the races, it is why they are so powerful, or at least believe they are. Your father rode right into the centre of the battle holding his sword high above his head, and from nowhere, a huge gust of wind was sucked out of the sky and connected with his sword. I will never forget it, as I watched from the safety of the rock. He leaned back in his seat, and then with all of his power, he thrust the sword forward, and I have never seen anything like it in my life." She smiled as her eyes lifted to her son.

"Oh Oatin, he was such a powerful man, I was in awe of him, and so proud to be seen as his wife. The wind came out of the sky, and blasted the battlefield, and yet not one Undine was harmed, the dust swirled up around them blinding their enemies, and when it swept away, there was not a single Summanu to be seen. I am not sure anyone knows really what happened to them. Pallum was there on the field, he will tell you, even to this day he has no idea what happened to the man in front of him."

"If he was so powerful, then why did he not use it to defeat the Summanu when they attacked our homeland, why Mother, because if he had, he would still be with us?"

It had taken many years, but finally, the one question she always expected was asked. Sarka understood and stood up. She walked slowly over to her son, he was an adult, and yet there inside him was still that innocence he had as a child.

"Oatin, it was after that battle your father struggled with his gift. One night shortly after, he asked me, did he have the right to act like a god? Your father saved many lives that day, but in order to do that, he also took many, and it mattered to him. Your father was a powerful warrior without the sword, and he told me, it was more honourable to face a man, and beat him fairly using his own strength, rather than the sword. He believed the sword had its purpose, but taking thousands of human lives with a flick of a sword blade, should not be one of them. Oatin, I agreed with him, the Summanu are our enemy, they would wish to wipe us away and take the sword, but those soldiers, were also to a degree slaves for their master. Like us, they have children and wives, mothers and fathers, and that was something I had never considered until I spoke with your father, which is why I agreed with him." Oatin considered it, and gave a slight nod.

"I can understand that, it makes a lot of sense." She smiled at him.

"Oatin, my son, you have grown to be so like him, you are as tall and as powerful as he was, and I am so proud of you for the man you have become, for you are so like him. Listen to me my son, that sword is yours, and I say to you now, take it, and use it with your father's wisdom to protect our people. The way I see it, I would rather that sword was in the hands of the man stood before me, than the hand of that butcher and slaughterer of the innocent, Balathral. Believe me when I say, that is the reason we lost our home, he wants that sword, and he wants those books, and if he ever gets them, all of Pangela is doomed."

It was a lot for him to take in, never had he seen his mother talk with such passion, and yet, he knew that she talked reason and truth. It gave him a lot to think about, and as he watched her face, she smiled, and pulled him close and embraced him.

"Tomorrow you will meet with the elders, and they will guide you." She released him, and he took a deep breath.

"Master Eliaston talked to me today, and he said I will have to adopt a new name, was that true also for my father?" She nodded.

"When he first took the sword, he became Andalyn, before that he was Renlyn. Oatin, he had a say, and was given the choice of which name he would use. He chose one that reflected his people, half his name was his people, and half the man he was before. That is something you will have to think about, but they will listen to you and be considerate to what title you use." In a way it came as a relief, it had given him great thought, and he felt relieved to know that he would have some form of input.

His mother needed to retire, and he wished to stay out in the air for a while. As he looked up towards the stars, she bid him goodnight, and left him alone with his thoughts. He paced the ledge, and looked out over the land of his people, he gave a sigh.

"Am I ready for this; how can any man live up to his reputation and name?”

“Do you not think he did not think the same, as did his father before him?” Oatin turned his head, to see Pallum stood by the door, he turned.

“It is hard for me to believe, for he was such a man of power. If I lift that sword, they will look at me the same way, and I do not feel I can match him.” Pallum gave a nod, and walked slowly towards him.

“I knew him well; he was a great friend to me and a saviour to my people. I talked often with him, for I admired the way his mind worked, not because he knew a great deal, but because like the dirt I walk upon, his responses were also simple. Your father did not cloud things, he took a simple path, and in that he gained the greatest wisdom. Oatin, no one expects you to be your father, for the truth is, no matter how hard you may try, it is something you can never achieve.” He shrugged as he watched Pallum.

“I know I cannot be like him; I am not sure any man can.” Pallum smiled, his bright white eyes almost luminous in the darkness.

“If I may offer you some advice? It is good you understand that, and I would say to you, be as simple as that which is before your feet, for within that is a power far greater than any man.” Oatin shook his head.

“I am not sure I understand you.” Pallum nodded, as he stood close to him.

“Look around you, and see all that has risen from the ground, do you think a seed worries when it is asleep in the dirt? It doesn’t, it cares not that it fell from the largest tree, and the reason for that is it knows that within time, a day will come when it is as tall as any tree that surrounds it.” Oatin understood.

“Like me, my father had to grow and understand his place, and in time, he became the man he was.” Pallum gave him a smile.

“I believe that day will come, for as I said, I knew your father well, and already I see a smaller version of him, but like him, you must learn. He read the four books often, and once told me, each time he read the books, he discovered something new he had not seen before. I believe that is the path all those who have walked before have taken. Oatin, consider my words, and rest, for tomorrow will be a day that will live in your mind for the rest of your life. Go, rest, and think on all you have learned this night." Pallum lifted a large white hand to his shoulder and gave it a squeeze.

"My greatest joy, has been watching the son of my friend grow into a man of honour, I am sure, was he here now, he would not argue with me."

As he walked to his room, he felt a little of the pressure he had felt lift slightly. Once again in his life, his mother and Pallum had given him much to think about. He lay in the dark with his eyes closed, and his mind brought back so many memories, as his father laughed and showed him things, or his mother sat holding his hand and talking to him of his father. For most of his life, Pallum had been there, teaching him the foods of the wild, how to fish, or even how to use a sword with skill. In many ways, he had already been trained for this moment in his life, and it felt comforting to know, that no matter what he faced, somewhere inside him was the answer. He awoke with a start, and sat up rubbing his eyes, there was noise in the house, it was Yandalla. She was very excited, as her mother helped dress and prepare her in her room.

This morning, he had to remain focused, and was only allowed water or bread, as later there would be the ceremony with the elders. He sat quietly outside until everyone was ready, Yandalla came first and stood with a large smile, she looked beautiful, with her new tight silken clothes, and flowers in her hair. Her mother had used powdered minerals to darken around her eyes, and it was hard to believe, she looked so much older now, she giggled as he pulled her into a hug.

"Have fun, and do not eat too much, it will spoil the dancing." She reached up on her tiptoes and kissed his cheek.

"I will be fine, and will tell you all about it when we get back tomorrow. I am not sure what, but I will find something I can bring back to give to you, so you will always remember this moment."

"Good, enjoy yourself little sister, and if you get to talk to Shengara, ask him to fix your tonk, so you will finally get my name right." He chuckled, as she smiled, and slapped his shoulder.

"Oaken, sounds nicer, and to me you will always be Oaken, for there is only Oaken and he is my brother." He nodded.

"Alright then, go on, have fun, and stay close to Pallum and mother." She smiled.

"I will."

She turned, and skipped across the path to where Pallum stood holding three horses, he lifted her up and she sat smiling in the sun, the bright flowers in her hair gleaming in the sunlight as she waved. He watched them leave, and then made his way slowly up the road towards the temple, feeling that today his fate would change, as he took the sword of his father.

When he entered the temple, he felt nervous, but he had no idea why. Master Eliaston met him, and they sat alone in the temple, where the sword lay before him, and meditated. The rest of the council then joined him, and for over two hours he recited the passages and prayers from the first two books of the winds. That was followed with the burning of incense, and more prayers, followed by another hour of meditation. In the final moments of the long day on his knees, he was anointed with dabs of a fragrant oil, and then Master Eliaston in his ceremonial robes stood up, lifted the sword still it its wrappings, and turned to face him.

"Oatin, son of Andalyn and Sarka, do you swear before the four books that you will defend and protect all of the people of Andalan, and the territories that surround it?" He took a deep breath, this all felt so serious, and so final. His head nodded slightly.

"I swear it." The old master smiled.

"The connection this sword brings will bring mighty aid to your cause, for it is the gift of Nuada. Will you use it only in need, and with great wisdom to the benefit of all?" He inhaled, his heart was beating fast, even though he had been sat calmly all day, his eyes viewed the sword, still wrapped in green cloth, his voice was soft.

"I will."

"What name will you take from this day forth, in defence of your people?" Oatin smiled, and looked up at the master. It was strange, but after a night of doubt, this morning it had come to him, and it was such a simple solution.

"I choose Oaken... Oaken of the four winds." The master gave him a big smile, and leaned forward to place the wrapped sword in his hands.

"So shall it be known... Arise a new man, arise Oakenwind of Andalan."

Holding the sword tight, he stood up, and Master Eliaston bowed with all of the council. It was done, the ceremony had been completed, and it was nowhere near as bad as he thought it would be. Master Eliaston gripped his shoulders with a smile.

"A name that is your true self, I feel you picked the perfect name." Oaken gave a slight chuckle.

"My sister told me this morning, it is who I truly am, and in a strange sort of way, I think she is right. Pallum told me, my father always tried to find the simplest of solutions, so all would understand, and when I thought of it, Oaken was right, it was simple, but to Yandalla that is who I truly am." He smiled.

"Your sister has deep wisdom, for I also believe that is who you are. All will know you have been blessed by us and the four winds have chosen you, now go into the world, and be the man you were meant to be."

Gently taking his shoulders, he turned him around, and then pushed him in the base of his back, and Oaken took a step forward, and then with a deep breath, he walked from the temple and into the light of the day, where a feast with the elders awaited him.

It felt strange in a way, because holding the sword he felt different, he had no idea of the power that had begun to build within him. Like his father before him, his mind would sharpen, his skills increase, and his ability to understand and show care would be greatly enhanced, for the true powers of the four winds, as written in the four books of the sky, would now be revealed.

The afternoon passed slowly sat on mats before a low table eating and talking, and yet even though he loved to hear the tales of his father with the council on Andalan, there in the back of his mind, he felt something building. The day passed in the bright sunlight, and with time, the elders grew weary and retreated into the shade. Oaken got up lost in thought, he had much to learn, and he felt apprehensive, as he walked alone to the edge of the high rock.

He stood on the edge of the high temple and looked down at the lands of his people, and then out across Undinalashka, somewhere out there, his sister would be having the time of her life. He had promised to meet them on the road in the morning, so for now, after the feast with the master, the rest of his day was free. He pulled at the new green cord of the sword, and slipped it over his head so the sword hung down his back, like he had seen his father do many times growing up, and thinking of his sister, with a smile, he turned towards the temple.

The sky across the mountains was dark in the distant south, and he hoped the rain would hold off, at least long enough for his sister to enjoy herself.

Chapter Three
A Celebration to Remember

In a large open square surrounded by trees, on its northern
most side, was a huge temple like building made of wood, that
was highly decorated with carvings of the life and the world
that surrounded the Undine. The Undine were a simple living
people, and most of their region was basic and very understated,
as they lived at ease, with the land that grew around them. The
large meeting hall of Shengara, was the only decorated building
in Undinalashka, and it was set in the very centre of the region.
The meeting hall was the focal point of the whole race, and once
a year, they gathered in celebration of their settling in their new
land.

There was a mighty feast, as food was carried in from all over
the region, and on the huge long lawn, families gathered in large
circles, all sharing food and reacquainting with friends they had
not seen for a while. Drums beat, flutes played, and the whole
atmosphere was one of happiness, conversations, and a great deal
of mirth and laughter.

For Yandalla, this was to be the highlight of her year, and Sarka
smiled, as she watched her daughter with her friend Shellena
excitedly talking, and pointing things out to each other. Their
excitement was obvious, as small groups danced and sang to the
rhythm of the drums, and Yandalla watched with a fixed excited
smile. Pallum walked with a proud smile, nodding to people who
bowed politely to him, and walked with great authority towards
the hall, and a meeting with his grandfather.

At the top of the four steps that led up to the large temple,
Shengara smiled as he saw his grandson and Sarka, with Yandalla
slightly to their side, he looked down as Pallum approached, and
gave a bow to his grandfather.

"My leader and master, I am happy to see you so well."

Shengara was tall, his hair dark grey with age, his skin was the
same bluish white, with a line of darkened blue, the scar of his

battles down the side of his wrinkled cheek. He was stern looking, and yet kindly in his manner, as he stood wearing the dark black robes of the race's senior, tied with a green belt of woven silks. On his hip was a mighty sword, a gift given him by Andalyn's father, and was the sword he defeated Balathral's father with. His smile was wide as he looked upon his kin, and his voice was deep with authority.

"Grandson, you grow in stature, I feel the power of a good woman and her daughter have strengthened you, although, I see your daughter is far too distracted by the events of the day to notice her frail old great grandfather before her."

Shellena suddenly realised who was speaking, and nudged the happily chatting Yandalla. She stopped and frowned, and then turned, and noticed who was stood before her on the steps, and her face broke into a wide smile. Shengara opened his arms wide.

"I have missed you little meadow flower."

He came down the steps, as she happily leapt into his arms, he was the most powerful of all the Undine, and yet as he swept Yandalla into his arms, you would not have thought it, as he hugged her hard.

"Great Grandfather!"

"You have grown such a size since I last saw you." His smile said everything as he hugged her, and Sarka smiled, for there was such love in his eyes.

"Tell me young Yandalla, how does it feel to finally be old enough to be presented to our people?" She took a huge breath.

"Great Grandfather, I am so happy, and excited, I have never seen such beauty in clothes, and the food was delightful. I just wish Oaken could come, he would love this so much." His eyes moved to Pallum, who gave a slight nod.

"He will be here later; he has something far more important at the temple." Shengara nodded, he understood and lowered Yandalla with a smile.

"Being presented at your first celebration is very important young flower, for this day marks your first rite as a woman of the Undine. All will see you and know of you, for you will have the respect of the mother who raised you, heaped upon you." She smiled, and glanced at her mother.

"Those would be big feet to wear Great Grandfather." He gave a roaring laugh, as his eyes moved to Sarka.

"Indeed, for your mother has great favour with our people, she is held in the highest regard by all of us. I would say young flower, out of the all the women that walk our lands, you have the best example to follow." Yandalla smiled as she looked at her mother.

"I know that Great Grandfather, I see the honour she is paid by everyone." He smiled and gave a nod, then lifted his arms.

"TO DANCE, IS TO FEEL JOY!"

He stepped down off the steps, and took Yandalla by the hand, and gave her a slight pull forward. She panicked, as he walked forward, with her a step behind him, onto the large space of green grass. The Undine parted, as Yandalla walked briskly at his side. He stopped and looked around at the Undine who all watched on, he shrugged.

"This is a celebration, and my granddaughter's first time, can an old master not enjoy himself? We are here to celebrate, so let us all enjoy it."

He swung around, bowed to Yandalla, who giggled with nerves, as she gave a regal bow back, and the music started. All of the Undine cheered, and then joined in, as Shengara, the fiercest warlord of the Undine race, danced with care, around his smiling and very happy granddaughter. Pallum and Sarka stood watching, as in the middle of the huge expanse of grass, surrounded by a wide empty circle, they watched their daughter, move with beauty and grace, as she danced with great skill, as taught her by her mother.

The Undine danced and laughed, as the joy echoed all across the field. Yandalla was having the time of her life, as young Undine men were greatly drawn to her, and respectfully asked her to dance. Shengara stood back, once again at the top of the steps with his grandson, and watched on.

"Your daughter is very beautiful, and her green eyes will attract a lot of attention, I feel there are many young warriors quite smitten with her." Pallum smiled.

"We are aware, and there are many eyes and ears to protect her should she need it, and do not forget her brother. I fear a few of our warriors may find the task of courtship hard with a younger version of Andalyn as her protector." Shengara nodded.

"I have heard they are very close, that pleases me, for many have told me he is a man of the highest honour. It cannot have been easy to raise the son of your friend, and seeing him in a younger version beside you each day." Pallum smiled.

"Andalyn as you know, I considered kin to me, he was like a brother, I admired and looked up to him. I see Oatin and Yandalla together, and I am greatly reminded of us as young men, for the bond between them is the same. It is easy, and at times it is hard to see him become his father, and on those days, I light the smoulder sticks, and think of him with great honour." Shengara nodded.

"I hear he has accepted his fate, it is a good thing, what name will he take?" Pallum smiled, and turned to his grandfather.

"I got word a little earlier, he has chosen to be Oaken of the four winds. I spoke with him last night, as did his mother, and we told him, pick something that shows who you are, and keep it simple. We both feel his choice is the perfect one." Shengara smiled.

"Many Undines struggle with the common language, and yet, he chooses a name only his sister could give him in her struggle with his ways of speaking. I find that a good omen, for it is the love of that beautiful young Undine, that will drive him to achieve great things. Oakenwind, it is a good name, it has the grit of the land within it, and carries great power with it."

High above the Andalan settlement, within the temple, Master Eliaston rolled up the grass mats, and stacked them neatly in the corner. He shuffled along with his arms full, as the smoke swirled into the air on each side of the three large stone steps that led up to the huge wall, draped with a tapestry depicting the regal figure of Nuada.

On the top step, four wooden stands stood in a row, three containing the sacred books of the sky. Each book contained the wisdom of the Andalan, and were placed in order, the books of air, then earth, spirit was missing as Oaken had it, and the final book of fire. It was quiet and calm as Eliaston walked back to the final mat, and then he noticed something in the corner of his eye, turned, and stood frozen as he viewed the scene.

There was no breeze, no wind, and the book of fire had opened, and its pages were slowly sliding up, then falling onto the next page, almost as if some invisible entity was searching through it, page by page. The old master turned his head, and viewed the outside, but the trees were still, nothing was moving at all, and yet he could feel a power growing in the air around him. He turned back to face the books, and slowly walked towards the base of the steps, as his eyes fixed on the figure depicted in the tapestry.

"My supreme elemental Nuada, what is it you seek?"

Behind him in the far off distance the thunder rumbled. The page stopped and fell flat to the book. Eliaston frowned, and then took a step forward onto the steps, he lifted his leg and stood on the second step, as the page came into view. The gasp left his mouth, his head snapped up to the tapestry, of a blurred figure within a bright light.

"NO!" The book lay open on the chapter, 'The Storm of Death.'

All the doors opened, and the wind rushed in, as the eyes of the old master, rolled back into his head. He shuddered and jerked, and fell back, landing flat on the mat on the floor. His body twitched and spasmed, as in his head, pictures flowed, and a loud ethereal voice boomed.

"PREPARE THE SWORD!"

Eliaston lay back on the floor, his mind alive, as images of screaming Undine, cages and smoke flowed through his thoughts. He saw Balathral with a blood covered face, scream with laughter, as he swiped a huge sword down, taking the head clean off a terrified and frightened Undine female. Her head fell, rolling down the blood covered steps, where below hundreds of other Undine heads lay littered.

Eliaston wailed in pain, caught in his vision, feeling the sorrow and the pain of the people of the Undine, and then the image that terrified him the most came into his thoughts. Metal bars on a wagon, and two pale hands holding them. The cage was filled and packed with Undine, but what frightened him the most, were the two green terrified eyes that looked out filled with pain from behind them. Eliaston jerked on the floor, and his eyes snapped open, he was shaking and sweating as the urgency swept through him, his throat dry and his voice low.

"Yandalla, Balathral is going to kill Yandalla, I have to get

Oaken."

Shengara stood, and proudly watched the celebration, the time for his speech would soon be upon him. At his side stood Pallum and Sarka, and in the midst of the whole event, Yandalla and Shellena danced with two fine, good looking men. As Shengara watched on, he noticed in the distance behind the tall trees, a column of smoke rising into the sky, and he frowned.

"Who is lighting fires, no fire should be burned on this day?"

As he spoke, there was a terrified scream, and he looked down. The dancers parted as a foaming sweating horse came galloping onto the field, and ploughed through the dancers, scattering them either side of the bolting horse. Sat leaning forward, with an arrow sticking out of his back, was an Undine warrior. It took a moment to fully understand, as the horse charged towards them, the warrior looked up.

"MASTER SHENGARA, WE ARE UNDER ATTA...."

From nowhere, another arrow whizzed through the air, and hit him right between the shoulder blades, he gasped, not able to finish, fell backwards onto the horse, and then crashed to the ground. Screams erupted, as panic engulfed the Undine, Shengara felt his rage rise, and took a pace forward, Pallum grabbed his sleeve and pulled back.

"Wait!"

As the Undine scattered in panic, of which Yandalla and her friend got swept in the surge, a wide row of Summanu soldiers appeared across the far bottom of the field. There were screams to each side, as more Summanu appeared, and instantly the Undine men drew out their weapons.

Penjin appeared holding his sword, and grabbed onto Yandalla's arm, he pulled her slowly behind him.

"Stay close, tell your friend."

Yandalla was shaking, her mother and father were at the other end of the field, and too far for her to get to them. She took hold of Shellena's hand, as a rider in a long red cloak on a white horse rode slowly down the field towards Shengara. Penjin holding up his sword, side stepped, Yandalla gripped the back of his jacket, and moved with him, she understood he was trying to move her slowly towards her parents, his voice was soft and reassuring.

"You are Undine, do not be afraid, I will protect you, for you are the sister of my best friend." Her lips were trembling.

"Penjin, I am scared."

"I know... Be strong, be like your mother."

Behind her, holding her hand fast, Shellena was shaking, they had heard much of the Summanu, but had never seen them, and now they had, the fear was coursing through them. The Undine men slowly pushed their families behind them, and nudged them back towards Shengara, as a line of armed Undine formed a line down each side of the wide gap.

Shengara lifted a hand as the lone rider came towards him. Either side of the field, Undine warriors had their swords drawn, Shengara had given the signal to hold, and so they all waited, their hatred obvious, and their tenseness showing. The rider approached slowly, and stopped with a smirk as he looked up at Shengara, and then slid from his horse, and dropped to the ground with a thump.

The air was tense, as Shengara looked upon him with hate, the man appeared unaffected, he walked to within four feet of the base of the steps and stopped. His eyes met Shengara's as he lifted them. His voice was almost casual, almost as if he did not care that he was addressing the legendary warlord of the Undine.

"The most revered Balathral, wishes me to convey his respects to you, Lord of the Undine. He has fifty thousand men swarming your boarders as we speak, your little empire here is over, as it now belongs to the highest of Gods, Bharl." Shengara sneered.

"Bring this Bharl to me and I will slit his throat, this is the land of the Undine, there is no god who can take this land. Speak your twisted words and then leave, before I have your men's throats cut." The Summanu gave a snort.

"This is no longer your say, Shengara, this land is ours, and I am here at the express request of our lord and God in this world, Balathral. Your choices are limited, your people will surrender and convert to the worship of Bharl, or they will die. What say you now?"

Shengara's eyes burned white hot with hate, before the Summanu could blink, and considering his great age, he shot down the steps at speed.

"THIS!"

Out came his sword, it swept into the air, and with one massive swipe, the head of the Summanu lifted spinning into the air, as the rage of Shengara roared into a war cry. The Undine roared with him, and there was a huge clash, as the fighters of the Undine showed no mercy or fear, as they stormed into the Summanu.

Undine and Summanu poured onto the large field, and the bloody fight for the land began, and in the midst, the women of Undine, lifted weapons from the fallen and waded in beside their men, with wild screams of hate. More soldiers poured onto the field, and after years of peace, and on their most sacred day, the Undine had made their greatest mistake, they had let down their guard to celebrate, and Balathral had taken advantage of it.

Two routes had been scouted through the desert, one to the west and one to the east. For years his men had died plotting their way through laying mats of woven reeds to create a stable surface to march on, and transport supply carts. Arriving at the most outward parts of the territory, they had gathered in number and sent out raiding parties. Quietly in the night, they slipped into the camps, and overcame the forward defences. By the time the Undine realised, it was too late, and Summanu were pouring in by the thousand across the border out of the desert.

In the midst of the battle, still holding hands and trying to follow Penjin, who was cutting his way through with a fierce and determined grimace to his face, Yandalla, holding a long knife, tried her best to help, stabbing at those who tried to harm Penjin. She was terrified, all she wanted was to be with her mother and father, and her thoughts were with Penjin as she tried to help. Bodies were falling all around her, and the screams of those wounded and in pain, were deafening.

Shengara waded into the fight with Pallum and Sarka at his side, as they cut down the Summanu fighting their people. It was chaos, as more and more people packed onto the field, and Shengara pulled women and children free, and pushed them behind him, his grunts and roars loud in his defiance against the Summanu. Sarka yanked at women, pulling them free, yelling and shouting.

"GET THE CHILDREN TO THE HIGH GROUND!"

Her greatest hope, was knowing her son was up on the rock, and the bridge could be pulled up to give safety and protection to all. She cut her way through, with a sword from a dead Undine guard, her eyes constantly scanning the crowd before her, desperately searching to see if she could see Yandalla. Her fear was at maximum, knowing her child was here somewhere, and she desperately needed to find her.

Yandalla plunged the knife into a leg of a Summanu, and he wailed out in pain, Penjin was struggling, and he needed help. As the soldier screamed out in pain, without even thinking, her instincts kicked in, and just as her father had taught her, her arm came up at speed, and the knife swept past his throat, opening it up, and he fell backwards. Still holding her hand, Shellena inspired by Yandalla, swept her knife across those fighting others, as the group of three protected each other, and pushed their way through up the edge of the field, towards the meeting hall, where her mother fought with her father.

The noise was deafening, but the Undine under the guidance of Shengara, were managing to form a long line, and were trying to push back against the swarm of Summanu, who were pouring onto the base of the field. Pallum was ten feet from Shengara, shouting his orders, as the line came together, along the side of the field. Summanu were dragging women kicking and screaming out of the fight, and dragging them off. Sarka had seen this before, and it was her greatest fear, they were here for slaves, and would take as many as they could. She knew of the vile horror's women were subjected to under the slave camps of Balathral, and her anger intensified, as she strove to cut her way through and find her daughter.

A huge soldier loomed up in front of them, and with a crashing blow, Shellena was hit hard in the face, and went sprawling backwards. Yandalla felt the tug on her arm and over balanced, she let go of Penjin, as she lost control, and he turned to look back. Yandalla screamed with all her might, as she saw the long silver blade cut right through Penjin, as she hit the floor hard, and smacked her head on something, and her eyes flashed with stars.

Not quite understanding what had happened, she felt herself dragged into the air, and her arms flailed outwards dropping the knife. She blinked, and her eyes focused again, and as she looked up, twenty paces away, her eyes met her mothers. Sarka saw her daughter lifted up onto a Summanu soldiers' shoulder, and as their eyes met, her greatest fears were realised, and she screamed out, Yandalla saw her, and reached out her arms, and screamed back.

"Ca yan Anna Ma!" She called to her mother in her father's tongue.

The blow as she wriggled and fought, came from nowhere, and as she felt the impact to her face, her last image frozen into her eyes was her screaming mother, and then everything went black.

Sarka was dragged screaming backwards, as the Undine closed ranks, her husband pulled at her, and she looked into his eyes, the noise was ear splitting, and she was so lost in her pain she could hardly hear him shouting at her.

"Get the women and children out of here and up to safety, Sarka, I am going after our daughter!" He had ten men with him and they all looked serious, and gave her a nod, and her mind cleared a little. Pallum dragged her into his arms and squeezed her hard.

"Sarka, I love you; do you hear me, I love you, and I need you to live so I can get Yandalla back?" She took a breath, and folded her arms around him.

"I love you too, save her Pallum, save our daughter."

He pulled back, and his face looked fierce, he was covered in blood, and his eyes shone whiter than they ever had.

"Sarka, we need to protect the people, and save as many as we can. Take the women and the children up to the high pass, raise the bridge, and talk to Oaken, we need his sword. There are too many, we need to save what we can. I will bring our daughter back; this is my truth to you." She swallowed hard, as her senses returned, and gave a nod as he released her.

"I will save your people, or at least as many as I can, that is my truth to you, now hurry, she went that way, help her."

Pallum gave a nod, and with his men, he ran from the field.

Sarka turned feeling dazed, behind her, a line of Undine forty deep had formed a wide row across the field, and were pushing the Summanu back. As they did, women and young boys and girls were dragged from the fight, and pushed behind them, the men of the Undine were protecting their families, as they fought with a great rage and determination.

Shengara was walking around, a huge slice down his arm, as he barked out his orders. Undine were pouring into the last defence, and Sarka understood him, behind the meeting hall was the only road up to the high pass. She was starting to get the picture, this was no longer about winning, it was about protecting what little remained. Shengara was clever, and was sending his units of archers up to line the pass, it was narrow, and would be hard for the Summanu to swarm it. It is what Andalyn had done, and because of that, his people had lived. As Sarka viewed the carnage and the fallen, she thought of Andalyn, and his voice echoed in her memory.

"Sarka, this is no longer about protecting a place that is simply rocks and stone, this is now about saving the people. They are the true heart of this place; it is their blood that makes this place a home. As long as one Andalan lives, our race can never die, and so now, the fight is to live." He was such a wise man, and she missed him, he really was the heart of his people.

Oaken came out of his house carved out of the rock face, and walked to the edge of the rock to look out over Undinalashka. Far below him smoke rose into the air, and he frowned, not understanding why.

"I thought fires were not allowed today?"

Fires were burning all over the land for as far as the eye could see, and he felt a strange feeling building inside him. He was not sure what it was, but without knowing why, he knew something was wrong. His eyes moved to the lower slopes, where down below he knew his family were gathered. There was no smoke, but he knew, something was most definitely not right, his words were quiet, and spoken softly, almost by instinct.

"Yandalla!"

Oaken turned, and as he did, he saw the old figure of Eliaston gasping in air, he looked red in the face, and was bent forward slightly. Oaken hurried along the front of his home, and onto the expanding rock that led to the road.

"Master... What is wrong?" The old man looked up and smiled, as he gasped in air, and patted his chest.

"Oaken, your sword is needed, a dark storm has arrived, and its name is Bharl." He took another huge intake of air, and up righted himself.

"The Undine are in great danger, I have seen things, terrible things brought to me by Nuada. Go to the bridge, sound the alarm, this place is about to fill up, there is nowhere else for them to run." Oaken nodded.

"Are you alright, can I get you something?" The old man shook his head.

"Do not worry about me, get to the bridge, I fear, soon, you will be the only thing to protect these people. Go... Leave me here, I will be fine, many suns have risen since I last ran, I need the winds back in me." Oaken nodded, and patted his shoulder.

"Fear not, I will help them."

Pallum strode fast, then turned, and Shaylil almost walked into him.

"Where do you think you are going?" Shaylil frowned.

"With you." Pallum shook his head.

"Shaylil, we will need Nutriana. Our people are heading up the pass, when the bridge is raised, there will be no way out. Oatin will need to come down to me, grab the boats, and take them to the beach, and let Nutriana know what has happened here, we will be needing her help." Shaylil looked at the large Undine men, and they nodded, Pallum lifted his arm to his shoulder.

"You fought with great honour today, and became a true Undine, but in this moment, it is not your skill with a sword I need, it is your skill on water." Shaylil understood, and gave a nod as he looked at the grim face of Pallum.

"Fight well... All of you, but stay safe and protect each other, fear not, the boats will be there." Pallum smiled.

"The same to you, young warrior, keep your back low, and move with speed, but no sound to be made. Many lives will depend on those boats, and one of them is my daughters." Shaylil understood.

"It will be done, bring her back safe."

Pallum smiled, and with his nine other warriors, he turned, and moved with great speed through the trees. Shaylil turned, took a quick look around, and then headed in the direction that would take him to where the boats were dragged up onto the land. From every direction, came the sounds of fierce fighting. Undinalaska was about to fall to the glory of Bharl, and he had to do all he could to help. Bent low, he ran faster than he ever had, Yandalla was at risk, and he knew Oatin would come soon.

Chapter Four

Rescue Plans

Oaken stood on the bridge, as all around him, men helped the weeping and crying Undine across and into their separated land. Many were wounded and injured, and all of the elders had come down from the high temple, and were attending to them, it all felt like a scene of chaos, and he felt helpless.

The pass was full, as the remaining Undine, protected by their warriors, fighting hard to keep the path open and secure. Archers lined the rocks either side, shooting volleys of arrows into the swarming mass of the Summanu. At the back of the line, he could see his mother hurrying on the young and weak, as Shengara with his arm heavily bandaged, stood on the rocks and gave his commands, as he controlled the stream of his men back to safety.

It took hours, and finally he hugged his mother, as she broke down and wept onto his shoulder. Once again, she had been so strong for the Undine, but as she saw her son, her fears for her daughter bubbled up, and exploded out of her. He held her close.

"She will return, it is already my priority, when these people are safe, I will go to Pallum, and we will get her and bring her home." Sarka sniffled, she stood up and took a breath, she had streaks from her tears down her bloody cheeks.

"Oatin, I have seen what they do to the women they enslave." He nodded.

"That will never happen, I will never allow it. Go, you need rest, I will wait until all here are safe, and then I will leave to find her."

She tried to smile, but it was hard, and yet he was so like his father, and it gave her great hope. She nodded, her face dirty and bloodied at him, turned onto the bridge, and with the rest of the people of the Undine, she walked across into the only part of this whole land, that Balathral did not rule.

Oaken walked off the bridge and onto the pass, Elden came up at his side, he was a burley guard, good friend, and well known for his force with a sword. He walked with Oaken as they made their way to the top of the high pass, the archers were doing well, but Oaken knew, they could not continue. As Shengara came up the pass, Oaken gave him a nod.

"Tell your men, this is the pass of my father, today, the Andalan will fight once again at their side. When I strike, they need to retreat to safety." Shengara gave a chuckle.

"You even sound like him, he too was good at giving me orders, but it shall be done, my people are weary from a hard fight." As Shengara turned to give out his orders, Oaken raised his hand, gripped the fabric bound hilt of the sword, as he let his mind relax. When he felt that strange feeling inside build, he pulled, and the sword gave a soft sound, as it came away from the scabbard, as he drew it over his head. Elden looked confused and stepped back from him, Oaken shrugged.

"What?" Elden pulled a bit of a face.

"Is that it? I did not expect gold, but it would be nice if the sun glinted off it, after all, it is supposed to be a sword of legend, a tip would have been sort of nice."

Oaken looked down at the sword, he thought Elden had a point, which was more than the sword had. The blade was dull, it was old metal that was for sure, but it had a sort of slight look of rust to it. It was actually sort of ancient and ordinary. Oaken looked up at Elden.

"It has not been used for a long time, when I get time, I will polish it up a bit. I never thought about looking at it before."

At the start of the bridge, on the Andarla side, Sarka watched feeling nervous, Eliaston at her side. She watched as her son pulled out the sword, and felt her heart start to beat, the old man smiled.

"He has no idea of the power he holds, yet in a few moments, he will." Sarka just nodded, her green eyes fixed on the blade, and in her mind, she spoke to herself.

"As it guided Andalyn, guide my son, and show him the path to saving his sister." She closed her eyes, and saw the memory of her husband, as he did the same for his people, and in her thoughts, she spoke to him.

"Andalyn, stand with your son this day, and watch over him for me."

Oaken felt the power within him, and it was stronger than it had ever been, he focused on his words and carefully picked each one, and then raising the sword with both hands, he gripped it firmly and spoke into his thoughts.

"Protect the Undine, and push back those who harm them." He swept the blade down with a loud whooshing sound.

Sarka watched as the dust blew up from the floor, and thundered down the pass, it lifted into the air, and swept above the Undine, and then bent low, and blasted into the faces of the Summanu.

The Summanu gasped and choked as their lungs filled with dust, and they felt their feet dragging on the floor. It was almost as if someone had taken hold of their ankles and were pulling at them. They had no idea what was happening, as suddenly, their legs were dragged backwards and they were lifted, coughing and choking into the air, and swept backwards at speed.

Elden watched as the dust swirled, and in front of the Undine, the whole of the pass was empty, and there was not one Summanu to be seen. Seeing their chance, the Undine warriors turned, and raced up the pass. Behind them, clouds of dust swirled across Undinalashka. Archers climbed down, and joined in the rush to reach safety and regrouped at the top. They patted his shoulder gratefully as they passed him standing proud, the broken tip of the sword facing the floor. He could see the weariness and deep sadness in their eyes, Shengara smiled, as he passed him, and slapped him hard on the shoulder.

"He looked that surprised when he used it too." He gave a roaring laugh.

"I owe you the lives of my people young Oak, my sword is yours when you need it." Oaken gave a smile.

"They are my people too, and one of them is out there, and I aim to find her." Shengara gave a sad sigh.

"We are bonded in our cause, for both of us hold a great love of her, for she is kin to us. Find her, and I will bring an army so fierce, none of the Summanu will stand in our path, for we burn with the anger of our defiled homeland." Oaken took a deep breath, his eyes fixed on the base of the pass.

"Rest your soldiers, and heal your wounded, for Yandalla and I have great need of them." Shengara gave a satisfied nod.

At the bottom of the road a single Summanu walked up and stopped, he stared up the long pass, and Oaken lifted the sword and pointed at him.

"THIS PASS BELONGS TO ANDALAN. ANY WHO TRY, WILL DIE BY THE HAND OF OAKENWIND, SON OF ALDALYN. GO TELL BALATHRAL, I AM COMING FOR HIM, I HAVE THE DEBTS OF MY FATHER TO SETTLE!"

Sarka watched, and heard her son, and felt a tingle run through her, Shengara walked off the bridge and stopped at her side, her eyes moved to his.

"That warrior out there, that is not his son, that... That iron in his words, that is his father returned, of that there is no doubt in my mind." Sarka looked back to the pass, where Oaken slid back his sword, turned, and walked back towards the bridge, she turned to Elden.

"As soon as he is back across, raise the bridge." He snapped to attention.

"Yes, Lady of Andalan."

She faltered slightly in her steps, and then smiled, as she walked back towards the place where all the wounded were being cared for, it was going to be a long few days, there was much to sort out.

All the wounded were carried up to the temple at the top of the mount, which was large and spacious. They rolled out the mats, and made a line of beds to rest the wounded on. Many of the women took charge, cleaning and bandaging wounds, some joined Sarka, who taught them better ways of cleaning and stitching the deeper wounds.

It was well over four hours later, when she came down to her home, and found Oaken with Shengara in his room, as he packed items he would need. She looked at the both of them, as Oaken rolled his sword inside his blanket ready to throw the whole bundle over his shoulder. On the bed was a small bag with a long strap, which had a sharpening stone, spare knife, and flint stones in it, she looked at her son.

"What are you doing?" He stopped, and turned to her.

"I am going after her, and I aim to free her and bring her

home." Sarka shook her head slowly.

"How... Oatin, are you mad, the whole of this territory is swarming with them, they are killing and burning everything?" He took a pace forward, and held her by the arms.

"Mother, they will take her from this realm into the desert, and then from what we know to Sumanula, where she will be sacrificed to Bharl. Balathral is not interested in Undine slaves, he aims to kill all of them. Only those none Undine will be enslaved." She stepped back.

"I cannot let you go, Pallum is already down there looking, I cannot risk you as well." Shengara took her hand.

"Sarka, Pallum knows his hope lies within these borders, he knows once he leaves here, he will stand out, and will not last long. Oaken, can move in the other places, he has more chance of mixing and finding her. I have a plan for Pallum, and Oaken will find him and deliver it, I told Pallum what to do if he found her and where to go." She looked at her son.

"I do not like this, it risks all of us." He could understand her, he remembered how she was when she found out his father had died, and already her daughter and husband were gone.

"I have the one thing no other has Mother, I have the power of the winds with me, and I will use that to find both of them, and bring them safely back."

"Oatin, how can you leave, you may have cleared the pass, but the rest of the land is filled with them, and they are all looking this way?" Shengara gave a chuckle.

"We want them to look this way, that way no one will spot him as he uses the water. I have reached out to the Animatre, they live on the cluster of islands to the east, and know all of the coast lands well. There are doors into all the lands that have never been closed, Balathral does not rule as well as he thinks he does. There are many ways to smuggle things in and out of the lands below us, and the Animatre are skilled in this."

It was hard to convince her, but she could see, he was going to do this no matter what she thought. Sarka left him as he packed a few spare clothes, and she returned a few minutes later with some tight bundled things, and handed them to him.

"There is a sewing kit, good needles and twine, just in case you get hurt, there are also wrappings and soap, it has the flame herb in it, so it will kill any infections. There is a change of clothes for Yandalla, she will feel dirty, get her away and then find clean water and let her take care of herself, and then dress as an Undine should." She lifted her hands to her neck, and lifted the twine, pulling it over her head.

"This was your father's, it is a small bead inscribed with the charm of Nuada on it, it has protected me since the day we were parted. Take it with you, and it will protect you and Yandalla when you bring her home." He gave a sigh.

"Mother, I cannot take that; I know how precious it is." She smiled, and lifted her arms to his head.

"It means everything to me, but it is a bead, you are my son, and she is my daughter, if this keeps you safe, I can part from it." He leaned a little, and it slipped down, and she tucked it into his shirt.

"If you do not wear that, you are not leaving, those are my terms Oaken of the four winds." He gave a little chuckle and looked down inside his loose shirt, where it sat on his chest.

"Taking a part of my father and yourself gives me hope, for the bond between all of us is strong." She stepped forward, and pulled him into a hug.

"There is no stronger bond my son, I love you, travel swift, stay low, and alert. I will wait here and ask Nuada to stay at your side until you find her." He squeezed her hard.

"All my life you have been strong for me, and now, I will show Yandalla the same strength, by bringing her home. At sun fall each day, I will sit and think of you, do the same, and we shall keep our spirits connected through Nuada."

Shengara went over things one more time, and then lifting his bag, he headed out towards the ladder down to the beach. When he arrived, Elden stood with a pack on his back, Oaken looked at him.

"What are you doing here?" Elden looked at him confused.

"I am coming with you, our fathers fought side by side, and so shall we." Sarka gave a giggle, Oaken looked at him.

"You do know we may be going out of the territory back to the old lands?" He nodded.

"That is why I am coming, I speak Andalan, Undine, Summanu,

and if we need to, Leyarken. I have pale skin and brown hair, and within a week I will be smelly and unshaven, I can pass for Summanu if needs be. You cannot take Undine, they will be easily spotted, and that will bring attention you do not need. You need me, I can walk in many places and fit in. I have also seen your sword, so I will not be disappointed if you pull it out again, others will be." It made sense, and Oaken gave a chuckle.

"How are you on water?" He frowned.

"I have never done it, but how hard can it be?"

Oaken pulled the rope and the ladder dropped down the cliff face. Elden climbed on, and began the long climb down, when his head disappeared below the floor level, Oaken swung around on to it, and looked at his mother and smiled, she looked upset and terrified.

"Mother, the Undine once came to our aid, it is time for those of my father's line to do likewise. We will see each other again, and when I next appear above this ladder, Yandalla will be with me."

She nodded as tears filled her eyes, and she watched him disappear below the level of the floor, as her tears dripped onto the dusty road, and she suddenly felt very much alone.

Shaylil waited as the waves lapped the boat, and Oaken with Elden ran down the beach to him. Oaken swung his legs up out of the water, as Elden scrambled in, and then Shaylil pushed, and the boat moved into the water, as Oaken grabbed the oars. Shaylil nodded to Elden, and took the rudder, and when the boat was out far enough, Oaken undid the sail line, and hoisted it up, Elden looked a little queasy, and Oaken smiled.

"You will get used to it, although, maybe we will see what you have eaten first." Shaylil gave a giggle, as Elden looked very pale and rigid in his seat.

On the large field on which the celebration had been held, the Summanu laughed as they ate the last of the celebration's food. They sat back watching those too old for anything useful, drag the dead Undine up the steps and into the meeting hall, which now had a deck and steps soaked in Undine blood.

With eyes filled with tears, the elderly Undine, lifted the bodies of all ages, male and female, and many of them familiar faces. It was heart breaking work as they tried to lie each of the dead out, inside the large wooden building, a special place that they had cherished. In those first days, all of the Undine had gathered in this spot, cleared the land, cut the wood, and then together, they built this meeting hall with their bare hands.

It was more than just a building, it was the centre of everything they had built here in this new land, that had spared them the persecution of those days before they came here. The Summanu had once again entered their world and violated it, and it made no sense, as for years they had lived here in peace, separated by the heat of the desert and not interfering with anyone.

The bodies were laid out with great reverence, as they tried to show them the utmost respect. Three of the women stayed inside, and washed their faces and combed their hair, so as their spirits passed on the journey from one state of being, into another, they would look their best. Many shed tears which washed the faces of the lost, as their quiet weeping sounded around the large interior, it was almost as if they wept for every race violated and destroyed by the Summanu.

After hours of back breaking work, the tired and worn out older Undine, had cleared all of the space of the dead, and entered the hall, to help take care of their fallen. Seeing the field cleared, the order was given, and the soldiers of Summanu got up from their feast, walked up the field, and closed all of the doors, wedging them together with broken spears through the handles. They stepped back, as other soldiers threw oil all over the walls, and the flames from a fire were thrown onto it. The building which was tinder dry, ignited quickly, and the soldiers stood back and jeered and laughed, as the screams from inside filled their ears. It was the single most evil, and hateful crime ever committed against the Undine, and it set the mark, for their treatment from that day onward.

Balathral had named the Undine, not human, and secondary to all others, their life was to be deemed as having no value, and to be exterminated on the spot. Balathral hated them, and wanted every last one of them removed from all of the lands. He even offered a reward for all Undine brought to him in the capital of his land, for sacrifice. Those arriving in Salanula City, would be paid one silver coin per Undine. In that moment, he placed a target on every Undine's head, knowing they would be rounded up, caught, and wiped out forever.

Their vile act of burning their people alive, was not unseen, as all over Undinalashka, some small pockets of the Undine survived, and gathered into small groups, avoiding the soldiers, moving into areas where the undergrowth was thick. They spread the word from group to group, to get word to Shengara, and some even joined forces with Pallum, and headed to the outskirts, looking for all those who had been taken as slaves.

Pallum had already worked out, that the only way to have brought an army through the desert unseen, Balathral would have had to seek out the remotest parts of the region. He had travelled all of the territory in the early days for his grandfather, making note of all aspects of the land, searching for herbs and much needed food supplies, so he understood what the Summanu had done.

It did not take long to discover he was right, and the old trails were well worn with the new marks of heavy cart wheels, so he set off on the hunt for the whereabouts of all those taken for use as slaves.

Oaken sat with his eyes closed as Shaylil steered, and Elden leaned over the side of the small boat and vomited repeatedly. The small boat with the wind in the sail, skipped easily over the choppy waves, and Shaylil watched the coastline of the land that was his home. For the whole of the journey, tall plumes of smoke rose into the air, and behind the trees, out of view, mass armies hunted and butchered or enslaved yet more of the Undine.

As the darkness began to fall, at the end of a day of blood and slaughter, the small boat came up onto a beach, where three people stood waiting. Two women and one man, gave him a polite nod as he climbed out of the boat, and pulled on the rope to drag it further up the beach. Elden fell to his knees and hands, and breathed in the air, glad to be in a place that was stable and not rocking from side to side. Oaken dragged the boat higher up the sand, as Shaylil spoke quickly to the people, and then turned, as Oaken walked towards him, Shaylil smiled.

"Oaken, these people are Nutriana." A very attractive woman with long flowing golden hair gave him a nod.

"Evander." A man of stern appearance, with short brown hair, yet kind eyes, gave him a nod, he returned it.

"And Tanaquilla." She was older, but had a resemblance of Nutriana, he assumed she was family or related in some way, he gave her the same smile and nodded.

"I am pleased to meet you all."

Shaylil knew these people, and quickly filled them in on what was going on, they already knew much of it, as they had encountered Pallum on their arrival, and Oaken was relieved to know that to a degree he was still alive. Talk was fast, they were out in the open and easily spotted, and now that they had met Oaken, and understood his urgency to find his sister, they guided him along the beach, to a hidden cave, where five guards stood on watch. He walked slowly, the sun was going down, and the sky was red, his mind moved to his mother, and in his mind, he spoke to her.

"I am safe, and with new friends who I feel can help me find Yandalla. I will return her to you, never fear."

Shaylil told him that these people were called Animatre, and lived on islands not far away, he soon found out it was twenty seven islands covering an area three times bigger than Undinalashka. Most of their trade came from the sea, which is how the Undine knew them, as they had traded with them when they lived in the lands of Leyarken, and re-established trade when they inhabited Undinalashka. They mainly bartered as the Undine had no use of money, and would swap fish and sea goods for fresh fruits and root vegetables.

The Summanu had approached them many times, as Balathral wanted to create a fleet of sea worthy vessels. Having seen their trade decimated when he enslaved the population of Shodalt, they turned him down, fearing he had set his sights on taking over their islands. Oaken felt it was a wise decision.

Inside the cave, with tallow sticks with wicks burning for light, Evander unrolled a large sheet of parchment, and Oaken was captivated, never in his life had he seen such a beautifully illustrated map, and he marvelled at the penmanship. Nutriana appeared amused by him. He studied the map as Evander spoke, noting all of the channels that ran inland, which they sailed their vessels along, he noted a line from the sea, that ran around to the wall of Andalan, and looked up.

"Is that a river?" Evander gave a nod.

"Yes, it is, and deep, it runs from the falls of Andalan. It is good drinking water, we collect a lot in barrels when we are there, for our belief is it is the sweetest water in all the land." Oaken nodded, he knew that, his mother talked often of it. Nutriana leaned over the map, her bright blue eyes sparkled, he had caught her interest.

"Why does this place appeal to you?" Oaken looked at the map, and placed his finger on a faint dotted line.

"Your friend here says that is the route that we think the Summanu took across the desert. If it is, and if the rumours are true, then the way I see things, it is the most likely route to take with the slaves, as it is the faster route back to Sumanula. They would skirt close to Andalan, because it is a land they have taken, as it would give them protection, and after trekking through the desert, they would need fresh water." He looked up, and straight into her eyes.

"I was ten when I crossed that desert and I have never forgotten it, the heat tears at your spirit, and cooks the skin. When we finally arrived here, the first thing we did, was wade into the lake to cool down and wash the dust off us, it will be no different for the Summanu." She gave a soft smile and looked up.

"He has a point, Father." Oaken suddenly realised, and looked at her.

"Sorry, I was not aware he was your father." She smiled at him.

"These are my parents; we live and work on the same boats." Evander gave a soft chuckle, and looked down at the map.

"You make a good point Oaken, we sail everywhere, we have not crossed the desert so have no understanding of the experience, although, you paint a severe image of your journey. I feel you may be right, so explain to me your thinking." Oaken stood up.

"No matter what Balathral has planned, that journey will be hampered and slow. The Undine can handle the heat, the Summanu won't, and the Undine people know that, so they will make it hard. The way I see it, they will stop for water, and when they see it, no matter how strict their leaders are, the soldiers will break for the water. That moment of break, could be a distraction for me to get to my sister if she is with them." Evander nodded.

"Yes, a boat will be faster, as we can skirt the edge of the desert and come inland and up stream. From that point, the distance they will need to cover to their leader will take several weeks, they will need a lot of water, no one enters the land of Leyarken now, so water will be scarce until they reach their borders." He looked at his daughter.

"It will be up to you, we can get you close to there but do not forget, it is bandit territory. You will be closer than they are, but after that, it will be on foot." She gave a nod, and looked at the map.

"The Leyarken will be open for me, I have already sent out word. I traded there for many years, before the Summanu cut off all the trade routes. Shodalt is not an easy land, I doubt we will be able to go the whole length of the river as we once did. Many boats have been attacked and sunken."

Oaken looked at them all, it was clear some plan had been hatched he was not aware of. It was obvious, Pallum had something in mind, he looked around the room.

"Am I missing something here?" Nutriana looked up, and smiled at him.

"Oh, didn't you know, I am coming with you, I will be your guide?" He shook his head, and gave a small chuckle.

"No... No one told me. It is going to be a long walk, will that be alright, after all it is not sailing?" She gave a small titter.

"The long walk will be fine, it will give me time to fill you in, you see, I am the one who runs all the smuggling operations in and out of Ranblate, Keytan and Shodalt. I know the towns along the river better than any, and there are a lot of people out there who hate Balathral, we should have help along the way."

Oaken smiled, he needed all the help he could get, and someone who knew the terrain as well as residents, could prove to be very useful. He looked back down at the map, they had a lot of distance to cover, but if their vessels were as fast as he thought, he knew he could be there ready when Yandalla needed him the most, and he had promised his mother, there would be no return without her.

"Alright, we can do this, when do we leave?"

Chapter Five

The Wind is Coming

It was after dark when a young Undine arrived at the cave, with news from Pallum. Oaken was relieved to hear he was safe and well, and had tracked down the slaves. There were two gathering points, where long lines of carts with steel cages were assembled, as the captives were herded into them, and had been left for the night. It was clear that they would start moving them out in the morning.

It was sad news to hear what was happening to the Undine, thousands had been slaughtered or burned alive in their homes, and Pallum had guessed that they had at least three thousand being herded into the cages, most of them young women and children, all men were killed on the spot. The news that there were many groups who had survived was a big relief, and the young warrior explained how Pallum had sent word out, to hamper the progress of the Summanu. Oaken gave the documents from Shengara to him to pass on to Pallum, and a personal message from himself.

The Undine once lived in the Leyarken Jungle, and so were no strangers to springing traps and guerilla warfare, and that was their current plan of action. It was revealed that before Pallum left, Shengara had spoken quickly to him, and the plan now, was to ensure fewer Summanu left Undinalashka alive. The Summanu numbers were vast, it was clear that this plan had been many years in the making, it was obvious, Balathral had been planning this since the death of his father.

Hearing the number of dead, was overwhelming for Oaken, these people were his friends and neighbours, and although they were of a different race, in his mind, they were also his people. His sister was one of them, or at least half Undine, but he had never seen her as a different race, she was Yandalla, the brightest person in his life. He walked outside the cave, as he needed some air, and walked onto the beach, it was pitch black, and he looked up at the stars, as the soft cooler breeze stroked his cheek. The moon was bright, and shone down on the water, as the gentle lap of the waves kissed the sand of the beach softly, there was a smell of burning all around him.

He took a deep breath, he felt mixed up, his anger mixed with his relief, as he knew he was closer to finding his sister, but he was also frustrated, as he wanted to move much quicker. Every moment she was away, would harm her, and he needed her back beside him. Nutriana appeared at his side, he turned to glance at her, it was very dark, and yet her eyes shone in her darkened face, her hair back lit by the moon, she felt very at ease and calm, and he liked that, in a strange way it helped him.

"I know something of what you feel Oaken, I lost someone dear when their ship went down. We searched for weeks in hope that some part of the wreck had been caught in the drift, but it was to no avail. Your sister is not gone forever; we will get to her." He knew that, but it did not make it easier knowing her life was at risk for every second she was away from him.

"I know, I guess I am feeling the tenseness of it all, we have never been apart, and she has always been there for me, I want to be with her and know that she is alright. I will be fine once we set off, I am not at ease sat around." She nodded.

"We will leave at dawn, you should sleep." He took a deep breath.

"I am tired, but fear sleep will not come soon."

"I know that, so, if you are awake, tell me, if you are Oatin, son of Andalyn, where does Oaken come from, it appears so different from other names your bearers have picked?" He was surprised at her level of knowledge, she appeared to him to be highly educated, far more than he would have guessed when he walked up the beach on his arrival.

"My sister is half Undine, her father is Pallum. Yandalla has trouble at times with the common tongue, as you know, the Undine have developed to fit their language, and some of our words are difficult for them to speak. Yandalla has always had trouble with words that end with 'in' to her it is easier to say Oaken, rather than Oatin. I had to pick a new name, and because I have grown so used to her calling it me, when they told me I had to use a name that was me, I chose Oaken, knowing she would never say my name wrong again. To her, that is who I am, and I guess, I like the way she thinks of me." Nutriana nodded in the darkness.

"I have heard talk of you many times, the people of this land hold you in a high regard. They have spoken of the closeness of you and your sister, many have noted your great love for her, and how you protect her. I have heard she is very beautiful, but most male Undine feel their hopes dashed, as they know they have to live up to your ideals. Penjin was one, you are probably not aware, but he was deeply in love with her, but feared he could not live up to your standards." Oaken shook his head.

"I did not know, my mother told me he was cut down protecting her, Shaylil is not aware of that yet. I owe Penjin for her life, I will make it known to his family when I return."

"They will be deeply honoured by that, for it is the mark of a man of honour." He felt the sudden pain again inside him, and put his head down for a moment, took a deep breath to calm himself, and then thought of something.

"Your name is not known to me, is it popular within your people?" She gave a little giggle.

"No, I fear I am the only one, my father named me. He told my mother I would be the most educated woman of our people, and then went on to explain, how he would ensure I had an analytical mind, and hold the gift of a searching mind to find answers in all things. I guess he was not wrong, for I have learned a great deal in my twenty four summers. Although, I will add, most people call me Ria." Oaken frowned.

"They do... Why?" She gave a giggle.

"You sound surprised, Ria are the three letters in the middle of my name, and I like it, as it sounds less educated, and makes life easier, it is not always helpful being a smuggler, and the most educated in the room." He considered the point for a moment.

"I suppose that makes sense, I can understand that, I have been in similar situations, I know how that feels, it makes you feel more isolated." She gave another giggle.

"It does... We have an early start, you should sleep, I feel I need some too."

She patted his shoulder and turned, and left him standing to the sound of the waves lapping up the beach. She was right, he needed to sleep, a great deal had happened and he felt weary. Oaken turned, and walked slowly back to the cave, and headed to his blanket roll. He lay back and closed his eyes, and all he could see in his thoughts, were those beautiful green eyes, in her pale white face, and her soft voice echoed through his head.

"Oaken, sounds nicer, and to me you will always be Oaken, for there is only Oaken and he is my brother." He gave a long sigh and relaxed.

"I am coming Yandalla, do not give up hope."

Far away across Undinalashka, curled in a tight ball, up against the metal bars, Yandalla's eyes snapped open, as she stared into the darkness, her voice was soft, and almost a whisper from her dry throat.

"Oaken?"

It was early when Oaken was shaken awake, he had not slept well, and sat up to feel the aches in his back. In the cave there was a lot of movement, as people prepared, and it appeared that at some point, more Undine had arrived, as a group of ten were busy talking with Evander. He was handed a tea, it was hot and sweet, and it appeared to heat up his body, as he stood and leaned back on the wall, as he watched and sipped.

Feeling a little more awake, and in need of air, he walked out onto the beach, and was surprised to see three large ships out to sea, Ria, was busy talking, as several smaller boats had come onto the beach. Elden came up at his side and stared out at the three huge ships.

"How can something bigger than a house not sink?" Oaken smiled.

"I think we will find out, one of those may be our way of making it across the desert before the Summanu." Elden shuddered.

"I was going to eat, but I wonder now what would be the point?" Oaken patted his shoulder with a smirk.

"Eat, take what strength you can, before you throw it over the side."

With a soft chuckle, he turned and looked around, everyone appeared to have something to do, except him. The men from the ship had wooden crates that they were taking out of the small boats on the beach, and carrying them up to the cave. Evander and Shaylil were talking and organising with the Undine, Ria was organising ship crews, and he was stood in the centre of all of it doing nothing.

Tanaquilla walked down the beach smiling with two cups in her hand, she looked different in the daylight, her hair was snow white, and she wore a dark blue tunic and pants. Her eyes were soft and kind, and she smiled a great deal, she came up and handed one to him, and then the other to Elden.

"Here, this will help keep your stomachs settled." Elden looked into the cup.

"I am not on it yet and my stomach is swirling; do they always move up and down in the water like that?" Tanaquilla gave a soft chuckle.

"Sadly yes, but in time you will adjust." He nodded, looked back, and then lifted the cup to his lips, Tanaquilla looked at Oaken.

"We will be taking aid to your people, Shaylil will be heading back with food and supplies." Oaken gave a sigh of relief.

"I am happy to hear that, I am worried, the water is their only way of getting things. Shaylil told me he was going back last night, but his boat is small and does not carry much." She understood that.

"They will be fine, we will make sure of it, the Undine have always been peaceful people, and we have done a great deal of trade with them. Oaken, there are many isolated groups still living, this northern shore is filled with dense lands where the Undine can hide and stay out of the reach of the Summanu. The south has suffered, and tales of brutal acts are coming to us, it is harrowing to hear what Balathral is doing, but as bad as all this is, he will pay." Oaken gave a nod.

"He will, I aim to assure it." She could feel the conviction in his words, and really understood, it did not fully show, but she could sense the anger buried deep within him.

"Oaken, my daughter is skilled in many things, and she can be of great aid to you, so I will tell you this, listen to her, and learn from her. She has run a very successful operation here for a long time, and has got supplies through their lines to many who are hiding and gathering their strength. Balathral has had everything his own way, because he has targeted a single race at a time, and your father understood that. He tried to unite all the races, and had he lived, I am certain he would have. Balathral can only stand if all the others kneel, and that is his weakness." Oaken considered it.

"So, if someone can unite them, then there may be a way to defeat him?" She smiled at him.

"The sword of the four winds in the right hand could do that, which is why Balathral fears it and wants it. Think of this, somewhere in Sumanula, there are all the people of the lands raided by Balathral, and they are enslaved. Oaken, the man who frees them, would have a mighty army. Get your things and be ready, you will be leaving shortly, we have injured heading our way, one of those ships shall remain here, and we will use it to care for the wounded and heal them. When we reach your people of Andalan, we will bring Shengara back here, his people need him where he can serve them better. Your job now is to focus on freeing your sister, and as many of the others as you can."

Tanaquilla's words stayed in his mind as he packed up his things, and headed to the boats. Within the hour he was on board the ship, which although smaller than the other two, was a giant compared to the fishing boat he had been using. He was taken below, and was to share a cabin with Elden, it had two bunks and a small table, it was plain and ordinary, but it suited his needs. He had been in the cabin for just a few minutes, when there was a knock at the door, Ria entered carrying clothing.

"Here, you wear the clothes of an Undine, your pants are skins, but are worn down, these are more suited. Wear this shirt, that thick cloth you wear will boil your skin, you will find these more to your comfort when we reach Shodalt. These jackets are sleeveless and long, they are good protection from the sun and the rain, and tie your hair back, the wind up top will have it blowing everywhere, put the cloaks in your packs for when we land."

She handed Elden similar clothing and smiled, then left, Elden looked down at the garments.

"These are better than my temple best." Oaken shrugged.

"The less like Andalan's we look, I suppose the better, she has a good point."

It was a little later, when he appeared up on the deck, and walked along taking everything in. Ria smiled as she saw him, dressed in his tanned coloured pants, white shirt, and a long padded waistcoat. With his hair tied back, he looked almost like one of the crew. Oaken leaned on the rail and looked out across the sea, above him, three masts flapped, as the sails billowed. In the distance, Undinalashka, looked tiny, just a low line of green, with the dark rock rising above it, mixed in with dark plumes of smoke, that met, forming a thick dark cloud over the whole region.

Below him, the white foam rolled up and away from the ship as it cut through the water, and he found it all quite impressive, never in his life had he known that boats could be so big that they could carry so many people. He turned and leaned back on the rail, and observed, as men with dark tanned skin, ran up and down the rigging, or heaved on large ropes to keep the sails taught. For him, this was a new experience, he had lived a very simple life, living with the Undine, he had never imagined that there were so many differences between races. His life and that of the Undine were similar, and he had always felt that was how everyone lived, he noticed Ria stood up on the higher deck, and watched, as she handled the wheel and gave out her orders. She was confident, and in ways many of the women of the Undine were not. His mother was, and Yandalla, they had a similar quality to Ria, Yandalla whilst very talkative, knew her own mind, and she had always tried new things to gain better insight, and then understood herself more because of it. In many ways, he had admired her, she was always unafraid of things and faced everything head on with a kind and curious nature, and yet at times, he had faltered.

He leaned off the rail, and made his way towards the steps, which was not as easy as he had thought, as the ship lifted and fell in the water, something by the look of it, Elden was very aware of, as he hugged the rail and retched over the side. Oaken smiled as he passed him and patted his back, then grabbed the handrail and made his way up the steps, Ria gave a chuckle.

"His sea legs will come; it just takes time." Oaken smiled, as he looked down, and saw the look of utter misery on Elden's face. Ria glanced at him, as he held the rail next to her.

"I suppose this is all quite new to you, this is a good vessel, it will give us the advantage and time to prepare. When my mother wakes up, we will go to my cabin, and I will go over the maps with you. I want you to really get familiar with them, so you know your way, we have a lot of distance to cover before we get to them." The ship rose up, and then crashed down again in the water, he held onto the rail tight.

"I feel a little out of things, I want to know as much as I can, Yandalla will be depending on me." She smiled at him.

"Have no fear, you will."

Yandalla sat up and as her eyes blinked open, she gasped in the dry stale air, and looked around at the packed cage filled with young Undine women, many of them with tear streaked faces, all with a look of fear in their eyes. Outside the cage, there were other carts, all filled with the same miserable dirty faces, gathered in the wide dusty space, as around her was a hive of activity. She felt movement and looked to her shoulder, Shellena was waking, her face was red and swollen, and she had a thick band of bruising below her left eye. Shellena opened her eyes, and jerked, her eyes opened wide and Yandalla smiled.

"It is alright, we are safe for now." Shellena looked around with wide eyes, Yandalla licked her lips, they were parched, and she tried to swallow.

"Shellena, this is bad, but do not be afraid, that is what they want. Mother told me that was how they ruled, they used fear to control everyone, so no matter what, hide your fear. We must be brave, we are Undine, and all of us were taught to be warriors." Everyone was looking at her, and she nodded at them all.

"I have fear, but my brother Oaken taught me, if I show it, others will know and defeat me. All of us must hide it, and face everything with grit and determination. Shengara will come, and he will bring Oaken, they will not leave us, my brother would never leave me." Others nodded at her, they knew Shengara, he was the hero of their people, and a powerful leader. One of the girls looked at her.

"You are his line; he danced with you?" Yandalla nodded.

"He is my great grandfather, he will come." The girl nodded, and felt a little hope.

High above them in the dusty rocks, Pallum looked down, as he hid in the rough grasses. His eyes scanned the long line of carts, it was hard to see who was in them.

"I need to be closer, at this distance it is impossible to see who is who, and my daughter is down there somewhere."

The Undine were laid in a long line along the top of the rocks, at the very edge of the desert, there were fifty of them, as Pallum had gathered more as he travelled. To his left about forty paces down a voice spoke quietly.

"I think I see her." Pallum turned his head.

"Where?"

"Tenth cart from that cloth building, she is at the front end, in the corner by the bars." Pallum slid back, and then bending low, he ran along the line, to the Undine who was looking out. He crawled up at his side.

"Show me." He pointed.

"There, look, she is the only one there in black pants, all the others have green." Pallum stared down and felt hope in his heart, and also great anger, but he smiled, and felt a huge surge deep within him.

"Yandalla, my daughter." He looked back.

"Bring bows, and parchment."

Yandalla sat looking out through the bars, there were men all over the place shouting out orders, and many others packing boxes and loading barrels onto other carts. Soldiers stood around looking bored, some of them clearly not enjoying the heat, as they pulled at their shirts or wiped their necks with wet rags. Yandalla licked her lips again, just seeing water used so wastefully felt like torture for her dry dusty mouth. Four men walked along the line of carts eyeing the women, one of them stopped and looked in, and the girl's shrunk back from the bars. The man was dirty and had bristles growing from his face, he smiled an ugly smile.

"Looks like our nights will not be so boring lads, look, we have entertainment." The men all laughed, and Yandalla felt her skin crawl, Shellena huddled closer to her and gripped her arm.

"Yandalla, I am afraid, I do not want my flowers taken."
Yandalla stared at the man with hate.

"They won't be, that is a gift meant only for Undine." In her thoughts she felt her fear, and whispered quietly to herself.

"Hurry Oaken, I am really scared."

As the men all jeered at them, winked, and blew kisses, the girls shrunk back away from the bars, shaking with fear, pressing themselves into each other and holding each other tight. Out of nowhere, one of the men jerked and fell forward, then another, and another, Yandalla jumped, as a man hit the side of the cage in front of her. His face looked shocked, as he breathed out a moan, and then slid slowly down the iron bars. His chin bumped on the bottom, and he gasped out air, and then disappeared below the floor of the cage, and rolled under the cart.

She looked up, and there on the hill was the outline of an Undine warrior, and even though the sun was behind him, she felt her heart leap, and gasped out of her dry throat.

"Anna Pa!"

It was almost instinct, she pushed her arm through the gap in the bars and raised it, her palm up, the greeting of the Undine, and watched as he pulled back on the string and aimed his bow right at her. Her eyes blinked as the arrow hit the cart just inside the cage next to her leg, she saw the roll of parchment, and without thinking snatched at the arrow, and it broke off. Shellena was up at her side, as Yandalla pulled free the small piece of parchment, and unrolled it, and looked at the Undine writing, she voiced it quietly, and felt hope in her heart.

"Yan fors ae cumten." She closed her eyes and felt the tears build, and the emotion swirled up and she gave a sob, Shellena hugged her arm.

"The wind is coming, Yandalla, Oaken is coming, he has embraced the wind, and he is coming."

Tears rolled down her bruised, bloodied and dirty cheeks, as she looked up and her father stood holding his bow aloft, in a signal of unity and friendship. They were not alone, her father was close, and somewhere out there, her brother Oaken was coming to get her.

"He is Shellena, I knew he would, Oaken would never leave me, he has always been my protector. Shellena, we have to live through this until he gets here, we have to be strong. I know you are frightened, we all are, but when he gets here, he will need us strong. We are Undine, never forget that, the land is ours, we understand it, and so we must find a way to make it work with us."

Chapter Six

Undine Spirits

With the appearance of her father, chaos ensued, the Summanu soldiers panicked and ran for cover. Yandalla saw the broken arrow implanted in the wooden floor, grabbed it, and wiggled it to free it. She tugged hard, and it came free, she leaned forward and slipped it under her top, and into the waist band of her pants. Shellena kept the shaft of the arrow with the feathers on it, and copied Yandalla, slipping it behind her into her pants.

There were frantic screams, and men ran around as more arrows rained onto the soldiers, she could no longer see her father, but it was clear, he had taken more of the lives of the Summanu. By the time the panic quelled, and the soldiers made it up to the top of the ridge, all the Undine had vanished, and the officers raged with anger. Yandalla smiled, she knew her people well, and she knew as they entered the desert, her father would follow her.

The carts jerked, and then moved forward slowly, there was a long pass of rough stone through to the start of the desert, and for the carts it was a tight squeeze. The cart moved very slowly, often stopping as it waited for the carts in front to lift up over the rough uneven rocks. The rock wall was inches away from the cart, and Yandalla saw the thick bunches of the succulent plants growing out of the walls. She took her moment, it was impossible for any of the guards to see them, and she jumped to her feet.

"My Undine sisters, milk berries, quick, grab as many as you can, they will sustain us for a long time."

The large clusters of pale green baubles hung all the way down the wall, and all the girl's stood up and started to pull them off rapidly. Yandalla pulled off a fat green round berry, and popped it in her mouth, and her tongue exploded, as the sweet flavour filled her dry inner cheeks. The berry popped, and she felt the moisture run around her tongue, it felt like nectar, and she quickly slipped in another, as she grabbed handfuls, tearing them off the walls and passing them back to Shellena. The girls gave little moans of relief, as they sucked the precious liquid, and grabbed as many as they could, Yandalla put some in the pockets of her long smock like top.

By the time the cart moved out of the rock passage, all of them sat feeling relieved, as the precious nutrients seeped into their bodies, quenching their thirst, and filling their empty stomachs. Yandalla smiled, as she looked at all the others.

"We will grow stronger now, and we have many left, including these."

She lifted a thick bunch of long purple berries off the floor from between her and Shellena, and the girl's gasped, she smiled a big smile.

"You all know what these do? We will use them, and make the Summanu pay, through the night terror death." They all smiled and nodded in agreement, some secrets of the land, belonged only to the Undine.

The cart moved onto the desert, where a road of mats had been carefully created, so that the carts did not sink into the soft sand. Understanding this, Pallum sent parties through the sand ahead of the carts, and set fire to the reed mats, and it caused chaos for the Summanu. The only way to get the carts through certain sections, was to halt the convoy, lift all the mats behind groups of wagons, and then lay them down in front of the carts to progress. The long breaks created ample chances for Pallum and his warriors who were used to the desert, to attack and kill more.

The result was, the Summanu soldiers panicked, and in a bid to speed things up, several units of the soldiers, attached long ropes to the horses, and helped pulled the carts quicker through the damaged sections. It was hard, hot, exhausting work, which left the soldiers weakened, and not as alert as maybe they should have been, and Pallum used it to the advantage of his people. The days in the heat dragged on for the Summanu, and they found it unbearable, as their sweat attracted many flies, and bugs, which would bite and sting, adding to the misery of the already weary soldiers.

Life on board the ship for Oaken was relaxed. When he came on board, he had slept little, but after spending several hours with Ria studying maps, he headed to bed feeling exhausted. He slept for most of the day, and it was late at night when he woke up. When he arrived on deck, it was quiet, the crew was lesser at night. Tanquilla was at the wheel, as he walked up the steps, she smiled at him.

"I take it you slept well, have you eaten?" He took a breath of the night air.

"I feel I needed the rest, a lot weighs on my mind, and as yet, I have not had anything to eat." She gave a nod, and looked to the man of the watch.

"Have Oaken brought food and drink." He gave a nod, and headed off down the steps, Oaken leaned on the rail, above him, the night sky was lit by thousands of stars. He gazed up in wonder.

"I have sat many nights watching the stars, my mother has taught me most of their names, like people, they stay in your thoughts, and you remember them, for they are beautiful." He looked down and at Tanquilla.

"This may sound silly, but how do you know where we are?" She smirked.

"I suppose for one who has lived on the land, it is an expected question. Answer me this, how do you walk through a desert in the night and not get lost?" He gave a nod, and looked back at the brightly lit sky.

"I see your point." She smiled at him.

"We are making good time, we will have travelled a great deal of the coast line, by this time tomorrow, we will be nearing the end of the island. There are shallow waters, so we will head a little further out to sea, and then move in a wide arc, and be able to turn, and start our passage down towards the river, at which point, we should be moving towards overtaking the Summanu with their slaves."

For Oaken, it could not come quick enough, his thoughts were somewhere in the desert, after a baking day and currently, none of the slaves had been fed or had water.

Yandalla sat in the darkness, she had slept a little after getting the juice of the milk berries, and felt revived. The camp was quietening down, many of the soldiers were resting in the cooler air, now the sun had fallen, Yandalla felt her moment was coming, she nudged Shellena.

"Slide over a little." She pulled the arrowhead out of the back of her pants.

"Watch for me."

Many of the girls were asleep, but a few were awake, they were not sure what Yandalla was up to, but they all became alert and looked around them. Yandalla looked down, and found what she was looking for, the boards were held in place with a thin shaft of metal. She took the arrow, and started to dig at the wood, Shellena looked down and then whispered.

"What are you doing?" Yandalla looked up.

"The metal sticks hold the wood in a little hole, make the hole bigger, and it holds nothing, and the wood comes off."

Shellena understood and looked out through the bars, as Yandalla began to dig away the wood around the metal. Undine arrows were sharp, and it cut through the new wood easily, and after a great time had passed, she had two holes wide enough around the metal spike, and dragged dust with her hand, and filled in the hole, so it did not look out of place. The others watched as she turned, and began to work on the board near the bars. She worked hard, and was alerted, as a group of guards walked down the line, with two men holding a pan.

They approached the cage, and she slipped the arrowhead back into her pants. Bowls were filled with a strange seed like sort of mush. Yandalla took it as the others looked down at their bowls disgusted. She looked at them and nodded.

"Eat, it is strength, it stinks and is not fit for any, but it will keep us in the living world."

She scouped a handful up and stuffed it into her mouth, it was vile and not cooked well enough, but she knew, she needed to stay strong. The others looked disgusted, but listened to her, and started to eat, they heaved and retched, but still swallowed. Yandalla finished and felt her stomach twist, but handed back her bowl. The guard nodded, and lifted a small bowl of water out of another barrel, and handed it to her. Those who ate, got to drink, and Yandalla was grateful, as she took the bowl and greedily gulped it down, before handing the bowl back. The others understanding, hurriedly swallowed, and handed back their bowls.

As the food detail moved on, Yandalla gave Shellena the arrowhead, and she began to dig through the wood on her side. The boards were wide, and deep, but they were only held in place with two metal pins per board, in a row of four double pins through the length of the boards. It was the start of what would become over a week of work at night. As dawn approached, they slept, they still had many hidden milk berries, and rationed them, two of the girls had little, and each day Yandalla ensured they got one each.

It took little time, and without realising, since they had left their homeland, all of the others began to look to Yandalla for guidance. In their mind, she was the granddaughter of Shengara, the leader of their race, and so all of them looked to her for leadership. Yandalla was Undine in all she did, her life at home was spent around many Undines, she spoke Undine as her first language, but unlike the Undine, Yandalla was also educated by her mother. The Andalan, were highly educated, they studied many areas of knowledge, philosophy, and military tactics. They were known as the truth holders, who studied the meaning of life, and to a degree they were not wrong. Yandalla had studied hard as a young girl, and was taught not just Undine, but Andalan plant lore.

As the days wore on, Oaken sailed east with Ria, Evander made several visits to Sarka and gave her news of what was going on. Pallum stalked through the desert with his fifty Undine, attacking whenever the chance arose. The days of the gruelling heat became more intense, and Yandalla could see how it was taking its toll on all of them. Some of the girls and women in the other cages grew sick, but rather than treating them, they were pulled from the cages, dragged up the sand dunes, and dumped.

Luckily for them, Pallum came to their aid, and had a line set up to secretly return them back to Undinalaska, and their secret places along the beach to recover. On the third day, the ship turned into the estuary, and headed down the river, and Oaken finally felt he was becoming closer to his goal. Yandalla was still many days away from the edge of the desert, where the men were starting to get tired of the relentless heat.

It was clear to all of them that the soldiers were becoming

weary, they were dirty hot and exhausted. In the heat of the middle of the day, the carts would stop, and the men would lie under them, or hang wide sheets to provide shade. As the cooler evenings started, the carts would move on again, travelling until late into the darkness. Yandalla spent her days watching everything, as she took note of all their movements, and routines, she knew Oaken would come, and in her mind, she had to be ready so she could help him. Whatever was to happen, she knew it would come fast, and so she got the Undine girls, to stand in the dark, and walk the edges of the cage going around in a circle to try their best to loosen their limbs, and stretch out their aches from sitting all the time.

The milk berries were running low, but had kept them alive and stronger than many of the others, although, there was always fear in the back of their minds. Some distance away, especially in the heat of the day, they would hear the screams and pleading of the women who were dragged from their cages, and violated by many men. Once done they were left for dead in the sand, brutally beaten and close to death. Yandalla cursed the men who did this under her breath, her green eyes watching, filled with her anger and hatred of the vile soldiers.

One afternoon as the carts stopped and sheets went up, two guards came down the line, they stopped as they looked into their cage, and one of the girls sat near the back door. One of the guards was big, filthy, and had a smile that Yandalla feared, he gazed at the girl known as Sintalla, and licked his lips.

"You will do nicely, when the sun goes down, I will enjoy toying with your soft sweet skin."

Yandalla shuddered, as she sat watching them closely, her back to the wall, where behind sat the drivers. They were not aware she understood them, she slipped her hand into her pocket and lifted out a large purple berry, and held it up as if she was going to put it in her mouth. The guard noticed and turned, and pushed his arm through the bars grabbing her wrist.

"Well, what have we here, have you been hiding secrets?" Yandalla smiled, and spoke sweetly.

"Na fan dit."

She smiled, Shellena looked away, knowing Yandalla had

called him an old bastard. The guard squeezed her wrist and she screwed up her face, then with his other hand, he reached in and took the soft berry from her hand. He let go of her, and she scowled at him, and snapped.

"Mine!" He laughed, then slipped it into his mouth, it tasted sweet, as he chewed.

"It is good, maybe later I will find out if you are as sweet as this." He gave a sinister twisted laugh, his eyes wandered over her body, and she felt the coldness run through her.

Yandalla frowned at him and he simply smirked, as he rolled his tongue around the inside of his mouth, and swallowed. Yandalla sat back, feigning anger at him, but deep down inside, she knew his hours were numbered, for he would not live through the day. As the men moved on to taunt others, Yandalla smiled at her Undine sisters.

"This box of bars keeps us in, but it also keeps them out. We must not let them in, we are Undine, we fight to protect each other, and make life hard for the Summanu." All of them nodded, and Shellena snuggled up close to her.

"He scares me Yandalla." She took her hand and gave it a squeeze.

"We are all scared, but we will not show them that."

Two hours later, there were wild frantic screams, the berry was starting to work. The guard ran around the carts screaming and yelling, many of the other soldiers looked panicked as they saw him. He clawed at his eyes as the hallucinogenic berry filled his mind with horrors, tearing at his eyes, as if they were filled with pain. In his head, the terrors of life were showing him vivid images, and fracturing his mind. He stared at everyone like a mad man, seeing them as monsters and demons, screaming at them and brandishing his sword as he slashed through the air at the invisible monsters. Yandalla watched on, knowing her girls were safe, this guard, would never again rape another Undine. In wild terror, he ran onto one of the dunes, as the soldiers watched on utterly horrified, as he stared at them like a man possessed. He waved his sword frantically as he swung at himself, as if trying to kill something that was living on him.

He sliced into his leg, terrifying the soldiers, and the blood sprayed out onto the sand. All the soldiers felt helpless, not knowing what was wrong with him, as they watched in horror, as he looked at his hand, then brought down his sword, hitting his hand, and cutting it clean off. The men below screamed with him in fear, and several of the younger Summanu fainted. No one knew what was happening, he had sliced off his hand, and yet he did not stop, it was almost as if he did not feel it. Then to their shock and terror, as he screamed out about the ghosts and the monsters, he plunged the sword straight into his stomach, and violently started to stir the blade round and around.

Many of the onlookers could do nothing but watch filled with horror, as his insides were sliced up, and poured out onto the sand, until with one last terrifying wail, he slumped to the floor dead. One young guard without realising had backed up against the cage, and Yandalla reached through the bars and tapped his shoulder. He jumped with shock, and spun around, she looked at him with her deep green eyes, and spoke quietly in the common speech.

"Undine not die, we slip into the body of those who kill us, eat their spirits, and make their body ours." She pointed.

"He kill many Undine, you will see more of that." He stepped back shaking, looking utterly petrified, she smiled.

"How many you kill?" She lifted her hand, and wiggled her fingers.

"Ta yan dis ten, bac see…. BOO!" He turned, and ran away wailing, and she giggled as did the others. Shellena sat back and laughed.

"He will tell all of them, this you must know?" Yandalla smirked.

"Oaken told me that when I was six summers, my mother shouted at him, as I did not sleep for long time. Yandalla never liked spirit stories, until now."

All the girls gave a soft giggle, and she sat back smiling with her dirty face, and bright green eyes dancing. She knew that at least some who had seen the gruesome death of their comrade, would not sleep easily for a while.

Eliason sat up and looked at Sarka, he wore a confused look as he wiped the sweat off his brow. He had taken to sleeping in

Oaken's bed, as he found the temple was too busy and noisy, and so Sarka had given him the space to seek peace. She found the house far too quiet without her family, and so the old man helped break the silence, and they talked a great deal, especially about his visions. She handed him a tea and he took it and sipped, Sarka watched on concerned.

"How are you, that was longer than the last one?" He sipped the drink, and thought about what he had just seen, his voice was quiet as he pondered his vision.

"I am not sure; I saw things I do not fully understand." Sarka frowned at him.

"Like what?" He took a deep breath.

"I saw Oaken, walk from a wood onto grass next to a vast river, and Pallum lies in the sands and watches." Sarka gave a slight shrug.

"That is expected, Oaken must be close to the river by now, and Pallum follows the carts picking off as many as he can, why do you not understand that?" He shook his head as he turned to look at her.

"I saw Yandalla, and she had spirits dancing around her, and as she pointed at the guards, they danced towards them, and entered their heads, making her smile. I have no idea what that means." Sarka looked at him oddly.

"Are you sure, Yandalla is afraid of spirits, Oatin scared her many times as a small girl?" Eliaston shook his head.

"That is what I saw, but it makes no sense at all to me, I cannot even speculate what the meaning of that would be." Sarka had no understanding of it at all.

"The Undine are spiritual people connected very much to the land, I have no idea what she has learned from Pallum, but could it be something to do with that?" Eliaston sighed.

"I suppose it could be, after all, their beliefs about death are that they go from one way of being to another, but I am not sure. I have never read anything about going into the head of a Summanu, they hate them, why would they?" Sarka shook her head, as she thought of her daughter.

"I have no idea at all." The old man scratched his head and frowned, he knew for sure, there was nothing in the books of the sky about it.

When the food came around, Yandalla was prepared, and as the bowl of thick stodgy mix was passed to her, she slipped out one of the purple berries and placed it on the bowl, some of the other girls followed her lead and did the same. The soldier noticed and grabbed the wrist of the young boy before Yandalla could take the bowl from him. He pulled it back and looked at the berry.

"Is this why all of you are in better condition?" The other bowls were withdrawn and the soldier took the berries off the food, and handed back the bowls minus the berries. The Soldier looked at Yandalla.

"How many more have you got, hand them over." Yandalla leaned back holding her bowl, and shook her head.

"For Undine, not Summanu." The soldier lurched forward, slipped his arm through the bars, and gripped her throat hard. She gasped for air; he stared at her with hateful eyes.

"Listen to me you little whore, you hand them over or you die."

She was starting to choke, as her air restricted, and she fought hard to breathe as her eyes filled with tears. Holding her bowl in one hand, she slid her hand down into her pocket, and pulled out the bunch of twelve plump berries. He was squeezing harder and she was starting to shake; she dropped the berries on the floor near the bars. He thrust her back hard with a smirk, and reached for the berries, Shellena pulled her back and held her tight as she gasped and coughed. Sintalla looked at the soldier with hatred, her eyes white and large.

"No right, Undine only." He smirked, as he looked at the fresh plump berries.

"No, you have no rights, you are nothing but whores and slaves, not even human. Hold your tongue whore, or you will be next for the men's party night." She backed against the girl at her side and he smiled.

"That is more like it, know your place whore."

They were fed and got water, as the smug soldier stood back and ate one of the berries, making the most of chewing and smacking his lips, in a show of his enjoyment, little did he know of the horrors to come. It was hard for the Undine not to smile, the Summanu thought they were so clever, and yet they had been fooled by their lack of knowledge of the earth.

Just over an hour later, as Yandalla walked around the cage with the others, which was not easy, but they had worked out a system, all hell broke loose in the camp. He had shared the berries, and several dozen men went into a raving madness screaming into the sky, as they attacked others, screaming at them that they were demons. The large soldier she had given them to, came out of the darkness screaming they were devils. He slammed into the cage brandishing a long silver knife, and waved it around wildly as he pushed it through the bars, and the Undine jumped back out of his way.

His eyes were wide open and filled with horrors, as he screamed at them, most of his words making no sense. His arm waved just above the floor, and taking her chance, Yandalla stamped down hard on his hand, pinning it to the floor, her eyes filled with her hatred of him. Sintalla seized her chance, and grabbed his hand as he raged, pulling at his fingers, the dagger came free, and with a wail of hate, she snatched it up and thrust it into his chest. Yandalla lifted her foot, and he staggered back screaming, as the soldiers who watched in terror did nothing, he turned, the dagger in his chest, and ran at the men screaming.

They scattered out of the way, terrified as he had a dagger deep in his chest, and yet he continued to scream and rage as he chased them, and Yandalla looked at Sintalla, her face bloodied with dry blood and dirty, and smiled in the darkness.

"We are Undine, we are strong."

Many thousands of Undine had died over the last week under the brutality of the Summanu, and even though it was only several dozen more, for Yandalla and her Undine sisters, it was a start to evening up the numbers. Her father had done his bit, and others all over their land were doing theirs, and even though prisoners, the Undine women would live up to their training, for they too, were proud Undine warriors.

Chapter Seven

Shade and the Apostle

In his time on board, Oaken had got to know Ria and her family much better. He found Ria good company, and really enjoyed his conversations, and her humour. They sailed down the river, and came to a halt close to the bank, and as the long boards were pushed out onto the grass, Tanquilla smiled at him.

"We have had reports from the locals, there is a heavy Summanu presence up ahead, and it may be dangerous to take this vessel further upstream. It is better that you make your start from here. It is not that far to where you were going to leave us, and there is a man named Arak that will lead you from here. He is Shodalt, and this is his homeland, he knows all the hidden paths, and where to avoid. This place is bandit territory, they raid the towns and Summanu for supplies to smuggle into Ranblate, and back to the high place where there are resistance fighters. He is the best that lives within these parts, and will take you safely." Oaken gave a nod.

"I appreciate all you have done for us, you have the gratitude of my people, and of the Undine." Tanquilla smiled.

"We all have a common bond, we strive against the Summanu, great evil has been done to many people. Oaken, it is time the Summanu understood, they cannot take what they feel is theirs, and learn that other races live around them in peace. Take the four winds to them Oaken of the winds, and reset the balance of all life."

Elden had finally found his sea legs, and now they had to leave the ship, he was in good spirits, and thanked many of the crew, as they had been understanding, if not amused at times by his violent sickness. They had taken him under their wing, and took good care of him, and he was grateful as he smiled and joked with them, before lifting his bag to leave the ship.

Ria hugged her mother, and then accompanied Oaken onto the

grass, and it felt strange to be back on land again. Ria took a deep breath, and glanced at him.

"From now on, staying safe, silent, and mindful, will be our way to get there as fast as we can undetected."

He understood, this was a new land he did not know of, and he wanted to be careful. In his mind, nothing could get in his way, he had to get to Yandalla at all costs.

Arak appeared to be a good choice. He was calm, experienced and yet he was cheerful, and very talkative. He was around Oaken's height, possibly a little older, and had short brown hair. His clothes were old and worn, but in a way, it made Oaken feel at ease, as he looked like he could survive out in the wilds. He checked they had food, and handed them dried fruit and meat leathers, as well as making sure they had plenty of water. Some of their journey would be through rough dry, rocky terrain, as they skirted the soldiers of the Summanu.

Ria wanted to keep the party small, she knew a lot of people on route, and so she would use contacts along the way. Once they had all the packs together, of which Ria had given Oaken and Elden packs with two straps so they could wear them on their backs. With the sword in his blanket roll strapped to the side of his pack, they set off across the dry grass and into the trees. They were heading towards a large area of rock, that separated the river from the wide plains of Shodalt, and its semi barren wilderness.

As they walked, Arak filled them in on all the current events, and Oaken was a little shaken when he heard about the proclamation that the Undine were to be considered none human, and were to be hunted and killed, or taken to him to sacrifice to Bharl. Arak explained that some of the half Undine in Ranblate had been hounded out, as bounty hunters sought them out. The rumours talked of how the Undine had been almost wiped out by Balathral, and all towns and villages within Undinalashka, were now under the control of the Summanu, who were allowing their soldiers to claim the lands as their own, and make homes there. Oaken said little and listened, as his anger simmered below the surface.

It was good to be under the trees again, and he had not realised how much he had missed it whilst out at sea. The air was cool and fresh as they climbed higher, the paths weaving around tall trees of rich scented pine. They came out on top of a high wall that looked down over the plains of Shodalt, and Oaken could see in the far off distance, the high range of mountains, that had once been the homeland of the Andalan. As he looked at it, he felt a strange stirring inside him, Ria noticed his gaze.

"That is the home of your mother and father, that is also the place you were born. The temple of the sky is in ruins, all the statues lie smashed and crumbled, and a great golden statue of Bharl has been placed, where once your father stood and spoke to his people." He was not sure how to feel, he felt an anger in his core, but also a strange inner longing to walk the paths he only vaguely remembered now.

"Bharl will never own or truly possess that land, for the sky above it is the true spirit of that place, and a day will come where the books of the sky will reside once again in their true place of rest." She smiled.

"I would like to see that day Oaken." He nodded.

"It will come... What now?" She turned, and looked to the path that followed the ridge.

"We head down, the river lies north, and as you can see, we have many miles to cover."

The walk was a long hot one, and as the day came slowly to an end, Arak found a sheltered place in the rocks, surrounded by trees, and lit a fire, as he reminded them, not only were there bandits, there were also packs of wild hounds, and fire kept them at bay. Oaken settled back on his blanket roll, as the flames flickered, and the huge chunk of meat cooked slowly over it. Elden watched the fat drip into the flames, licking his lips, he had worked up a hunger.

The day drew slowly to a close, they ate their meal, and settled down in front of the fire. Ria and Elden were soon asleep, as Arak sat up on the edge of the rocks, and looked out through the trees into the falling darkness. Oaken lay back on his rolled up blanket and stared into the flames, his mind lost to his thoughts of his mother and Yandalla. Arak watched the darkness, and could see the large fires of the Summanu burning in the distance, there were more and more each time he came into the wide plains. He was not aware that Balathral having achieved his aims, had withdrawn many of his forces back to Andalan. He turned to see Oaken staring into the flames.

"Your sister is very precious to you, what about your parents?" Oaken lifted his eyes from the flames, to see the dark silhouette of Arak.

"My father died when I was ten summers, my mother lives." Arak nodded.

"I lost my parents, and have no other siblings, many of the people of this land were slaughtered before the Undine arrived and faced the Summanu." Oaken understood, he had heard many such tales from his mother and Elaiston.

"I am sorry to hear that." Arak shrugged.

"We live the life we are given, and do the best with the little we have. It has become a skill, spotting each opportunity to prosper is a way of life here, we barter and fight, and hope we survive another day."

In a way it made sense, the whole land was filled with small pockets of people hiding from the Summanu and trying to get by. It was not unsimilar to his own people, without the help of the Undine, they would be left in the wilds to fend for themselves.

His thoughts drifted, as he considered everything, all his life he had been told of the Summanu, and the madness of their leader Balathral. Shengara had killed his father and ended one war, and now there was no real war, just death and destruction. Balathral had raised a greater army than ever before in the history of these lands. What would it take to stop him, would killing him end all of it, or would the people of the Summanu just find another to replace him?

At some point, lost in thought he drifted, and when his eyes opened, Elden was by the fire, adding more wood as the pot hanging above it started to steam. Ria was just a little distance from his side, curled up in her blanket, Elden smiled as he noticed Oaken look at her.

"She had a long day yesterday, she sailed most of the night and then took the watch after Arak, it is still early, we should let her sleep more." Oaken sat up and stretched his limbs, the floor was hard and he was feeling the pains of it.

"We have time, and need to plot our course for the day, let her sleep a while longer."

Elden poured the water into a cup, he was making tea, behind him, Arak slept wrapped up in the long coat he had on his pack. Elden handed him the tea and he took it and sipped at the cup, it was hot and he was not that awake yet. Breakfast consisted of bread and cheese, with some dried fruits, and as the others ate, he sat on the rock and looked out over the land. There was smoke in the distance, Ria came up at his side and sat down, still chewing, she lifted a scope and looked down it.

"We were right, they are all heading towards the falls to take on water. It looks like a lot of the Summanu are heading back, the road south is busy." She handed him the scope and he held it his eyes.

He had never used a scope before, he had heard of them, Eliaston had told him often of how he would use one to look at the stars, so for him it was a novel experience to look down it. The scope was not powerful, but the shapes of the marching armies were just about visible enough to understand where they were. He panned the landscape in front of them, and something caught his eye as he swept across the rough uneven territory. He moved the scope back slowly, and found what he had seen, it was some sort of carriage, with two drivers, it was moving slowly, and had red markings painted on the doors. Oaken took the scope away from his eye, and looked at Ria.

"Who are they, and what do those symbols on their carriage mean?" He pointed, and handed her the scope, she lifted it up and looked down it, and gave a sigh.

"That is the carriage of an Apostle of Bharl, they are known as the Order of Apostles. They travel the land looking for those who did not convert in hope of making them see sense, because only Bharl can protect them. The carriage looks like it was built in Keytan, and not very well by the look of things, you would think in a world ruled by Bharl, they would find them a more suitable form of transport. My mother hates them, she believes they are the vilest of all Balathral's fanatics." It interested Oaken that there were people who want to do that.

"Do these people do this without being forced to, you know, do they choose to do it?" Ria nodded.

"It is their choice, but Oaken, nothing in these lands is free, they make a lot of money collecting donations to build places of worship that never appear. Whoever they are, they will be well fed, and have plenty of precious metal in their pockets." It made little sense to him.

"I do not understand that, I live with the Undine and I know their culture, but I was raised in the ways of Nuada, and I have seen things that help me to believe. I see Yandalla who shares both of our cultures, and she respects both, so I do not understand why anyone would embrace another cultures god without proof." She gave a chuckle.

"Really, look to the Undine and what is happening to them. Oaken, they are being slaughtered in the name of a god they have no use for, Bharl. The instinct to live is strong in all cultures, and the Shodalt and Keytan have suffered, it is not hard to pretend you love a god, when there is a sword at your throat. Strong men lead, but they are few in number, and behind them, there are many helpless and weak to follow them." He gave a long sigh.

"So, what is the solution, replace Balathral, because that would not be an easy task?" Ria turned and face him.

"Oaken, look out there, look at all that barren land. You know, there was a time during your father's life when out there were thousands of homes and farms. People worked hard, but what they had was the fruits of their labour, and then along came Balalaran, and his son Balathral. Those people fled and live in hiding unable to work the land they own, because they lived in fear of the Summanu. Ranblate, is the only place they are safe, because Balathral takes sport from seeing them suffer. I have been there, I have seen what it is like, and it is rough and violent where your life has no meaning. Good women who once had an honest living survive by selling their bodies, and then smoke the fume of plants at night to hide their feelings of shame and self disgust for what they have had to do. Young girls are bought and sold openly in the streets, and either enslaved, or forced to sate the drunk men's lust. Good men who once worked hard, live in a cup filled with the strong brews of sugars, that ferment and intoxicate their minds. Their homes and farms lay wasted, because the Summanu demanded they worship a god they did not know." She took a deep breath and calmed herself, he could see the anger in her eyes.

"Many of those I once called friend, now in their shame, they hide from me. Don't you see, their lives may be ruined, but they were a once decent people, they opposed Bharl, and they have paid a high price for it. Oaken, if you are asking me should the one who replaced your father, and carries his sword fight for them, my answer is yes, because who else do they have?"

There was such a power of conviction in her words, and in many ways, she reminded him of his mother. She too, had fought to keep the Andalan together with the force of her beliefs, and she had done it. There had been moments where the pressure was on, and the Andalan had faltered, and it had always been his mother that at the very last minute, had always pulled them back together. He smiled at her.

"You sound like my mother." She gave a slight smirk.

"That is a high compliment, my mother holds her in very high regard, she has told me often, more women should look to her for inspiration." Ria took a breath and lowered her voice.

"Oaken, we are here to save your sister, and yet beside her, in front of her, and behind her are many other women. All of them are heading to their death, or the houses of Sakanula, where their bodies will be sold by Summanu men, without asking them. This whole land is filled with women who suffer terrible things because their men are not strong enough to defend them. Let me ask you this, does that sword in your hand have the power to defend everyone, because, if it does, in my mind, it should?" She gave a sigh and got up off the rock.

"We will need to leave soon, we have a long walk ahead of us, it will give you time to think."

She walked away down the path, and he felt her words still echoing through his mind, as he asked himself one question. He had set off thinking only to save his sister and help the Undine, but should he do more? He gave a heavy sigh, and spoke to himself.

"This task is more suited to my father, the sword is still his, and he had the power and the wisdom I lack."

He wearily stood, grabbed his things and shouldered his pack, and they set off with Arak leading. It took about another hour for them to reach the bottom of the pass, and head onto the wide plains, which had once been filled with life. As they walked over what was a dust filled and rocky land, he noticed the burned out remains of what he assumed were once homes. He spotted the charred timbers, of where a home once stood, and it was clear, that around each of them, the land had been cleared of all the rock. He could see how at one time, each of these plots would have been filled with growing crops, not unsimilar to some of the small homesteads of Undinalashka.

As the sun rose, they stopped for a break, up ahead there was a ravine, and Arak told them the terrain would be become difficult and hard going, as this was the edge of the bandit country, and they would need their wits about them. They sat together and made a small fire, and heated up the water to make a refreshing tea. Ria had brought many herbs from her land, and he found they had a reviving effect on him. She had surprised him a great deal since they had met, and her mother was right, she was very intelligent, and very at ease in these lands. Her confidence wore off on him, the more he was around her. He found her good company, and in a strange way, educational.

They were sat in a circle eating, when somewhere behind them, there was a faint scream, and it sounded like a child, Oaken turned, and looked behind himself. He continued to chew as he stood up.

"Did anyone else hear that?" Ria sipped her drink.

"This land is filled with screams, the plain is flat, sound travels a long way."

Oaken felt unsure, he took a few paces forward towards the edge of the ravine, he was sure he heard the clash of steel. His ears strained as he walked closer, Arak got up and followed him. When Oaken reached the top of the steep side of what was a good sized drop, and looked down, he was unsure of what he was looking at.

Down below in the bottom of the ravine was the carriage he had seen earlier, and a fat man in brown robes squatted, his head bleeding. At his side were two children, and he was holding onto them, as they shook in terror. All around the carriage were dead bodies, the floor splashed red with their blood, and stood in the middle, was a small white skinned figure, who was holding what looked like a torn sheet, and they were cleaning their sword.

Arak appeared at his side and looked down, the white skinned figure was a woman, and he recognised the black waistcoat type garment and short skirt, there was no doubt, she was Undine. What confused him, was her hair, it was short and messy, most Undine had long hair that they plaited either side of their faces, and yet this woman had cut all her hair off. Arak gave him a nudge.

"Come on, saving the life of an apostle is good paying money, and the Undine will fetch a good price."

Oaken blinked and reached out, he grabbed Arak by the sleeve, and Arak turned back to look at him.

"What... Come on, hurry, if she gets away it will be a sad loss." Oaken held tight and frowned.

"What do you mean, she is Undine?" He pulled his arm free and nodded.

"I know... Oaken, stop wasting time, if we sell her to a night house, she will bring good silver, even Balathral will pay good coin for her."

Oaken felt shocked, as Arak turned, and headed onto the slope pulling out his sword. He could not believe what Arak had in mind, his sister was half Undine, how could he even think of selling her? Ria walked up and looked down; she took note of the scene.

"What is that idiot doing, is he deliberately trying to get himself killed? Oh Smit, he knows these paths better than any, and we will not find one better than him, what an idiot." She was so calm, but Oaken's insides were twisting.

"He said she is worth a lot of money, especially to the night houses, Ria, she is Undine." She nodded.

"I know, and that idiot is going to get himself killed, she already took out eight, does he really think he is that good? My money is on the girl, this is her territory, and if she is not selling her body, then she must be good."

Oaken did not know what to do, he could not believe she was so calm, he looked down the slope where the rock was sliding as Arak slithered down at speed with his sword out. The Undine appeared to be unconcerned, she examined her blade, and then dropped the cloth, and turned to face where Arak came slithering to the bottom.

The Apostle, had climbed back in the carriage, and pulled the children in with him, and the doors closed. Oaken felt tense, he was annoyed at Arak, and could not let an Undine be harmed.

"I have to stop him." He stepped onto the side, as Ria frowned.

"Why Oaken? Look, if he is so stupid, let him face her, it matters not, he will not survive her."

Oaken could not believe it, this country was insane, his feet slithered as the stone slipped, and he held out his arms to try and stabilise himself, this was nowhere near as easy as Arak had made it look.

At the bottom of the valley, the Undine turned, and looked at Arak, as he reached the bottom wearing a wide smile. She stood like frozen stone, her short sword held firmly in her hand. She was small, lean, very toned, as her short tufted hair blew in the slight hot breeze, her eyes fixed on Arak. He gave a little giggle, as he walked onto the road like surface, his sword held firmly in his hand.

"Oh yes my pretty, you are nice, you have a good ass, good legs, shame you are not bigger in the chest, but still, you will fetch top prices." She spat at the floor.

"Summanu fan dit!"

She raised her arm, and her sword came up in a stance of defence, Arak swung his blade from side to side, and smiled.

"A few well placed nicks, and they will bring this hound to heal. Little cuts heal fast, but do not worry my pretty, I will not harm the look of the package, after all, that is where the value lies."

Oaken was sliding at a fast pace, leaning back, and doing his best not to go head over heels, and end up flat on his face. The rocks slid from the sides, creating a large cloud of choking dust, he tried to keep his eyes on the girl, but it was not possible, as he shouted out.

"ARAK, just leave her, she is not our enemy, the Summanu are." Arak smiled, as he took a step forward, and raised his voice.

"Stay out of this Oaken, you had your chance, she is mine now, and this is good business."

The Undine curled her lip, her eyes fixed with hate, and without so much as a blink, she bounded straight up into the air, and came hurtling at Arak. He brought up his sword, and they collided and rang out. She came landing back on her bare feet, she pulled a long knife out of a scabbard on the back of her belt. Arak laughed as he spun around to face her, she struck like lightening, swiping the knife right across his side, and around to his stomach, and let out a wild Undine war scream. Ria gave a nod of approval as she watched from above.

"I was right, if she lives here without selling her body, she has to be bloody tough."

As the dust cleared, Oaken watched Arak flop to his knees, as his clothing stained, as blood ran down, pooling on the floor, in a large puddle of red. She stood frozen, her back to him, as he watched Arak fall forward and hit the floor. The Undine bent over, and slipped her blade into the back of his jacket, she gave it a flick, and it cut clean through. She reached down and grabbed the fabric, and then with the flick of her wrist, the sword blade sliced through the rest of the cloth, cutting a section of it off. She lifted it, and began to clean her long knife, wiping it down, and making sure all of it was off, before reaching back, and slipping it back into the scabbard.

Oaken took a step forward, and her head whipped around fast, and he felt himself catch his own breath, as he stared at her. There was no doubt she was Undine, but what caught him off guard were her eyes, they were a deep intense blue. Apart from his sister who had green eyes, he had never seen an Undine that did not have white eyes. He lifted his hands as she stared at him, and nodded to her.

"Ca Baska!" She frowned, and tilted her head slightly, his ability to talk Undine, clearly surprised her. He took a deep breath, and another step forward, his hands still up.

"I am not here to hurt you; I told him to leave you alone."

She looked unsure, she clearly had little trust of people, but he could not blame her for that, he had thought Arak was a good guy, but he was going to try and catch her so he could sell her. She watched him very carefully as he moved closer, he turned his head slightly, and looked to the carriage. He could just make out what looked like a man with a shaven head watching him, he turned to look at the Undine, she had not so much as moved, he gave her another nod.

"My name is Oaken, what is yours?" Her voice was soft and

low, not unlike Yandalla's.

"Dar len eah ae lune." He nodded, and thought of it, he smiled and lowered his hands.

"That is a long name, shade below rock in moonlight... I suppose in my language that would be Night Shade?" She watched him carefully, but gave a slight nod.

He was not dead yet, so he had lasted longer than Arak, which was so far good. He lowered his hands, and nodded to her, and spoke in the common tongue.

"I mean you no harm, I have a sister who is half Undine, her name is Yandalla, she is a prisoner of the Summanu, I am heading to try and rescue her." The Undine smirked.

"Shen tey!" He smiled.

"Yes, it is foolish, but she is my sister, how can I leave her?" She nodded, and relaxed a little, then surprised him as she spoke in the common tongue.

"Save Undine, need many." He took a deep breath, and agreed.

"She is my sister and only fifteen Summers, I cannot let them hurt her or the others with her, I have to find a way to help them." He could see she was thinking about it; she took a moment.

"You have way?" He smiled.

"I did until you killed my guide, although, I did tell him he was a fool, and to leave you." She nodded.

"All men fool, want coin." Oaken relaxed a little more.

"Not all men, some of us who live with the Undine see their value in more than just coin, they are good people, and I have many as friends." She nodded.

"Undine gone; all kilt."

He smiled, she was so like Yandalla, much fiercer, but he could not help looking into her blue eyes, and feeling the same life and the same spirit as his sister, he pointed to the cart.

"I am going to check on those people to make sure they are alright."

She scoffed and turned back to her blade and started to wipe it. Oaken walked over towards the cart, the door was closed, and a frightened looking fat man stared down at him.

"What are you doing, she was going to take the children, go and kill her?" Oaken looked back at her, she was knelt down checking the pockets and bags of the dead for things she could use. He looked back at the fat Apostle.

"What happened here?" The man looked almost lost for words.

"What happened... Can you not see? I was robbed, they took my horses, and they were going to take the children. My driver jumped down and they killed him, and as they grabbed at the children, she appeared and killed them all. She wants the children, now go and kill her." Oaken nodded his head.

"So, if I hear things right, she saved your life, if she had not shown up, they would have killed you and taken the children, am I right?" The man stared at him in utter disbelief.

"That is not the point, she would have killed me to get the children." Oaken shrugged.

"Maybe, but you are still alive, and there are eight dead men who would have killed you for certain. I heard saving the life of an apostle is worth money, you should thank her and reward her." The apostle screwed up his face.

"But she is Undine, she is not even human." Oaken reached up, and gripped the front of his robes, as his face reddened.

"Listen to me man of Bharl, I have a half sister who is the kindest and most beautiful soul I have ever known, and she is half Undine, just like that girl there. Now pay her, or I will slit your throat just for insulting my sister, and give her all your gold." He pushed hard and the old man went sprawling back with a squeal into the carriage, and the children gave startled wails.

Ria walked with Elden up to the side of the carriage, she smiled at him, and he looked at her not understanding why she looked so happy.

"What?"

"I wondered what would push you over the edge, and I knew a man of Bharl would find it. Good, you needed the push, it is about time you got angry, you will need it."

The apostle appeared at the window looking frightened, he swallowed hard and handed over a small black bag of coins, Oaken gave a nod, and snatched it out of his hand. He turned and walked away, heading back towards the Undine who was sat wiping her blade, and polishing it up. Oaken stood in front of her, and held out the bag, she looked up at him, and he smiled.

"He is worthless, but you saved his life, if not, he would be dead, this is your reward." He dropped it into her hand, and she stared at it for a moment and then looked up.

"You no normal, who is you?" He shrugged.

"I am Oaken, I am trying to save my sister, in a land I do not know, with no guide, and honestly, I am learning more about myself each day. My guide is dead, I have food and water, and could use the help of someone I can trust. Tell me Shade, can I trust you, and if I do, will you help me free some of your people?" She dropped her hand, and slid the money into a small bag on her belt.

"You have meat?" He smiled.

"Only in dried strips, but if we can hunt it, we can cook it." She stood up.

"Give meat... Then walk." He smiled, and looked back to Ria.

"I need meat leathers, give me a few, I think she is hungry." She nodded, and looked at Ria and smiled.

"Me hungry."

It was good to have a new guide, however there was a problem. The apostle, was named Jenmar, and he was accompanied by two children around ten to twelve summers of age. One was a boy named Caleb, who it appeared was to be trained as an apostle. The girl was his sister, her name was Meda, and all of them were stranded. The horses had been cut free, but with the appearance of Shade, they had bolted, and ran off. The Apostle and his two charges were stranded in a very hostile area.

The other problem was, Jenmar hated Undine, although to be fair, Shade hated the Summanu, of which Jenmar was a symbol. Ria walked up to Oaken as he stood pondering his problem.

"This is unexpected Oaken." He gave a sigh.

"What do we do now, they are stranded, I am not keen on leaving children out in the wilderness? To be honest, after what he said about the Undine, I would have no problems leaving him here to the mercy of his god Bharl, just not children." She agreed.

"Our other problem is Shade, she hates his guts, if you look at it, he is a supporter of those killing the Undine, the fact he is alive is a miracle." Oaken nodded, she handed him a good quality belt with a sword on it.

"Here, take this, not every occasion will require your gift of

Nuada, this will serve in those times." He took the sword and fastened the belt around his waist; she made a good point. He looked at Shade who was happily sat eating her dried meat.

"I want to trust her to guide us safely, do you think we can?" Ria gave a nod.

"The Undine stick to their word, and you have made a deal with her. If I am honest, I trust her more than I do the apostle, I think the way he fauns all over those children makes me cringe. An Undine who hates him and watches him, might be a good thing."

Oaken agreed, there was something sickening about the man, and he really did not trust or like him. He knew he could not leave a man to die out in this barren land, but he could not deny, he was not thrilled about taking him along. It took some time to organise, but finally the apostle accepted that he no choice but to leave his carriage, and seek the protection of the group, as his only means of getting to a village.

Shade looked at the maps and understood what they were trying to do, her use of common tongue was not easy, but with some translation into Undine, she could communicate enough to arrange a new route with them. She did point out that the way Arak was taking them, would lead them well out of their way, and they would be late to meet the carts when they turned up. Oaken was happy, she had appeared to have kept her word, and so once the apostle had packed a bag for himself, and one for each child, they set off up the other side of the ravine.

At the top, Shade picked up a bag made of woven grasses with a blanket roll. She had a short bow, and a long thin pouch again made of woven grasses, in which Oaken could see arrows. Shade led the way, walking in front, which she was happy with, as the apostle was not that fit, and so lagged at the back with Elden. Shade was alert, she noticed things very quickly, and several times they stopped and took cover, as bandits or soldiers passed by.

By the time the night came, they had changed course completely, and Shade had led them into a tree lined slope, where there were large rocks scattered amongst the trees. It was a place she knew well and had used many times, as one rock in particular was higher up, with a large overhang. It was large enough for all of them to shelter under, Jenmar collapsed, it had been a very long time since he had walked anywhere.

They gathered together and lit a fire, under the shelter, Elden had found some salted meats in the carriage, so he put his pan onto boil and added the few fresh vegetables he had, and made a thin meaty broth. Shade added some wild herbs, which caused a stir, as she bent over, and Jenmar noticed her lack of under garments, and became quite excited. She noticed him looking and sneered at him.

"Steng hem!"

Oaken noticed it, and turned as Shade dropped the herbs in the pan, looking at Jenmar with disgust. She walked out from under the overhang, and sat on a rock just in front of him, and took out a stone to sharpen her knife. Ria looked at him and raised her eyebrows at him, she understood some Undine. Jenmar looked at them all, and shrugged.

"If she has nothing there to hide it, why complain when a man looks, after all, if she cared at all, she would cover it." Ria looked at him.

"With what, I wear pants, but without them I have nothing to cover me, no Undine does, do you?" He looked appalled.

"Yes, I do, I have a loin cloth below my robes." Ria appeared interested.

"Really, show it to me." His eyes opened wide.

"I will not, it is not decent." Ria smirked.

"Neither is rape, and yet it appears Bharl allows it, I am sorry Jenmar, do not talk of decency, when out there as we speak, the men of your god are raping and butchering a whole race of Undine." He looked at her his eyes wide.

"Bharl the almighty is a merciful god, had they converted they would be alive." Oaken turned around and looked at him, his dislike for this man was growing by the moment.

"I heard of no choice for the Undine to convert when the Summanu ran into their sacred space, and started to hack them up. They have lived in peace separated from all the other territories for years, they were happy to be free of war and away from the evil that walked in Pangela. They wanted to be left alone in peace, they did not ask Balathral to send his men to rape and kill them. I feel Jenmar, you should be wary of talk of the glory of your god around me. I have seen nothing good to date in following this Bharl." He shrunk back and said nothing, which pleased Oaken.

Shade stood up and went tense, Oaken caught her movement in the corner of his eye, and turned to her. She was stood frozen, her hand on the hilt of her sword. She was a little way down from the entrance, and so the others had not seen her, he stood up and walked softly to her side. She was listening carefully, her head giving little twitches, he had seen Yandalla do it many times as a child when she hunted the hopper bugs. He kept his voice almost a whisper.

"What is it, what do you hear?"

Chapter Eight

Fates of the Winds

He was relaxed, and now suddenly he felt the tension in the air, as he watched Shade, knowing, like Yandalla, she had very keen senses. Shade turned slowly, her ears straining to pick up on every sound in the area. She spoke very quietly, as her head twitched, as if something had touched her.

"Soft feet, careful, slow, not Summanu, animal me thinks."

Oaken tried to listen, but could hear nothing, he stared into the trees below them, but there was no sign of anything. Shade moved forward, and stopped, she moved her head from side to side.

"No fear us, not harm."

Oaken had no idea why or how she could work that out, he could see nothing and not sense any kind of danger at all. She sniffed the air, and froze, her head moved very slowly, as she sniffed the air again. Her blue eyes glinted in the dim light, and she gave herself a quiet nod, as if understanding something he did not.

"Calthra!" He blinked, she said cat, what did she mean? He frowned at her.

To his left, a large cat jumped up from the grass, and it was big, he jumped back with surprise. It was golden and covered in black spots, Shade looked at it and smiled, she let go of her sword hilt.

"Leyarken."

She smiled, as the cat jumped down and walked towards her, it stopped and sniffed at her leg, then walked past her, and into the overhang. Elden stood up, and squealed in fright as he saw it, the two children panicked, and gripped tightly to Jenmar, who sat holding his bowl of stew looking terrified, Ria saw the cat and gave a big smile.

"Vesta, I was not sure my message would get to you."

Oaken stared lost for words, as the cat sat down, and then suddenly, it stretched, and from nowhere there was a completely naked woman. He swallowed hard, never in his life had he seen anything like this, the naked woman embraced Ria.

"We got it, but you were not where you were supposed to be, we have spent all day looking for you. We got your scent an hour ago." Oaken frowned.

"We?" She turned and smiled, he swallowed hard, she was amazingly beautiful, and naked. Shade gave a giggle and leaned into him and whispered.

"Steng hem." He turned, and looked at her as she smiled, he frowned.

"No, I am not... I ... Just, you know?" He lifted his hand.

"She was a cat one moment, and then... Well?" Ria giggled.

"She was a naked female." Oaken stammered a little.

"I have never seen anything like it, that is all... It surprised me... A lot." The woman smiled.

"You must be Oaken, I am Vesta, and that behind you is my husband Zeron?"

He turned to see a naked man stood behind him, the man smiled, and walked under the overhang, Shade leaned over, to have a really good look, and he looked at her.

"Who is the pervert now?" She giggled.

"Mmm, Yan tee!"

Her eyes were wide open, and it was obvious as Shade looked at the muscular body of the man, she highly approved. Jenmar had his hands over the children's eyes. Ria walked over with a giggle and hugged Zeron. She looked at Oaken.

"This is Vesta and Zeron, I sent word to them to try and get them to meet us, they are from the Leyarken territory. They are split spirit beings, and change their shape at will."

They both stood by the fire smelling the pot, Elden whose eyes were fixed on Vesta, spooned out a bowl of hot broth, and lifted it up to her, she smiled at him and took it. He handed one to Zeron, and both of them sat, held their bowls up, and licked at the broth. Elden noticed, and put the spoons back down on the rock, Vesta lifted her eyes from her bowl.

"This is good, we thank you." He smiled, and Shade gave another giggle.

The two Leyarken, sat with Ria and talked of what they had

seen since leaving their land. For them, a lot had changed, it had been a long time since they had journeyed out of their land. The Leyarken had chosen to remain in their own territory and guard the lands they had, and so far, Balathral had not entered the jungle, although the last time he had, the Undine had lived there. He had suffered a lot of casualties to his men from surprise attacks, as Undine attacked and then disappeared back into the jungle. Zeron put his bowl down, and leaned back on the wall as he licked his lips.

"We owe the Undine, for they shared a land in peace with us, and played a big part in pushing the Summanu out of it. It is why we are here, our people took a vote, and decided to help them in their hour of need, as they did us." Ria gave a slight smile.

"Shengara will appreciate that, he favours your people highly, how is Aisie?" Vesta smiled.

"She is content, and is as always a fair guide to our people, she misses her husband, but understands the needs of his people."

Oaken was still trying to understand the complex act of changing from an animal to a human. How did something as big as a person manage to squeeze all of themselves into a cat? It made no sense to him, because even though what he saw was big for a cat, it still was not big enough to fit a whole human inside. He was supposed to be on watch, although, these two had just appeared and walked past him, so he wondered, what else was out there he had no idea about? Shade was sat on a large rock a few large paces outside the overhang, he moved over to her side, she nudged up a little to let him share the flat area.

"All quiet, no moves." He nodded and breathed in; his mind still preoccupied.

Zeron appeared a few moments later, and walked down the path a little way, he bent down, and picked up a bag and some loose clothing. He walked back and gave a nod as he passed, and Oaken turned to watch, he handed a long robe to Vesta, and she pulled it on, which answered one of the other questions he had floating around his head. Shade sat smiling, she approved greatly of Zeron, it was clear.

The time passed, and he stared into the dark, unaware of the group behind him, and lost in his thoughts, when Shade turned to him.

"Sister, you big love for her?" He gave a slight nod, as the thought of her came into his mind.

"Yes, she means a great deal, I love her deeply." Shade nodded, as she understood.

"Hear words, they big power on Summanu, Jenmar." Oaken lowered his voice.

"I feel he is not to be trusted, but I could not leave him, I did not like what he said about you." She turned to look at him and smiled.

"Made good feeling, think me like sister." He gave a shrug.

"I meant what I said, I live with the Undine people, and you are one of them Shade." She shook her head.

"Have no people. Anna Ma kilt, Anna Pa sell me." Oaken felt his breath caught in his throat, and he swallowed.

"He sold you... He was your father, how could he?"

"He bad man, kilt now... Me kilt him." The shock hit him again, and he blinked, he could not believe his ears, she smiled at him.

"Is right, he bad Shodalt, me run, me live."

In a way it made sense, he had wondered why she was alone in the wastelands, and not with others of her kind. Knowing her mother died, and trying to contemplate how a father could even consider selling his daughter, just filled his mind with so many questions, he had no idea where to begin.

"Shade, you should go to the Undine, they will accept you, and you will have others like you around you. Shade, you cannot be alone forever." She smiled.

"Me like Oaken, he good man, Jenmar like my Anna Pa, he no have child's." Oaken nodded.

"Do you think he will hurt them?" She glanced back.

"Me here. know, me kilt him."

Oaken had no doubt in his mind, he had seen how quickly she took out Arak, and there were eight others dead. Somehow, he was glad she liked him, he was starting to understand, those she did not like, did not live long. He turned to her; his voice low.

"Life is hard, it cannot be easy to be so alone? Shade, I realise you do not think so, but the Undine will welcome you to them, especially now, as they have suffered many losses." She gave a smile as she looked at him.

"Summanu bad, Undine lose, then, me only Undine. Me lone, be lone when Summanu win. Me live, know dirt, tree, rock." In a way he could understand that. She patted his shoulder, and stood up.

"Sleep now." He gave a nod; she left him alone staring out into the darkness.

He watched as she smiled and left, she was so like many others he knew from the Undine race, and not unlike Yandalla. She was medium sized, and thin, and yet as she passed him, he saw the muscle tone in her legs and how although her body was quite lean, like all Undine, she was very powerful. As a child there had been many occasions where Yandalla and he had wrestled, and even though small, for her size she had great strength. Shade was very like her, and he felt reassured to know she had tagged along with them. Ria walked out from under the overhang, and crouched at his side, she handed him a tea.

"Here, it will get cold tonight, there is little cloud cover." He took it, and held it with both hands, she was right, there was a chill in the air.

"I think our new guide trusts you, she appears very relaxed around you." He gave a slight yawn, and blinked as he lifted his cup.

"I have no idea why, but I like her, she feels fair, which probably sounds strange, as we have not known her long. I have a strong sense; we are safe with her." Ria nodded.

"Maybe she just recognises the loner in you, I think it is something she understands, and I also think she too feels she is safe with us." He gave a slight nod.

"Possibly, she does not like Jenmar, she really does not trust him."

Ria turned to look at her, she was sat in the corner out of the way, her bag wedged behind her, and one hand on the hilt of her knife. Her eyes were closed, and yet, somehow, Ria felt Shade was aware of everything around her.

"I trust her instincts, she has survived in this land alone, and that is no easy feat. This has become a hostile place to live, the terrain is not easy, and the land is filled with some pretty severe bandits. Shade has navigated that alone, and if she is cautious about someone, I think it is wise to pay attention." He had been thinking the same. Ria patted his shoulder and stood up.

"Vesta and Zeron have offered to take the watch, so get some sleep, we will need it tomorrow, we have a long walk, and some difficult terrain to cross. I will fill you in about things at first light."

Across Undinalashka, over eighty percent of the small villages had been attacked and set alight. Shengara had arrived back on the high mount, and stood with Sarka as they both looked at the smoke still rising through the canopies of the trees in the moonlight. Areas of the land glowed orange and red in the darkness, where new buildings burned. His eyes glowed white, and were focused on the land he saw as the home of his people. Sarka stood at his side and let a long sigh pass her lips.

"This is so wrong, you lived here in peace, Balathral has no right to do this."

Shengara stared at the place where they had all been gathered, knowing the smoke he saw was the place where his people had been slaughtered and burned.

"He wants all of us dead, he wants control of everything, which is why I have gathered every last Undine together, and we will for a time leave this land." Sarka turned to look at him.

"How do you mean, leave?" Shengara gave a slight smirk, as he turned to face her.

"I will leave capable men here to protect you, but I have spoken with Evander, and I aim to take the two ships we have off this land in the water, and take my best fighters up the Keytan River. We will return to Leyarken, and gather with Pallum who has more men going to his aid, and we will take this fight to the foot of the high steps in Salanula, capital city of Sumanula. I will face Balathral, and in front of his people, I will kill him as I did his father. I will prove he is not a god, but a man with a corrupt mind." Sarka shook her head slowly, as she spoke.

"Shengara, that is suicide, Balathral has thousands of men at his disposal, your people will be wiped out long before you get to the high temple of Bharl." He stared down at the smoke over his land.

"Sarka, staying here is the real suicide, nearly all of his forces are here. Boats move faster than legs, I can be in his cities long before his armies leave my lands, and head back to protect him. My people are down there, attacking him in small groups to create chaos and have Balathral think there are more of us, just like Pallum in the desert. As long as we fight here, the Summanu will not leave, and that will give my people the chance they need. We owe you a great debt, you have nursed my people and helped them recover, this will not be forgotten, the Undine and the Andalan will always have peace side by side."

Shengara owed the life of his people to the Andalan. They had advanced medicinal knowledge, and Sarka had supervised many of his people who had arrived, teaching his people new ways to clean and sterilise wounds. In the past, many died not from their wounds, but the infections that arose from them, and with the Andalan taking his people in, they had seriously increased their chances of survival.

Sarka had not really understood as she stood with Shengara, but leaving his wounded here with her to heal, if all went ill, some of the Undine would live, and his race would survive. Those left behind, were the real future of his race, because there was no way Balathral could reach or attack the Andalan, because they were separated by a wide and mighty drop. Eliaston had made sure that the Andalan people were placed at regular intervals all around the large mount, so that no area of the mount could be bridged and breached without them knowing. For now, the Andalan were not Balathral's priority, the complete removal of the Undine was, and that could be his greatest mistake.

Far away in Sumanula, Balathral decked out in robes of deep red and embroidered with elaborate patterns of golden thread, sat on a huge golden throne. Twenty steps below him, Tallif, the general of all his armies knelt before him.

"Your holiness, son of Bharl, all goes well in the undying lands, and they appear to die better than expected." Balathral smirked at the humour.

"I hear there are still small groups running wild in the trees."

"There are, but we are sweeping across their lands and rooting them out, and all will face and feel the touch of our swords." Balathral smiled.

"You stay until every last one is dead; I want that race wiping away forever."

"It is as you wish, and three thousand sacrifices are currently on route, to offer to the great lord Bharl, and their blood will bring high honour to the people of Summanu." Balathral moved on his throne and looked excited.

"All women I hope?"

"Indeed, they are your mightiness. The wombs of the Undine will be opened up in praise of Bharl, to ensure no Undine is ever born in these or other lands again." Balathral gave a satisfied chuckle.

"Our people have enjoyed the sight of sacrifice; I am pleased we will have so many more offerings. Our people need to witness the power of a god, as I slit the Undine from top to toe, and pull out their infected and inferior organs, and show their soiled souls to our people. They will praise the mighty power of the high and glorious God Bharl."

It was a chilling thought, as Balathral sat and talked about the slaughter of an innocent race, almost as if discussing the weather, or the food for the next weeks menu. His utter contempt at naming the Undine not human or a life form, showed how cold and unfeeling his blood ran, and even for some of the Summanu, it was chilling to comprehend what their armies were doing. They may not completely agree, but they would never speak of it, for to do so would bring about their deaths, such was the fear of the rule they lived under.

As the night wore into the early hours, Shengara walked around the mount. He visited the temple where many of his people lay wounded, and knelt at the side of each of them. He told them of their bravery, and he was grateful to them for doing their best to protect their race, then laid his hand on their brow. With his eyes closed, he would give them the blessing of the land and the sky, which was the traditional way of their people to ensure their safety and survival always.

In doing so, he made them one with the earth and the sky, and so no matter what they faced in the future, they would know that their leader had favoured them highly, and charged them with the care of land of their people. For an Undine, there was no greater honour, and even though wounded, he could see in their eyes, their undying loyalty to their race, and seriousness they held having received it from him personally.

As Shengara spoke to every injured Undine, on the beaches below the high cliff, the Undine warriors gathered. Some came down from the high walls, and some from within the trees, as they waited for the boats to come across the water and land on the sand. Two thousand Undine, heavily armed and ready, crossed the water in the darkness, it appeared like a lot, but compared to the forces of the Summanu, it was little, and they knew that they would face overwhelming odds if they wanted to face Balathral.

Every one of them knew, that they may be going to their death, and yet they still volunteered and climbed up the rope ladders onto the ships. As they manned the boats, away across the on the other side of the land. Within the dunes, another two hundred Undine had met up with Pallum and were working in groups, some attacking and some resting, ensuring the Summanu had no rest in the cooler hours of the night, and the exhaustion was starting to show. All over Undinalashka, small groups were working within the cover of the dense trees to appear out of nowhere, and strike at the Summanu soldiers, and then disappear without a trace leaving lethal traps behind them.

Summanu soldiers would run into the trees, only to find pits filled with sharp spikes, that they fell into, or spring loaded traps, that would swing large groups of long sharp spikes into them, impaling them where they stood. The Summanu wounded were stacking up at a slow and steady pace, and the officers of the Summanu were scrambling to find answers, as they knew Balathral would never accept anything other than the complete annihilation of the Undine.

It was dawn when Shengara removed the sling off his heavily bandaged arm, and gave a smile to Sarka.

"May the four winds ever blow in your favour Sarka of the Andalan, and if this is the last that we meet, know this, you are the most honourable of your line, and I have felt a privilege knowing of you." She smiled, but her heart felt heavy, for she did not want him to go.

"You honour me greatly and know this Shengara of the Undine, you are a glowing example to your people, for you have ruled with great honour and been fair in your judgements. If you fall, you will be remembered always as the hero of your kin, but please, do not throw away the life that has been bestowed upon you freely. Watch your shadow, and walk with a sure foot my friend, for I have a great desire to sit with you as we once did, and talk of life and its meanings." He nodded his head at her, knowing her deep feelings of sadness he was leaving.

"Hold the winds safe for me until I return, for I would wish to blow with freedom around my people once more." He swung around onto the ladder, and slowly descended leaving her alone at the top of the rock, and Sarka lifted her eyes to the two boats anchored out to sea.

"May the blessing of the four winds give you strengthened force, within brisk sails, and the sun of the sky light your way to freedom my friends." She turned with a sad heart, and walked back to her home, feeling more alone than ever before in her life. She stopped and looked south, trying to hold back her tears.

"Stay safe my husband and children, the winds blow around you."

Chapter Nine

The Coming Storm

It was still dark when Shade woke Oaken up, and handed him a drink, he sat up, and shivered a little, Ria smiled.

"We have a long walk through some difficult terrain, it will get hotter as the day moves on, we will need an early start. Vesta and Zeron will travel ahead of us to search the trail for enemies, find news, and they will report back if they find anything."

She was not wrong about the distance. Shade's skin was white as snow, which in the darkness appeared to glow, which was good, as when they set off it was pitch black with few stars in the sky, and the ground was rough and uneven. Oaken could hardly see the floor or even where he was putting his feet, and found it easier to stumble along, his eyes fixed on Shade who was a few paces in front.

It had felt like forever, when the sun started to come up, and as it rose in the sky and he looked back, the slope lined with trees they had made camp on, appeared a lot further away than he thought it would be. All around him, the floor was dusty, uneven, and rocky, although it was clear that where they were walking was some form of carved out depression, that had served at some time as a roadway. Either side were the remains of what had once been villages, although, now there was little to show that, as everything had been burned out of existence.

Dark coloured patches on the rocks and earth, marked out places where buildings had one stood, with stumps of burned out wood sticking out of the earth. Burned, dried, worn by time, preserved by the fire and weather proofed, and he could see what were once the doorframes of houses or barns had stood. There were little signs of life, just a few scattered and ancient weathered and twisted trees, but apart from that, everything was dried out, and reduced to the dust that blew up in breeze and tasted dry. His first impression of Shodalt, was it was nothing more than a barren, deserted landscape.

Twenty summers ago, this had been a fertile land filled with an abundance of crops, and a land of green that stretched for as far as the eye could see, and now all of it had gone. Erased and left for dead, a land of nothing, no life, no people, and no water. The rivers that once flowed through Shodalt, had been diverted, dug by hand by the slaves of the Summanu, and now all water ran into Sumanula, to feed their crops and their expanding population. New lakes and dams had been created, and all to the praise and glory of Bharl. Shodalt was a soulless and desolate country with no god, as Bharl demanded all fall to their knees before him, or die.

When the day moved to the midway point, and the sun was at its highest, they stopped, much to the relief of the party. They had reached a steep incline surrounded by large rocks, and took shelter in the cooler shade behind them. Jenmar who was not used to walking was struggling and had fallen behind, and Elden had hung back with him to assist him. Oaken sat back, and sipped from his water skin, as he wiped the sweat off his face and the back of his neck, Ria looked red in the face and hot, Shade looked completely unaffected.

Jenmar arrived, he was bright red in the face and dripping in sweat, he was a large man who had lived a life of greed and laziness, and so for him, a man who was in every way unhealthy and unfit, it had taken the greatest toll on him. Oaken was unconcerned with Jenmar, who sat back against a rock panting and rubbing his feet, staring at Shade with malice.

"If that creature had killed the two who were stealing the horses first, we would not be walking." Shade looked up and noticed him looking at her, she scowled at him.

"If kilt you first, me have quiet." Oaken smirked, he could almost feel the hate vibe coming off her. Jenmar rubbed at his sore feet.

"Being dead would be better than this Bharl forsaken land." Shade pushed the cork in her water bottle, and stood up.

"Shen tey!" Ria smiled, as Shade walked out from the rocks, Jenmar looked across at Ria.

"What did she say?" Ria loosened the buttons on her shirt, sat back in the shadow of the rock.

"She said you were a fool, an idiot. Jenmar, you are lucky she came along; I know you hate it, but she is the reason you are alive, you should be nicer towards her." He scoffed.

"How do you mean, because if you mean I should treat her as I would you, Bharl says that is wrong?" Oaken looked up.

"No, Balathral says that, a so called God would have the wisdom to understand a living being. Balathral has deemed them unworthy of status because Shengara killed his father, it has nothing to do with gods, it is the words of an angry man." Jenmar stared at him.

"Do you not think he has the right to be angry, that butcher cut off his father's head. Tell me Oaken of the Andalan, would you not feel the same and proclaim all of the Undine unfit for purpose if you were in Balathral shoes?" Oaken felt the jolt inside him, and his annoyance, he cooly looked Jenmar in the eyes.

"The child of Balalaran killed my father, so should I name all Summanu and followers of Bharl unworthy and put them to the sword, because if so, you would be dead?"

"HA!"

Shade leaned over the top of the rock and looked down at Jenmar, Oaken smiled as the Apostle of Bharl felt caught in his own trap. Oaken looked at Jenmar awaiting his response, he looked at ill ease and squirmed a little.

"The Andalan are well known for their culture, and follow a god of their choosing, unlike that kind." Oaken leaned back and closed his eyes.

"I have lived with the Undine, and they have a deeply beautiful culture. They may not have a named god that suits us, but their faith is in the land and what grows from it. I find their culture to be quite rich, their ceremonies of being joined to each other is quite beautiful to witness, and they show deep commitment and respect to the women of their race, who they see as equals. The Summanu from what I have read, treat their women as second class and beat them, the men of the Summanu treat women as objects to use for spawning male children to fight for Bharl. I have read a great deal about how the new born females are left to die for they have no worth to a valiant warrior, I will not deny Jenmar, I find that hard to accept, as do the Undine who see all life as precious."

"And yet their leader took the head of the great and glorious lord Balalaran. If you ask me, that does not sound much like seeing life as precious."

"Shengara was watching his people being butchered, and yet the death of one man, ended the war, brought peace, and settled the lands from turmoil, and all whilst saving his people. It appears to me, one life taken, spared the life of many." Jenmar looked offended.

"He was hardly a man; he was a god sent down by Bharl." Oaken shrugged.

"Then why did he bleed and die, surely a god would not have died?"

"HA HA!"

Oaken looked up where Shade sat wearing a huge smile, Jenmar gave a frustrated sigh and lifted his bottle to drink, Ria looked at Oaken and gave a smirk and winked. The two children sat several feet away from Jenmar, who appeared too busy with his aching feet and own cares to notice them. They looked thin, undernourished and dirty, it was clear that compared to Jenmar, who was fat and well tailored, they got little from him, as his needs came first.

Shade slid down from the top of the rock, and squatted in front of them, she smiled and held out a water skin, they appeared reluctant to take it. Shade frowned and shook the bottle.

"Is hot, need water."

Meda licked her lips, she clearly wanted a drink, Shade smiled at her, and gave a nod to urge her to take the water skin. Caleb looked at Jenmar, and then turned to look at Shade, his voice was soft, and his throat was clearly dry.

"We cannot be served until our master has fulfilled his need." Shade gave a sigh, and turned to Jenmar.

"Give water, or they kilt."

Oaken looked up, and saw Shade staring at the fat bald apostle, who was far too preoccupied with his own drinking. Oaken watched, as Shade stood up, and pulled out her knife.

"Give water to child's, or me kilt you!" Ria had stopped, and was staring at the children, she smiled a kind smile.

"Meda, it is alright, you must drink, Shade is right, your master will allow it, because he knows out here you will die if you do not drink." Shade nodded, looked down and shook the skin.

"Drink, me watch, keep safe."

She gave a soft smile, and Meda blinked, and then reached for the water skin, and took it, Shade gave a gentle nod to reassure her it was alright. Meda took a huge gulp of the water, it was clear she was really thirsty, and she swilled it around her mouth and swallowed and then smiled, it was obviously needed, she handed the skin to Caleb. Shade sat down cross legged in front of them, as Caleb drank, and opened her bag. She pulled out some pieces of dried fruit and dried meat strips, and handed it to them.

"Eat, make leg strong."

She nodded, as they took the food and ate the dried foods greedily, they were hungry and it showed, Meda smiled again, and Shade leaned forward and patted her leg softly.

"Me take care, good now." Ria slid up to Oaken's side, leaned in, and spoke quietly.

"I think Shade is growing maternal." He nodded.

"She has reason to be, I feel her on watch for them, and I think those two will be fine now. I cannot deny, I do not like the way they have to serve him and wait on him hand and foot. He is fat and lazy because they do everything for him, they are not his charges, they are his slaves. I think Shade is the perfect person to watch over them, they have no idea how fiercely loyal the Undine can be, it gives me reassurance they will be well taken care of." Ria nodded at his side, as she watched Jenmar reach into his bag, pull out a large chunk of malted bread, and stuff it into his mouth, she gave a shudder, as he devoured it.

In all the time they sat in the shade of the rocks recovering, Jenmar paid no attention to the children at all, and when it came time to leave, Oaken noticed how the children lifted the bags and slung them over their shoulders, and Jenmar carried nothing. He turned to Elden, who had two bags, one filled with food from the carriage.

"Give that bag to Jenmar, you have carried it enough today, ease your load, and rest a little, we will all need our strength in these lands. Jenmar lacks stamina, carrying a bag will enhance him."

Elden looked at Jenmar, and sighed, he knew that they were already slow enough, behind him Shade gave a little giggle. Elden lifted the bag.

"It is alright Oaken, I have broad shoulders, I can handle three times this. Weighing him down will slow us up even more, and we need to get to Yandalla."

It was true they had been slower than expected, but Oaken felt it was unfair that everyone including the children had bags to carry in this heat and dust. Elden did make a valid point, but it angered him that Jenmar had everything his own way.

They moved on into the heat, walking on the rough terrain, and Shade veered off the roads and into the wilder lands. She stopped, and slipped some soft slipper like shoes out of her bag, and then slipped them onto her feet, she smiled at Oaken.

"Feet hard, stone harder." He gave a chuckle, turned and walked onwards.

Slowly the landscape changed, as the surface got harder, and more compacted, littered with rocks and sharp stones. The land stretched out before them looking flat, but it was misleading, as they would come across deep gulleys with steep sides, which had been carved away by the fast flowing water that once ran toward the sea. Shade would point down into the dried up river beds, and then point south.

"Big water once, now go, robbed by Summanu."

It was a startling reminder, as Oaken looked at the white dead trees, that were once thick, bushy and vibrant, and were now reduced to bleached white skeletons worn slowly away by the hot dusty winds. From what his mother had told him, this had once been a very fertile and productive land, the ruined evidence was scattered all over of the many farms that had once thrived here. Balathral had swept his men across the land, and killed everything, including the earth below their feet. Ria noticed him looking around as they trudged on, the dust billowing up at their feet.

"Greed is a terrible thing, and those who gather all the wealth, suffer like an addiction. Sumanula is a beautiful realm of fertile life, it is the biggest territory on this continent, filled with woodlands, fields and many farms. Balathral has it all, and his land has always prospered because of it, and yet his greed drove him to own more, and in his rush to take everything, he killed all he desired."

"It makes no sense to me Ria, if he has so much, why take all this and destroy it, my mother told me this was a rich land filled with life, but all I see is a dead land, slowly being devoured by the desert." She smiled.

"It is an illness, one they cannot cure, it matters not to Balathral that he rules his own land like a god, and it is a land of rich bounty. To him it is not enough, and in his mind, it never will be, that is the problem of the rich and powerful." Oaken nodded, as he looked ahead at Shade with the two children.

"Yes... They are far too greedy." Ria gave a giggle.

"To a degree yes. Oaken, those who have most, fear losing it all, and in their fear, they continue to take more and more. No territory is free from it, the rich and powerful sit in their high seats and plan ways to have more, and eventually, they take all that there is, and leave everyone poor, desolate and starving, and yet, it still is not enough. Balathral has taken every territory now bar mine, and a day will come where he will build boats, and set out to land on my homeland and take that for himself, and if he ever does that, he will find it still is not enough, and will look to the oceans and new lands to conquer. What he does in the name of Bharl has nothing to do with the worship of a god, it is the excuse he uses to line his own coffers."

"It is insane, he has enough to live many lifetimes in comfort, he does not need to own any other lands." She nodded as she walked at his side.

"That is true, the problem is, if you told him that, he would laugh and look at you like you are the insane one. To him, there is no infinite point, it has never been about ownership, it has always been about the power to control everything, think about it, who can stop him? Oaken, many have tried and all have failed, the laws are written by the powerful and greedy to only benefit the powerful and greedy, there is no law to stop him." She stopped and looked back, Jenmar was lagging behind again.

Standing with the hot wind blowing to his back, he looked south west and into the slowly falling sun. In the far distance, he could just make out the tops of the vast mountain range, which was the start of his ancestral homeland, Andalan. As he looked at the grey rough outline, he felt something stir deeply within him, that was where as a small boy he had lived, parts of which still lingered in his mind and his dreams. That was where his mother met his father, married, and brought him into the world, it was the place his father lived and died for.

He felt a tug at his shirt sleeve, and snapped out of his thoughts, blinked, and then looked down, Caleb looked up at him with a dirty face.

"Shade said something like 'Yan Fors' and told me to tell you. She has gone ahead and we must hurry, she said danger."

Oaken looked to where Caleb was pointing, Ria turned with him to look, and gave a gasp, he understood Shade, she had told Caleb to say the Undine words for 'The Wind.'

"Oh no, that is the one thing we do not need."

In the distance, Oaken could see the sand lifting and stirring into the air, as a thick dark cloud of dust blew across the land, there was a really big dust storm coming. He looked at Ria.

"We need to move, and fast." She nodded and turned back, Jenmar was many paces behind them with Elden, she lifted her arm and pointed.

"Elden... Dust storm, we have to hurry!"

Up ahead, Shade was rushing around, picking up large stones and stacking them into a wall like structure as high as her knees, on the floor. Meda was using one of Shade's knives and was stabbing at the ground. Oaken understood, and hurried up to her, and started to lift more stones, she was creating a large circle. Meda was inside the circle loosening the hard compacted sandy soil and pushing it up against the stones, Ria jumped in, and pulled out her knife and started to dig at high speed.

Caleb did his best to help with the rocks and stones, they were strewn all over, so it was easy to collect them, as Oaken and Shade rushed back and forth, lifting them up and carrying them into place. Ria was digging frantically as Meda pushed more earth up the inside walls of the circle, and the wall was growing. Elden arrived, and started to help with the rocks, and Caleb joined in with the digging, as across the wide plain, the dust storm came closer, and the wind began to pick up.

The wall was at least as high as Shade's knees, and inside the hole was getting deeper, as the loose soil was pushed to the sides. Shade gave a nod, and grabbed at her woven bag, and pulled out a wide sheet of yellow waxed, fabric, Oaken understood, and grabbed the other end of it. The sheet flapped in the building wind, as they pulled it over the circle, Caleb held onto a thick dead branch Shade had cut, and held it upright in the centre, as Elden helped pile rocks on the sheet edges on the outside of the circle, to hold it taught, and down.

Shade was moving fast, pulling rocks towards her as she pulled at the sheet and then placed them on it, the dust was already starting to swirl. Inside, Ria was still digging, even Jenmar was helping, he may be lazy, but even he knew of the dangers of the storms. Oaken nodded to Elden, as he pulled his scarf over his mouth.

"Get inside, we are almost done."

He nodded, they were almost around the whole of the wall, with just a wide enough space to slip under the sheet, Shade grabbed his shirt, which was starting to flap, he looked at her.

"In, me no big, can wriggle in."

He nodded as she held the sheet, and slipped under, and saw the group huddled around the upright branch, as the fabric violently flapped around above them in the strong wind. He clambered over the low wall and slipped down into the hollowed out hole, and sat back waiting for Shade. She wriggled in holding a rock, and then leaned over the wall, pulling the loose flap to the floor and dropped the rock on it, took some she had ready off the top of the wall, and dropped them on top. Shade slipped down into the centre of the tent like structure. She slipped in between the two children, placed her arms over both of them and pulled them close, they were frightened, and it showed, she smiled at them.

"Safe now... Sleep, wind big, take time go."

It was unnerving to sit in the makeshift tent shelter, as the wind howled above them. The sheet was tight, and yet it still shook and flapped, which was really loud, and Oaken could see how the children would look up at it with frightened eyes. Ria was close to his side, they were all so cramped, they were shoulder to shoulder, and she leaned slightly on to him. As the storm got closer, inside the tent got darker, and everyone sat huddled, listening to the sand storm blasting thick clouds of swirling sand and dust over everything. Ria gripped his arm, and huddled closer, it was clear, she too was afraid.

Time appeared to slip past slowly, and Oaken drifted into his thoughts of home, growing up with his sister and mother. His mind slipped into his memory of Yandalla when she was twelve summers old, as they stood outside their home, under the overhang as a large summer storm blew in from the ocean.

The rain was heavy, and the drops large, as they pelted towards the earth. Both of them stood looking up at the stone roof edge, where the water running down the rock poured off it like a waterfall, creating a curtain of water. The water hit the floor, and washed into the cut channels, that sent it to drain in the deep well. As they stood watching side by side, the whole of the sky lit up, in a bright vivid purple, and Yandalla, jumped with a squeal. She grabbed his arm and pulled herself close.

"Oaken... I not like this." She swung around him, and snuggled into him, and he pulled her close.

"It is just the thunder, Eliaston says it is the warm clouds of the sea, meeting with the cool clouds of the mountains, and when they bump, it causes sparks, nothing more." She shook in his arms.

"What if it is Bharl, they say he hates us, and will one day come to kill us?"

He smiled, as he looked down to see her looking up at him, with those deep green eyes. Yandalla had an innocence to her, even though she was actually immensely clever.

"Yandalla, Bharl could never cross the sands of the desert, Nuada would never allow that. This storm is driven by Nuada's winds, to push back the cold flowing from Sumanula, you should never fear the Summanu coming here, it will never happen." She shook her head, and looked at the flowing water.

"Oaken, I am not sure, I have dreams of them coming, I fear them more than anything." Oaken gave a jolt, and opened his eyes in the darkness.

"She saw it?"

He took a deep breath and blinked his eyes; the tent was still flapping but not as badly as it had. There was little light and he could just make the dark shape of Shade and the children; they were curled up together on the floor facing him. She was holding Meda close to her, and Caleb was curled into her back.

He looked down, and Ria was fast asleep on his shoulder, and had slipped her arm around his waist, almost the same as Yandalla used to do when she felt restless, and would fall asleep sat with him. He lifted his arm carefully and pulled it around her, and leaned back and closed his eyes again.

Had Yandalla dreamed of the Summanu attack four years ago? He knew the Andalan had seers, Eliaston was one, and he had heard that there were some within the Undine who could see times ahead of them. If Yandalla was half Andalan and half Undine, the odds were, she may be able to see things before they happen. He relaxed and breathed in letting the memory of that time float through his head, was it the look in her eyes that made him realise, and why had he not acted sooner?

The truth was, she was twelve summers and he had not taken her seriously, but as he lay in the darkened tent with the wind blowing across the fabric above him, he was starting to understand more of the things Eliaston had taught him of the ways of an Andalan. Yandalla had a gift he did not possess, and in many ways, he felt that was probably why he had not taken her seriously, but the truth was, her vision came true, and he regretted not listening more to her, because if he had, she would not be in danger now.

He seemed to drift in and out of sleep as he wearily waited for the storm to pass, he was drifting when he felt movement and jerked fully awake. Ria was waking up, she snuggled and squeezed his waist, and then yawned, as he looked down at her. She realised where she was and whose shoulder she was lay on, and jerked back as their eyes met, Oaken smiled.

"Morning, evening... Possibly night, I have no idea to be honest, although it is dark." She leaned back on her own pack.

"Sorry, I did not realise." He gave a soft shrug.

"There is no harm done, you looked comfy and restful, I did not mind." She looked a little embarrassed.

"It is not like me, I am normally more alert, I did not mean to fall asleep."

"I am not sure any of us did, but it has been a hot day, and we have had a difficult walk, I think we were all tired." She twisted and reached for her laces on her pack, and untied them.

"I won't deny, I hate sand storms, they rattle me a little, it is easy to get lost and buried in them. I was a little panicked when I first saw it coming towards us."

It was understandable, he looked up at the cloth tent above them, it had sand on the outside and was sagging a little, but Shade had worked fast and he was impressed, although, he was not sure why, she lived in this land, so knew how to survive out here.

"Well, it sounds like it has passed us by now, so we should be safe to get out of here, I cannot deny, it is too hot in here, I could use some cleaner, les stifled air." Ria lifted her skin and took a long drink, and nodded, it was clear she wanted to.

"If we had been able to wash, it would not be so bad."
He smiled, there was a scent to the air that added to the unpleasantness of their confinement.

Getting out was not as easy as Oaken thought it would be. The problem was the hurriedly made stone wall, was on the inside of the tent, the waxed fabric had been stretched over it. Outside, sand and dust has been swept across the flat landscape, gathering where ever there was anything to impeded it, and so all of the outside, had large mounds of sand pushed up against it. Oaken began to understand why Shade had built it the way she had, the sand piling up against the wall, also trapped the cloth, which prevented it from being blown up, ripping the fabric off.

The only way out, was to dismantle some of the inside wall, and then pulling up the cloth, dig a way through, in order to crawl out. It was hard work, but the sand was so dry and fine, it was like digging through salt. He finally crawled out onto the surface, and turned to hold out his hand, so Ria could follow him through. He pulled her out and both of them stood up in the total darkness, and looked up to the sky with awe.

High above them, the stars were bright in the complete darkness, above them were millions of dazzling white stars. Stood in the cooler air and breathing deeply, Oaken marvelled, above his home had always been a great view point, but here in this vast country wiped clean of everything, in the darkness, he could see for miles. Every minute spot in the blackness was filled with twinkling light, it was breath taking. He turned his head slightly and saw Ria looking up wearing a large smile.

"To be honest Ria, never in my life have I seen so many stars, my master has taught me many of them, but I fear, even he is unaware of how many there truly are." Her voice was soft, and she breathed in the cool air.

"My grandfather told me, each one was a marker for a lost life of a good being, and I fear, this vision of wonder, is there only because Balathral, has killed so many." It was a startling thought.

"Yandalla is not one of them… Not yet." Ria looked across at him in the darkness.

"How do you know? She has been with them a while Oaken, as much as I hate it, you must be prepared to face the fact she may not yet make it." He breathed out slowly.

"If all the stars are a token of the lost, then I know she still lives, for there is no star up there, bright enough to be hers. Yandalla lives still."

Chapter Ten

Dealing with the heat

The chaos of the purple berries, plus relentless attacks in the dark, had left the Summanu on edge, which meant they had grown colder and crueller towards their captives. The meal ration had been halved, and large covers had been thrown over the cages, trapping them permanently in the darkness. Small circles of light would illuminate inside as the sunlight shone through the holes in the old heavy sheets, but apart from that, they were deprived of the sunlight.

Tonight, was dark so there was no light at all, there was a small rip near to her face, so Yandalla had taken to leaning against the metal bar, trying to see anything outside of the cage, in the light of the burning torches. They had removed a great deal of the wood around the metal spikes, but in the darkness, it was getting harder, and the arrow head was growing dull with constant use.

Most of the others were asleep, she was hungry, they had not been fed a lot of food to begin with, so half a ration had not filled her, and her stomach whined constantly. As she drifted in her thoughts, she became aware of a strange sniffing sound, and looked at the sheet. She was not sure if she was dreaming, and turned her head to get her ear close to the sheet, and heard it again.

Yandalla leaned back from the bars, she was unsure as to what it was. She could sense something close, and wondered if it was some sort of wild hungry beast, looking for an easy meal, after all, in a cage there was nowhere to run. Her eyes focused on the sheet where there was the sound of sniffing, she tensed, unsure as to why, but she felt unnerved, she had never sensed anything like this, and had no idea what it was. The sheet moved, and she tried to lean back more so as to be out of striking distance of anything that could fit through the bars, her eyes fixed on the spot where the sheet moved. It moved again, but this time closer to the floor, she held her breath and prepared, as the sheet moved again, and then lifted up, and she swallowed hard to hide her scream of fear, as a black head with glowing yellow eyes came under the cover and looked right at her.

She had no idea what it was, but it made a soft sort of whining sound, and the rest of its body came under the sheet, and she felt her breath trap in her throat. It was a large dark cat, and it clearly had its sights set on her, she tried to push back a bit, two of the others had seen it, stood up, and were pressed into the back metal bars with fear. What happened next, brought Yandalla to her feet in sheer shock, the cat grew in size, and then turned into a woman.

The tall women stood between the sheet and the bars, and looked at Yandalla almost eye to eye, as Yandalla looked up at her. The women smiled, and her voice was Undine and quiet.

"Ca baska, Yandalla of the Andalan and Undine."

It was so startling; she had no idea what to say as she stared at the dark naked outline of the women. She took a deep breath, and spoke with a dry hoarse voice.

"Do you know me, for I am sure we have never met?" The dark figure leaned flat against the bars.

"I know who you are, you have the same scent as he does." It made no sense to her.

"Who are you, and why do you know of me?" She slipped her hand through the bars, and held it out in a token of friendship.

"I am Vesta of the Leyarken, and I know of you, as last night I talked with your brother." The shock hit her hard, and she reached out, and took hold of the woman's hand and moved closer to the bars.

"You were with my brother, is he alright, is he safe?" It was impossible to make out the woman's features, but she felt that she smiled.

"He is safe with friends and heading across Shodalt, he is heading towards you, and plans to meet with this line of carts at the falls of Andalan. He is coming Yandalla, and he has the sword, but he is worried about you."

Yandalla felt her face smile, but she had not enough liquid in her for the tears to form in her eyes. Her emotion deep inside her was strong, and Vesta gave her hand a soft squeeze.

"I am here to try and help, my partner Zeron has gone to your father, for he knows of Pallum. Yandalla, he is coming, you must hold fast, for he will get you safely away from them. His determination is fierce, and drives the power of the four winds within him." She nodded; her smile fixed to her face.

"I knew he would come; I have felt him." Vesta nodded, and looked at the others in the cage.

"I am but one for now, tell me, what are your needs, for I am here to help." A voice came through the darkness from the other side of the cage.

"We need water, or we will die." Vesta looked through the darkness.

"I am alone and but one, and can only move in spirit form, but I will see what can be done." Yandalla gave a sigh of relief.

"Tac yeat." It meant thank you in Undine.

Vesta dropped to her knees, and morphed back into a large cat, as she stood on the thin ledge at the side of the cage under the heavy fabric. Yandalla watched as she sniffed the air, and then carefully slid out from under the cloth, and disappeared. She took a huge breath of air, and felt some relief, Oaken was coming, and her inner turmoil settled a little. She turned into the cage and noted how all of them faced her in the dark, even Shellena was awake, Yandalla slipped down to her knees and took her by the hand.

"We have hope." Shellena squeezed her hand.

"I knew he would come; he would never leave you Yandalla, that is not who he is."

Outside the cage, in the middle of the desert, all the flat carts containing the cages were stopped in a long line, all with the heavy sheets pulled over them. Vesta as her cat form, walked silently underneath them out of sight, looking around the camp for signs of life. Wooden poles holding more canvass sheets had been erected, held by ropes with wooden stakes, under which she could see long lines of sleeping men. She tried not to breath in too much through her nose, as the stench of the Summanu in this heat, was raw and turned her stomach.

At the end of one of the long lines, she saw a row of tents, this was her intended target, and as she drew level, she slowly looked out from underneath the cart. Her eyes scanned all around, the men that were on duty were gathered around a large metal basin, in which wooden logs burned, as they quietly spoke to each other. They were in deep conversation, so she slipped out from below the carts, and ran as fast as she could across the gap, and in between two of the tents.

At the back, out of sight, she sniffed at the back of each tent, which was not pleasant, but it allowed her to find the one tent that was unoccupied. Scratching at the sand, she dug down, creating a space that was small, but enough for her to slip her long lean body under. Lifting her head through first, she looked inside to make sure it was really empty, and when she understood it was, she crawled inside, and changed her form. She gave a slight smile as she examined the contents of what must have been the tent of someone high up, noting the food and water slings, and also the bottles of wine.

She moved quietly, gathering together the water and some of the food, there was nothing to put them in, but saw a padded cushion. Vesta worked fast, biting the seem, and tearing at it with her sharp teeth, the insides which was a cloth bag of feathers fell out. Holding the empty cover, she picked up the two water slings, and dropped them inside, then added a loaf, some fruit and a small block of cheese.

Vesta turned, seeing the bed, where a long black cloak was draped over the end, it was perfect, and she moved fast, grabbing it, and swung it over her shoulders. Holding the bag of water and food close to her under the cloak, she slipped up the hood to hide most of her face, and then got ready to leave. Her ears were at their most alert for any signs of movement outside, she turned to head for the loose door flap, and then stopped as she noticed a glint of light flash.

On the end of the bed, next to a large leather bag, was a silver dagger in a sheath. Vesta picked it up, and looked at it, there was no doubt it was well made, she gave a slight smile and slipped it inside the bag. Pulling the cloak tight, she walked to the flap and sniffed the air outside. With the long black hooded cloak on, she blended well into the darkness, and after checking the guards were still busy, she hurried over to the carts and slipped in between them. Making her way carefully and slowly, she arrived undetected at the cart that held the cage in which Yandalla was prisoner.

She lifted the sheet, and slipped the bag inside, as she looked around to make sure all was clear. The bag slid through the bars and Yandalla gave a little squeak, as she grabbed it and pulled, and spoke quietly.

"Thank you, Vesta, I owe you a great debt, it was a big risk to come here." The bag came through, and she excitedly pulled it onto her lap, on the other side of the fabric Vesta whispered.

"It is not a lot, but if you share it equally, it will help all of you." Yandalla gave a huge sigh of relief as she pulled out a water sling.

"Vesta, tell Oaken, we owe him and you a great debt, and we will repay it." Vesta smiled.

"You owe us nothing, just live through this, it will not be long now, he is closer. I will go now, but will remain close."

Yandalla nodded, as she pulled on the cork of the water sling, Shellena pulled out the other sling and handed it to Sintalla.

"Stay safe, and be wary Vesta."

"I will."

The other girls gathered in the dark, it was hard to see them, but Yandalla could feel their excitement, she took a huge gulp of water, and gasped with relief as she handed the bottle to Shellena, and licked her dry lips.

"Water has never tasted as good."

She looked into the darkened bag, and slipped in her hand, and felt the cold metal of the knife. Yandalla wrapped her fingers around it, and pulled it slowly out, even in the darkness she could feel the quality. Shellena leaned into her.

"Is that a weapon?" Yandalla turned, and lowered her voice.

"It is a knife, and it is also a way to cut holes in the darkness."

Her mind was already working, if she was to cut holes in the material above the cage, no one would see it, but it would allow more light into them, she handed the bag to Shellena and stood up. Sintalla had taken a drink, and passed the water sling on to one of the others, as all of them waited to have their turn, licking their lips with excitement. Yandalla looked at Sintalla.

"Help me, I need to get up to the top."

Sintalla crouched low, and Yandalla slipped onto her back, and stood up. She reached up for the top bars to steady herself, and then lifted the knife. Holding the bar and sheath with one hand, she slipped out the knife, and shoved it up into the sheet. The knife was very sharp and went straight through, and Yandalla dragged her hand to widen the cut. Slowly moving around the cage, Yandalla cut several long holes into the cloth, and the cool draft blew in, as she pulled them apart with her hand. Just for a moment she stopped and gazed through the sliced hole, and smiled. High above her, she could see the stars twinkling in the dark sky, and they had never looked as beautiful to her. She had looked at them all her life, and yet there, in that dark cage, as she peered through a slit that was a little bit bigger than her hand, they were the most stunning she had ever seen them.

Vesta walked slowly down the line, there was another tent further down she wanted to slip behind. As she approached it, a guard stepped out from behind one of the carts, and gave a startled jump as he saw her, his sword came up, as she turned.

"What the hell are you doing?" He looked at her bare feet below the cloak and was suspicious, his eyes slid up the cloak, she was turned slightly away from him.

"Who are you, no Summanu has feet that thin?" She moved slightly, as he lifted his sword.

"You better talk quick, or you will feel the edge of this blade, what is your business here?" Vesta slightly loosened the cloak and turned more from him, as she lowered her voice to a soft whisper.

"You should be on your way, those who mess with the spirits of the dead Undine, will suffer their fate." He stared at her in the darkness, and swallowed hard.

"You are no spirit, I can see your cloak, and it looks solid enough."

"Really, then take hold of it, and feel the truth of the spirit contained within it."

He did not like how calm this stranger was, he knew they were not Summanu, but out here in this wide desert, who could it be? They were not Undine because the skin on their feet was not pale enough, but who else could they be? He nervously stepped forward.

"I am done with this, come here, and I will take you into the light."

He lifted his hand with his other arm ready with his sword, grabbed the shoulder of the cloak, and pulled. His heart almost stopped as the cloak fell away and hung limp in his hand. He was so shocked, he did not see the shape of the black cat, as it tore away up the side of the tent. He held the cloak limp, and felt the chills run down his spine, it was empty, but how could it be? His voice was strained and quiet.

"Oh, bugger no, you had a body shape and voice, oh hell, what is living out here?"

Yandalla felt a little burst of joy, and she used the knife to cut the fruit into equal pieces and shared it with her Undine sisters. It had been such a long hard day, and yet now, in the middle of the night, all of them sat on the floor and ate their share of the food. It was not really a lot, but to them, sat huddled close in the dark, it fell like a banquet.

Far away in Shodalt, Shade stopped and looked down into the deep ravine, she had been hoping it would still have a little water left in it. She gave a sigh as Oaken walked up at her side, and looked down.

"I was really hoping to see some sort of flowing river, cool water about now would be really nice."

It was dark, but the temperature was still pretty high, as the heat trapped in all the rocks radiated out around them. Shade gave a little chuckle, and started to make her way slowly down the steep side.

"Stop use eyes, use head." He smirked, as she made her way down the steep edge, as Ria came up to him holding Meda by the hand. She gave a long sigh.

"You have no idea how much I miss swimming." It had crossed his mind, after all, she lived most of her life on a boat.

"I have no idea what Shade is doing, I cannot deny, I would have been happy to find a small pool, let alone a river, this heat is not helping."

Down below them, Shade reached what was a dried up river, she looked up and down in the darkness, her ability to see better than most of them, due to her Undine heritage, gave her a big advantage. She dropped to her knees as Oaken watched on, although, to him, she was almost as dark as the shadows, the only thing that allowed him to even spot her, was the whiteness of her skin. Ria frowned.

"Is she sniffing the floor?" Oaken gave a shrug, as he watched.

"I have no idea; I am beginning to understand that Shade knows things we will never understand. If you're asking me can she smell water, all I will say is, I hope she can, because we need fresh supplies and soon?"

Shade crawled along the dusty floor, her eyes scanning the dark hard earth, she stopped and sniffed the air in front of her. She leaned back on her haunches, gave a slight nod, and smiled. Oaken watched from above, as Shade pulled out her knife, and started to dig, scouping up piles of sand and tossing it at her side. He had no idea really what she was doing, but somehow, he understood that if there was water in this dry and arid place, she was possibly the only person who would find it.

He stepped off the rock and started to pick his way between the large rocks and shale sides of the steep drop, as below Shade dug away at a fast rate. Holding onto anything that would give him a hand hold, he slipped and slithered, he could not understand how she could walk down steep banks without sliding, and yet she did.

As he reached the bottom, she was bent over, reaching into what was becoming a deep hole, he walked slowly towards her, and immediately noticed how her skin glistened. She was still digging as he arrived at her side, and as he looked down, he saw the glistening light of water, as it reflected the stars in the sky above.

"How do you know how to do this?" She leaned back, and looked up, her face was dirty, as she smiled.

"Undine, know."

He supposed she was right; they were an instinctive people who knew the lands in ways none of the other races ever would. Shade stood up, and rubbed the dirt off her damp arms.

"Give time, water come good."

He gave a chuckle, she was so simplistic, and not one for using too many words, and yet he found her approach to all things interesting. Little really concerned her, she knew what to do to live in this hostile place, and that was all that really mattered to her. Just like Yandalla or Shengara, she did not concern herself with greater power or control over anything, she lived as one with whatever was around her, and he felt lived better than most of them.

Shade walked over towards a large rock, and sat down, pulling out a cloth to clean her dagger, he turned to her, and watched, she looked up at him.

"What in head?" He smiled, as he walked over towards her.

"You surprise me, I have lived with the Undine for almost my whole life, and understand their rituals, their culture and their love of the land, and yet being around you, I see much Undine, but something more also." Her bright blue eyes glinted at him.

"This strange to me." He frowned at her, not really understanding why she would think that.

"How is it strange, I find your ability to live here quite extraordinary?" She cleaned her blade with her cloth.

"You Oaken, man of wind, yet no know this thing." He shook his head.

"No, I don't." She gave a little chuckle.

"Think you make wind, but don't." She slid the knife back into her sheath, and stood up, as she looked at him.

"Wind not come if ask, wind come when not ask.... Need meat." He stared at her, as she turned, and walked off up the dry river bed, his head filled with confusion.

"Shade, you make no sense, how can the power of the wind come when not asked?" A little way up in front of him, she turned and looked back, and pointed up at the sky.

"Air come in me, and go out, me no ask, it does it."

Oaken stood staring at her as she wandered along the river bed heading away from him, as he thought of her words, his voice was soft, and just to himself.

"Is she talking about breathing?"

The realisation of the moment hit him, she was, she was talking about breathing, she did not ask to breathe, she just did it without thinking. Was she trying to tell him that the power of the winds was not something he controlled, like breathing? Did she mean the power of the winds just naturally happened somewhere within him, he was starting to think she was, and that was actually really surprising.

He remembered that day with the oil burners, and Eliaston, and how with just a push of his arm, they all blew out. He had not thought for a second, he could do that, it just happened as a reaction to him. There was no intent behind his action, if anything he was following Eliaston's instructions, and yet without even knowing, the power had flowed out of him, snuffing out all of the light. He looked up to the river bed, Shade was no longer in sight.

"She is talking about the force of the four books and sword, it is why I am my father's son, it flows out of me without any thought at all. I did not realise, well, not until this moment I didn't. That was what Eliaston was trying to teach me, I do not will it, as the power is not just within me, it is also a part of me. Hell Shade, you are amazing."

Ria had found a reasonable and a little more stable path, and with the two children she made her way down the dried up river bed. Oaken was stood in front of the hole lost in thought, she came up at his side and peered down into the what was actually a deep hole.

"Good, we really need that, and if it is filtered through the soil, once it settles, it should be drinkable." Oaken blinked out of his thoughts, Ria turned and smiled at him.

"You look puzzled." He gave a nod.

"Shade baffles me, she just told me that like breathing, the force of the wind just flows from me without any thought at all. I find her to be really intriguing, she appears so simple, and yet her abilities with everything around us, is uncanny." Ria gave a shrug.

"Not really Oaken, she is half Undine after all."

"How does that make a difference?" Ria looked at him a little puzzled.

"Oaken, the Undine are Earth, they literally are the personification of all things natural. Hell, you live with them, how can you not see that?" It was an interesting question; he looked back up along the empty river bed.

"I have never really considered it if I am honest, I have just always marvelled at their abilities with the natural landscape."

"Oaken, the Undine are a very special race, they harness the power of the earth in many different ways. Look at their buildings, they do not simply pick a site and build, they feel what is below their feet, and when they find a strong and powerful connection, that is where they erect their buildings. Look at the scatter grounds where they lie the remains of their people, it is poor ground, so they burn their dead and then scatter the ashes on the weakest soil. You could say, the Undine really do return to the earth, because all their scatter grounds in the past have over time created some of the most fertile pastures. Shengara has even had a lot of success in holding back the desert and reclaiming the land back to grow on again." She smiled and patted his shoulder.

"You still have much to learn, the Undine are the true definition of earth as a people, it is why they must survive what the Summanu are trying to do to them. If they die out, all the lands will suffer the loss of their wisdom. Caleb told me Shade has gone hunting, it will be dawn soon, I think I will make a fire, if she finds something, we will want it cooked fast."

It was not that long before Shade arrived back to find a good fire burning, it was the one good thing about this land, there was no shortage of dead wood, as most trees had died and were they stood in the sun all day drying out. Shade carried a decent sized skinned animal, but Oaken had no idea as to what it was, and something told him he would be better off not asking. She had skinned and gutted it outside of the camp, so it had no head or legs, and therefore there was no real way of identifying the beast.

She fixed it on a thick stick, and then wedging it into the earth, she leaned it over the flames to cook. Whilst the meat cooked, she pulled some seeds from her bag and two small flat stones. Placing the seeds on one of them, she used the other to grind the seeds down into powder, which she then sprinkled over the meat, and left it to cook.

Seeing the flames, and with the smell of meat in the air, it was not long before Jenmar appeared with Elden, and the fat apostle sat close to the fire and watched as the meat sizzled. Shade sat away from the fire in semi darkness, and once again went back to cleaning her knife. Ria settled down next the children close to the fire, and Oaken stood a little back close to the hole that was filling with water, and gazed into the darkness.

Was Ria right, were the Undine connected in ways he had never really understood before, and did that mean that Yandalla was also like Shade? His mind drifted as he slipped into his memory of the past, and he remembered sitting on the grass in a wide clearing filled with white flowers with his mother and Pallum, as Yandalla, who was only a small child at the time lay sleeping wrapped in a green cloth. His mother was sat right behind him as she faced Pallum.

"So, it is true, Shengara has pronounced her the union of the earth and sky?"

"He has, for she has both spirits within her. Sarka, this is a good thing; she connects our races, and also the land and the clouds within which rise the winds."

Oaken was watching his sister as he relaxed with a full stomach, his mother moved and he felt her leg touch his, so looked up. His mother was looking directly into Pallum's eyes.

"You say this has happened before, and that Shengara had a child with a Leyarken, if that is true, then she would be an aunt to you, so where is she?" Pallum gave a nod.

"She remains in the land of her mother in the centre of the Leyarken Jungle. Her name is Almae, and she is treated like a princess, for she is the daughter of Aisie, sister to the lord of the Leyarken." Oaken watched his mother puzzle it out in her thoughts, her eyes still fixed on Pallum.

"If she is half Undine and half Leyarken, then doesn't that join her as spirit and earth?" Pallum smiled.

"It does, and with Yandalla in the circle, there is the protection of the joining of earth, spirit and sky. Sarka the powers of the earth have united with two more of the elements, Bharl who is consumed by the fires of the heavens, will not stand long if we unite." She gave a slight scoff.

"Tell that to the Shodalt, or the Keytan, both their lands have fallen, as has the land of Andalan. I fear if he does rise up again, the Leyarken and your people will not last long, he grows in strength everyday Pallum. I am glad there is a desert between us and him, and I hope it holds him back forever."

Oaken came out of his thoughts, as Shade stood before him holding the pieces of steaming meat, he blinked and looked at it, and she gave a slight nod.

"Eat, make strong, think Yan tee when done." Oaken frowned as he looked at her, Shade turned to look at Ria, she turned back and smiled.

"You, her, should Yan tee." He gave a gasp of utter shock.

"Shade, it is not like that, we have done nothing." She shrugged.

"You should, she, mmm, Yan tee for you." He shook his head.

"I do not think so, and Shade, keep your voice down, she may hear you, it will offend her."

Shade gave a shrug and walked back towards the fire where Jenmar looked at the meat and licked his lips, Shade was making him wait until everyone else was served. He sat silent, his stomach groaning, but saying little, he knew full well, one wrong word, and Shade would not share the meat with him, and he was feeling very, very hungry.

Chapter Eleven

Blown by the Winds

Vesta sat with Pallum; she smiled.

"She is doing well; I think she has all the girls in the cage with her well organised, and she is watching out for them. She is dirty, but I expected that, but to be honest, Yandalla is in better shape than some of the others." Pallum appeared to be pleased, and he swelled up with pride.

"She is my daughter, and somewhere deep inside her, there is the strength of my line. She will find it, and when she does, others will look to her for guidance." She gave a small smile as she saw the pride in his face.

For Pallum, it was important that his daughter was doing well, but the fact she appeared to have been the one helping out the others, was a source of great pride. He had been raised to ensure his people survived. He knew Yandalla had watched both him and her mother all her life, and he had always hoped the example that they set would guide her.

Pallum was more aware than most of the devastation the Summanu had inflicted on his race. Over the past week he had managed to set up a supply line back through the desert back to Undinalashka, as he sent back injured, and got fresh supplies of men and food. Most of the North West, along the sea edge, had safe zones, and around the area that surrounded the mount of the Andarla was secure, but the south of the land had been purged of all life, and burned to the ground. Even now, a week on, the villages and surrounding forests burned. In five days, thousands of Undine had been put to the sword, by the Summanu. Pallum took a deep breath.

"I need all of those young girls to live, after all we have suffered, they will become the future of our people, they are the future mothers of our people, and every time one dies, our race will take longer to recover."

It was a chilling thought for Vesta, she had heard many of her own line talk about the danger of the Summanu, in her land, all of her people had retreated into the centre of their jungle realm. The Leyarken Jungle was filled with thick dense plant life, which was hard for human like forms to navigate, it also had many steep valleys and ravines lined with trees and vines, which acted like a barrier of protection. The Leyarken had little trouble moving around their realm, as they had the ability to walk in their spirit animal forms, so they could easily slip under the plant life and navigate the land with ease. Vesta looked at Pallum as he sat by the fire, waiting for the dawn.

"Pallum, Balathral will kill all the women he can, have the Undine enough men to stop him? My people fear that soon, only our race will be free, and when that happens, Balathral will burn everything down to reach us and wipe us out. He has cleansed the south of your land; you know, soon he will pour everything into the north. Pallum, I have to ask, without the Andalan, can the Undine really survive this?" He gave a soft smile, and lifted his eyes to her.

"We are about to find out, in a moon cycle or sooner, your people will know, one way or the other."

Around the fire, everyone sat eating the meat that was surprisingly succulent, even if they had no idea what kind of animal it was. The two children were really enjoying it, and chewed with big smiles on their faces, Shade sat by the fire watching, with a soft smile on her face. She lifted a cloth and put her hand onto the hot ashes and pulled at something. It was obviously hot, and she blew out her cheeks as she flicked it with her hand into the rag, and then reached for another. Oaken noticed and leaned over Ria.

"What is that?" Shade looked up at him with a smile.

"Meat rocks, me like." He frowned, and turned to Ria who was chewing.

"What are meat rocks?"

She smirked, as Shade blew on her fingers, and flicked the meat rock into her rag, and lifted it up to show Oaken. He looked at it, and saw what looked like a very large black egg, it was probably from a large bird. He frowned and looked at Shade.

"It's an egg." Shade frowned at him.

"Shen tey, is meat rock." She pointed at the blackened oval object.

"It hard, has bird meat inside." He gave a smirk, as he looked at her.

"Shade, we call them eggs." She gave a snort.

"Eggs, Shen tey, meat rock better."

Ria snorted a laugh, and looked away from him, he sat back watching Shade looking very confused. She lifted the hot egg out of her rag, and cracked it on a stone, then peeled away the burned shell, revealing the white cooked inside with a smile. She stuffed it into her mouth and chewed, wearing a very happy smile, and nodded at Oaken.

"Meat rock good." The two children who had been watching, giggled.

When the meal was over, enough time had elapsed for the hole to fill with water. As the sun rose, they could see the crystal clear water, and Ria knelt down and began to fill all of the skins. She dropped them into the hole, and they bubbled as the air ran out filling the empty pouches with cool clear water.

"Shade is clever, the fine sand and grit, filter out all of the impurities, I am glad we found her, she knows this land better than any, and how to live here."

As they filled their skins, the hole refilled, and once everyone had a full water sling, all of them lay down and put their lips to the water to drink their fill. Once done, Oaken washed his face and hands, and felt the relief, as the wind and sand had burned into his skin, and the water cooled it. Refreshed and revived, he looked at the map with Ria.

"Shade has done good, the river we would have taken had it not been too dangerous would have been quicker, but we would have had to snake quite far south, before heading north again, and some of that land is dangerous. She has taken us straight across country, and as much as this is a hostile land, we will soon be across it and into the greener belt of Shodalt, and under trees again."

Oaken looked down and studied the map, he would be glad to be away from this bare land of rocks, dust and hot sand. He traced the line of green, and the river that ran from the lake to the Andalan falls, he was a lot closer than he had realised, Shade had driven them hard, and they had crossed a vast span of the country.

It was not long before they picked up their bags, and set off once again across the flat dry landscape. With full stomachs and filled with water, all of them felt good, and the pace was better, even Jenmar was keeping pace with them. Elden walked at Oaken's side.

"It will be nice to walk in the dappled shade, I am sure Jenmar will complain less, although, if his bag was not filled with so much metal, he would find walking less of a strain." Oaken's eyes moved to glance at Elden.

"His bag is filled with metal, you mean coins?" Elden nodded.

"Trust me, he had no intentions of leaving his money in that carriage, Jenmar likes his comfort too much. Oaken, I do not trust him, his soul rings to the sound of coins, when we reach the falls, how can we be sure he will not inform the Summanu of our presence?" Oaken understood him, he had been thinking the same.

"I am not sure yet, for now do not let him out of your sight, especially when we reach the trees, I do not trust him at all, and I would not be surprised if he does not try to slip off and head for help." Elden nodded.

"I am on him, do not fear, he will not evade me."

By the time the sun was high in the sky, in the distance they could see where the ground rose up, and the lines of green growth started. Oaken looked beyond the trees, where the ground rose steeply to the high plateaux that was the homeland of his people, and the place he was born.

The dark red stone of Andalan rose into the clouds, and he smiled as he remembered those days of mists as a young boy, where he had run outside to see all of the cobwebs filled with tiny droplets that sparkled like crystals in the pale light of the morning. Inside he felt a deep stirring, and a strong sense within him drew him in, as a yearning to walk those paths again grew within him.

"Home, empty." He moved his eyes to where Shade stood

looking at him, and pointing at the mountain.

"What do you mean?" She dropped her arm.

"Me live there once, learn words there from old man." Oaken narrowed his eyes, he did not understand.

"What old man?" Shade shrugged.

"Name not know, me went when Anna Pa kilt." Oaken looked back to the mountain.

"Was he Andalan?" She nodded.

"Old man, good man, got kilt, so me left."

Oaken was sure his father had gotten everyone out, as far as he or his mother knew, no one had been left behind, so who was it that had taken in Shade and helped her? Shade gave a giggle, and he looked at her, she bent her arm back and forth like a wriggling creature.

"Live in water hole, put kilt slithers in buckets for Summanu, make them terror." She gave another chuckle.

"You put dead snakes in their water buckets, Shade, did you live down the well?" She nodded.

"Many places down hole, old man shows."

His mind drifted, as he remembered sitting in the temple with Eliaston, as he talked of Andalan, he always looked so happy talking of his home.

"The place was a labyrinth of passages and homes below ground. I never understood why your father did not go underground and attack back from places they would never find. He told me the Andalan belong in the light in the sight of Nuada, and yet I often wonder if Nuada would have minded that much. I am sure they would have been happy to see us fight for the temple from hidden places."

He snapped out of his thoughts, as around him there was movement, they were rested enough, had taken water, and they were back on the move. Shade appeared to be happy as she walked towards the green trees, and the Andalan mountains, although he too was feeling a little more uplifted. He was getting a lot closer to where at some point, Yandalla would arrive, and he really wanted to get there and prepare before the Summanu came.

The group continued on with renewed hope, as the trees of green and the promise of softer earth and shade loomed before them. The day once again was hot, as the sun burned down on them, but as the treeline grew closer, they pushed hard, and as the evening approached, Oaken looked down relieved, as he walked on spiky grass, and through the low shrubs and small trees, almost with relief.

By the time they were deep under the canopy, of what was a very ancient woodland in the cooler air, the day was heading towards an end, and he felt exhausted. Shade appeared in higher spirits, and her pace appeared to quicken, which took its toll on all of them, and after several hours of walking in what were much nicer conditions, she stopped and pointed along a thin path off to the side of the track they were on.

"Rest soon, not far, then safe."

Oaken did not really care, he would happily stop here, and it appeared the rest would also, but Shade turned with a smile and walked onto the fine hardly worn track between thick bushy trees. No one was really paying that much attention, most of them had their heads down watching the path, which was narrow and not always easy, as low growing branches snapped at their legs. Without any real warning they walked out into a clearing, and Shade stopped and looked back at them.

"We here, we safe."

Oaken looked up, and in front of him was a small dwelling like building made of heavy stone, which had a very thick wooden roof that had grass growing on it. There were no windows, just a door, and it looked heavy set, and made of iron, held together with large heavy type bolts.

"What is this Shade, where are we?" She smiled.

"Home... Me." He frowned, as he started to understand her.

"This is your home... You know, where you actually live?" She nodded.

"One, me many."

He walked towards her as she headed for the door, behind him, the others were just happy to be able to stop and slip off their packs and drop their bags. Oaken arrived at the iron door behind Shade. She smiled at him as he came up at her side, but spoke Undine rather than the common tongue.

"This was once where rich men hid things, no bandit can get in here, it is why I made it mine when the Summanu came, they not find a way in." He nodded as she bent low, and pushed one of the stones, and to his surprise, it moved, and swung out like a small door. She grinned at him as she looked up.

"Open with head, no eyes."

She pulled on something inside the hole in the wall, and Oaken heard a strange sliding nose, and with a loud click, the door moved, and swung open to reveal a small gap. Shade stood up and then with her toe, she swung the stone back into place, and grabbed the door, and pulled it open. There was no key hole or handle, she simply grabbed the edge of the door and pulled it open, and then stepped in.

As soon as he entered, it was clear that the inhabitant lived a simple life. There was a small table, with a shelf on the wall, on which was two metal plates, three stone bowls of different sizes, and two wooden carved beakers. There was a stone fire place, with a metal bar to hang things on, at the side of which were two iron pans, one deep and one shallow. There were several barrels stacked in a corner, which he assumed she used for salting, and another shelf filled with small glass jars of dried herbs. A hook on the wall held a long thick black cloak, and in the corner was a long stuffed heavy fabric bag of something, which he realised was her bed. On the floor were several mats of woven reeds, one under the bed, one in front of the fire, and two by the table. In the far corner was a broom made of fine twigs, and he noticed how well swept out the floor was, it was stood next to a tall stack of cut logs, which had an axe at its side.

There really was little in the way of possessions, and he thought of his room in his own home, which had a raised wooden bed, books, and a trunk of clothing. Shade had so little it was actually quite startling to realise anyone could live with less than he had. Everyone came in, and looked around, it was not a huge space, but there was room to move around, but no chairs, so they had to sit on the floor.

The inside of the door had a handle, and as soon as everyone was inside, Shade pulled the door closed and slid in three thick large bolts that went right into the stonework. She was right, this place was secure, the walls were thick, and roof which was wooden appeared to be made of heavy timber, and the whole of the room was cool, much cooler than outside, which was nice, as all of them were overheated.

The children sat on the bed bag, and everyone else sat on the floor and leaned against the walls, Shade lit three tallow candles, and then started to build the fire. Ria wiped her face, and loosened her top as she watched.

"So, this is where you live, how long have you lived here?" Shade struck the flints, and the dry moss ignited.

"Big time, is safe, night dangers."

"Dangers... Are there wild animals here?" Shade gave a chuckle.

"Me kilt wild beasts... Your word, me no know, I call Brighem." Oaken lifted his head.

"Bandits, is this bandit country?" The flames flickered, as she looked back at him and nodded.

"Bad men, not get here, we safe." Ria appeared to understand and looked at him.

"I know of some of these parts; we have had problems in the past. They attack boats from the shore, they fire at them and try to board us and take our goods and enslave the crew, we are always well prepared. I was not aware they were inland though; I thought they were just along the river."

Shade opened the lid of one of the barrels, and took out some preserved meat, she stroked the excess salt off it, and looked back.

"We close for river, wash and walk."

The meal comprised of boiled salted meat, with many dried roots and leaves, some of which neither Oaken or Ria recognised. Shade used many herbs, and the food she made was surprising tasty. The two children tucked in, and ate their fill, including Jenmar, who had been much quieter around Shade, although she controlled the food at the moment, which probably had a lot to do with it.

Once they had eaten, and after the sand storm and walking in a hot dusty land, Ria asked about the river, and it was clear, everyone felt a need to wash and get clean. With Shade's windowless house locked up, she led them carefully along narrow paths, it appeared she had many traps around the place, which had in the past killed several bandits.

The plant growth was dense here, with small palms and long

grasses, above which grew large canopies of the many different types of trees. Oaken noticed many of them bore fruit, which possibly explained why Shade had also taken up residence here, food came easily. The path wove from side to side, and at times it was hard to stay on track. Shade led them easily; she was on her own patch, and it appeared knew it very well indeed. He could not see much, but knew he was slowly walking up a slope, large rocks started to appear in the thick of the plants either side of him, and it was clear, they were heading towards a rocky terrain, and he could hear falling water.

The plants broke apart, and Oaken stepped out to see a wide ledge, to his right was a high wall, over which water spilled and fell down into a water fall, filling a wide pool, which overflowed into a stream. From there, it ran towards the edge of the ledge, and then ran over falling to somewhere out of his range. They were not very high up, but it was a wide plateau that looked to the trees down below, where in the distance he could see the wide river snaking its way towards the high rock walls of what he knew was Andalan in the far distance.

As the others appeared, Shade crossed the stream on the stepping stones, and walked along the rough rocky terrain, Oaken was not sure why, but she walked right past what looked like a deep pool below the waterfall.

"Are we not washing here?" Shade turned and lifted her white arm, pointing to what looked like rocky steps a little ahead of her.

"Pool up first, then cold one." He frowned not quite understanding, Ria gave a slight chuckle.

"Wow, this pool is beautiful, what else does she have, come on, let's go see."

Oaken watched Shade ahead of him as he followed, she stopped at the top of a small group of rocks, turned and smiled, and then without any warning, she pulled up her top, dropped it on the floor, and then slid off her skirt, and stood naked looking down at her feet. Oaken stopped as he realised, and Ria bumped into his shoulder.

"Come on, hurry, I am covered in dust, and really looking forward to this." He turned to her.

"She is naked." Ria frowned and stared at him.

"Well yeah, she is having a bath." He nodded at her.

"You go; I can wait." She gave a little giggle.

"You are not embarrassed are you, do you not have communal bathing in Andalan?" He shook his head.

"NO!" Ria moved past him.

"You must be the only race that doesn't, because that is the first time I have ever heard of any that does not share bathing spaces." He was actually really surprised.

"You haven't?" She shook her head, and walked on towards where Shade had disappeared as she slipped into the water.

"Come on, get over your surprise, we need to get clean, or at least I do."

It took a few moments for him to overcome his mixed and confused feelings, in which time, Ria made it up the rock, to discover Shade sat back with her eyes closed, up to her neck in warm steaming water. The upper levels had three hot springs on them. Oaken gave a sigh feeling a little nervous as he walked towards the incline, and up ahead Ria stripped, which was something he had not expected at all, and as much as he did not want to look, the sight of her tanned body held his gaze.

That changed when he suddenly realised, he had to undress and climb into a pool with two naked women. Elden appeared quite happy, the children did not hesitate, and so he slipped off his shirt, took a deep breath, and did his best to hurry, and slid down into the water. That moment of hitting the water impacted on him, and he gave a moan of happiness as he slid down feeling the warm liquid surround him.

Every inch of him reacted after walking across the hot dusty plains, and he felt the joy of feeling all the dust that had found its way into the fabric of his clothing slowly get washed away. He leaned back and opened his eyes to see Ria smile, and she slipped under the water and then dug her fingers into her scalp and rubbed out all the dust and grime from her hair. It looked too inviting, and he followed her, taking a deep breath, and sliding down below the warm water.

His scalp came alive as he rubbed his fingers into it, as days of itching came to an abrupt halt, he felt the dirt from his hair flow away, and it felt glorious. With his embarrassment fading into the oblivion, all he cared for was getting clean, and like all of the others sat in a wide circle around the pool, he busied himself with the task of rubbing his skin to free it from the dust and the dirt of his days walking. He came back above the water feeling utter relief, and took a long drawn in contented breath. Being clean felt almost life changing, as it had been a good while since he had been given the chance to bathe.

Shade again led the way, after she felt she had cleaned herself thoroughly, she stood up, and strolled out of warm pool, and walked back towards the waterfall, and deep cool pool. Oaken watched as she waded out until it was up to her waist, and then dived under the water, and disappeared. She emerged with a gasp, and her face wore a wide smile, and with that everyone followed her and climbed out of the hot spring pool, and headed for the colder waters of below the falls.

For a moment it fell like everything had faded away, the heat, their dirtiness and their mission and need to stay alert. The group became adventurous, and fooled around in the water, and for the first time in a very long time Oaken felt a sense of ease and inner peace. He had a swim, enjoying the cool water, and then sat on the side of the bank, and washed his clothes, which were far dirty than he had at first thought. Ria who had washed her shirt and slipped it on wet, as it was still hot outside, walked through the water with her other wet clothing, and laid them out on the rocks close by to him.

"It is nice to be clean again; I find Shade to be more and more useful." He looked across the pool, where she lay higher up on a flat rock, next to her washed clothing, as she dried off.

"She is quite resourceful; it surprises me considering she has raised herself here alone. I find her to have a wild almost feral streak, and yet at the same time, a strong sense of morality. She will rob a bandit and kill him, but will protect a child, and show a level of care that shows her great intelligence, because she is very bright. She is Undine in so many ways, and yet she rejects the notion of being one, and she is something else, and I am unsure of what that is." Ria could understand what he meant.

"Oaken, Shade believes the Undine will be wiped out, I cannot deny, because even though she has only been with us a short time, I feel I trust her, and I agree with a lot of what she says. She knows how to survive where others cannot, and that is a rare skill, especially when it is as instinctive as it is with her. What if there is some truth to what she says? I cannot deny Oaken, it bothers me, because she understands the Summanu in ways we do not, she has survived in a place where they exterminated or enslaved everyone." He nodded at her.

"She has, and I feel that maybe it has clouded her judgement. Ria, her mother was a full Undine and she died, and then the Summanu came and killed most of the men and enslaved the women. I think she feels that the Undine are not strong enough, she does not understand them as we do, she has not seen their strength, and the power they hold as a community. I think if she did, she would see the hope all of us have that one day we can push back the Summanu." Ria turned to him, and lifted her eye brows as she looked at him.

"You think they can be pushed back, to be honest I have considered what we are doing is trying to save the women of the Undine, so that when the Summanu leave the land of the Undine, the men that survive will able to rebuild their people. Oaken, pushing back the Summanu, is impossible, there are two men in the past that were capable, one was your father who is now dead, and the other is Shengara, but he is older and not as able as he was. We all hoped the desert would be a boundary that would contain Balathral, but as we have seen, he is determined to rule every inch of this land." Oaken twisted his trousers, and squeezed out the water.

"I have thought about it a lot as we walked, Balathral has proclaimed himself as a god that has come to this land, and because of that he is feared, and everyone abides by his rule. Once I have Yandalla free, I aim to prove Balathral is just a man, and not a god, and then his rule will fail, and his empire will fall." Ria gave a snort.

"Are you insane, how on this land do you think you can do that?" He shrugged.

"Not sure yet, but I have a gift of the winds according to Eliaston, who is someone I deeply respect, and so I have to believe that I can in some way bring Balathral down. Ria, I have the gift of the air, you know the water, the Leyarken carry the power of spirit, and both Shade and Yandalla hold the power of the earth, there has to be a reason we all came together at this time, and the third book of the sky talks of when the earth, air, spirit and water rise up against the fire, to bring back peace. I have read the chapter several times and will read it more, but I think it is a prophecy of what will be, and if it is not a task meant for us, it is a task we must begin. I have questioned why I was given the sword of the winds, and the only thing that makes sense to me, is I am to play a part in the downfall of Balathral, and so I aim to try."

"You pick a hard fight, if that is your aim." He stood up and slung his pants over his shoulder.

"I know, and yet knowing Shade will be with me, I feel more assured." She gave a slight nod.

"I am assuming you have talked to her of this, how can you be sure she will help you?" He gave a smile, and turned to look back at her on her rock drying in the sunlight.

"I have a strong feeling she has a score to settle, and somehow, I feel we walk the same path. Once Yandalla is free, I aim to head to my homeland, for I feel a yearning to walk there, and when I do, I know the land of my people will guide me. I have felt it since I left, and seeing it as I do in the distance, I feel the pull to return home. I think Ria, the winds are blowing me towards what was always destined for me."

Chapter Twelve

Growing Understanding

Lying naked in the warm sunlight felt surprisingly good, as his clothes dried on the rock at his side. His eyes moved to the side, where Ria lay back with her eyes closed, her wet shirt stuck to her skin. It was hard not to notice her shape; she was without doubt a very beautiful woman. There was a soft giggle behind him, and he turned his head, Shade sat up on the rock just above him and smiled, as she lifted her eyebrows. He felt embarrassed, and turned his head back, as she chuckled to herself.

The last few days had been hard, and suddenly stopping and feeling completely clean again, he gave a happy sigh, closed his eyes, and simply relaxed, it was so nice to stop and rest. Ria gave a soft moan.

"Oh, this is so nice, I have missed the water, and that dust was testing my sanity."

Oaken opened his eyes and turned his head, Ria was looking at him, she smiled.

"You look more at ease now, see, there is nothing to worry about, and how wonderful is it to be clean again?"

He sat up, and looked around, Shade was just to his right above him sunning herself as her clothes dried, Elden was sat on the edge of the water, watching the children play and smiling to himself. The children were enjoying themselves, swimming in the pool, to him, it felt like the first time they had acted as children should. He thought back to Undinalaska, and how all the children would head to the beach and splash in the waves, he had watched Yandalla so many times splash with her friends, and he felt it was nice. Caleb and Meda were doing the same, there was a slight breeze across his cheek, as something to his side moved, and he blinked.

"STENGHEM!"

Ria sat up fast, as he realised Shade had jumped from the rock, he looked down as she marched up the beach holding her knife, and pointed it at Jenmar. Jenmar was sat on a rock looking fearful as Shade marched right up to him screaming.

"NO! No right… Yan tee Fent ae!" Oaken gasped, and Ria turned to him.

"What is happening?"

Oaken noticed Meda stood at the edge of the water, she had lifted her top and was trying to hide herself. He looked back, as Shade spoke through gritted teeth at the Apostle, she was clearly very angry, but he was too far away to hear her words. The reaction of the Apostle was enough to tell him, whatever it was that had happened, Shade had made a serious threat to him, as he looked terrified. Oaken swallowed hard, she was as aggressive as a wild boar when provoked.

"I am not sure what he did, but she accused him of a vile act." Ria frowned.

"Vile act, whatever do you mean?" Oaken watched, as Shade turned slowly, and walked over towards Meda, and then helped her dress. Ria stared at him.

"Well?" He came out of his thoughts, and looked at her.

"The word she used is not one I expected, she is very angry, and I may be wrong, but if you ask me, a man like Jenmar did something very sickening to her as a young girl."

"Like what?" Oaken watched the gentleness of Shade, as she spoke to Meda, and helped get her damp clothes on.

"Ria, why do you think Jenmar is creepy?" She gave a slight shudder.

"I am not sure, there is just something about him that feels foul and sickening, he makes my skin crawl at times." Oaken looked at her, and gave a slight nod.

"Follow that thought, and imagine yourself as young as Meda." Ria gave another shudder, and rubbed her arms; he could see the golden hairs lifting on her arm.

"Okay, I am more creeped out than I have ever been, I wish I had never asked." Oaken stood up and looked down at her.

"I think it is time to get dressed, the mood has changed, and I want everyone dressed now." She nodded and reached for her damp pants.

"Yes… I think you are right; I am not sure Jenmar is safe at the moment, Shade is very angry, and honestly, I am not sure any of us could stop her if she exploded. I fear Jenmar is in great danger." Oaken slid on his pants, and picked up his shirt.

"Had he not touched himself, he would be safe." Ria looked up and gasped, Oaken nodded.

"That is the Undine word she used; the fact she knew it surprised me." Ria was shocked, and looked down at Jenmar who was still sat on the rock.

"You cannot be serious?" Oaken looked down, as Shade walked Meda into the trees.

"Shade was pretty serious, why do you think that was? I get the feeling when Jenmar leaves us, he will be going alone. I am not sure Shade will ever allow him near the children again." Ria was starting to put everything together; she lifted her boots, stood up and took a deep breath.

"I think you are right; she has become more and more protective of those children with each passing hour." Oaken nodded at her.

"Maybe she has good reason, I will not deny, I trust her instincts."

They walked together along the path back towards the house in silence, as they approached the open door of Shade's home, Ria grabbed hold of his shirt sleeve, and pulled Oaken back.

"Oaken, wait."

He turned to her and looked her in the eyes, it was clear something was troubling her, she swallowed hard, looked down and then looked back up at him, her voice was soft and quiet.

"I know you talk to Shade, can you tell me, was she hurt as a child, is that why she got so angry?" It was not a question he knew how to answer, he took a moment and chose his words carefully.

"All I know is, her father betrayed her, I know nothing else, but looking at her anger, I cannot deny, I think something horrible happened to her. Why else would she react like that?" Ria nodded looking sickened, her voice almost a whisper.

"Poor girl, I have heard so many stories of the vile things the Summanu do to young women, it turns my stomach to think of it." Oaken gave a slight nod.

"Then help me stop them Ria, help me find a way to end their rule of fear." She gave a sigh.

"You are but one man, the odds of stopping them are greatly against your favour, you will be walking to your death." He shrugged.

"Maybe, but one man can make a difference, Shengara did with one sweep of his sword, and it stopped the war."

"Oaken, Shengara led a raid in the night, he came in under darkness and attacked Balalaran to kill him." Oaken nodded, and then smiled.

"So, there is a way to do it then?" She rolled her eyes and looked at him.

"You really do mean to do this then, don't you?" He nodded and smiled.

"Once I have Yandalla free, I aim to bring down Balathral, but I cannot do it alone Ria." She shook her head.

"You are insane, look, free Yandalla, and then we will talk." He gave her a wide smile.

"Thanks, I knew you would understand." Ria smiled, and started to chuckle.

"I think I am as insane as you are."

They both started to chuckle as they turned and walked in through the door, inside Shade was busy preparing food, she looked up as they walked in together.

"We eat, then walk, dark good friend."

Oaken nodded, he understood her perfectly, in the dark they would be safer, but also, it would be harder to slip away under the cover of night in a strange land, which would keep Jenmar close. Shade understood things better than he realised, she knew, at some point, he would try to alert others, and she intended to stop him.

As Oaken and Ria sat on the floor to eat, in the desert as the sky darkened, and the camp settled, over the dunes, dark figures slipped soundlessly down into the back of the camp behind the tents. Yandalla was hungry, the food ration had become smaller, and all of them once again, felt the pinch of hunger in their stomachs.

She lay on her side along the bars, and looked up through the rips in the canvass, at the first of the stars that shone down, trying to take her mind away from the hunger she felt inside herself. All felt quiet and still, as the days had past, and after the terrible chaos of some of the men going mad and defiling themselves, the nights appeared less rowdy, as the soldiers of the Summanu feared the nights.

There was a soft thud as she stared into the darkened sky, she blinked, and then realised someone was above them, and they were pulling at the gap in the canvass above her. She sat slowly up, others had noticed and were all looking up, as the gap in the canvass slowly tore, and a white face appeared and smiled. Yandalla felt her heart thump in her chest with shock.

"Anna Pa!" He smiled.

"Hold fast daughter and keep quiet, I am here."

His arm slid in, and she jumped up to reached out to it, and he took her hand in his. Yandalla felt her first tear in over a week fill her eyes.

"Anna Pa, I am afraid… Ca yan!" He squeezed her hand tight.

"I am trying to help you, but now is not the time, but it will be soon my brave daughter, they still have many numbers before we can get you. Your mother sends you her love, and your brother is coming, stay strong my warrior daughter, the earth is here with you in the power of your spirits, it is with all of you, be strong."

She nodded unable to speak. He released her hand and there was movement, and then a long thin bag of woven grasses came through the hole, and down to her.

"Eat, stay strong, milk berry bread will give you the power of the land."

She took the bag and lowered it, Shellena took it and looked up as a water skin came through the hole, and Yandalla took it. Shellena looked up at the white face.

"Leader Pallum." He looked down at her white eyes in the darkness, she took a breath.

"My family… Do they walk this land, or have they joined it?" He gave a soft nod, understanding her concern.

"Your mother was wounded, you father fights with Shengara, your brother is now one with all things, I am sorry." She took a deep breath in, and gave a soft nod.

"Tac yeat." He nodded, and slid back from the hole, and she felt the soft hand of Yandalla slip into hers.

"He is one with all, and within you." Shellena nodded and lifted her hand to wipe her eyes.

"My Anna Ma and Anna Pa live, I did not know, I will live too Yandalla, and I will live for my brother." Yandalla smiled in the dark.

"We all will, all of our sisters here will, my father and brother will ensure it." One of the girls handed both of them a pastry filled with milk berries and herbs.

"Eat, we grow as one, and stronger."

Pallum turned at the top of the hill, and looked down on the darkened camp, as his men returned from feeding the others.

"They all have food and water, we have done what we can for them, now we bring the sun to their night, go, take more souls from their God Bharl."

As the night drew in, and the air cooled slightly, the Summanu prepared to pull down their tents and shelters, and once again start to move out through the darkness. The day had been the hottest they had endured, and already they felt their strength had been sapped, and wearily, they prepared for the struggle of moving through the darkness in the soft sand.

As the darkness thickened, all along the top of the sand dunes, a line of light appeared, lighting the top of the dunes, as if another sunset was happening. It went mainly unnoticed, until a line of fire a mile long appeared on the horizon, and before the Summanu understood what was happening, a hail of blazing arrows came hurtling down into the camp.

The canvass sheets of the tents and the shelters ignited, as the oils painted on them to keep out the water, burst into flames, and within a minute the whole of the long line of Summanu was in utter panic. Arrows whizzed through the sky, hitting men, and setting them ablaze, as they ran screaming through the camp. The tents all around them burned, and the whole of the night became one brightly lit mass of screaming and terror laden wails of fear.

The commanders tried to bring order as they yelled out their orders over the chaos, but were met with arrows, and the men ran wild, and crawled under the carts seeking protection, using their prisoners as a shield to save them. Many hid whimpering, covering their ears as their fears ate them away from the inside.

The trip through the desert had become a living nightmare, as each day, more and more of them died, their bodies left behind them to rot into the ever shifting sand.

Balathral, had named the Undine as inferior, and yet, the convey in the desert had seen a third of them wiped out in the surprise raids. The Undine, led by Pallum, carefully plotted each move, and attacked when least expected. Back in the land of Undinalashka, the Summanu still ruled, as they tried to hunt down the last of the Undine, but in truth, most of those capable of fighting, were already on route to Keytan. In the Heliospan Desert, the Summanu had found that the Undine were not the inferior race Balathral had named them, to be more precise, they were proving to be far more superior.

As the arrows rained out from the sky through the darkness, Yandalla and her Undine sisters could only sit in their cage listening to the screams and wails. After almost an hour, Yandalla could take no more, she wanted to see, she needed to see what was happening. She jumped up and reached through the bars, grabbing the large canvass sheet, and gave it an almighty tug.

"My Sisters, help me, we must see this, for we watched as they slaughtered many of our land, let us watch as the land rises against the Summanu." She tugged with all her might.

Shellena, and then some of the others got up and came to her side, they all reached through the bars and helped to pull at the fabric, and slowly as they heaved, it began to slip, and lift on the opposite side of the cage. Heaving and panting, all of them joined in, giving their all, as the canvass slid slowly up revealing the desert sands, and the brightly lit night, as flames roared in all of the temporary shelters. One side of the cage was open and the smell of the burning filled the cage, as Yandalla stood in the mass of her Undine sisters, her face dirty, her hair unkempt, and her green eyes filled with life, as she looked out at the carnage.

Dead Summanu lay scattered everywhere, many lay wounded and pleading for help in the sand. They were as dirty as she was, caked in sweat and filth from the long journey through the searing heat. To her surprise, she noticed how many of them looked as frightened as her sisters had looked, on the day of their capture. Below her feet, under the cart, she could hear the frightened whimpers of the young men, who wept and moaned, for like her, they too wanted to go home, and it felt startling to hear it.

She had seen what she wanted, and as the others stood and viewed the carnage, she turned and walked back her corner, sat down, and pressed her back into the bars. She closed her eyes, as her thoughts drifted back in her life to her mother and father when she was but ten summers old. In her mind, she saw her mother, and her soft kind smile, as she sat on the floor with her father in front of her.

"Yandalla, my daughter, you are made of two, I am Andalan, as is your brother, and yet your father is Undine. You are the proof that races can live as one, we all look different, but inside, we are the same. We all fear something, we all bleed and feel pain, and we all have a great ability to love. We live on Pangela, and yes, we may be different races with different looks, but it is one land all our feet walk on, and all of us belong to it, do you understand me?"

Yandalla sat, her bright green eyes fixed on her father as he smiled at her, and she thought of what her mother had told her. She looked up into the white of his eyes, that radiated a light that appeared to burn brightly.

"Anna Pa, if Yandalla is two, why my tonk not work?" Sarka gave a chuckle, and turned to Pallum, he was smiling at his daughter, he leaned forward and took Yandalla's hands in his.

"Yandalla my daughter, you are raised within the land of my people, we speak with the voice of the land, it is a way that makes us use ourselves differently. Because you learned to speak Undine first, your tonk developed a way of speaking. The common speech is not easy for all of us, but in time, you will find, you will adapt and the words will work. You are young, and have a life to learn all things." She gave him a smile, and her mother watched her with eyes of love.

"Yandalla, there are many who find when they speak Undine, their tonk does not work also." Yandalla's eyes opened wide.

"Really?" Sarka gave a small giggle, and nodded.

"Even I have trouble at times. Yandalla, it does not matter what words we use, what matters is that we all talk, and share what we have learned, for deep inside we are all the same. It is in understanding that, you realise, that to talk is to join as one for everybody."

She opened her eyes, and noticed Sintalla was watching her, she smiled.

"I can tell when you think of home, it shows on your face." Yandalla took along deep breath.

"My parents taught me all I know, and here in this place, I have thought of much of the words they have spoken to me." Sintalla appeared to understand her.

"What words have stayed in your heart?" Yandalla brought up her knees, and leaned forwards onto them.

"I realise how young I am, and how much my parents and brother have protected me. I hear the sadness of the soldiers as they cower below us under the cart. They are as frightened as we were when the Summanu came. I owe my life to Penjin, he died fighting to protect me, and he was the same age as those who cower below us. Something is wrong Sintalla, we all hate each other, but why? We are a different colour of skin, but we bleed the same, get hurt the same, fear the same things, and we all care for those we love the same? Below me is a soldier who screamed for his Anna Ma, I want my Anna Ma also Sintalla, I miss her, and I am scared she will get hurt when I am not there. We all hate what is the same, and I want to understand that."

Sintalla gave a slight laugh, and leaned back on the bars, as around them the chaos continued, and men screamed and wailed as they were struck down, from the precision of the Undine warriors high up in the dunes. In the midst of the fire and madness of the dark, Sintalla sat back and stared at Yandalla, she was white skinned, had green eyes, and yet she radiated the power of an Undine, she gave a soft smile.

"I will tell you this Yandalla. Yes, you are young, I am three summers older, and yet as I sit here, I know in this cage of misery, I have learned much from you. There is no doubt in my mind, you truly are of the line of Shengara, for you use words as he does. Two summers ago, he stood on the steps of the meeting house, and looked out at his people, and I listened, because he is a man I admire greatly. He said, dying is easy, living in peace is the hardest thing to do, your words are different, but the meaning is the same. I have no idea what will happen, I want freedom for all of us, but here in this place, I swear to you now, wherever you go, you will not be alone, for I will follow you until my death, if needed, Yandalla of Shengara."

Yandalla looked around, and all the other Undine were watching and listening, somehow in all of the chaos that surrounded them, they had turned to listen to her words. All of them were dirty, and all of them smelt, in one corner was a large wooden pail, which was their only means of passing the food they ate, and it stunk. All of them had undergone a transformation, they had been forced to live with the humiliation of being in open view to do what was their normal bodily tasks, and it had shamed all of them.

Their journey locked in a cage had been the worst days of all of their lives, and yet in some strange way, they had bonded deeper than maybe they would have living in Undinalaska. Yandalla had called them sisters, and in her innocence, it had impacted on all of them, and united them in a common bond. As Yandalla sat with her knees pushed up to her chest, and she gazed into the faces of each of them, all of them gave a slight nod of agreement with Sintalla. She was the great granddaughter of Shengara, an Undine who had become a living legend, and seen as the wisest of all the Undine, and for the first time in her life, she felt the responsibility of her line. She looked back to Sintalla.

"We are sisters, all of us, if we use our minds, and stick together, all of us will make it through this. I am of Shengara's line, but I have a lot to learn for I am still young in the eyes of the land we walk on. My brother Oaken, he will come, and I will follow him, for I believe in him." Shellena leaned into her.

"Then we will follow him too." Yandalla smiled.

"He would like that, for there are days when life presses him down, and he feels lonely. I do not want him to feel that way, which is why I have always been at his side."

Over the dunes within the world of shifting sands, Pallum walked away from his attacking men with Zeron.

"We cannot keep this up, the further we get from our home land, the longer the journey takes to get back. The Summanu swarm our home, so we cannot replace, what we use here easily, when Oaken arrives, all we will have left is our swords and knives, and a will to use them. He must attack before their soldiers arrive, if he does not, there is no hope of saving our people. Scouts have seen many Summanu preparing to leave, soon they too will walk on the sands, and we do not have arrows to match their numbers. This night has gone well, it is all I can do to slow them, and lessen them." Zeron nodded at his side.

"Vesta will return to Oaken; I will head to my father and our people; we have the means to make what you need. It is good Shengara heads towards Keyton, but there are many Summanu there, he will not find it easy. I will ask my father to let his people run free, for now is the time we all united, for if we do not, the Leyarken will be next. I would rather walk to the fight, than be burned in my bed, it is time Pallum to reunite the pacts of old, as written once before by Andalyn." Pallum agreed.

"Andalyn was a wise man indeed, he saw this happening long ago, he is greatly missed. How close is Oaken, he cannot be that far away?"

"He should be somewhere close to the green belt by now, the Undine girl has him walking at good pace, much faster than the bandit, so he is making good time. He will be at the falls long before you are, but be aware, they have many soldiers waiting there, the water source is good, and they are making the best use of it, two miles south of the falls there is a large army encampment."

Pallum considered his words, as his keen eyes, saw through the darkness and watched his men along the top of the dunes, where they still fired at any target that moved.

"It pleases me to know he has an Undine guide, and yet I know nothing of her, what did you say her name was again?" Zeron gave a shrug.

"I do not know her real name, Oaken named her Night Shade so the others could liaise with her. She appears to like the name, Oaken is fluent with her language, which to a degree won her over, Ria knows some, but the others have no understanding of her, which Vesta thinks works to Oaken's advantage, especially with an apostle amongst them." Pallum considered the point.

"It concerns me to know a Summanu is with them, it concerns me he may try to take the life of his Undine tracker, Balathral's new proclamation, will cause many problems for my people. One of my scouting parties took out three hunters looking for riches off the lives of Undine a few days ago." Zeron gave a smirk as Pallum spoke.

"Fear not for the life of Shade, I feel there are few who can match her, she truly is an Undine warrior of the highest skills. There are some fierce bandits in that area we know of, and they are terrified of her, she does have quite the reputation, few will tangle with Shade and win."

"And yet, I know nothing of her, we could use fighters of such skill, it puzzles me she has not come to us, and lives in such a hostile barren wilderness. You say her mother was Undine." Zeron nodded.

"From the little we know of her, her mother raised her mainly in the ways of an Undine, her father was Shodalt, and a well respected farmer, until the Summanu swept across the land. It appears he turned on everyone, her mother died when she was seven summers, the rumours are he sold her to pay a gambling debt in Ranblate, and shortly after her owner died, and she ran free. Her father died a little while later and she disappeared completely until a few summers back, when bandits tried to rob her, and she killed all three of them, and now she is with Oaken, and guiding him faithfully. No one knows of her line or where it came from."

"I see, I find her story curious, I would care to know who her mother was."

"I can ask Vesta, but I doubt Shade will tell her."

"Please do, she interests me."

Chapter Thirteen
Spirit

Shade stopped in the darkness, Oaken could see her shortly ahead of him, her pale skin appeared to glow through the darkness, she turned and looked back.

"River close, be wary, bad men here."

They had been walking through pastures and woodland for many hours, Oaken looked back at the group, Ria stood close with the two children, Elden was not far behind her, with Jenmar, who appeared to be walking faster, Oaken felt all the walking was doing him some good. He turned back to Shade.

"Maybe we should rest here and gather our strength." Shade walked towards him, and pointed to her face.

"Eyes now, better than legs."

He understood, and could see how alert she was. The group gathered close by, and sat down to rest on the soft warm grass. Elden walked up to him, and looked back as Shade sat with the children.

"She seems twitchy." Oaken gave nod.

"This is bandit country; we need to be on our guard." He looked at Elden stood at his side.

"How are you holding up, we have not spoken for a few days properly?" Elden gave a shrug.

"I am enjoying this, it is nice to be off the rock and meeting folks, to be honest I never thought I would have much of a chance, and so for me this is a valuable experience." Oaken gave a chuckle.

"Bathing naked with women, was that valuable?" Elden smirked.

"I was never going to object, Shade and Ria are not unpleasant on these eyes, I was just glad the fat Apostle stayed dressed, I fear no one wants to see that." Oaken sniggered, as Elden smiled.

"I won't deny, I am relieved he did not join us, although, were you not a little embarrassed, I cannot deny I was?" Elden smiled.

"Honestly lad, you were embarrassed to stand naked with those two fine young women, I just thought they will laugh or look, they did neither so I was fine. I have no idea why you felt embarrassed, especially with that sword you have, hell, if I had to pull that thing in front of those two, I would die of shame." He gave a mighty laugh, and Oaken smirked.

"It is a good sword, Elden; it is linked to the four winds." Elden nodded.

"I understand that Oaken, but them two have heard of the legend, trust me, no one will be impressed when you pull it out. Have you cleaned it yet?"

"Not yet, I have meant to do it, I have just not really had time." He looked at the bundle on his pack.

"I would sneak off somewhere, and try to make it look a little more impressive, people have expectations you know?" He gave a chuckle and patted Oaken on the shoulder.

"Have a rest lad, I will take a watch from here, I need a break from our Bharl loving apostle and his wittering's." Oaken gave a slight nod, and then walked the few yards to where they all sat, as he sat down, Ria handed him some fruit leathers that Shade had provided.

"Eat, these are really tasty and they will give you good energy."

He took the food and sat back, Ria and Shade were sat side by side, he had not really considered it, but as he watched them both, he could see that Elden was right, they were in a way, both very attractive. Ria looked up, even in the dark her blue eyes sparkled.

"What are your thoughts?" He gave a smile, his eyes locked on hers

"Nothing that relates to our task, just random things, personal things."

She gave a soft smile, as she looked at him, and he felt a little uncomfortable, it felt like she understood him better than he did her. He looked down at the fruit, and Shade gave a soft giggle, and nudged Ria's shoulder, she smiled and looked down.

The rest period was long, because once Shade had eaten, she slipped off into the dark, Ria pulled out a map, the moon was bright, so they could see it reasonably well. Oaken watched as he followed her finger on the map, and she talked him through things.

"According to Shade, we are better off taking this trail, it weaves a little, but with care we should be able to skirt past any groups of bandits. There is a town not too far away, and Vesta has good influence there, the Leyarken have done trade with some of these people in the past. If we are lucky, we may get a small boat to float down the river, which will speed us up." Oaken frowned.

"Won't that be dangerous; you did say boats get attacked?" She gave him a smile.

"Oaken, I am ship's master, and the way I see it, if we have a small enough boat and go at night, because the moon has risen tonight, we will have several days to travel, and in one day we can cover three days of walking. It could be a risk, but I think it is worth it, after all, you do have the sword of legends." The words of Elden echoed in his thoughts; he gave a slight cough.

"You know it is just an old legend, and ancient, it is not that impressive, it is just an old damaged sword." She frowned at him in surprise.

"It controls the four winds, Oaken, I hate to point out the obvious, that is pretty impressive. There are books filled with stories written about it on Animatre, when you pull that sword, people will remember it." Somewhere behind him, Elden sniggered. She smiled a huge white smile at him.

"To be honest Oaken, don't think me childish, but I am actually really excited to see it." Elden stood up, and walked further back to the trees, Oaken could hear him quietly laughing. He looked at her.

"You are, you know, really excited about it?" She nodded, her eyes wide and sparkling with excitement.

"Back at home, my father has three big paintings of it, as your father wielded it in battle, and the sun illuminates the whole picture as it bounces of it. I will not deny Oaken; I have read everything there is about it; I would pretty much do anything to wield it with my own hand." He swallowed hard, and his voice lowered.

"Really?" She gave him a very knowing smile.

"Oh yes, you have something I greatly desire to see in use." Elden laughed out loud in the trees, and somehow, Oaken suddenly felt like he was caught in a trap. Oaken noticed movement, Jenmar got up and was about to walk off, he looked up.

"Where are you going Jenmar?" The apostle turned and scowled.

"If you must know, I have to pass soil."

"Be careful, this is bandit country, do not stray too far. Elden is up to your left, close to the trees, stay where we can see you, just in case. Bandits care not you are an apostle, as you noted before Shade found you." The apostle looked unpleased.

"Caleb!" The boy moved and Ria stretched her arm and gripped him.

"Stay there, he is a fully grown man, there is no job for a child required." Her face turned to Jenmar.

"Your days of service Caleb, are over, or least whilst I am around, they are."

The Apostle stormed off across the grass, angrily muttering to himself. He arrived at the treeline and looked back, then muttering, walked just inside the line, and saw a smooth level area. With a grumpy sigh, he lifted his long robe, and pulled at his loin cloth, then squatted, and screwed up his face. It had been some time since he had been, and it was painful, as he squatted, and panted.

Elden leaned against a tree trunk and cringed, as small squeals and grunts echoed behind him, Jenmar groaned and gasped for air, his face red, with sweat on his brow. Behind him as he made low whining sounds, sticks snapped, but such was his pain and effort, he did not hear them. A voice brought Elden back to attention.

"Well, well, what have we here then?"

Elden slid his hand down to his waist and went for his sword, and from nowhere a long white arm reached out and softly took hold of his hand, he turned, and Shade smiled, he nodded understanding.

Inside the edge of the woodland, Jenmar panted, as behind him four people stood partially hidden in the darkness. Jenmar looked back, saw them, gave a grunt, and suddenly, everything unloaded onto the floor, two of the men shuddered and looked repulsed. He panted, the pain he felt was intense, as one of the men came forward a little.

"I hope you know, shitting on my path requires a hefty payment, Apostle?" Jenmar swallowed hard.

"I am a man of little means, and afflicted with a great appendage. I am in great pain, and I suffer a lack of regularity." One of the men stepped back, and pulled a hand to his mouth.

"Gawd that stinks!" The man who had spoken smirked, his face still obscured by the heavy darkness cast under the trees.

"No apostle is poor, not one we have crossed has been honest, we know the cost of your service, do not lie to us." He came forward and stopped, in front of Jenmar a bright white figure was framed between the trees.

"Is mine, no touch."

There was a faint sound of metal sliding, as Shade pulled out her sword, the man with a hand on his mouth turned white and dropped his hand.

"That is her, she is that spirit that sliced up Brogaram, that apostle is not worth death, she took eight, right in front of us. Let's leave it Granth, my life isn't worth some fat old Bharl worshiper shitting in the woods." The lone bandit lifted his sword and pointed at Shade, he turned to look back at his men, all of whom appeared reluctant to move forward.

"Spragg, are you telling me, that little girl is the phantom spirit that wiped out half of my men?" Spragg nodded rapidly.

"Do not be fooled Granth, she is thin, but she is powerful." He smirked.

"She is Undine, we could get a lot of coins for her skin." Spragg shook his head fast.

"There is a big bloody difference between wanting it and getting it, Granth, if you are taking on the spirit, you are on our own, I want to live." Shade leaned slightly to one side and looked at Spragg, she gave a soft nod.

"Me know you." He nodded quickly.

"I did nothing, I backed off, I let you have what you wanted." She smiled.

"You smart." She up righted herself, and looked at Granth.

"Listen friend.... Leave." He gave a cocky smirk.

"And what if I don't want to?" Shade shrugged her shoulders.

"Then get kilt."

On the floor between them, there was a resounding long high pitched whine, and then an almost explosive splatter, as Jenmar pushed hard, and brought instant relief to his insides. He panted rapidly, Shade smirked, and pointed at the hot steaming pile with her sword.

"You take that, me no want." Granth stepped back looking appalled.

"That is disgusting, what the hell have you been eating?" He took more steps back, and Spragg nodded with relief.

"Yeah, Granth, leave em be, it is smart, we live to fight another day." Shade watched as the group turned, and began to walk away, a few yards down, Granth turned and looked back.

"This is not over Spirit, we will meet again, and our blades will touch." She nodded.

"Me know." He gave nod, turned, and walked back into the darkness of the wood. Shade looked down at Jenmar, her face carried her disgust.

"You owe coin. Bury that." She turned, and walked back out from under the trees, where Oaken stood quietly with Elden and Ria, Shade smirked, and looked back.

"He no man, Shade has bigger shell slimes on food plant."

Ria smirked, as Shade strode past, and Elden tried not to laugh. Shade bent down and lifted her bag; she looked back at the others as they walked towards us.

"Go now. Not safe."

It was a little longer before Jenmar walked slowly down from the trees, he looked in pain, Elden sniggered as he lifted his bag. Jenmar glanced at Elden, and scowled.

"Laugh all you like; I have an affliction." Shade slung her bag over her shoulder.

"Bharl, kilt all Undine, and my Anna Ma, eat less, talk less, make better." She started to walk, and Ria with the two children followed her. Oaken looked at Jenmar as he lifted his heavy bag.

"You know Jenmar, she could have let them rob you, and yet she did not, she protected you. Shade is right, you complain a lot, and yet at meal times you are always there and get fed well, you eat more than the two children in your care. Tell me, is Shade so wrong? She shared food with you at her home, and has guided all of us safely, and yet you still mutter how she is not to be considered a person. I ask you this, who is acting better, the greedy apostle who would allow children to starve, or the Undine who has nothing, yet has shared everything? I understand you feel Bharl is a saviour, but as an Andalan, who lives with the Undine in peace, I can never agree with you." Jenmar gave a twisted scowl.

"Are you telling me that your fake god Nuada is better?"

Oaken turned back, and lifted his hand, he gave a flick of his wrist, and from nowhere, there was a blast of wind, and Jenmar was lifted off his feet with a squeal, and crashed into the floor. Oaken leaned over him, and looked down at Jenmar.

"You just felt Nuada, tell me, did he feel fake to you?" Ria came running up looking worried.

"What is happening?" She looked at Jenmar lay on the floor, looking shocked, Oaken gave a sigh and turned.

"It is nothing, just two men talking about faiths. Come on, we need to move, it is no longer safe here." He walked off leaving Elden to help Jenmar back to his feet, Ria looked back.

"Did I see that right?" Elden gave a nod.

"You did, and that is why we know he is the son of Andalyn." Ria looked back amazed, and seeing him with new eyes.

With everyone finally ready, Shade led the way walking with Caleb and Meda, Ria followed, and behind her a few paces was Oaken, Elden took up the rear with a very quiet Jenmar. They walked on as the night sky changed, and the first signs of dawn approached, it felt like they had covered a good distance, but Oaken would not know for sure until he consulted the map.

Caleb walked silently lost in thought, he glanced at Shade, and then looked away, Shade smiled.

"You talk small." He looked up at her.

"We have to remain silent with the apostle." She understood.

"Me not apostle." He smiled, and looked at Meda who was watching him, he looked back up at Shade.

"Is what you said true, did Bharl kill your mother?" Shade kept looking ahead.

"Me love Anna Ma, but she sick." He nodded, and Shade took a deep breath.

"Bharl man say make better, but kilt her." Caleb swallowed hard; his voice seemed quieter.

"He killed her... How old were you?" Shade took another long breath.

"Me seven summer." Meda looked shocked.

"That young, what did you do?"

"Anna Pa sold Shade to bad man, so kilt him." Meda looked so shocked; she could not believe what she was hearing. Shade looked down and smiled at her.

"Bad man, Bharl apostle, did bad thing, he kilt now, me live."

Ria walked behind listening, she had thought so, and yet hearing Shade talk so openly to the children was hard to hear, Caleb, looked up at her with a sad look.

"I am sorry Shade I did not know, which is why I asked." Shade lifted a hand and patted his shoulder.

"Long past, me find Anna Pa, he kilt now, me not angry." Caleb appeared to understand, he looked at her as she walked, she truly was an Undine warrior.

"He did not touch Meda, I did not let him, I would never do that." She looked down at him and smiled.

"You good man, like Oaken." He gave a big smile, and nodded.

"We like him, he is kind to us and has protected us, as have you." She nodded.

"He good man, me like too, he not Yimp Bellashen like Bharl man."

Ria gave a gasp and snorted a laugh, and Caleb looked back at her. Ria tried to hold in her giggle; she leaned forward to speak quietly.

"I think she called him a bloated goat." Ria giggled, Caleb looked up at Shade, she was watching out of the corner of her eye.

"Me did, Undine word, not know others."

Caleb felt his tummy wobble, and looked at Meda who had a hand on her mouth hiding her giggles. Behind them all, Oaken walked with a big smile, he felt it was apt and followed as he silently laughed to himself.

The children did not talk much, Oaken watched thinking this was the most they had ever spoken, he liked how they felt safe with Shade, and so had opened up to her. He liked how she had grown so protective of them, but again, as he heard another part of her story, he realised what she had gone through. In many ways he fully understood her, especially her protection of the children, in her own wild way, she was trying to prevent a similar event for Meda.

As dawn started to rise, they came to a rocky outcrop, and on the top of it sat Vesta, Ria smiled as they walked up the path, and Vesta nodded to Oaken.

"I saw you coming, and so waited here, I have a fire and food for you, we are two miles from a town, so thought I would set up camp for you."

They came into a clearing and saw the fire crackling away, with an animal butchered, skinned and cooking. He felt some relief, as all of them felt tired, hungry and weary, again they had walked many miles. He dropped his bag, and relaxed, the others put down their things looking hot and really tired, he walked to the edge of the rock and looked out where a few miles in the distance was a small town of scattered buildings. Shade came up at his side and looked out.

"Me not safe." He understood.

"Fear not, I will protect you, no one will harm you whilst all of us are around." He felt she understood that, she turned with a frown and looked at him.

"What Spirit?" It was a word from the common language she had never heard before.

"A spirit, is a ghost, a phantom, a shadow of the dead." She looked a little confused.

"Shade, some people believe that when we die, you know, kilt, part of us inside comes out, like air. Some believe it rises to Nuada, and those that get stuck down here, well, I suppose they are spirits. Some say they look like us, but can be seen through, like air, but bright." Shade gave a nod.

"Like Nyen Diran?" He smiled.

"Sort of, they linger, and people fear them." It made sense to her.

"Me no kilt, me no spirit."

"We know that, but the bandits think you are, and they fear you." She nodded.

"Good, eat now."

Oaken ate whilst he took first watch, and was replaced later with Elden who had eaten his fill. He sat down and leaned against his bag, and Vesta came over and sat at his side.

"I met with Pallum, he has a group of Undine and they attacking whenever the Summanu let their guard down. Pallum has found Yandalla and he is watching over her, he got to sneak in at night and speak to her, as did I. Oaken she is doing fine, she needs a bath, but she is healthy, alive and for now safe." He breathed a sigh of relief.

"I am happy to hear that, I worry about her so much." Vesta smiled.

"She has been forced to grow up, and from what I have seen and heard, her Undine warrior spirit is showing. Oaken, she is very intelligent, and has been taught by not just Pallum, but Sarka, and it is starting to show."

"It pleases me to know she is thinking things through; she will avoid mistakes putting her in danger."

"Oaken, all the slave girls are in large metal cages on carts, there are eighty seven of them. Yandalla has seventeen in front of hers, and they travel in a long line. They are slow and heavy, pulled by six horses each, and they are surrounded by guards at all times. You are few in number, but Pallum will meet up with you, and he had two hundred when I left him. Oaken, it is still not enough, they have huge numbers in front and behind them, Pallum has killed many in the desert, but more arrive every day, it's like every man on Pangela is now Summanu."

"Let me worry about that, Yandalla is my sister, she will walk free." Vesta understood, but she still felt he was making a big mistake.

"The cages are iron, and they close with large locks, they will not open with a sword."

"I know of locks, Master Eliaston has many to hide the four books of the winds, to open them, I need something much smaller." She nodded.

"Good, because honestly, Pallum explained them, and it made little sense to me, he told me you would know of them." Ria turned to look at them across the fire.

"We have them on the vessel, if I can see one, I may be able to open them with a fine shaft of metal. It is not easy, but it can be done, although, the last time I opened one, I did not have thousands of Summanu trying to kill me." He nodded at her.

"One of them will have the keys, that is the one we will need, we will watch and hopefully learn who, then we work out how to get the keys off them. All we need now is to get to the meeting point, we are low on supplies and will need goods. We will stop at the town and restock." Ria looked across the fire at him.

"What happens to Shade, she is Undine?" He smiled at her, as he watched, she lay sleeping next to the children.

"She is only half Undine; her skin is pale and her eyes are blue. She wears Undine style clothing, we will need to get her something else, and maybe a head cover. In daylight we are fine. It is at night we have problems; her white skin radiates light like Yandalla's does, no wonder they call her a spirit, from a distance she looks like one."

The sun was rising as Sarka brewed a drink, and walked out onto the wide ledge that looked down upon the land of Undinalaska. Fewer fires burned now, and the forces of the Summanu had been reduced, it appeared that the Summanu were withdrawing some of their forces, and leaving patrols to ensure no Undine returned. The land of the Undine was now under the control of Balathral, and in many ways, she felt he had won, as now there was only one race left in their homeland, the Leyarken would be next.

Eliaston shuffled out and lowered into the woven chair, and sat back sipping his drink, as he watched Sarka stare into the distance, knowing her husband, son and daughter were out there without her, the old man understood her concerns.

"They live, if they did not you would know." She turned to him.

"I know that, but for every moment they are away, they all face danger." He nodded in agreement.

"I watched you when Andalyn rode into battle, you were the same then, and I say once more, if their death was planned in the four winds, I would know, and I have seen nothing that would make me believe one of them would fall."

"Yet knowing that, I still find it does not comfort me." He gave a smile.

"There is little comfort for a mother who loves her family, they will return, and you will hold them, that will be the moment your unease goes away."

He was right as always, his many years of watching their people had taught much, and in times of need, he had always spoken with great recall and wisdom.

"I am glad you here Master Eliaston, you have eased the quietness left by Yandalla's absence, I am missing the joy she radiates around here."

"What, even when she ran naked to the temple?" He gave a giggle, and she smiled.

"I am amazed you remember that, she was five summers old and so excited to know that her first day at temple had been approved. I bathed her and she simply could not wait, once she was dry, she was off leaving her clothes on her bed, she had such joy and life within her that day."

"I would say, every day, she has changed little as she has grown." Sarka took a breath, remembering was painful, and she turned away so he would not see her tears.

The old man was no fool, he understood her, and sat back sipping his tea, and allowed her the space to release some of the pain she was trying to hold in. Sarka was a powerful force within the Andalan people, but at the moment, she needed a space to simply be a woman and a mother, and he gave her that, for it was important she allowed some of it to flow.

Chapter Fourteen
Doing Deals

Shade stood and pulled a long face, she was clearly not very happy as she looked down at the white shirt tucked into Oaken's spare pants, which were a little on the baggy side. They were loose, but with the addition of her sword belt, her pants were successfully held up, even if they did look a little ruffled at the waist. She looked up as Ria smiled at her.

"Not good." Ria gave a sigh, as Shade pulled at the pants, obviously feeling uncomfortable.

"Shade, please, we have to hide as much of your skin as we can, so that you are not mistaken for an Undine." She looked up and frowned.

"Am Undine." Ria gave a little nod.

"I know, and I can see how proud you are, but Shade, there are people in the town who will want to capture you, and sell you to the Summanu. These clothes will hide your skin, and with your blue eyes, people will just think you are a pale Shodalt." She shrugged at Ria.

"Try catch; me kilt them."

"Shade, we need to blend in and not stand out, so if there is no killing, that helps. Right now, it is time for socks, and then some shoes." She shook her head.

"No foot bags, not like."

"Shade, please be nice, just sit down, and let me do them for you."

Shade gave an exasperated sigh, and flopped down on to the floor, as Ria crouched down, and rolled the socks on to her feet. She wiggled her toes as she watched, as Ria tried to slip on a pair of boots.

When she was finally dressed, she stood up and looked very uncomfortable, Oaken appeared to approve, and he lifted up a floppy hat and plopped it on her head, and felt she looked like a farmer. Shade looked up at the brim and then at Oaken.

"Me feel bad." He smiled.

"I know, but it is only for a short time."

Ria wrapped her arrows and bag with an old canvass shirt, and with some tying and tucking, the woven basket style look was covered, and it actually looked like a reasonably good bag. She was finally ready, unhappy, and feeling very uncomfortable, but she accepted it was only for a short while. Jenmar smirked at her as she walked onto the path and she glared at him, as he took his chance to get his own back.

"Well, I must say, it is an improvement to match your manner, you look like a man." She scowled at him with hate.

"Na fan dit." Elden leaned into Jenmar.

"I know what she called you, and it implies your aged, and have no father. Seriously, what is wrong with you, why provoke her, she is as wild as rock bear?"

"She is an abomination in the eyes of Bharl, he will strike all of them down and cleanse this land, and free it of the inferior." Elden looked at him with disgust.

"You know what I think is an abomination? It is a man who has had his life saved twice by a person he sees as an enemy, and has no care in his heart to show gratitude. You disgust me Jenmar, without Shade, you would have died, it matters not to her if you live or die. In her eyes, you are Summanu, the race that wants all Undine dead, and yet she faced four men in the forest alone, and just her presence, meant you lived."

He walked off leaving Jenmar behind, as Oaken and Ria lifted their bags, there would be a three mile walk into the town, and they needed to get a move on.

Riverside, was a small town, a rural town, which had a dock that stretched out into the wide river. In days long past, it had been a very important and busy town on the river, where crop traders would buy from the local farms, pack the goods in crates, and then send them up the river to be sold. These days, it was more a smugglers outpost, where goods and contraband came in to be transported across land to places like Ranblate, and some of the other towns of Shodalt. There were smugglers and bandits all over the place, hence Shade's transformation, as in towns like these, anything and everything was for sale for the right price, and currently, trouble was the last thing they needed.

Ria was interested in a man on the outer edge of the town, her father had recommended they speak with him, he had a lot of contacts as he had lived most of his life on his farm. Ria was quite sure he would help them, Oaken was not that convinced, after all, the man she wanted to meet, was name Hammerhead. Vesta appeared interested in him, as she walked in her long robe at their side.

"I find his name to be a strange one, and not one known to me." Ria understood and gave a smile.

"He is a blacksmith, and runs a smithy on his farm, he has made parts for my father many times. My father says he is a man of honour, who deals straight, and we should be able to trust him." Oaken looked sideways at her.

"Should be, that does not sound as confident as you were last night?"

"Times have changed Oaken, and people change. Life here has got much harder than it used to be, and people have to earn a living the best they can, and that is not always on the side of complete honesty. We are lucky, in the sense that we have been able to avoid Summanu patrols, people here do not have that luxury, and in one raid, they can lose everything. Around here, people bury their coins to keep them safe until needed, that way, bandits and soldiers do not get everything. Hammerhead is well known for his goodness; I hope that has not changed."

On the approach to the town, was a wide dusty road, on which either side was fenced, and behind them, were fields of food plants. Just before the town, the road forked, and Ria took the left hand fork, which skirted the far end of what for the region, was still a large town. Hammerhead lived on a small plot of land a few minutes out of town, he had a small house, besides which was his large hut, in which he ran his blacksmith trade.

As they walked along the road to his home, his door opened and he stepped out onto a small wooden porch, holding a large black hammer. Ria slowed her pace, and the rest of the group followed suit. Vesta lifted her hand to Oaken, to allow Ria to approach the tall wide muscular man who stood in front of his home. He had a thick beard, and shortish scruffy hair of grey streaked jet black, his skin was tanned, and his eyes dark and piercing. Ria stopped a few feet in front of him, as the rest of group hung back, and he surveyed all of them. His eyes moved down to look at Ria.

"You keep strange company, Andalan's rarely leave their land, let alone associate with Undine and Leyarken, and as for you, where is your boat, I see no masts over the houses at the harbour?" Ria gave a smile; he was very perceptive.

"I came over land, your town is no longer a safe haven for the boats of my people." He nodded, as if he agreed.

"You have grown since I last saw you, I see more of your mother and less of your father now, although your stance is very much his." She looked surprised.

"You know who I am?" His eyes lifted to the group.

"That I do, although, I never thought you would fall in with an apostle, I know him too, I cannot say I agree with the friends you gather, although the Undine is well known. You can fool most, but she has my respect, even if she is dressed like a man. What is your business here? I am closing shop, if it is work you need, I am no longer your man? There is nothing here for honest workers, they have all left, as will I."

The place did look run down, and most of his field was cleared. Ria could understand his position, many of the towns of Shodalt had fallen to the bandits, it was growing to become another region like Ranblate.

"My father told me to come to you, I need a boat, no sails, one that cuts the water fast and quiet. He told me out of all men around here, you would know how to acquire one quietly, we have coins." He gave a smile.

"That is all that matters to most these days." He lifted his eyes to Jenmar.

"I know what you need, it will not be easy, but it can be done for the right price. Stay in the hut, he is not welcome in my home, the old hut leaks, but with him in your party, my trust lessened as you arrived." Ria was grateful, and she did understand, the Summanu were hated equally as much as they were feared.

"I appreciate your kindness, and we welcome the chance to rest a while." He nodded.

"This will take a little time, settle your group out of sight, and then come alone to the house, and we will discuss terms."

"Thank you, we will talk soon."

Ria turned, and walked back to the group, Hammerhead did not move, and his eyes did not leave them once, as she explained the situation. They made their way to the old hut, which contained what was left of an old forge.

Oaken leaned on the door, behind him, inside the rough built shack, with one brick wall, which contained the forge, the others settled. The air was filled with rumbles, storms were coming which were long overdue, he could feel the tension in the air and felt the soft breeze on his cheeks, as in the distance, the clouds darkened. Shade sat outside, still wearing her hat, which looked a little comical, she did not like the feeling of the forge, and preferred to be outside where she could see everything surrounding her. Ria came up at his side.

"I will not be long, and with hope, we will find a boat quickly." He reached out, and took her arm, she turned and looked at him.

"Be careful Ria, I am not sure I am keen to have you in there alone, I would much rather be with you." She gave a soft smile.

"I will be fine Oaken, and if needs be, I can take care of myself." He nodded.

"I want you safe, it worries me to know you have to do this alone." His face was quite serious, and she actually liked that, her smile was caring.

"Oaken, I will be in the house, and if I get into trouble, I will yell out, and you can come and save me." He nodded which amused her, she was joking, but he appeared to be very serious about it all, and that pleased her to know he cared enough to worry. Ria headed over to the house, and Oaken watched, Shade looked up at him and chuckled, he noted it.

"What?" She smiled a big smile.

"You need Yan Tee... Both want, why no do?" He gave a sigh.

"Mind your own business and worry about your own Yan tee. It is not like that, we are friends." She giggled.

"Me Yan tee lots." He turned away and tried to ignore her, as she giggled even more, sat just in front of him on the dusty earth.

Inside the house, Hammerhead made tea and they sat at the table, as Ria explained a little of what they were trying to achieve.

She held back enough, including that Yandalla was half Undine, and Pallum had a group tracking the convoy of metal cages. She looked at him across the table as she finished the basics of their journey.

"So, as you see, we need supplies, swift transport to be there in time, and a means of unlocking the cages."

Hammerhead sat back in his seat as he thought about all she had told him, Ria lifted her herbal tea, and sipped as she watched him. He rubbed his beard and gave a sigh.

"I can help you, it will not be easy, but I can get you a boat. I hope you have coins, because the way things are, it is the only way to buy silence?" She nodded.

"We have some coin, fear not." He leaned forward onto the table.

"That coin is for them, if you want me involved to do this, there is another price to be paid." Ria leaned back, and frowned.

"My body is not part of the deal, neither is Shade's." Hammerhead blinked as he suddenly understood what she was saying, and his face broke into a wide smile.

"Is that what you thought?"

He sat back in his chair, and gave out a loud roaring laugh, his cheeks popped forward with his smile, and he bellowed his laughter out, Ria did not quite understand, she looked at him confused.

"We hear everything is for sale in town, I just want it known, there are somethings that no man can afford when it comes to me, or Shade for that matter."

He just roared out his laughter even louder, as he looked her, and his face turned red with the power of his amusement. He slapped the table making the cups jump, Ria found it all odd and did not understand the joke at all. Hammerhead took a huge intake of breath and tried to calm himself, he tittered, as he composed himself and kept breaking into chuckles as he looked at her.

"My, you are funny, Nutriana, you are a fine looking woman, I am old, but not blind, and I mean no insult, but as much as most men would favour the idea, it is not my desire." She nodded, and breathed a sigh of relief.

"So, what is it you want?" He breathed in a relaxed.

"What I want is peace, or death. They killed my wife and two daughters, and life for me has been tough since, so this is my deal. Take me with you, that is your payment to me. When this is all done, allow me to sail off this land of hate and demons, and find me a place on your islands as far away from this dung hole as possible. That is what I ask, give me a place of peace, and I will make sure those locks undo quicker than any of you can." Ria understood him, her father had spoken of what a good man he was, and currently, he was surrounded by evil.

"Hammer, this will be no easy task, we may all die." He gave a smile.

"I am already dead inside, everything I had to live for was taken and slaughtered, dying for me is a release, it is living I struggle with." She felt the power of his words, and her emotions surged, he was so sincere, and it impacted on her. Ria took a breath and nodded.

"We have a deal; pick any island and I will personally escort you to it." She reached out her small delicate looking hand, and he gripped it firmly with his huge hand and smiled.

"It's a deal." She smiled.

"Yes, we have a deal." He smiled a wide smile, and sat back in his seat, his face changed and he suddenly looked serious.

"You are aware the apostle will sell you out?" Ria smirked.

"All of us have no trust of him, especially Shade, she will kill him if he even tries." He gave a nod.

"As will I, to be honest, he does not have to leave here, I am quite happy to dispose of him for you." Ria gave a chuckle.

"We are at a town, at some point we expect him to run, he really has no idea what we have planned, most of our conversations have been out of ear shot. We only let him travel with us so we could protect the children, it is our hope he leaves without them." Hammerhead breathed out as he considered the point.

"I have heard things about the apostles, the odds are he bought them, he will not let them go easily." Ria had thought something similar.

"Shade has taken a strong liking to them; I doubt he has the power to take them." Hammerhead gave a slight smile and nodded.

"I know of her, although I know her as Spirit not Shade, I know some of her story, I can understand why she protects them. Good, with her looking out for them, I feel they are far safer than they were. I will tell you now, if the need arises, I will deal with him, you cannot afford for the Summanu to know of your plans, and he will sell you all out."

Ria returned to the hut, and smiled at Oaken as she walked in.

"We have a deal, we will have a boat, he has promised, and I believe his word is his bond." Oaken nodded at her.

"Next time, we stand together, no more going alone, it is far too dangerous." She gave a smile.

"Why do I like that you were worried about me?" He gave a sigh.

"Just be more careful, we all need to protect each other." Ria gave a nod.

"I will, I promise, next time, we go together." Shade turned and looked back at him, she smiled at him and raised her eyebrows, he frowned at her.

"You are too smart for you own good, worry about your own life not mine." She gave a giggle, and turned back to watch over the fields.

Hammerhead left to go and arrange things and they all settled down. Caleb helped Elden set a small fire in the forge, and they cooked a pan of stew using dried meats and plants gathered by Shade for them. It was cooler in the hut which was nice, and the humidity of the day felt like it was rising fast, and as Oaken predicted, by mid afternoon, the clouds rolled in, and the temperature plummeted, as the skies lit up with a mighty storm, and the rain pounded on the roof.

The rain poured down, and it was heavy, and soon large puddles appeared outside of the hut, as the water ran in torrents down the path, as it washed off the baked land. Ria placed pots out to catch what water she could, they would need their skins refilling for travelling, and with the power of the heavy rain, it was not long before all the pots filled, and she replenished their water supply for travelling.

Shade climbed up to the loft and sat on the ledge of an open window space, and watched the town, she knew it well, and she was well aware how things worked. It would have been noted that they had travelled down the road, and onto Hammerheads land, and she knew it would not be long before someone decided to investigate, to see if there was coin to be earned.

Two hours later, Hammerhead returned, he had made the arrangements, now he needed to pay, he needed 200 hundred coins, Oaken turned to Jenmar.

"Pay him." Jenmar recoiled, sat on a bale of hay.

"Why do I have to pay him? The funds I have are merge, I am an apostle, I carry little." Elden gave a smirk.

"Seriously, I have lifted your bag. Jenmar, do not try to fool us, we know you have a greater wealth that you admit to, just give up the money."

"My bag is heavy as I carry the words of Bharl."

From high above, the figure of Shade dropped like a cat, and landed with a soft thud, and stared with malice at Jenmar. She reached behind her, slid out her knife.

"Pay or get kilt." He looked shocked and scared; she took a step forward towards him. Caleb and Meda watched on nervously.

"Me save you, pay!" Jenmar swallowed hard.

"This is robbery." Hammerhead gave a nod.

"It is no different from the way you acquired your wealth. If you ask me, the girl looks pretty angry, I would pay if I was you, plus, I don't want blood all over my place. If she is going to slit your throat, I would prefer she did it outside in the rain, it will wash the blood away easier." Shade nodded, and gritted her teeth.

"Me kilt you and take it." She took a pace towards him, he squealed in fear and snatched at his bag.

Oaken smirked, as Jenmar quickly undid his bag as Shade leaned in holding her knife ready. He tried to hide what he had, but it was not easy as the money clinked as he rifled through it, Jenmar had far more than any of them realised. Shade held out her hand, and he counted out the two hundred, as her hand filled, she passed it to Hammerhead, and held it out again so he could continue to count out the rest mumbling insults.

When the money was counted, Shade smiled at him, and Hammer bagged up the coins, Jenmar frowned at all of them, and complained.

"This is robbery, you are supposed to protect me." Oaken looked at Shade.

"You lived, you were protected, I could have allowed Shade to just kill you and take all of it." Shade smiled.

"You not kilt, you luck." Ria smiled at her, and her eyes moved to Jenmar who was not at all happy.

"Jenmar, we have shared our food, protected you from the sand storm, defended you with the bandits and guided you safety. We shared what we have to get this far, you should share what you have to get us further. I know if we leave you here alone, you will have your throat slit within the day by the bandits who live in that town, so stop complaining. All of us are in danger, and you have just helped us find safe passage." Shade turned, and walked towards the doors.

"Want kilt him, save food." The strange thing was, no one disagreed.

Ria walked outside with Hammerhead and Oaken followed, Shade leant on the wall with Vesta, they appeared to prefer the rain. Hammerhead looked at them, and then leaned to check inside, Jenmar was still sat at the far end mumbling as he fumbled inside the bag, he spoke quietly.

"One mile south, the river bends into the land, there is a wide beach there. Meet me there at dusk, and I will have the boat ready, be on your guard, others saw you, and they will come sniffing. They know apostles always have coins, if you want my advice, ditch him, only trouble follows an apostle, and as long as you have him, he will bring you woes." Shade leaned off the wall.

"Me know place, will be there." Vesta pulled up her gown and slipped it off, she handed it to Ria, as she stood naked in the rain.

"Look after this, I will go with Hammer and make sure he has extra protection, they will know a deal has been made, and they will watch for him." Ria took her gown and put inside her bag.

"I will be happier knowing he has a guard, take care, both of you, and we will see you at dusk." Hammerhead lifted his large hammer, as Vesta changed into the black cat, he smiled at the group.

"Never get tired of watching that happen, it fascinates me." As they headed off up the road to pay for the boat, Shade walked over.

"We go now; others not watch yet."

Oaken turned and looked back over the fields, he had no idea how she knew, he just trusted her, although it was still raining quite hard. They walked into the barn, and lifted their things, as Oaken looked at Elden.

"We are leaving, grab your things, and Elden, keep your sword close, we do expect company." Shade smirked at the moody face of Jenmar.

"Bag lighter, walk fast." He grumbled, as he stood up, and slung the strap of the bag over his shoulder.

"If this place was safer, I would be done with you and your kind, all of you are abominations, and should be exterminated." Shade pulled at the shirt she was wearing, and pulled it over her head.

"Me Undine now." She smiled at Jenmar.

"Me kilt you, not other." She slipped off her pants and boots, and then looked at Ria.

"Me like foot bags." She looked down at her feet and wiggled her toes, Ria smirked.

"My gift to you Shade, keep them."

"Me like, Tac yeat."

Oaken smiled as he lifted his bag, she had such simple tastes, and lived such an ordinary life, and yet she found simple happiness in a pair of socks.

"I would take them off Shade, after all, it would be a shame to ruin them in the rain."

When they had all picked up their things, and Shade was back in her normal clothes, which she had been wearing under the new clothes all the time, they packed the shirt and pants away, lifted their bags and headed out into the rain. Oaken wore a cloak, which he had been given by Evander, as did Elden, both of which were dark brown, Ria had one too, and Shade cut two really large leaves and handed one each to the children, then cut herself one. They were surprising good at sheltering them, as they walked off down pathway, which was a torrent of running water. Oaken noted she had taken her new socks off and was once again in bare feet, it made him smile to think she wanted them safe and dry in her bag.

Shade led the way, she knew where they were going, but he could also see how alert she was. She expected trouble, which probably explained her change of clothes, she knew, there were few who would tangle with her, and in a way, that was also a protection. It was a long time till dusk, but with the rain clouds above, it was really quite dark, and he knew, once in the trees, that would also be of help to them.

As they trudged through the rain, and rapidly forming mud, once again Oaken had time to think. Last night he had pushed Jenmar over using his hand, and the power of the winds came out of it, and blew Jenmar off his feet. He had not thought about it, he was simply angered by the words Jenmar had spoken, and also how ungrateful he was. There was a part of him that had hoped that being with them, Jenmar would realise how a great deal of what Balathral said was wrong, and yet he was so blinded by his own dogma he could not see it. He had to ask, was he equally as blind?

He knew of his father's ability; his mother had spoken often of it. In many ways, it was because of that he had wanted to grow up to be like him, and yet he felt now he had no understanding at all of what was happening to him. Three of the four books were back at his home, and he wished he had all of them so he could again read the passages and find some meaning in them. How could he do something without wanting to?

A picture formed in his mind of Shade stood on the empty river bed, looking back at him, as she pointed to the sky.

"Air come in me, and go out, me no ask, but do it."

According to Shade, using the four winds was as simple as breathing, but how did she know? He really was struggling with all of this, it was no different than his time in the temple, even now, he really did not understand how he could have blown out all the wick lamps. He gave a sigh and muttered to himself.

"How can I have a gift that only works when I am not thinking of it, it makes no sense at all?"

"Maybe it is driven by intention and not thought, have you considered that?" He looked up, and realised Ria was right at his side, he turned to her, as their feet squelched through the muddy water.

"How do you mean?" She shrugged.

"Shade was right at the river bed; it is as simple as breathing. Oaken, I get the impression you think that you have a power you can control as you will it, but I am not sure it works that way. Shade breathes, it is not her will, her intention is driven by her reaction, it is a part of her as it is all of us. We all breathe, it is a living part of us, so have you considered that the four winds are not some gift or special power, but actually who you are? Think about it, we do not stop and decide we are hungry, or tired, it is within us, your body intends to eat or sleep because it knows instinctively the body needs it, just like breathing. Shade is clever, she lives on those things, to her it is normal and she does not question it, and you shouldn't either. Jenmar made you angry, and because he insulted Shade, who to be honest, appears to me to have become a good friend to you, she is like your sister, and so your instinct was to lash out at Jenmar, so your body reacted. Shade understands that, and I would think, so does Yandalla."

Just the sound of his sister's name made him smile, he looked ahead where Shade walked with the two children ensuring they held the plant stems right to keep them dry. Ria was right, he had grown fond of Shade, and he hoped she did see him as a friend, for in truth he felt he was.

"Shade is wild and untamed; I am not sure Yandalla will become as wild as she is." Ria gave a slight nod.

"You said it yourself, your sister has always understood you, so her instincts are well advanced. She has also been trained by an Undine warrior father, Shade is not fierce because of her survival, she is fierce because she is Undine. They are a race made to last, no matter how bad this gets, my father is convinced they will make it through and survive, and for the very reason that they are fierce. They live as one with all things, and if you think about that, look at sand storms, floods and thunder, all of them are as natural as an Undine, and are the same force as flowers, food and beautiful seas. Yandalla is connected to the land in ways we may never understand, she may surprise you by what she is capable of as she grows."

"You seem to hold the Undine is awe." She nodded.

"I do Oaken, I find them a magical people, there is a reason people refer to them as the undying race, and that is because they will live forever as part of this land. Balathral may think he rules everything, and I say let him think that for now, but if you ask me, attacking the Undine was the biggest mistake he ever made."

"You do, why would you think that, he is slaughtering them as we speak?"

"Is he though, a great many of the female Undine are captive not dead, and yes many of the males died defending their land, as have many Summanu. If what Vesta says is true, Shengara has a lot of men on my father's ships, and there are a great many wounded being cared for in safety by your people. Do not believe all you have been told by the corrupted such as Jenmar, I believe a great number of Undine still live, they are too skilled to fall easily, and the Summanu have never won by skill, they have won because they breed fear and use superior numbers. The Undine are not easily frightened, they are spiritual and clear minded, which I may add, is why your father held them in such high esteem. If I am right, something is going to happen that has been long overdue, and honestly, it excites me a little." Oaken looked at her and frowned.

"How can any aspect of this current situation even remotely be considered exciting; people are dying Ria?" She chuckled as she looked him, the water dripping from her hair.

"Oaken, the Undine are returning to their homeland, they are currently on route back to the Leyarken Jungle, and when they get there, they will do something only they have the power to do, and it will be spectacular."

"How do you mean, what is spectacular about heading back to the jungle?"

"Oaken, read your four books again, the Undine will rile up the Leyarken, and when that happens, all hell will break loose. There is a good reason Balathral has not attacked them, they are two spirit, he will not fight men, he will fight wild and ferocious animals, and only the Undine can trigger that. Shengara is a very clever man, and if you ask me, he knows exactly what he is doing, after all, his wife and daughter are Leyarken, and his granddaughter is Undine and currently a prisoner. The one thing I know about the Leyarken people, is family to them is very sacred, and it is the one thing they will die to defend. Shengara like Shade, is using the same force as you do, he is running on instincts, and his are telling him, he needs to go home."

He could not say he fully understood all of it, but he knew Ria did and trusted her a great deal. So, if she told him that

Shengara was doing the right thing, he believed her. She patted his shoulder.

"I saw what you did last night, you are Oaken of the four winds, you and Shade have far more in common that you realise, you too can be quite wild when you need to be. Honestly, last night was the most attractive thing I have ever seen a man do; it surprised me." He looked at her and swallowed hard.

"It was, why?" She gave him a very lovely smile.

"I want to see more of your wild side, oh boy, let those winds flow, I really want to see that." Behind them Elden gave a loud giggle, Ria smirked.

"He gets it, you will too eventually."

Chapter Fifteen
River Race

It was still daylight, when Shade led them up a path into the rocks, she stopped, and pointed downwards as Oaken came up to her side.

"That meet place."

He looked down, there was a long expanse of golden sand, which formed an arc around the rocks, and the river flowed fast where the sand met the water. The rest of the land behind the beach that rose gently upward, was thick with trees and tall rocks.

"It looks well sheltered, but I cannot deny, those trees are dense, it would be a good place for a trap." Shade gave a nod to him.

"Me watch, see, then know." Oaken understood her, and thought of Ria as he looked at Shade, her blue eyes were intense, but very intelligent, Shade turned and saw him staring at her, she smiled.

"Me say, Yan tee for Ria, not me." He sat back and smiled.

"I was not thinking Yan tee, I was thinking how clever I think you are." She gave a giggle.

"Me know big; Anna Ma teach good." He smiled.

"I like how close you were to your mother, Yandalla my sister, she is very close to our mother. I have watched her all my life being taught many things about life, and our people. It saddens me you lost your mother so young, I cannot imagine Yandalla not having my mother with her." Shade sat back and took a deep breath, her voice softened as she spoke, and put her hand on her heart.

"Anna Ma mean big, teach all, me miss on bad day." He understood that.

"What was she called, she sounds so special, and I do not even know her name?" Shade looked down at the floor, her voice was so soft, it was almost a whisper, and he could feel the power of emotion sweep through her.

"Ae Lune yan."

It made sense, in the tongue of the Undine, it meant Moon Flower, he knew the plant well, for it grew only in the shade, and flowered in darkness, and it was a beautiful pure white flower.

"I know the flower well; it grows in my home between the rocks. It is a beautiful flower and name. Knowing the Undine as well as I do, they must have felt the beauty within her to name her that." Shade looked up, and a tear ran from her eye.

"Tac yeat... Me no know that."

He smiled at her, and in a strange way, he could see the beauty of her own mother within her. Oaken reached out, and touched her hand.

"I feel a great honour knowing you told me Shade, Tac yeat, for sharing that with me."

She nodded, but kept her head down, for a moment she was a daughter, and he realised, one who still grieved for a mother she lost. He left her alone to compose herself, and walked back to the group as they settled.

"No fire, this place is probably hostile."

It was not raining as hard, but they were all wet and chilly, the thought of no fire did not uplift their spirits. The day slipped past slowly, so they huddled together and chewed on dried meats and fruits, as they tried to keep as quiet as possible, Shade kept watch.

As the light started to lower, by which time they were starting to dry out a little, Shade jerked, and looked back. Oaken spotted it, and their eyes made contact, and it was clear there was something not right. Silently, he moved towards the edge of their lookout, they were around twelve feet above the beach, as Shade pointed.

"Brighem."

He stared into the darkness under the leaves, it was not easy to see, but there was definitely something there, as shadows moved around the trunks. Shade lay down her eyes fixed on the trees.

"Apostle, no luck, they take coin." He was starting to understand that, Jenmar was a walking target, and as long as he was with them, trouble would follow. He looked at her as she stared out.

"What do we do, it will not be long before Hammerhead shows up, he does not know there is a trap?" She turned slightly, and smiled.

"You, me, kilt them."

Shade slid back into cover, moved along the edge, and around to the side that fell down into the fast flowing river. She peered over the edge, four feet below them, the rocks jutted out from the drop. It was not very even, but it was wide enough to walk on, so they could move to the corner and look around at the beach just below them. Oaken understood, he slid over to Elden, who had joined them.

"Shade and me will go over the edge, and around this way. Take Ria and the others, go down the path we came in on, then work your way around. Elden, take your time, and stay quiet, they know about Jenmar and want to rob him, which is the reason they are here, they know apostles have coins. Watch Ria, and keep her safe, and hold back, even if it kicks off, because with Hammerhead there will three of us, and Vesta is with him, so we have a huge cat. Watch, and only enter the fight if we need help." He nodded.

"Use your normal sword, you know, do not embarrass yourself without a reason, keep that rusty old thing hidden. I think you have impressed Ria, don't spoil it." He giggled, and Oaken smiled.

"Keep everyone safe for me, get ready to run for the boat as soon as there is clear passage."

Elden headed off to organise the others, and Oaken followed Shade over the edge of the wall, and down onto the rough rocks just below. It was wide enough, but very uneven, Shade had bare feet, he was wearing his boots, and felt her footing was probably far better. Below them, the river flowed fast, and it felt much louder, as the water rushed past at high speed, rolling over rocks, and lapping up the side of the rock face.

He slid his hands along the wall, gripping with the tips of his fingers, and yet Shade simply walked along with perfect balance, as if she was idly walking down a road. She reached the end and peered around to look up the beach from the water's edge, she already had her hunting bow out, and held it back, as she watched the tree line. It was very clear to her now she was lower, she could see them stood back waiting for the boat. She leaned back and looked at Oaken.

"Brighem. Many bad men." He nodded.

"When you say many, exactly how many?" She leaned around the wall and watched, then moved back and looked at him. She looked at her hand, then lifted it up, and opened and closed it three times.

"Many." He was a little surprised.

"There are fifteen, that is a lot to fight Shade." She frowned.

"Kilt them, then easy."

It made a weird sort of sense, as they killed them, there would be less to fight, although, he was not sure she fully understood his point. In order to make the fight easier, they had to face fifteen first, no matter how he looked at things, it was still a lot. She smiled at him, he felt she sensed his apprehension.

"Cat good, iron hand good, you good, me kilt rest."

Yeah, there was no way he could make her see how hard a task that would be, and he decided to leave it, after all, Ria and Elden were somewhere in the trees to give them support.

Upstream, there came a whistle, and he looked back, Hammerhead sat in a very long narrow boat, at the front, sat on the edge, was a large black cat. Oaken signalled that there were men waiting and he nodded, and then steered the long boat closer to the cliff.

Vesta jumped off the boat and landed on the rock with a low growl, she looked up, and then jumped upwards, and headed back up to the top. Oaken looked up and watched her, as she jumped with skill from rock to rock, and disappeared out of sight. Hammerhead steered the boat around, and then cruised at speed into the beach, the front of the boat hit the sand, and it drove upwards onto it.

Shade tensed, as soon as the boat hit the sand, there was movement under the trees, and she loaded her bow. It looked like it was going to get violent fast, as Shade saw them walk out from under the trees in a long line, as Hammerhead got out of the boat, and pulled it onto the beach. He stopped and looked at them, as they came to a standstill twenty or so long paces from the boat, in the centre was Granth. Hammerhead gave a sigh.

The group behind Granth looked pretty well built, it was obvious from their clothing they were used to living it rough. All of them were well armed, unshaven and grim looking, Hammer partly expected this, and gave another long sigh, as he stared at them all with dark eyes.

"What do you want Granth?" Shade saw him, and tensed, she looked back at Oaken.

"He mine." Granth stood staring at Hammerhead.

"You know how it is? Old Slade told us about the boat, they have an apostle, and you know what he carries. Leave and do nothing, and we will give you a cut, we have no quarrel with you Hammer, we just want the coin." Hammer nodded.

"The problem is, my friends promised him shelter, as much as I would love to watch you slit his throat, I am bound by my word." Granth gave a smile.

"We reckoned you would say that, pity really, I like you, killing you would feel like a waste. Last chance Hammer, get back in the boat, they will not be needing it." A short scruffy one at his side nudged him.

"Just kill him, and we get the boat too."

From nowhere an arrow whizzed through the air, it hit the scruffy man right in the eye, he gave a grunt, lifted off his feet, and was slammed back into the floor. Shade smiled.

"Hit eye kilt, if no kilt, no see, all good."

She leapt out from behind the rock and landed on the sand. As Oaken moved around the rock ready to jump, Shade was already on the beach moving forward, loading her bow and shooting, and four lay dead with arrows straight into their eye sockets. The bandits spread wide, some realising it was the spirit, turned and fled, unfortunately for them, Vesta in cat form leapt from the rocks, and landed on one of them.

Shade took down more, as Oaken landed with a soft thud, and drew out his sword. One bandit drew out a long sword, and raced at Oaken, another larger one headed for Hammerhead, and Shade smiled as she dropped her bow, and stared at Granth.

"Me kilt you now." He smirked, and pulled out his sword.

"I don't believe in ghosts and spirits; you are just some Undine bitch that should be dead."

She smiled, then charged at him with speed. Oaken lifted his arm and defended as the bandit came fast, he whipped his sword around at him. As the blades met and clashed, close to the trees, Vesta mauled one of them on the floor, tearing at his throat. Oaken saw Shade jump into the air, somersault clean over Granth's head, land behind him, and before he even realised what was happening, she drove her blade right through him from behind. Shade grabbed his arm, and pulled herself right up to his shoulder, and whispered in his ear.

"You spirit now."

She pushed, and he fell to his knees, as Oaken lashed back hard knocking the bandit off balance, as he fell back, Oaken went for the kill, and pushed his blade deep. The bandit went limp, he took a breath and looked up, the large bandit lay flat on the side, his face mashed in. Hammerhead stood watchful, his large hammer in his hand as it dripped blood on to the sand, the others fled. In the trees. Vesta could be heard, as she ripped and clawed at another bandit.

Elden and Ria appeared with the others, she smiled, as she rushed over and handed him a bow with a quiver of arrows.

"You alright? Here, take this, it may come in handy, two of them had bows, but once Shade appeared they panicked, dropped them and ran. I picked them up; they could be really useful. Nice sword play, you are good." Oaken nodded.

"Pallum trained me well, I have had lessons since I was twelve." She looked around the beach.

"You looked good, I was impressed, I see Shade let her natural side out again. She is like some sort of collector of souls, wherever she walks, she releases them back into the land."

As Jenmar appeared with Caleb and Meda, Ria turned to the boat, Oaken followed her as she inspected it, she appeared a little excited to be going back onto the water. Behind them the others gathered together, watching the trees, just in case. Ria eyed the boat carefully.

"This is a first rate boat, and absolutely perfect for us, it is fast, silent, and sturdy enough to take a bump or two." Oaken frowned.

"Take a bump, we will be in water!"

She nodded and crouched down, and pointed to the centre of the front of the boat, where there was a wide piece of timber, that looked like it had been bent to follow the underside of the central column of the boat. Oaken noted, how it went right under and along the whole base of the boat.

"See Oaken, that is good thick timber and perfect for these waters, there can be rocks, so this is under the boat and the rest of it sits on top of it. It is thick, so impacts will do little to damage it, as it protects the very base. It is needed in some of these waters." He did not fully understand, but Ria knew boats and she was satisfied, so that was enough for him.

Ria started to get organised as he watched. The boat was really long, but narrow, they would all sit in a long line down the boat, and there were paddles lay down the insides. At the back, was a long rudder like paddle, on a tilting hinge. The rudder appeared to move from side to side, but it also leaned into the boat lifting out of the water, he worked out it was for in shallow water, so it could still steer, but not drag on the bottom.

Ria pulled everyone over quickly, after all, there were still a lot of bandits in the area, and judging by the loud growl and screams in the trees, Vesta had found others. Ria looked back, and hurried the others to get to the boat.

"Jenmar, you sit up front, Shade next. Meda and Caleb, you sit next, then Elden. Put your bags at your feet, they will be safe there. Oaken you next then me, Hammer, you go at the back and steer, and I will guide the boat with the paddle and instruct the others. Let's get going, Vesta is busy, so there will be more. Hammer help me push the boat back out."

Everyone clambered in, and sat in a long row, as Hammerhead helped, and they both pushed the boat out and pulled it around, as the boat drifted out into the water. Ria waded into the water, and whistled loudly, then climbed in, sat down, and pulled out her paddle. Jenmar looked back, he did not look at all comfortable.

"Why do I have to sit here, would it not be better for the Undine to sit up front?" Ria gave a sigh.

"We need to balance the boat out, you counterbalance with Hammer at the back, it will keep the boat even in the water so we get more speed."

The large black cat came bounding out of the trees, sprinted up the beach, Ria screamed out, as Vesta leapt into the air, and landed with a thump on the free seat and the boat wobbled, which unnerved Oaken, and he gripped the side.

"PADDLE, AND FAST, LOOK!"

Out of the trees other bandits were appearing, no one needed any more instruction, they grabbed their paddles, dropped them into the water, and began to push the boat forward, as Hammerhead steered out into the centre of the river. The boat moved really swiftly, as it glided over the fast flowing water, going with what was already a fast flowing current. The bandits screamed up the beach, but there was no way of stopping them, the boat was too fast, and gliding down stream at a really fast rate away from them. Shade turned, and looked back looking panicked.

"No good way." Oaken frowned, and looked back at Ria.

"What does she mean, not good way?" Ria smiled.

"This is the fastest route, it will half the time it takes down the other fork."

"Other fork, what other fork?" She pulled on her paddle.

"The river forks behind us, it is a calm run, but it winds and weaves, this fork takes the path of least resistance, and goes direct. It might get a little choppy, but this is the perfect boat for it, paddle strong, listen to me, and we should be safe enough." Oaken looked forward at Shade who was shaking her head.

"We get kilt!" She pointed down the river, in the direction they were going.

"Big, big water!" He felt his heartbeat quicken.

"What do you mean big, big?" She looked panicked, and her eyes opened really wide.

"Get kilt. Water make kilt!" Ria sniggered.

"Shade we will be fine, I have done this before, stop worrying. If we do not paddle, we might get kilt, so paddle like the Summanu, are after you."

Oaken's heart was racing, as he saw the panic on Shade's white face. He watched, as she turned around, slung her paddle into the water and paddled like a maniac. Feeling terror inside, he sped up his own paddling, the speed of the boat rapidly increased. It was getting really dark, and suddenly up ahead, he could hear the loud roar of falling water, and he started to sweat, and breathe really fast. He took a deep breath in.

"So, you have done this before, you know, the river?" He took another deep breath, as he pulled back the paddle in the water.

"I told you, I did this a good few years back alone, I mean, I have never done it in darkness, but that sort of adds to all the adventure." His heart gave an extra big beat.

"Ria, it is going to be pitch black soon, and that sounds like crazy water ahead of us."

"Oaken stop doubting, you need to let go a little, the moon will be full tonight." He pulled back hard, and lifted the paddle.

"Ria, I hate to point out the obvious, but it has been raining all day and the sky is covered in cloud."

"Stop worrying, we will make it, one way or the other."

"You are as mad as the white one down there, do you know that?" She gave a giggle.

"Life is an adventure Oaken, after all, if things get bleak, we can use the four winds." The roar of the water was getting even louder, and he could hardly hear Shade as she shouted back to them.

"WE GET KILT!" Oaken looked up, and his heart almost stopped.

Up ahead, the river suddenly narrowed through what looked like two walls of rock, the water rolled and foamed and then disappeared, and judging by the roar, it fell down a good height. Ria screamed behind him.

"Hammer, keep it straight, we have to go right through the very centre." Oaken paddled like crazy, as his eyes fixed on the water ahead, Ria screamed at the top of her lungs.

"PADDLE FASTER, WE NEED THE SPEED TO HIT THE CENTRE, AND PASS OVER."

Everyone was paddling as fast as they could, but sheer living terror spurred them on, as they raced towards a white wall of rolling water. Hammer steered watching, his focus intense, as the long white boat, which was not that deep, shot across the water caught in the current, and headed directly into the centre. Ria screamed through the deafening roar of the water.

"PADDLES IN, AND HOLD ON!"

Oaken held his breath, pulled in his paddle, as the boat hit the centre of the wall of water, lurched up steeply, then crashed into the water as a huge wave engulfed them. The boat suddenly dropped steeply, and they came flying through the wall of water, and crashed down into the raging river, faster than any of Shade's arrows.

Oaken breathed out and felt sick, as the boat flew down the river, and looked back to see the six foot high water fall, churning up sticks and branches. Ria smiled, she was soaked to the skin, but actually enjoying what was for him a terrifying experience. The boat raced on, and Hammerhead steered from behind, as large boulders loomed up on both sides of the river, as it twisted at high speed.

He was dripping wet, and yet sweating with panic, and he was convinced, Ria was insane, her brain had gone bad, and she was now hell bent on killing all of them. Shade was silent, and paddling like a crazy person, the two children were hugging each other hanging on for their life, and behind them, Vesta cowered in the bottom of the boat, cats do not like water. He paddled like crazy, his eyes focused on Shade trying to match her stroke for stroke, as the boat leaned from side to side, twisting through the current, barely missing large sharp rocks, mumbling to himself.

"I am mad, that is what this is, all this heat. I have gone mad with terror, no one who is sane would be in this boat, it is like the desert sickness, too much sun, and the brain boils. That walk, it was too much, I have damaged my head with sun, and the heat has taken my sense away."

Jenmar was not even paddling, he was so terrified, and was leaned over hugging his bags, and wailing out to Bharl to save him. The roar of the water was so loud, as it echoed up what was a steep canyon either side, and the water was now flowing faster than the wind across the mountains of Andalan. The boat was set right in the centre, travelling at a speed Oaken did not even think was possible. They raced so fast, the sides were starting to blur, and Ria kept screaming to keep paddling, and he could not deny, he had to ask.

"HOW MUCH FASTER DO YOU NEED TO GO!?" He really wished he had not asked.

"Oaken, we need to be quicker, the next bit is far harder, and if we do not speed up, we will be smashed to pieces."

His arms screamed they ached so much, and he really was

not sure he could do much more. He heard Ria scream to Hammerhead.

"THE FRONT IS TOO LOW, LEAN BACK ALL OF YOU, WE NEED THE FRONT END UP, BEFORE WE HIT THE NEXT WALL." He tried to lean back, but it made paddling harder. Ria screamed over the water.

"JENMAR, LEAN BACK, THE FRONT IS TOO LOW, IF YOU DO NOT LEAN BACK, WE WILL NOT MAKE IT. WE NEED THE FRONT HIGHER IN THE WATER!?" He did not move; he was too busy hugging his bag of coins and wailing. Ria screamed, and Oaken could hear her fear.

"JENMAR, SIT BACK. OR YOU WILL KILL US ALL!?" He looked to the front as Shade glanced back, Oaken looked straight at her.

"SHADE, PULL HIM BACK; WE ARE TOO LOW!?"

The boat was flying at a huge speed, dodging rocks, and twisting, as it headed toward another huge wall of water in the distance, she gave Oaken a nod, and turned to face forward.

Shade pulled in her paddle, and then leaned forward, she slapped her hand hard on Jenmar's back, gripped hard, and yanked him upwards. To the horror of all of them, she stood up, gained her balance, and then heaved the fat apostle up, and before anyone could scream, she lifted him up in the air, and tossed him right over the side, into the water.

Jenmar went screaming and flailing into the ice cold river, and was caught in the fast flowing current, as they swept past at high speed. Everyone was utterly shocked as Shade turned and looked back.

"LIGHTER NOW, WE LIVE!"

She plopped down in her seat and lifted her paddle, as everyone was so stunned, they had no time to think or even consider what had just happened. The boat hit the wall of water with the front high, and cut right through the swirling mass of foam and water, Ria screamed again.

"HOLD ON TIGHT!"

They came crashing out of the other side, and dropped a great height. Oaken saw the river rushing towards him, dropped his paddle in the boat, and gripped the edge of the seat for dear life.

It crashed into the water below, the boat hit, went slightly under, and then as the back hit the water, the front end shot up at high speed. He gritted his teeth with terror, and held the bench seat, Shade had turned and was sprawled across the children holding them in the boat. A huge wave of water came funnelling over them all, and then they were once again, snatched by the current, and whipped through the swirling rapids, and onwards through more rolling water down the mighty flowing river. He sat trembling, not knowing if he was cold, or just being utterly terrified, as everyone breathed hard and sorted themselves out on their seats. Ria leaned forward, her hair hanging limp and soaked, with a smile, and patted him on the shoulder.

"See, we live." He was simply frozen on his seat, lost for words, his mind swirling. Hammer chuckled as he watched and steered the boat, and kept it on course shooting through the canyon.

For over an hour, in the darkness, Ria instructed Hammerhead, as she talked him through the fast flowing canyon, watching the rolling white of the foam in the water. There were a few scary moments, where the bottom of the boat scraped a rock, and tilted suddenly, but with Ria guiding them, they managed to keep the boat upright and straight. With tired arms, they paddled onwards, flying at a really fast pace, until just before dawn, the waters appeared to calm, and Hammerhead turned the boat for the bank of green grass.

They hit the bank and all fell back in the boat and groaned with relief, there was no doubt, that had been the most frightening ride of Oaken's life, as the large black cat sprung onto the bank and instantly Vesta changed and became the naked female they were all now used to seeing. She sat on the grass with relief, and then flopped back and lay still. Elden climbed up, and lifted the shivering children out of the boat, they were really frightened, and he held them tight. Shade stood up and looked back.

"Need fire. child's cold."

Oaken sat up and breathed a long sigh of relief, he was shivering and had not even noticed. He grabbed his bag as Elden offered a hand, and he took it and clambered up onto the bank with shaking legs. Hammerhead and Ria came last, and Hammer helped lift the boat up onto the bank, and tip it over to drain, it contained a lot of water. Jenmar's bag was still in the front, and he dropped it on the bank at the side of the boat, and walked to where Shade was busy building a fire.

The camp was quiet, as the fire was built up, everything they had was soaked, and the blankets were hung on branches to drip dry, as they sat around the fire shivering and trying to get warm. Oaken sat lost in thought staring into the fire, the pictures of Shade lifting up Jenmar and just tossing him out of the boat stuck in his head. His mind swirled, she was so thin and small, how could she have such strength to lift him so easily? Nothing made sense to him, the ride, the water, the loss of Jenmar, it just felt so much to contemplate, that he could not really fit it all into his brain. Ria slipped down behind him, and her arms came around him.

"You are shivering quite badly."

She pressed her body into him and held him tight, as she leaned her head on the back of his shoulder. He felt the warmth of her body against his and came out of his dreams. She talked softly.

"Are you alright, I felt the shock you felt as she threw him out?" How could he answer, he did not really know himself how he felt? He put his head down and she leaned into it.

"I feel you are disappointed in me Oaken." He lifted his head up.

"No, I am not, I understand why you choose that route, I wish you had warned us first, I will not deny, I was really afraid tonight."

"Fear is at times a good thing, my dad has always told me, it motives people and brings out their true instincts, Shade's as we know is survival, as is yours." He turned to her.

"I have to live, Yandalla is dependent on me." She smiled, her face was close and her blue eyes sparkled.

"So, who are you dependant on Oaken of the four winds?" That was easy to answer.

"I was raised to be like my father, I can only depend on me, there is no one for me, as I have others to look over, and ensure they are safe." She gave a soft nod, as his words resounded on her.

"I find that sad Oaken, everyone should have someone they can turn to." He shrugged.

"Shade doesn't, like me, she has no one." Ria considered the point for a moment, and then her eyes looked into his.

"I think that was true when we met her, I am not sure it is true now. She has come to trust you, and I think she also looks to you, she certainly did in the boat."

"If she had looked to me, Jenmar would have stayed in the boat."

Her body heat was seeping into him, and he felt he was starting to finally warm up as the fire raged in front of him, he noticed his shirt was starting to steam. Ria appeared to snuggle into him.

"I am not sure I disagree with Shade, Jenmar was never meant to stay with us for so long. He was a walking target for us, the people of the Shodalt have suffered a great deal, and they resent the Summanu and especially the apostles. His constant rubbing of their noses in the dirt of how Bharl was the almighty force for everyone, annoyed a lot of people, after all, Bharl is the reason they lost everything. The boat was too low, I may have got us through, but it was hard sailing Oaken, what Shade did, saved all our lives. Her instincts are keen, and she knew his removal assured our lives." He breathed out and leaned back into Ria.

"Do you think he lived or died?"

"If he did, he will be injured, and go to the Summanu, and tell them what little he knows. If not, we are free of a very dangerous man, and the two children can now relax, for they are no longer slaves." He turned to her.

"They were not really slaves Ria, they were training to be apostles." She smiled at him.

"You have an innocence at times I find very attractive, but really Oaken, you know Shade's story. Apostles buy children, not to train, but for their own sick needs, Meda was not quite old enough, but he was willing to wait. Shade noticed straight away, which is why she hated him the moment she set eyes on him. He only lived because we arrived on the scene, she would have killed him and taken care of the children whether we were there or not. I would think she spotted him and tracked him, with every intention of killing him, after all, she knows what was in store for them."

"I am not convinced of that Ria." She snuggled in close to get warmer.

"Really, then ask her, she can hear us and she is listening." Oaken looked up, and Shade was sat on the other side of the fire between the children, her eyes were set on him.

"He bad man, like Anna Pa."

It felt a little shocking to hear it, and yet somewhere deep inside, he knew Shade was right. He closed his eyes, as the heat of the fire and the warmth of Ria radiated into him.

"I am tired, I really need some sleep." Ria slipped back and stood up.

"The blankets are damp, and it will be cold for several more hours, we should sleep in pairs for body heat. Caleb, you sleep with Elden, keep each other warm. Shade, take care of Meda, and stay close to the fire for warmth. Vesta is with us, so no beasts will come near."

As Oaken lay down close to the fire, Ria snuggled into him and pulled the damp blanket over them, he pulled her close, and she felt the heat from the fire on him fill her with warmth. She lay still, as he curled around her back, and looked across the clearing as the river ran past behind them. She spotted Shade looking at her, and she smiled, Shade winked, she understood, even if Oaken didn't.

Chapter Sixteen

Belthaz

Sleep came fast, but was not easy, his dreams were haunted by pictures of Yandalla sat in the darkness. He opened his eyes to a mass of blonde hair, he was not even aware he was hugging her, but he could feel the heat that radiated between them. There was movement, and he leaned back and looked up, Shade sat smiling watching him.

"Is good, you good."

He frowned, and then noticed some animal hanging over the fire cooking. She must have risen early and gone hunting. He pulled back slowly and tried to free himself from the warm body of Ria, she gave a little moan as he slid back, and pulled the blanket back over her. He felt stiff and ached, as he stood up, the dampness had got into him.

The sun was up, and he took a look around, it was dark last night when they arrived, so there had been little to see. They were in a small open glade and the sun was warm as it shone from a blue sky. Hammerhead was sat against a tree wrapped in a thick fur, he held his large hammer tight in his hand, all the others were still sleeping. He noticed Vesta was a cat again, and Meda was snuggled into her fur, deeply asleep, he smiled, as he moved to the fire and sat beside Shade. She had a pan boiling with a strong smelling herb in it, she poured some into a cup.

"Drink, make warm, give strong."

He cradled it in his hand as he yawned a wide yawn, and then lifted it to sip. His eyes opened, it smelled strong, and appeared to really open his senses, she smiled at him.

"Sleep good, she good." He gave a sigh.

"It was just for heat, we were wet and cold last night, all of us needed body heat." Shade gave a chuckle.

"Reason good, but lie." He frowned at her.

"No, it is not, we needed to keep each other warm." She sipped from her cup, and then rolled her eyes.

"You smart, and Shen tey, same time." She turned and looked at him.

"Ria good women, why you no see?" He shrugged.

"I know that, we are good friends." Shade gave an exasperated sigh.

"Shen tey, she like, you like, yet Shen tey." He frowned at her.

"I am not an idiot, I like her too, she has become a good friend." Shade shook her head, and gave an even longer sigh.

"Me friend, she more." He was not at all sure about that.

"Shade, that is not how things work, you know, people just don't say Yan tee and jump on each other, there is a process." She leaned back and stared at him.

"Take walk, talk Ria, me know."

"I am not awake yet Shade, it was a rough day yesterday, I ache all over."

"Drink, make strong."

He gave a sigh, and sipped at his tea, it was strong, and yet it had a sweet sort of taste, although there was a slight bitter tang of aftertaste. The fire was built up, and the cooking meat smelled good, Shade refilled his cup and then attended to the meat. He watched as she spread some seeds and herbs on a flat rock, crushed them and ground them with another flat stone into powder. She scouped it up into a small wooden bowl from her bag, and then mixed some water with it and made a thick greyish paste.

It was fascinating for him, as she had another flat stone on the fire, onto which she poured a little paste, and then using the back of her carved wooden spoon she smoothed the paste out. The mixture appeared to inflate on the hot stone, and she flipped it over using her dagger creating a flat form of bread. Shade smiled as she lifted it off the stone, and then cut some of the meat off the cooking animal, and rolled it up in the bread. She handed it him with a smile.

"Eat, make strong."

She took some more paste and started again. It smelt really good, and he bit down and felt his mouth come alive, and suddenly realised how hungry he actually was. Shade gave a nod.

"Good." He nodded as he chewed.

One by one they slowly awoke, and each of them got a cup of Shade's strong brew. Shade showed Meda how to make the bread, and it was nice to see her, as she instructed Meda, and crushed and ground more seeds, her eyes never leaving Meda and showing her how to perfect the flat breads. There was plenty of meat, and with Meda helping and enjoying herself, there was plenty of bread to eat. Oaken ate three, and found himself stuffed, but feeling more alive.

Ria sat at his side, and he felt she was much closer than normal; she appeared to be really happy after her long sleep. When they had all eaten, Ria checked out the boat. It had a few scrapes and scratches, after all, they had bumped one or to rocks, so she treated each scrape with a coating of bee's wax, from a block she carried in her bag. The inside of the boat was drained, and free of all the water that had splashed into it. Oaken inspected the bows she had taken from the bandits, they were good long bows with a good selection of arrows, and he knew they would be useful. Once all checks were done, they gathered again by the fire, the sun was getting hotter and the day was warm, which was good, because all their things were laid out to dry. Hammerhead tore a whole leg off the animal, and sat chewing, as Ria planned out the rest of the day.

"The river is not that bad from here on down, we are through the worst of it, what we face is nowhere near as bad. The problem we have is there are two towns on route, they are not big, but they have been known to harbour Summanu." Elden looked up from his plate.

"Do they have look outs?" Hammerhead belched, and rubbed his chest.

"Shadrak is the most likely to be a problem, but we are quite far off. It would be wise to pass the place in the dark, I heard they have a lot of soldiers camped there."

Oaken tried to look at the map, but it was wet and the ink had streaked, so it was not really that clear, Ria leaned into him and pointed with her finger.

"I want to take it easy, we need to save our strength, just in case we need a fast paddle to escape. This boat is great quality, and is very fast, we have covered a lot of ground. As you can see, if anyone in Riverside tried to follow us, this high rock plateaux has no path across it, and we cut right through it, so they will have to travel in a wide arc to get ahead of us. If we take it easy and enjoy the rest, we will not reach Shadrak until dark, and with luck, if we stay in the middle of this wide part of the river, we should shoot through quite quickly unnoticed." Hammerhead took another large bite and chewed.

"A lot of traders travel that stretch of water. Pull the blankets over yourselves and stay low. I can paddle and steer, and if anyone looks, all they will see is one man and boat packed and covered, as if moving goods to trade, which is normal for those parts."

Oaken gave a nod, to him that felt like the best idea, he liked that one, it made the most sense to him. All he wanted to do was get down the river fast, and then set up ready to find a way of getting Yandalla out of her cage. It was agreed, and as the day wore on, they repacked all of their things, rolled up their now dryer cloaks, and slid the boat back into the water, and loaded it up ready.

They set off mid afternoon, and it was hot on the river. The water moved fast, but it was very smooth, so they guided the boat into the centre, and swept on down at a good pace, but taking it easy. It was not long before Oaken started to enjoy himself, he enjoyed the relaxed stroke of the paddle, and the gentle flow of the boat, as it glided across the water. The banks were rocky and steep, large bunches of flowers and berries hung down, filling the rock faces with greens and yellow, and occasional splashes of red. It felt strange, his first encounter of Shodalt had be one of a bleak baked desert, and yet here the wilds felt lush and full of life. Maybe that could explain a great deal of the absence of people, maybe they had moved west out of the desert into greener lands, he knew he would if he lived here.

Everyone appeared to be more relaxed, Meda and Caleb sat up front, and Shade sat behind them pointing things out and talking quietly to them. Vesta was dressed and human again, and leaned forward as she paddled, and talked softly to Elden of her life in Leyarken. Ria rested each of them, allowing them breaks to not paddle, with the river so calm, they needed less effort. When it came to their turn to rest, she moved forward, pushed him to the side a little, and sat down beside him. She smiled as she handed him some dried fruit.

"I have enjoyed my trip, and enjoyed my time with you, have you thought more of what you want to do when you get your sister?" It felt like an odd question.

"I have not really had much time since we left Shade's home, but if you are asking if I intend to go on and go after Balathral, my mind is still set on finding a way of doing so." She nodded.

"Can I ask why you would risk your life so easily...? I suppose what I am asking is, Oaken, do you have no reason to live, is there nothing you would not risk at all?" The question surprised him, he really had not expected it.

"Ria, I am uncertain as why you would ask that, I have many reasons to live." Her blue eyes sparkled as she looked at him.

"Like what, you talk so little it is hard to know?" He sat back, and watched her, she appeared to be really serious.

"They say I am future of my race; my mother believes I will one day lead the Andalan, I also have my mother, Master Eliaston and Yandalla to care for, I have much to live for."

"Do you? Oaken those are the duties that have been thrust upon you, I am asking about you, is there nothing at all you would like for your own happiness, is there not some woman you can return to? There must be someone who will comfort you, and be just for you, is there no wife or companion in your future?" He had never thought about it, and just shrugged.

"I suppose there are Andalan girls, my mother has often told me of a few who appeared to have their eyes cast my way, I have not really thought about it. Yandalla has friends she tells me want to be closer, I know she wants me to favour Shellena, her friend, and she often makes fun of me because I have no wife. The Undine pair early, my father did not pair with my mother until later, I guess, I thought I have always had time for that later, and continued my studies." She smiled a soft smile.

"I feel we are similar; I have never given it much thought either, but recently I have. It is all very new to me to suddenly feel, and I am unsure of what to do."

He could understand that, he saw how some of his few friends agonised over it. Penjin was madly in love, but would tell no one who it was. When they sailed, it had appeared to be all he could talk about, his great love of an Undine.

"I suppose Ria, what would you like to happen?" She looked down at the bottom of the boat, and her voice dropped to a very low and quite tone.

"I want you to notice me." He strained his ears.

"What, I did not really hear that?" She looked up, and looked saddened.

"Oaken, I have found myself caring greatly for this person, it has really surprised me, and all I want, is for him to notice me." He could understand that.

"Well, if you ask me, I would say he will. Ria, you are very beautiful woman, trust me, he will notice." At the front of the boat there was a loud laugh.

"HA! Shen tey." Oaken frowned, and turned to look down the boat, he shook his head and turned to Ria, she was smiling at him.

"You think he will find me beautiful?" He leaned back, and looked at her.

"What, you don't, Ria, have you looked in a polished plate, trust me, no man alive will not notice?"

Hammerhead, who was not far behind them stifled his giggles, Ria appeared quite pleased with his answer, so he was at least relieved he had found a good answer for her. All this talk, reminded him greatly of Yandalla, and her endless talks of falling in love.

Ria sat back smiling lost in thought, and Oaken drifted with the soft pace and smooth passage of the boat. His thoughts drifted to the river, and Shade, he turned to Ria and lowered his voice.

"Do you think Jenmar lived?" She snapped out of her thoughts and looked at him.

"I am not sure, he could have been swept over the falls, or found his way back, it is hard really to know which. If he is, and came out on this side, he will find help as there are many patrols inland, if not, it will be a long time before he finds anyone to aid him. For now, that is not my concern, getting you to your sister is." He nodded, he supposed she was right, but he could not help wondering exactly what had happened to him.

As they came close to the town of Shadrak, they moved into the bank, and climbed onto the soft sand and weed, to rest up and eat. It was close to nightfall, but nowhere near dark enough. The day had been pretty relaxed and easy going, and everyone was not really paying that much attention to their surroundings. Shade was, and soon picked up on a few individuals stalking through the trees, it was clear to her they were watching, with no intent to attack.

Shade did not like it, she trusted no one, and knowing that they were not that far from a town which housed Summanu soldiers, she felt they should pack up and leave. Ria agreed, as did Hammerhead, so slowly they got up, and Oaken suggested they tried the other side of the river until it was fully dark. There was a wide spot on the bank just down river on the other side, the boat was light, so it could be hoisted up.

It appeared to be the right compromise, after all, it was still too early to move safely downstream, so they loosely loaded the boat back up, untied it, and paddled across the river. Hammerhead, Elden and Oaken lifted it full of their things, and carried it deep into the trees. The group sat back in bushes and waited, the children slept, as did Elden, and Hammer dozed.

As the light started to fail and darken, across the lake, Shade noticed burning torches in the trees. Ria slipped up at her side and took her telescope, she placed it against her eye looked at the lights moving across the river.

"There are Summanu soldiers, quite a lot of them. Your instincts were right Shade, someone was not happy to see us, but who could it be, it is impossible for anyone to get over the pass that fast? No one from Riverside could get here faster, the only pass is two days walk that way to get to the summit, and then it would be at least two more days to get to the town." Oaken looked at Shade.

"How far is this town from here on foot?" She considered the question.

"Make food, eat, rest time." Ria smirked.

"At least an hour, maybe longer."

"What about by river?" Ria shrugged.

"The river is fast, so I would say a third of that time. Why, what are you thinking?" He smiled.

"In the dark on foot, with a fast pace, we could get past the town easily. Hammer was heading east when we met him to find new work. Everyone back at the town knows that, so he could take the boat and meet us downstream from the town. We could move quickly under cover, then get silently past the town. If they stop him, he has a reason to be on the river, after all, he has his bag of tools with him." It did make some sense.

"Oaken, he will not be protected, what if they try to attack him?"

"Send Vesta with him, she is black at the moment, and not easily spotted as an animal, and she senses people very quickly, so he will be well warned."

It was a good idea, and Ria was a little surprised at Oaken. It made the most sense, and as they sat with Hammerhead and discussed it, he agreed that with Vesta, he would be safer than alone. If anything happened, she would be able to get away and alert the others very quickly. Shade knew the area, and she thought it was better, but felt it was better left until the morning when they had light to see properly, which swung the agreement.

They settled down for the night as the moon rose, and soon Oaken was fast asleep, as Ria took first watch with Elden. The night was cooler but nice, the day had grown warm after the rain cleared, and as it peaked, the night fell, and the cooler air came as a relief. When Hammerhead took the watch, Ria and Elden made up their beds on the opposite side of the camp to Oaken and Shade, and settled down to get some sleep before the dawn broke.

It was chilly when they rose at first light, but there was no fire, as they knew that others were looking for them. They ate a cold meal and packed their things. Oaken and Elden helped lower the boat back into the water and tied it to the bank, Hammerhead would give them a good head start, and then he would paddle down river slowly with Vesta.

Shade led the way, and very soon they found themselves on a track that led in between the trees of a rich and fertile woodland. The track was narrow, and occasionally they came to a small flat wooden bridge that crossed over a wide stream. Oaken walked along at a good pace, Shade appeared faster than normal, and he felt she was uneasy in this region, which he could not understand why, as the land and life around them was beautiful.

Everywhere he looked, tall slender trees stretched up the sky, stretching out their delicate branches, filled with thousands of thin pale green leaves. The light came through the canopy, casting beams of bright white down through the dappled green of the woodland, illuminating patches of soft grasses, and ground cover plants of flowers in blues, white and purple. It felt refreshing and calming, and it reminded him greatly of some of the many parts of Undinalashka.

Shade was very alert, she scanned the trees ahead, and was constantly looking around watching everything, and tensing at the slightest sound. She kept the children close; they appeared relaxed, actually more relaxed than he had ever seen them. He could not help but ponder, was the removal of Jenmar a benefit for them, did Jenmar's presence oppress them so much they could not be natural?

He noticed how Caleb talked more to Meda, and she smiled and giggled far more than he had seen to date, and he had to question, did they feel safer now than they had before? He turned to Ria, she was slightly behind him, her eyes were set looking forward, she did not even look at him, as she walked holding her long bow in her right hand, her left on the strap of her pack. It was almost as if she had not noticed him, to be honest she had said very little since camp, which was not like her, she was usually more talkative as they travelled.

It was almost noon when they rested, and Shade looked out through the trees and watched. Oaken sat with her, and viewed the river, and the huge wooden bridge that crossed it. The river was much wider here, which he was relieved about, after all, Hammerhead would come down the centre of it, and that meant he was harder to reach from both sides. Shade had talked of how the river here was at its deepest, and as they watched the bridge, hoping to see Hammerhead, Oaken turned her.

"I feel you know this place well, have you been here before?" Shade stared across the water at the bridge.

"Bad time, not good." Oaken nodded.

"Sorry, I did not realise." Shade did not move.

"Time gone, is past." He looked back at the camp.

"Shade, is it me, or is Ria really quiet, she has hardly spoken since last night?" Shade's eyes stayed fixed on the water.

"Is you... You Shen tey." He frowned at her.

"What does that mean?" She gave a slight laugh.

"If ask, you Shen tey."

"That makes no sense at all, how does asking a question make me an idiot?"

"If no know, you Shen tey." She turned, and looked at him.

"No speak from inside, Shen tey."

He had no idea in the slightest what she was talking about, and gave a long sigh, something was not quite right, everyone appeared weird today, and he could not for the life of him work it out. Shade looked back at the water.

"Use head, think words."

He slid back against a trunk and took a deep breath, trying to work out what it was Shade was saying, but he could not deny, nothing she had said, made any sense at all to him. He sat back, and his thoughts drifted, the group did feel quieter than normal, were they all just really tired, he could not deny, being soaked, had left him aching, and he did not really want to walk this morning? Shade tensed, and spoke quietly, he blinked and looked at her.

"What?" She slid back slowly from the edge, and shrunk back into the grass.

"We go, not safe."

She slid back into the trees and headed back to the others. Oaken moved up a little and looked out across the water. On the bridge, stood in the very centre was a tall figure in black robes, he could not see the full details of him, but from a distance he looked like a taller, slenderer version of Jenmar. The main difference being, that whoever this was, he had on black robes. Jenmar had worn a pale brown robe of a similar fashion, so it made sense to Oaken that whoever this was, he was something to do with the apostles, he breathed a sigh.

"We just got rid of one, and now another one pops up."

He looked back into the trees and Shade was moving around lifting bags, and handing them to the others, it was like she was in some sort of rush to leave. It bothered him, but why, and was Shade actually afraid, it seemed like she was? He glanced back at the bridge, did this person scare her? He was about to leave, when something caught his eye, and he stopped. Along the bridge, low against the rail he saw something moving, and watched it.

"Is that a cat?"

The animal walked up to the man's side and sat down, it was a soft golden colour, and it looked like it had some form of black markings. He did not really understand why Shade felt she needed to leave, so he tuned, walked into camp, and picked up his bag. Shade was already on the path, she turned, and looked back as she took Caleb and Meda by the hand.

"We leave, walk fast, need boat."

She was definitely acting strange, her sudden urgency was worrying, he lifted his bow and slipped on his pack. Shade was already moving, and much faster than before, he looked at Elden who shrugged, it was clear he thought Shade was acting odd also. Ria was a few feet behind Shade, and moving just as fast, and with Elden at his side, together they walked out of the clearing and back onto the path.

"Elden, is it me or is everyone acting strange?" They walked quickly side by side.

"I won't deny, everyone is much quieter, and if you ask me, something has got Shade spooked. She just walked towards us, grabbed her bag and said, 'We Go' then started handing us our bags. I reckon she is scared of something, not sure what, but I felt it, and to be honest, having seen her fight, if she is scared of something, we should take note of it."

It did make sense, and she was going at a much faster pace than they had for a while, he gripped his pack and moved quicker. Shade was already getting too far ahead, so he picked up his pace and hurried, no doubt at some point she would say something. Was it the man on the bridge, did she know him, he was starting to think she did?

Her words of bad times swirled in his mind as he followed her and Ria, he knew she had suffered, and had to consider that maybe this man on the bridge was some part of that. Whatever it was, Elden was right, Shade was not acting normal, and he felt that Shade was actually afraid, and if that was true, it did not bode well for any of them.

They moved at a really fast pace, and as they approached the area of the bridge, Shade moved off the path and into the trees, there was no doubt in his mind, she was avoiding something. Caleb and Meda were almost running to catch up, and Ria took their hands, Oaken did not understand it, so he picked up his pace. He ran wide of the trees, overtook Ria and the children, Shade was moving further ahead of them, which was not like her at all. He started to run, leaving the others behind him, and caught up with her, as she moved along, staring ahead, her hand on her sword hilt.

They were past the bridge and on the other side, and he knew soon that Hammerhead would be coming down the river, and he had to do something. Shade knew this place and he needed her, because if she deserted him now, he had no idea which way to go or how to get to Yandalla. He reached out his arm and grabbed her, and gave a gentle tug, she tried to shake him free, but he held on. She stopped, spun around ready to pull out her sword, and he noticed.

Her eyes, they gave her away, and she looked beyond scared, she looked utterly fearful, and for a moment it threw him completely. His voice was soft; he did not want to spook her more.

"Shade, please wait... I know you are afraid, but wait. I hope you know that no one will hurt you whilst I am with you?" She took a deep breath, and blinked.

"No understand, bad man, very bad man."

He nodded at her, and could hear the others coming up behind him, and as much as he had got used to hearing her speak his language, he changed and spoke Undine.

"I know you are afraid of this man; I think he has something to do with your father, or at least his death. Dar len eah ae lune ca yan, help me understand." He released her arm, as she looked at him, and responded in Undine, which the others really did not understand at all.

"The man on the bridge is a very bad person, he is the son of the man my father sold me to, and I kilt." Oaken nodded, it made sense.

"This man's father did bad things and hurt you, I understand now." She swallowed hard and took a breath.

"Oaken, he took my flower when I did not want to give it. It hurt very bad, so I kilt him." Everything made sense.

"The black robes he wears, he is an apostle, isn't he?" She gave a nod, and spoke the common tongue again.

"Man name, Belthaz, son of Frenalk. He high apostle." Ria gasped, and looked back, but the trees were too dense to see through.

"That is Belthaz, head of the high order of apostles, what the hell is he doing here?" Oaken tuned and looked back.

"Do you know of him?" She realised he had asked her a question, and turned back to him.

"I have heard of him." Oaken stared at her, waiting for more, but it did not come. He held out his hands, and shrugged.

"AND!!" She gave a scowl.

"And what?" He could not believe she did not know.

"Ria, if you have heard of him, then tell us, we could really use a little more so we know what we are dealing with." She looked for a moment like she was going to say nothing, then let out a long audible sigh.

"He is obsessed with Bharl, loves human sacrifices, is a cold bloodied killer and loves to watch people suffer. He enjoys violating females in the most horrible of ways, especially children. He is ruthless, and some say so cold, he can freeze your heart simply standing near you." Her tone was cold, and her face emotionless, yet he felt she was angry.

"Oh... He has a pet Leyarken called Lithana, but never mention her near Vesta. Lithana killed her brother by tearing out his throat, when he was ten summers." Caleb appeared shocked, as did Meda, which Oaken did not fully understand. Shade gave a nod.

"Lithana, bad Calthra." He wanted more, but to be honest, for now he had heard enough, and he understood Shade and their situation better.

"Right, in that case we keep moving, and head to the meeting place, the sooner Hammerhead appears, the better, we need to get as far from this Belthaz and his cat as possible." Shade nodded.

"We go."

Oaken gave a nod, and they all started to move again, this time not as fast, but at a good pace, his mind raced, the more he learned of the things that had happened since his father had sent them into the desert, the more he wished he had never left home. His mind swirled as he walked fast, and he could not help but ponder, why it was the Summanu were so violent to peaceful people.

He also thought about the manner of Ria, it was like she had completely changed overnight. Her smile had gone, and she had become really quiet, and it confused and puzzled him, and he could not deny, he missed her laugh and his talks with her as they walked. Something was not at all right, and he wanted to know what that was.

Chapter Seventeen

The First Rule of War

Hammerhead came around the bend in the river, and saw the bridge, he was not going very fast, as he had opted to take his time, which would allow the others to get well ahead. Vesta peered over the bow of the boat, and could see the long line of Summanu on the bridge, all holding up long spears.

Hammerhead dipped his paddle in the water to slow the pace of the boat more, it was clear, they intended to stop him. As he came into view, other boats appeared with soldiers in, and they paddled up the river towards him. He looked down the boat at the cat form of Vesta.

"Do you understand me when you are cat? I hope so, because I think you need to get out of sight. I am not sure they will be too thrilled to find a Leyarken happily sat with me." Vesta slithered down under the front bench, which had a canvass over it.

She bit into the canvass and pulled it down, to hide her from sight. She lay across the boat as low as she could, under the seat, hidden in the shadow. Hammerhead watched carefully, and steered the boat slowly towards them, and the right hand river bank. Two boats came either side of him, both filled with Summanu soldiers, Hammerhead nodded.

"Greeting, friends, is there a problem, the last time I travelled this river, it was open and free of other boats?" The head soldier looked at him, lifted his arm and pointed.

"We are to escort you to the bank." Hammerhead looked at the bank. and back to the soldier.

"As you wish, is there a reason a man of trade is to be waylaid?"

The soldier ignored him, and gave the front of his boat a push, to ensure it moved in that direction. Hammerhead lifted his paddle and gave the boat a little help as he leaned on the rudder, he saw a long wooden jetty, on which stood a tall man dressed in black. Hammerhead guided the boat up to the side of the jetty, and looked up at the figure dressed in black. He was cold looking with narrow eyes, his jaw appeared very set and square, giving him and even sterner look. His voice was devoid of emotion, and Hammerhead felt himself shiver, as he sat in the boat below, looking up. The tall man stared at him like he was filth.

"Where are you from, and what is your purpose to use this river?" Hammerhead smiled.

"Riverside has fallen to bandits, and so I am heading to my brothers in Millerdale. I am smithy, and I have heard that the Summanu are building and are in need of workers of metals. As you see, all I have left in this world are my tools." The man stared at him, and it was clear he was deciding his fate.

"We have had reports that you have been seen with others, where are they?" Hammerhead sat back.

"I have had a long slow journey, others have paid me to take them down the river, there has been several that accompanied me and left at different points."

"I am interested in an Undine." Hammerhead understood, and he nodded.

"There was one, but they were half Undine, not a full one, I left them several miles back, they paid me by hunting." For a moment he appeared to be pleased, and it showed in his voice.

"What was her name?" Hammerhead frowned.

"Her name, don't you mean his? The half Undine I carried was a young man, I will admit he was lean and sort of small, and he had very short hair, but he was clearly male. His name was Gritten." The tall man frowned.

"We were told you had a female Undine with you, one once known as the Spirit?" Hammerhead shook his head.

"I know of who you speak, many bandits lie dead because of her at Riverside, no one in their right mind would give her a boat ride. You are aware she is very hostile and dangerous? Slit your throat in your sleep, no, I would never go near her, it is not worth losing your life." Hammerhead hoped it was enough; the tall man was hard to read. It was clear he was thinking about it, he turned abruptly, and started to walk along the jetty.

"He can go, he is another worthless Shodalt, but he does have the skills needed." The soldier in the second boat looked at Hammerhead.

"You heard him, get on with it, and hurry, they are fallen

behind back in Millerdale and he is not happy." Hammerhead nodded and lifted his paddle.

"If you get out of my way, I will do." The soldier frowned, and then pushed his boat away from Hammer's.

"Go on, get lost."

Hammerhead pushed the paddle against the jetty, and pushed hard, the boat turned towards the centre of the river, and he began to paddle. He wanted to be as far away as possible from all of them, especially the man in all black, he was cold, and he gave him the shivers. He stroked hard in the water, and picked up speed, and as he reached the centre, he turned the tilla, and headed into the current, and the boat picked up pace.

As he shot under, above him on the bridge, all the soldiers stood holding their spears downwards, and he was not completely sure they would not throw them. He shot under at speed, and did not look back, somehow, he felt the ice cold stares burning into his back, and all he wanted, was to turn the corner of the river and get out of sight as fast as he could.

Vesta stayed hidden under the bench, below in the dark she had felt a sense, and smelt the air, and for the first time in a long time she had smelt a scent she had never forgotten, and her thirst for revenge was strong. It was very difficult, because her instincts told her to snarl, and jump up and go after Lithana, but she knew she could not because she would endanger all of them. As she lay in the dark below the bench, she knew now who she had aligned herself with, and all she needed to do was wait for the man in black to appear, and she knew Lithana would be with him. It had been many years, but she could bide her time a little longer.

Ria watched from the bank with her scope, Shade sat back under the trees in the semi darkness, her eyes alert, almost as she was sensing the movement of every leaf for miles. The two children sat eating fruit they had picked from some of the trees, and away from all of them, Oaken sat leaning against the base of a tree with Elden who was dozing.

In his thoughts, he tried to put together what he knew. Shade's mother was named Moon Flower, it was a name of honour, her mother must have been an Undine of honour, for only those of the highest reputation would be named directly after a flower. It made little sense, if she was such a high member of the Undine race, how could she end up married to a drunken Shodalt?

Shade was highly adaptive and very skilled, especially in combat, she had told him that her mother trained her. Moon Flower died when she was only seven years old, and yet somehow, she had trained Shade to a more than competent level. Oaken knew Yandalla had been trained from a very early age, Pallum had given her lessons long before her friends had been taught, his mind slipped back to a memory from his past.

Yandalla looked up at Pallum.

"But Anna Pa, Shellena and the others are going to swim in the pools, they do not have lessons." Pallum patted her softly on the head.

"You are my daughter, one day you will have the responsibilities I do, swimming can wait, study hard and learn fast, and then both of us will swim together." She looked down, and gave out a long sigh.

"Yes, Anna Pa." She turned with her head down, and walked onto the path back to the house, Pallum gave a smile as he looked at Sarka.

"I will make it short, and she can be like the frogs in the pool after."

Oaken came back to his senses, he was right, Moon Flower had status, she must have, otherwise she would never have trained Shade to such a high level so early in life. Understanding that posed another question, was that why her father sold her, did he believe her to be of great value? Another thought came to his mind, he sold her to the man known as Frenalk, who was the head of the order of Apostle's, why would he not simply sell her to the first person that offered, after all, there was a good trade in children in Ranblate, his mother had told him often of how sickening it was? He closed his eyes and leaned back; his words slipped out without him realising.

"She is of a line of high Undine, nothing else makes sense." Elden jerked.

"What... Did you say something?" Oaken turned to him.

"Not really, I was just thinking out loud." Elden blinked, and sat back.

"I wish the boat would hurry; it has all the food in it."

The sun was rising high in the sky when finally, Ria spotted the boat, as it came around the bend. She stood up, turned, and walked into camp and picked up her bag, she looked at the two children as they finished eating.

"Hammer is here, grab your stuff."

She glanced at Oaken who she knew had heard her, then turned and walked to the bank. They all got up and lifted their bags, Oaken walked to the bank, and stood at the side of Ria. He could see Hammerhead in the boat, and Vesta's head was peering over the front. He glanced at Ria.

"You are quiet, are you unwell?" She did not look at him.

"I am fine."

"Really, because you do not appear so, if anything you appear nothing like yourself at the moment?" The boat came sailing in towards the bank.

"Nothing like me, you do not even know me, how could you think you do?" Hammerhead looked up, he was sweating slightly, he nodded.

"I think you should hurry; this is one place I feel we should not hang around."

Ria stepped into the boat, as Shade came out of the trees, Vesta leapt out of the boat growling, and ran for the trees at high speed, Oaken stepped forward into the boat.

"What has got her so riled up?" Ria snorted.

"Oh, you are capable of noticing some women then?" He frowned, and turned back to her, but saw Hammerhead looking back up the river.

"Vesta has a score to settle, but I feel she held in her anger. Some beast will suffer her wrath, but for now that is not our concern, they are onto us, and they know about the spirit and are looking for her. I say we get moving, that man gives me the jitters, there is something about him that bothers me a whole lot, and I would rather be where he isn't."

It did not take much more, and once Shade was in the front, they pushed off, and started to paddle quickly, Hammerhead stroked hard in the water, and soon all of them were matching his pace, and the boat was moving swiftly and quietly, as it glided at high speed down the river.

As the evening approached, once again, they pulled into the bank for a break. The day had grown hot, and all of them were tired, hot and red faced. Oaken could feel the skin on his arms burning from the day of hot sun. Hammerhead dragged the boat up on the low bank, so it was completely out of the water, and then covered it with the large green canvass.

As everyone sat down feeling utterly spent from the fast pace, Hammerhead pulled a short handled axe out of his bag, and handed it to Shade.

"We need wood with no smoke." She took the axe, and stood up.

"White skin tree."

As Shade wandered into the trees with the axe, Hammerhead, used a broad knife from his belt to cut away the turf, and then started to dig a hole. Ria walked to the edge of the water to wash her face and arms, and Meda joined her, Oaken opened the backpack to see what provisions they had, it was mainly dried goods. He saw the bow on the floor and picked it up.

"We need better food; I will go look for something." Hammer nodded, as he prepared the hole to make the fire in.

"Stay close, we have no idea who is around, this stretch of river is not as safe as it used to be, so stay alert." Oaken nodded.

"I am well aware, have no worry."

He wandered into the trees, Shade was not far in, shaving the bark off a dead tree with the axe blade, he walked up to her, and looked down, she had several good pieces of old broken dead branches.

"I am going to see if there is anything we can hunt to eat." She smiled, and pointed.

"That way, beasts roam." He glanced in the direction of her finger.

"Good, I am starving." She nodded.

"So me."

It had been a long time since he had hunted with a bow, he remembered when Pallum had shown him how to stalk properly. He took his time and walked softly, his eyes set on the woodland in front of him, trying to stay low so as not to startle anything. He had not walked far, when he noticed a large rodent like animal.

He had no real idea of what it was, but it was big and fat, with a round body and small head, and had a short thick tail. He crouched low, and silently lifted his bow with an arrow fitted. He looked down the arrow and sighted it, pulling back just a little more on the string before letting the arrow loose.

CLAP!

He blinked with surprise, as all the birds in the trees above got startled, and flew into the air. The arrow slipped and fired, missing the animal as he jerked, and the beast ran off. He turned to look back and saw Ria not far off behind him holding her bow, he stood up feeling angry.

"Why would you do that, I was trying to get us food?" She smirked.

"No, you were trying to kill us, do you even know what that was?" He looked back, to where the animal had once stood, the place was empty.

"No, I did not know what that was, I have never seen anything like it, but that is not the point, it was made of meat." He turned back; he was starting to feel a strong anger brewing inside himself.

"We all need good food, why is that problem all of a sudden?" She walked towards him.

"Around here they call them wood mules, where I come from, they are known as Bog Rats. They have glands all over their skin, so if you kill one, and then skin it, by the time you are done, all of the meat is covered in a dangerous toxin, which is fatal to people. The Summanu use their skin to poison arrow tips, which is probably from what I have heard, what killed your father." He felt the surprise hit him, and felt useless.

"I did not know... Sorry, I was trying to help." She gave a slight shrug.

"We have food, I shot six fish, the river is full, and they are close to the bank. Come on, Shade is getting the fire going." She turned to walk back, and he took a step forward.

"Ria... Are you angry with me?" She stopped with her back to him.

"It matters not." He took a step forward.

"It does to me, just tell me, because to be honest it has been bothering me all day."

"I just told you; it matters not." He did not understand her at all.

"When things do not matter, people tend to be nicer, and to be honest, you have been cool with me all day."

She turned and looked at him, her eyes sparkled with life, she was tanned, and her hair flowed down from her shoulders, and shone in the dappled light.

"If you told Yandalla, or your mother you were going to face Balathral and try to kill him, do you think they would be upset, or worried?" He gave a frown.

"What has that got to do with this?"

"Just answer the question, would they try to stop you?" He really had no idea, he had not really given it that much thought, and tried to find and answer.

"They would probably not be thrilled about it, but both of them know me, they know this was something I felt was important." She gave a slight nod.

"They would tell you how dangerous it was, tell you to think more, and not just run off without planning it all out?"

"Probably... Why?"

"Tell me Oaken of the winds, would they be worried for your safety?"

"I suppose so." Her eyes shone with life as she looked at him.

"Why?" He frowned, to him it was pretty obvious.

"That is a stupid question, of course they would worry, they care about me." Ria gave a nod.

"I am glad you understand, I am glad you notice, because if I am honest, I think they would be more than a little worried. I think the thought of you facing that monster, and throwing your life away, would terrify them." He was trying to work all of this out, but it was confusing him more.

"Ria, why does my mother and sister's concerns have anything to do with the way you have been acting?" She turned away from him, and started to walk back to the camp, her voice drifted.

"Because you can notice Yandalla, and your mother's feelings, but you have no idea at all about others, and I really wanted you too." He gave a long sigh and sagged where he stood, his voice dropped to almost a whisper, as he spoke to himself.

"What in this world does that even mean?"

Utterly confused, he walked slowly back to the camp, everyone continued as normal, and Elden smiled as he handed him a plate of cooked fish. Sat in the grass he was finding being out in the wilds was not that big an adventure, if anything it was a reminder of how little he knew of the land that he lived in. He had spent most of his life in the study of Nuada, and studied little of the races of the people who also inhabited the islands of Pangela.

The simple truth was, he knew of the races and a few of their abilities, but he knew nothing of their interactions, or the lives they lived. He had no idea what animals surrounded him, or what could be hunted, and it was abundantly clear he had no understanding of the interactions of others, especially women. He lifted his food and chewed, but his appetite had been lost, and he ate only because he knew his body needed it.

With his plate empty, he lay back on the grass and closed his eyes, he felt tired and weary, and suddenly very isolated, it had not been the easiest of days, and he wanted to just end the day and somehow start a new one as it had before. He closed his eyes and drifted, as his thoughts formed in his mind.

"I miss you Yandalla, you have such a better and more instinctive idea of all this, I wish you were here to cheer me as you always have." Yandalla jerked and sat up.

"Oaken?"

The cart was still moving, there was word that the edge of the desert was not far away, and for the whole day the cart had bumped along. Most of the other girls were sleeping, the food from her father had been rationed, and they had tried to make it last, as the Summanu had cut their ration to little, and everyone was feeling weaker.

Yandalla closed her eyes, and she could feel a strange sensation, in her mind there were pictures, of people sitting around a fire eating. A large man, a young woman with golden hair, two children and... her breath caught inside her, an Undine with coloured eyes. She had no idea what she was seeing, the woman had blue eyes, but she was Undine, and like her, accept hers were green, but she had never in her life seen any other Undine with eyes of colour, and she felt shocked.

She sat back feeling a mixture of emotions swirling inside her, the Undine with blue eyes spoke.

"Calthra." The golden haired girl reached out her hand, there was a leg on the floor, and she grabbed it and shook it.

"Oaken, Vesta is back, wake up." Yandalla's mind exploded with the shock, and she gasped, then the image went black.

"Oaken?"

The girl had definitely said it, he was out in the wilds with others, strangers to her who she did not know of. Yandalla swallowed hard, her heart was beating rapidly, she looked down at her dirty pants and tried to breathe again, she had been holding her breath, and not realised. Her voice was quiet.

"Was that real or a dream?"

She really had no idea, she had dreamt things in the past, but had always doubted they were visions, although her nightmare of fire sweeping through Undinalashka for years had finally happened. It felt so real, and she could smell the smoke of the fire still in her nose, what was happening to her, was the hunger playing tricks on her mind? Her lips were dry, and she licked them, maybe it was the cart, the cramped conditions or the lack of water and food, it had to be tricks of the mind.

The cart rocked as it slipped on the sand, and she blinked back into full reality, they were still prisoners, and for now she believed Oaken was coming for her, maybe that was all it was, just a hopeful dream.

Back to reality, she slipped out the knife, between them a lot of the wood around the metal shafts had been dug away, but there were still others to be finished, and so as she looked around, she decided to occupy herself until they stopped, and dig away some more. In her heart, she knew she had to be ready, because the metal cage could not be broken, she was sure it would not open for a wind. She leaned over the still sleeping Shellena, and stabbed at the wood, and then using the tip of the blade, she started to dig into the timbers.

Ria pulled out the robe and handed it to Vesta, and she slipped it on and sat down, there was still some fish left, and Ria offered it to her, Vesta smiled and shook her head.

"I have eaten, and I seldom eat cooked things, it spoils the flavour."

Elden gave a shudder; raw meat was not something he enjoyed. Shade gave a smirk, as she watched on. Vesta looked at them all.

"Passing the last bridge was not easy, but I feel this next time will be harder. Many things change here. This town you know as Millerdale, is very different, I see now why the fat apostle was coming here. The great Grand Master of the order is building a massive building, the people here call it temple, and it will span across the river. As I speak, they have built out with rocks into the water, and the river runs narrow, and it has what they call gates on it that hang above the water. All the roads are watched with many Summanu, and apostles are coming from everywhere, to meet in praise of the Grand Master, as he names ten, who will rule each of the new territories." Oaken frowned.

"Ten, there is only eight territories within Pangela?" Vesta shook her head.

"Balathral is redrawing up the boundaries, and creating ten new territories around Sumanula, in truth there will be eleven. This master named Belthaz will shortly move to Undinalashka and build another order there, although, according to some, it will become two territories, named Balthan, and Balate. A road of wood is to be built to bridge the desert, and join Andalan with the Undine world. He has decreed that Undinalashka is a dead world, and out of the ashes a new world will arise in praise to Bharl." Ria looked concerned.

"Why does it bother me knowing Balathral will rule the shore of the nearest land to my home?" Vesta gave a nod.

"That is not all, he has boats, and he is looking for more boat builders, and has demanded my people surrender their land to him, or suffer the fires of the wrath of Bharl. He will kill everything to get what he desires; his overkill policy has gone too far."

"It is the first rule of war, according to the first book of winds." Everyone turned and looked at Oaken, he stared at all of them.

"Well, it is, you cannot have too much overkill, that is sort of the point of it. When you have the mind of a mad man like Balathral, everything has to die, he means to rule, even if it is a land without people." Shade gave a nod.

"Me said, me last Undine, soon all dead but me and him. Me will kilt him, and live quiet." Ria looked at Shade, and shook her head.

"That will not happen Shade, others will fight, and he will fall." Shade gave a smile.

"Five fight, where others?"

She had a point, they had walked through the land of Shodalt, and all they had seen was destruction, and groups that preyed on each other, and killed each other. There was no unity in the land, it should have rose up like it once did at the side of Shengara and Andalyn, and yet this time it had not, it had sat back, watched others suffer, and eventually surrendered to the forces of Balathral, and converted to the praise of Bharl. Oaken took a deep breath.

"You will never be alone Shade, I will not let that happen, we will stand side by side until our end, I have told you that. We are friends, and we stand as one." Shade smiled.

"Me lone, then Oaken and friends. All good, not bad, me friend too." Ria smiled and looked at Oaken.

"The river is out; we may as well ditch the boat and move out on foot." He gave a nod.

"Yeah, we have time." Hammerhead looked around the group.

"What are you saying, that is stupid? Look the boat is light, we pick it up and take it with us, then when we get passed Millerdale, we jump back in the river and carry on to the lake. Walking around that lake will double the time a boat will." Ria gave a shrug.

"I suppose so, but it will be hard to remain hidden carrying a boat. We have made good time, and it will be useful when we arrive at the lake, you are right, going across it will be faster than around it." He gave a nod.

"Can I ask all of you something?" Oaken looked up.

"Yes, that is what we do." He gave a nod and smiled.

"Call me Ham, that is actually my real name, I sort of hate the name Hammerhead, it makes me sound sort of stupid." Elden smirked, and Ria giggled, Oaken gave a nod.

"Alright Ham, I am sure we can do that."

Chapter Eighteen
Sold Out

"We need a break, can we take a few moments, I am exhausted?"

Ria held the boat up above her head, as the others stopped, they were well past Millerdale, and they had been walking for most of the night. Ham turned around still holding the boat, at the back, Oaken was red faced and sweating, he gave a nod, and between them, they took the weight, and Elden and Ria relaxed their arms.

The boat was lowered slowly to the floor, Ria stepped out of the way and shook her wrists, glad to have her arms below her shoulder level again. She sat down on the grass, Shade was up ahead and had stopped, and was watching, she turned, and came slowly back towards them, Ria gave her a smile.

"Sorry, but I am done in, this pace and carrying the boat up hill, it is too much, I need to rest." Shade nodded, as she looked around the rocky path covered in trees.

"We safe, go long way round." The boat hit the floor, and Oaken let go, and stood up, he looked over it at Shade.

"How far are we from the river?"

"Half day."

It was further out of the way than he wanted to be, but once they had seen the massive scale of the new temple being built by the Summanu, he had agreed with the others, that there were just too many soldiers, and so they had taken a wide arc to avoid any contact with any living people. Shade knew this area well, and so had led them up the slope, and away from the town. The path they used had once been a goat herders track, it was rough and worn, and not really that wide, but it was just wide enough for them to carry the boat in the moonlight. It had been a hard walk up hill all the way, and all of them were tired and exhausted from carrying the boat as well as all of their other things.

This part of Shodalt, like many other parts, was empty of

people, nearly all had either fled, been killed, or joined the Summanu. With the boat upside down, Oaken with Elden and Ham, sat on it and relaxed, as Ria sat on the grass at the side of the path and rubbed the tops of her arms. Shade leaned on a tree and watched the path, her eyes scanning the horizon for signs of life, of which there were none. Vesta in cat form was ahead of them checking the trail. Meda who was carrying what was left of their food, handed out dried meat and fruit, and so taking a moment as the dawn rose, they took their chance to eat.

Tiredness was creeping in slowly, and Elden soon snoozed quietly with Ham. Caleb and Meda curled around the legs of Ria, as she sat with her back to a tree and her head nodded, as she slowly drifted between being awake and asleep. Shade moved to the edge of the steep slope and watched below as the sun rose, her bright blue keen eyes alert, and aware of everything happening. Oaken came up and sat beside her, he looked down on the wide river and the roads either side.

"Many Summanu eyes." He gave a slight smile.

"They are looking for you, this man Belthaz, he means to capture and hurt you." She gave a slight nod.

"I kilt his Anna Pa, me knows." Oaken gave a long sigh.

"There is too much death, I am tired of it. Balathral means to wipe out every Undine, but I have no real idea why. The Undine want peace, as did the Shodalt and the Keytan. I have no idea why he wants to kill a whole country of people or enslave them, when all they want is peace."

"Is why." Oaken frowned and turned to her.

"What, he wants to kill them because they want peace?" Shade gave a gentle nod.

"Anna Ma told me, fight, no bother you."

Oaken turned and stared down the slope, he could see the roads filled with tiny figures, running around like ants. He smiled to himself, many times now it had been Shade's simplicity that had helped him.

"Did your mother think if they all fought him, he would leave them?"

"She right... Me fight, they no try." It made some sort of sense.

Shade was right, and Moon Flower had given her some good advice. He had seen how the bandits were afraid of her reputation, even though there was more of them, they still walked away into the forest. Was that what Shengara was trying to do, was he raising an army so that Balathral would finally learn, and people could live in peace?

The Undine had stood by his father's side and fought against the Summanu, and then the Undine retreated into the desert and lived isolated and in peace. Well, they had before Balathral ordered their land cleansed, was all this chaos down to the simple fact that they had gone through the desert? If they had stayed and defied Balathral all these years ago, would they have been left alone?

Eliaston had once told him how when you stood up to a bully, they would leave you alone after that, but as long as you tolerated their behaviour, they would continue it. Was Balathral the same, if he was to raise an army like his father did, would Balathral finally back down and stop?

He was uncertain, hell, he was uncertain about everything these days, he really did not know what was the right thing to do in any situation, even Ria appeared different with him, and he really had no idea why. He leaned forward and rested his head on his arms, he felt tired, not from lack of sleep, but the world around him. He felt Shade pat his shoulder.

"Go sleep." He shook his head.

"There is no point, I lie in the dark, and my mind fills with questions I cannot answer."

"Sleep, answer come." He was not convinced, he turned and looked at her and she smiled, her blue eyes held so much life as she smiled at him.

"Hold Ria, sleep, make better." He gave another long sigh.

"Of that I am not sure, she is mad at me, it is better I sleep on the other side of the camp." Shade frowned and shook her head.

"No mad, Ria like big." He leaned back.

"It is not like that Shade, we are friends." Shade gave a smirk.

"Still Shen tey… Ria like big, Oaken like small, like big big, you see." He was too tired to argue, he got up with a smile, and patted her shoulder.

"You are a good friend Shade." She nodded.

"We friends, good." He smiled.

"Yes, we are."

He walked back to where everyone was sleeping, Vesta was lay on the ground watching him, and he nodded as he came close to the boat. Ria had slipped and lay down, and Meda and Caleb had moved slightly away, and were curled together. Oaken saw the blanket that Ria had used to pad her back against the tree, he lifted it, shook it out, and then covered her over to keep warm.

Oaken moved over towards the boat, he sat down and leaned against it, he felt so mentally exhausted, and closed his eyes. Across the camp, Ria opened her eyes, pulled the blanket tight, and then closed her eyes and smiled.

His mind was so full of thoughts, Eliaston and his belief in him, his mother's love and faith in him as she saw him as his father. Pallum's words echoed all the time in his head, and in the middle of it all was Yandalla. He could not explain the power of the bond between them, she was his half sister, and yet it felt like she was a part of him. He could not explain it, but it felt like they were connected in some strange and powerful way, which was why he had to save her, he could not lose her.

Oaken's mind felt full, and his body ached from keeping his arms over his head carrying the boat uphill, and as he sat with his mind swimming, the tiredness finally overcame him, and his mind and thoughts started to fade as he drifted into sleep.

It was not long before the sun rose higher, and the day began to heat up, and the tiredness took its toll. Shade relaxed, Vesta was on watch, so she made her way into camp, and curled up using her bag as a pillow. It was early morning and all around Shodalt, people were rising to start their day, as the whole group slept deeply. Vesta, still in her cat form sat in the trees, watching over the group, her yellow eyes alert, taking note of every sound and scent. She sniffed the air, and for a moment, the fur along her spine started to rise, her head moved from side to side, as the scent grew on the slight breeze. Vesta stood up on all fours, and walked slowly across the camp, the scent growing stronger, and what concerned her, was it was scent she knew well.

Walking softly and carefully, Vesta walked as she followed the scent up the slope behind the camp. She kept low as she stalked through the long grass, her eyes fixed forward, her body tense, as she expected trouble. She came to the top of a steep banking, and peered through the tall grass, across what was a rocky top to the slope.

Lithana sat in naked human form with her back to Vesta, almost as if unaware of Vesta's presence. Like Vesta, her senses were keen, and she was aware that Vesta was close, possibly observing her, she smiled to herself.

"Why hide, we both know that we sense others more than most?" Vesta stared at her, she did not trust her, but unlike many, she was not afraid of Lithana.

Her form changed, and she stood up, and walked naked onto the top of the rock and stood behind Lithana.

"I am not hidden, no Leyarken can be hidden to another, we both know that." Lithana stood up slowly, and turned to face her.

"I knew you would come; it was expected." Vesta stepped forward.

"You have changed little Lithana, apart from the many scars you wear on your skin. Tell me, are they battle scars or were they made by your new master?" Lithana gave a smirk.

"Spare your concern, we both know there is unfinished business between us." Vesta gave a nod.

"You killed my brother, Brennar, and sold out our people to the Summanu." Lithana shook her head slowly.

"Brennar was an accident, he came at me with others, what was I supposed to do, let him and his pack kill me? What I did was to defend myself."

"He was young, you were much older and knew better, you once served the house of Aisie. You should have known better, you knew they were no match for you. Why did you not pat them down and prove your authority, there was no need to kill any of them, especially by ripping out their throats?" Lithana gave a long sigh, as she faced Vesta.

"I told you, it was a mistake, they rushed me and I responded on instinct, before I knew what I was doing, it was done." Vesta stared at her not believing anything she said.

"Was selling out our race to the Summanu on instinct too? Lithana, you gave them a route into our world, and many of our race died. Had it not been for Shengara and Andalyn, we would have been wiped out as the Undine are at the moment?" Lithana lifted her hands almost in a pleading manner.

"Vesta, we were once friends who trusted each other, is there no trust left between us so I can at least explain?"

"That was eighteen winters ago, and that time has gone with the loss of many to the Summanu. You know the rule of our people, I aim to take you back to face Aisie, and allow our people to decide." Lithana smiled at her.

"I used to admire your sense of duty, for one so much younger than me, you always had what it took to serve the people of our land, but you lacked the power to stand. I will not return Vesta; I have my place in the world now." Vesta could not believe her.

"How can you call that a place in the world, is being the pet of a master of evil better than the green valleys of our home?" Lithana gave a slight chuckle.

"Even now you understand so little, Vesta, our race is doomed, when the Undine fall, which they will, our people will be next. They will burn in their homes, as Bharl wipes away everything. My master has no understanding of the power and tolerance of our people, he cannot truly harm me, these lines on my skin are nothing, you know that. Vesta, a time will come when I am the only Leyarken left alive, I will be our race."

"Lithana, how can one who was so wise become so stupid, you will never be the last, you will die long before our people do?" Lithana turned, and walked towards the edge of the rock.

"It matters not who dies first, our race will die, as will the lines of your friends, Balathral will wipe everything not aligned to Bharl from this land. Their policy is convert to Bharl, or die, no one will have a choice, as they go to each lodge with swords. A time will come when you must choose, and your choices will be life or death, and life will mean turning to Bharl, he is the most powerful God." Vesta took a step forward.

"We live in a world where the spirits of our people walk with us, our memory of our race is well documented, how can you reject the whole line of our Leyarken past, in favour of man made god?" Lithana spun around, and her eyes burned.

"You dare lecture me on the power of a spirit, you fool, Bharl is now in control, he is the supreme ruler. Vesta, would you rather die than simply say the words in favour of Bharl, and live?" Vesta nodded.

"Yes... Yes, I would, my ancestors have deep meaning in my

life, Andalyn proved that Balalaran was simply a man and no god, when he led the revolt and gave Shengara the edge to cut off his head, and show the world he bled like all men. Bharl is made up by the Summanu, the clouds flashed long before Balalaran came to power, before him, no one knew of Bharl, and since his death, his son has continued with the lie, as has your master, who educates with fear, not belief." Lithana bit her lip, and tried to hold back, and snapped back in anger.

"It makes no difference what lies you speak, all the races bar the Summanu will die, I would rather live the lie of Bharl, than be burned in the valleys below the trees. Vesta, we were once friends, I came to offer you a chance to live." Vesta shook her head slowly.

"I would rather burn in the trees than be a slave to your master." Lithana nodded.

"I expected your answer, although, I did hope you would change your mind. Vesta, Jenmar lived, he is battered and cut, and has a broken arm, but we know of your party and the gold you stole. My master has ruled your lives forfeit, and as we speak, they are bound and will face Balathral on the high steps of Sumanula. He will show their blood to Bharl, and he will rejoice, it looks like this time, you aligned yourself with the wrong spirit. That white spirit is much desired by my master; she will not survive long enough to reach the high steps."

Vesta suddenly understood what was happening, Lithana had lured her away from the camp, she knew that Vesta would catch her scent on the breeze and follow. Her heart rate quickened as the shock hit her, and before she realised what was happening, Lithana morphed into her cat form, and sprung at her.

Unable to think, Lithana pounced right at her, and more out of instinct than anything else, and still in her human form, she twisted, and ducked, then punched out. Lithana was hit in the stomach, twisted, and before she could land, Vesta gathered her thoughts and became her cat form.

As Lithana landed, Vesta launched herself at her, her teeth bared and her growl loud. The two wild cats met, they intertwined with great power, and both of them rolled into the grass, scratching and biting. They snarled at each other on top of the steep incline, down to the camp, where far below, a Summan soldier held out a long pole with a lasso on it, and slipped the loose rope around the head of the sleeping Shade.

He pulled back hard, as Shade's eyes burst open, and her head lifted to see her assailant, the soldier pulled the rope tight, and it tightened around Shade's neck. He yanked her head forward as she sprung from the floor, and threw her off balance as the noose around her neck tightened restricting her airways. Others came forward with other poles, and a second noose went over her head. Shade tried to grip the rope around her throat, as she staggered gagging for air.

The pole was too long, and she could not reach the soldier, as tears filled her eyes and she struggled to breathe. All around the camp, other soldiers slipped out their swords, and pressed them into the throats of the group, as they knelt on their chests, pinning them to the ground. They were all caught, and were trapped, unable to fight as their weapons were taken.

Shade snarled and growled, her temper flaring as she struggled, and fought like a wild animal. She grabbed one of the poles and the rope got tighter, and gripping it firmly, she pushed with all her might, and the soldier holding the pole fell backwards into the smouldering ashes of the burned down fire. Ham lay back, two soldiers on his chest, as ropes were slipped over his wrists, and two soldiers pulled fast on them. Elden lay with a smile as he looked at the soldiers who held him, as close to his side, Oaken lay still, sweat on his brow, lost to a dream. Elden's eyes moved to Oaken.

"Wake up, Yandalla needs you."

Somewhere close to the edge of the desert, in a cage that was moving slowly, Yandalla looked east, her small white hands gripping the bars, her pale dirty face pressed up to them, as her green eyes stared out at a canvass sheet. In her thoughts a connection was developing and she closed her eyes.

"Oaken, I am with you, they need you, help them."

Shade had one pole free, and was tugging at the other as she gasped for air. Others were trying to apply more nooses, but she was twisting and bending, as the soldier holding the pole staggered. Her growls and snarls filled the whole of the clearing like a wild Leyarken, and her eyes blazed a vivid blue with hate.

She pulled hard on the pole, and then pushed back hard, and the soldier staggered back, unable to believe her strength for one so small. She dragged and pulled, and he was yanked sideways, as he tried to hold onto the rope that was taught around her neck, but his balance was not steady, and he was starting to fall, as others tried and failed to loop other ropes over her neck.

Ria lay back, a large soldier on her waist as he held a knife to her throat, and his other hand slipped behind him, and started to run up the inside of her legs, he smiled a sick smile.

"It is a long way to Sumanula, and for all the time we travel, I told the others, you are mine. I think I got best part of this job, and I am going to enjoy every moment of it, making the most of your soft Animatre skin."

She cringed, as his hand moved closer to the centre, she was pinned down and unable to stop him, and for the first time in her whole life, she was terrified.

"OAKEN WAKE UP!"

Deep in his mind, lost in a trance, a white figure grew out of light and smoke. She walked slowly towards him, and he smiled.

"Yandalla." Her face was so white, and her eyes as green as the grass, as she smiled.

"I am here, but your friends are in great danger, my spirit is with you, but Oaken, you need to wake up, the wind is calling, can you not hear it?"

He frowned at her, as she lifted her left hand in front of him, and he could see all of the smoke that was surrounding her, was flowing onto her palm. Her right hand touched his and she smiled, as she pulled it up, and then slid the swirling ball of smoke onto his palm. Her voice was soft, and almost ethereal.

"Yan fors ae Cumten." He smiled, as he felt the power in his hand.

"The wind is coming." She smiled.

"You are the wind, as I am the clouds of the world that awaits you... WAKE UP!"

Oaken's eyes snapped open, as a man's voice screamed to the sound of snarls, as he looked up at the sword. A pole with a man clinging to it swept across and crashed into the man sat on him, and both of them shot sideways, and he felt the pressure leave his chest. He looked sideways, where Shade pulled at the ropes on her neck with one hand, whilst swinging a pole around her with another. His thoughts crashed together as he felt the danger, and without thinking, he thrust his arm forward, and all those surrounding Shade were blasted from their feet and went reeling backwards.

The sudden awareness of the moment hit him, and he leapt to his feet, there were Summanu all around him, and he saw Ria looking at him with tear filled eyes of terror, as a soldier ran his hand on her most private parts between her legs laughing, his temper flared.

"Get your filthy hands off her." His wrist snapped, and the man was lifted and flung into the trees, as Oaken looked around at the shocked faces, Eliaston's voice echoed in his mind.

"Calm your mind, and bring up that feeling once again, but this time, focus on it so you understand its true feeling and true power."

He felt a power surging inside him, and it was far more powerful than he had ever known, he took a deep breath in, as Ria crawled over to the terrified children and pulled them to her. Oaken closed his eyes as behind him, Shade had both of her nooses off and was swinging with the pole at the soldiers, as she moved slowly backwards, almost back to back with Oaken. He felt the power with his eyes closed, and one soldier seeing his eyes closed stepped forward with his sword, Eliaston spoke in Oaken's mind.

"I want you to push your arm quickly away from your chest, and as you do, open your eyes." He breathed in.

"Alright Oatin.... NOW!"

The solider stepped forward to lunge with his sword, as Oaken's eyes snapped open and his hand pushed out hard, and there was a bright flash of white, and the winds came down into his hand, then exploded out of it.

All around them, the group watched, as Summanu soldiers were dragged screaming into the sky, and exploded off in every direction, as the dust swirled around all of them. Everyone sat dazed simply staring at Oaken, unable to fully comprehend what he had just done, his hand dropped to his side, and he turned, saw Ria, and then rushed over to her. He reached out his hand and pulled her up on her feet.

"Are you alright?" She looked at him, her eyes filled with tears, and then she threw her arms around him and pulled him close as she burst into tears.

"I was so frightened, Oaken he threatened to do terrible things." Oaken lifted his arms, and pulled her close as she wept, and held her softly in his arms.

"It is alright, I am here, you are safe."

Behind him Shade smiled as she rubbed the red marks on her neck, her voice was a little strained and croaky.

"Now, no Shen tey, now close. Good."

At the edge of the desert, all of the Undine girls trapped in a cage with Yandalla, moved to the opposite side of the cage and shielded their eyes, as Yandalla stood holding the bars, and pure white light flowed out of her. The light filled the cage and was blinding, so much so, the other Undine were afraid of it. As Ria hung onto Oaken and he comforted her, in his mind the soft words of his sister spoke.

"You are wind, and I land of spirit, we belong, and together we will heal everything."

Ria took a breath and slipped back and looked up into his eyes. He smiled at her as her tears stopped on her damp cheeks.

"Are you better now?"

She gave a sniffle and nodded, and as she looked up at him, she lifted up on her toes, and kissed him. Oaken felt her soft lips, but did not back away, his arms tightened as he held her, and the kissed continued. Behind him Shade smiled and then winked at Elden.

"Hmm, Yan tee!"

Caleb and Meda both sniggered, as Ria held him tight and they both continued the kiss. Up on the hill there was a loud squeal, and all of them turned around, Ria and Oaken broke the kiss, and turned to look. The trees vibrated and then parted, and the large black cat sprung out, and landed at speed on all fours The cat morphed into Vesta, she looked around, she had three lines of blood scratched down her cheek, she looked at them all stood staring.

"Did you see her, which way did she go?" Oaken shrugged.

"All we saw was you, have you been fighting too? That cut will need looking at, it looks deep."

Vesta lifted her hand to her face, and felt the coolness of her own blood, she wiped it, and continued to look around, as she turned, they noticed the long scratches down her back.

"I had her, and she was losing, I know she is wounded and has gone to ground, but this place reeks of her soldiers, so I cannot pick up her fresh scent." Ria took a step forward, and reached for her bag and a clean cloth.

"Who was wounded?" Vesta turned and looked across at her.

"Lithana... She tracked you all, Jenmar told Belthaz about you all, and they came to kill you, are you sure you have not seen her?" Elden looked at all of them, and then back at Vesta as Ria walked over to her with the cloth.

"Hold up... Did you say Jenmar, did he survive being thrown out of the boat?" Vesta nodded as she sat down, and Ria crouched and looked at her face, then dabbed it with a cloth, Vesta winced, and then looked up at Elden.

"He made it to land; he was not in good shape with a broken arm. I am not sure how, but he made it to Belthaz, he was carrying gold pieces for him, which is why Belthaz is after us." Shade kicked out at a rock, and sent it flying.

"Na fan dit! Me should kilt him." Elden patted her shoulder.

"Do no worry about it, the next time we see him, I will hold everyone off, whilst you take good care of him for us." Shade smiled, and her blue eyes sparkled.

"Mentee. Me like." The group gave a giggle, and Ham stooped and picked up his hammer.

"Not really sure what you did Oaken, but I am grateful. We should not tally and get a move on, we need to get to the river and fast, it will not be long before that cat limps home, and when that happens, we will have a whole load of trouble following on behind us." Shade picked up her sword and daggers.

"Me kilt them." Oaken smiled, somehow, he thought she would, he looked at Ria as she got up.

"Get your things, are you going to be alright now?" She gave a smile, and nodded.

"Yes, I am better than ever now."

Shade gave a giggle, and when he turned to look at her, she

lifted her eye brows and smiled a very cheeky smile at him.

Within the hour, they were heading down hill and away from their camp, they had not had much sleep, but it was enough, and combined with sense of urgency within them all, they made swift progress carrying the boat.

In the distance, Oaken, who was at the front of the up turned boat and was following Shade, could see where the land turned and the river was wider, his eyes followed it into the distance, where just below the horizon he saw the lake that would take him straight to the falls of Andalan.

The high mountain range was growing bigger, as they got closer, and his eyes were fixed on it at the end of the lake, its top lying hidden by cloud. It was his homeland, and the place he was born, and he felt the growing power inside him, beckoning him to return home.

For most of the day, they ploughed onwards leaving the town and swarming masses of the Summanu behind them. Oaken knew that they were now onto him and his party, and understanding that the large bag of gold they had belonged to Belthaz, it was clear, that they would not stop until they found him. The rocky path began to litter with weeds, and soon they found themselves on a weaving path of sand and shale, as they moved closer to the treeline, Shade slowed her pace and looked back.

"In trees, rest."

There was a gasp of approval behind him, it was clear, they had done enough for today, and everyone was starting to feel exhausted. Ten minutes into the trees, Oaken could hear the sound of running water, Shade led them on paths he was sure she knew, and slowly they wound their way through the trees and thick low palms, toward what looked like a huge rock that rose out of the forest floor. The noise grew louder, and suddenly, they walked into an open glade, where before them was a wide pool, and Shade stopped.

"We rest now."

There was a collective gasp as the boat was put down, and all of them walked to the edge of the pool from a natural spring up the rock. He crouched down to wash off the sweat of their long walk in the hot day. Oaken sat back on his haunches as he felt the cold water run down his neck.

"That feels so nice, I can hardly feel my arms." Ham nodded at his side.

"I cannot deny, I am used to using my arms to work, but never in my life have I felt such aches." Oaken nodded.

"We cannot be far from the river now, we must get there soon and keep moving, time is not on our side." Ham lifted his arm and patted his shoulder.

"We will get there, have no worries, and we will get to your sister in time." Oaken took a deep breath.

"I hope so Ham, I cannot deny, I feel a really bad feeling about this apostle, he aims to find and kill all of us. I am starting to think, this apostle is more dangerous than Balathral." It was a sobering thought, Shade walked up to his side.

"He bad man, me not fear Bharl, me fear Belthaz."

Chapter Nineteen

The God problem

As the group settled next to the large pool, Shade hunted as Ria and the children gathered wild fruits. Across the land on the western side of Pangela, Shengara stood on the deck next to the wheel, where Evander steered the ship, into the river opening, heading east towards Andalan, and the land of Keytan.

"We will need fresh water and food, once inside the river I will drop anchor, then we shall send out boats with scouting parties to restock" Shengara looked at the riverbank, lined with the thick thatch of a heavily wooded woodland canopy.

"My warriors are suited to this land, they will spot foods your people have no knowledge of, I will ensure you have enough for each party."

As Shengara turned, behind him, there was an almighty screech, and his head snapped around, as he looked in the direction it had come from. His face turned to a smile, and a snow white eagled soared through the sky, its wings stretched in a giant wing span, as it glided in an arc towards him. The large eagle flew low, and then swept up to the rail of the ship, and its large white talons gripped onto the rail, as Shengara felt the emotion surge up within him.

"My daughter."

The eagle gave a nod, as all the crew stared on in awe, for the giant snow white bird was mightily impressive, and they watched as it opened its wing span of easily two men's spread arms reach, and it dropped to the floor, its talons clicking on the wooden deck. There were gasps of amazement, as Shengara unclipped his long black cloak, and the large white bird morphed into the form of a very beautiful woman, with the purest of white long hair. She smiled at Shengara as he wrapped his cloak around her naked form, and snatched her into his embrace.

"Anna Pa, you have returned to me." He held her tight, his voice soft and still commanding, but softened by the joy of being reunited.

"It has been too long, but as I vowed to your mother, I have returned to the homeland we once shared with her people."

He released her and looked down at her, as tears formed in his eyes, and she smiled, her white eyes almost translucent and radiating the light of the love she held for him.

"My mother awaits you, but allowed me to take the form of flight to meet you. I bring greetings from the people of Leyarken, and need to talk with you urgently." Shengara gave a sniffle as he smiled at her.

"Likewise, I have messages for your mother, come, we shall talk alone, for there is much I wish to say to you."

As a young man living in the Leyarken jungle, long before the Summanu attacked, Shengara had fallen deeply in love with Aisie, and had sworn his loyalty and love to her. She was the daughter of the pack leader Arorgarth, a mighty and powerful Leyarken, who presented himself as a ferocious lion.

Aisie was special, she could take the form of many animals, although her main form was that of a golden panther. Most Leyarken had only one form, although there were others who could change the skin of their chosen animal form, like Vesta, who most of the time was a leopard of gold with black spots, and yet she could force her spots to cover her whole skin, and present as a black leopard when needed.

Almae, the daughter that came from the union of Aisie and Shengara, who in her human form looked more Undine, was blessed with snow white hair, and could at will become any animal she chose, but it was always an animal of pure white colour. The ability to become more than one spirit animal was highly revered by the Leyarken, and when Arorgarth was slain, the people chose Aisie, as their new leader, believing she had more powers of protection to keep the pack safe in the heart of Leyarken, and to date, they had been right.

Below decks in his room alone with his daughter, soft words of love and separation were spoken between a loving father and his daughter, then they sat back and Almae smiled.

"Anna Ma has missed you; she yearns for you to be with her again. I do not bring good tidings, for there are troubles, and the young cubs live in fear, for the Summanu have fenced the borders of our land, and placed symbols on wood on the posts. Anna Ma has read them, and Balathral has ordered the land of Leyarken as the property of Bharl. Anna Pa, he has demanded we all praise Bharl, or he will burn the land until there is only the soot and ashes of what once was our home. Our people are afraid, and with news from Zeron, from the outside world, there are many who fear that we will all die in our beds." Shengara gave a solemn nod.

"This was my fear, hence my return, Balathral has raided our lands and burned our trees, as he aims to wipe the Undine race away forever. There is much I need to talk about with your mother, but aid will come to yours and my people. I have a large amount of my best warriors, and it is my aim to meet with your mother and tell her, the winds are coming, for the sword of the four winds has found another hand." Almae gasped.

"It has... Who?" Shengara smiled.

"It has returned to the hand of Andalyn, in the form of his son who has chosen the name of Oaken of the four winds. Your nephew Pallum walks through the dessert as we speak, attacking the Summanu who have imprisoned many of the women of our land, one of which is Yandalla." Her eyes opened wide.

"Anna Pa, this is not good, Yandalla is of the royal house of both Undine and Leyarken, and Balathral has her captive." Shengara nodded.

"Almae, she is also the daughter of Sarka, Yandalla is of the line of three houses fused by the land over time. Her brother is heading to free her as I speak, which is why I need to get into the land of our people and speak with your mother." Almae understood the great importance; she bit her lip as she thought.

"I must take this news to Anna Ma, time is short, and you must hurry, but I fear there is great danger in the lands of the Keytan, for the land is swarming with Summanu. Much has changed in these lands since the great war, the Ketonia are little more than the slaves of the will of Bharl. They toil in the misery of their lands, to grow the food that feeds the soldiers of Balathral." Shengara smiled.

"They have not been slaughtered, so that will provide the making of an army." Almae shook her head.

"They live, they work hard, but the light of their spirit has been extinguished by the Summanu, few try to leave, and those that tried, have found themselves hanging on the walls of Balathral as a sign to those who would try in the future. Anna Pa, there are no places to hide from the followers of Bharl, Anna Ma has taken the few with a will to resist into our lands, and they live quietly in the borders of our northern land, but they will not leave to fight, they live afraid to set foot outside the trees, for they know, to do so is death." She put down her head, and her voice dropped to almost a whisper.

"Anna Ma fears we will die by the flames of Bharl, for there is not the will to fight such overwhelming numbers." Shengara stood up, and his daughter lifted her head, her eyes the purest of white, her tears sat softly in the base of her eyes like glittering diamonds, he smiled.

"Return to your mother, and tell her, her lands will neither burn, or fall to the Summanu, this I swear before you my fairest daughter. Tell her, I bring the winds and the light of this land, prepare for us." Almae smiled and stood up, as she saw the power and pride of her father, he pulled her close and held her softly, his voice low.

"Fly now, fly back to our homeland and take my words in your care, I will walk in the fair green lands of Leyarken soon." He kissed her softly on her head, and turned to open the window, his cloak hit the floor, and he watched as the huge white eagle soared high into the sky.

"Fly free my child, for I am coming, and I carry the sword that slays Summanu gods."

Elden sat back against the tree and rubbed his chest and then burped.

"I have never eaten a snake before, you know, I did think it would taste somewhat slimy and slippery, but that was rather good, not at all what I expected."

They were sat beside the pool, close to the trees, with a smokeless fire made by Ham. Shade had returned with four very large green looking fat snakes, or 'scare slithers' and she had prepared and cooked them, which at first had repulsed some of the group. Hunger got the better of them, for the thick slices hung on sticks over the fire, and the fat dripped and sizzled, all of them had felt their stomachs groan, and their will to refused faded.

Oaken sat back at the side of Ria, his stomach full and his head tired and weary, Ria leaned on him.

"Are you still thinking about her?" He gave a sigh.

"How can she walk into my dreams Ria, and then hand me the wind I needed, it makes so little sense to me, and why was she so surrounded with bright light?" Ria shrugged at his side.

"She is Undine and Andalan, maybe the light has something to do with her Undine side, either that or she has a gift like yours from Nuada. Honestly, I do not know, I am just glad she could, because you waking up saved all of our lives, and if she helped to do that, I will thank her when we free her." He turned to her.

"When we free her?" She frowned at him.

"Yes, I told you on the beach, I will do everything I can to help free your sister, it is why I am here Oaken." He closed his eyes, and leaned back more into the tree.

"I feel utterly exhausted and I sleep, but I see so many things in my dreams, I wake feeling I have not slept at all." Ria moved off his shoulder.

"Come, lie back on your pack, take off your shirt, roll over and relax. I have oils that will help you calm yourself as I rub them into your skin, and you will sleep deep and free of all dreams."

He frowned at her, and gave a sigh, she gave him a hard stare, and he yielded, and gave a huff, as he pulled off his shirt and lay face down, resting his head on his pack. Ria reached into her bag, and pulled out a small bottle of purplish oil, she rubbed some into the palm of her hands, and then pushed down on his back and rubbed her hands towards his neck. Oaken gave a long moan of happiness and she smiled, Shade turned with a smirk, and looked at Elden who was watching with keen interest.

"Mmm, Yan tee!" She giggled, as Oaken gave out another happy moan.

Lithana stood naked, her body blackened and torn, her wound bloody and dark, as she faced the rage of Belthaz. He lifted his hand and struck her hard, and she was smashed downwards into the floor.

"That was my gold, and those children were to be mine, the girl is untouched, have you any idea how hard it is to keep one girl untouched in this waste of a landscape? That girl cost me ten lives of a Shodalt man, she was mine, and you were ordered to bring her back." Lithana was already in pain, and she felt it more as she slid up from the floor, Belthaz stared at her.

"You had one task, find them and take my men to them, they had that Undine bitch and because of your incompetence, she escaped again." He turned to the stern face faced solider at the door.

"Breg, ready the fleet, they have a boat that they carried, at some point, it has to touch water, and when it does, I want the boat and everything in it. Take Jenmar, he can identify all of them." Belthaz looked down at Lithana.

"Get out of my sight, and stay hidden until I need you."

She morphed into a cat, and scurried across the floor with her head down, Breg stepped to one side and allowed her to pass, then turned and followed her out of the door, Belthaz walked to the window and gazed down the river.

"I have not forgotten you Dar len eah ae lune, you are like your worthless father Yendee, had you not killed him, I would have. I know you are out there, and I will find you, and then you will pay for the death of my father, as I hang you up, and spend weeks peeling each layer of your white skin away bit by bit. I will have my vengeance, and it will be long, slow, and sweet." His eyes burned in his face with his hate, and yet he smiled a sick and sadistic smile.

Ria blinked away the sleep, and opened her eyes fully, Oaken was sat staring into space beside her, the old book held firmly in his left hand. She sat up and yawned and rubbed her eyes, and then leaned on his shoulder.

"How long have I been asleep?" Oaken blinked out of his thoughts.

"Everyone is sleeping." She smiled, he had not really heard her, he was so lost in his thoughts.

"What are you reading?" Oaken gave a sigh.

"I was reading the third book of the winds, but my mind got sidetracked." She nodded at his side, and her eyes moved down to the book.

"I thought the books could not leave the temple." He looked at his hand, and lifted it slightly.

"They cannot, this is a copy, my father's parents copied them, my grandmother copied the first two, and my grandfather the second two, they belonged to my father, and he left them for me." It made sense to her,

"What side tracked you?"

He placed the book down and got up, and she frowned unhappy he had moved. Oaken walked to the fire and threw two more logs on it, he turned and looked back at her as he lifted the pan filled with water to boil.

"My father studied these books for all of his life, and he made notes in the margins. I was reading a passage on the high steps of Salanula, and at the side he had written, 'long before Bharl, the ancients.' I have no idea what that means, and was trying to work it out." Ria gave a smile and nodded.

"You doubt Bharl is real, like Nuada is to you?" Oaken smirked.

"I know he is not real, but that was not what I was pondering, what caught my attention, was, knowing he is not. Knowing the High Steps of Salanula, are older than Bahalaran, who the books clearly state brought Bharl forth, I have been wondering, who built the high steps, and for what purpose?" She smiled and leaned back on the tree, as he lifted two cups and sprinkled the dry leaves of the tea into them.

"Oaken, my father has said there are texts from long ago on our main island, that mention the high steps, and that is many generations before Balalaran. He too thinks Bharl is a cover for the brutality of Balalaran and his son." She watched as he lifted the pan, and poured the water into the cups.

"Oddly enough, those same texts talk of the Andalan, and their life of worship and search for spiritual wisdom, so in a sense, your people have been around long before many of the others, but I will add, they also talk of people who came from a land destroyed by great floods, and they settled in Jandaria." Oaken stood up with the drinks, and looked confused.

"Where is that, I have never heard of it?" She gave a giggle.

"It is the land we know as Sumanula, but according to my father, it was once named Jandaria, and it was a barren and rocky wilderness." He nodded as he walked over, crouched down to hand her the tea.

"So, these new arrivals renamed the land?" She gave a nod, and lifted her tea to her lips, she looked over the cup.

"They were a very wise race with great skills, my father thinks they built the steps, and dug the water channels that brought water into the region, and they prospered." She gave a slight chuckle.

"He once told me, that shortly before Bahalaran took power, one of the parts of the steps collapsed, revealing a thick core of metal, and they rebuilt it, but struggled, as their workers of stone found it hard to work out how the steps had been built. I remember him telling me, Bharl was fake, the only reason the lightning strikes the steps, is because of the metal that runs down the core of the steps, as it draws it down to it." Oaken frowned and sat back looking at her.

"How... The light falls from the sky, no one knows where it will hit?" She nodded and her eyes grew large as she looked at him with a big excited smile.

"I know... I said the very same thing, and so he showed me." Oaken narrowed his eyes.

"Showed you... How?" She gave a little giggle; she was loving this.

"He took me outside and hammered a tall spike of metal into the sand on one of the beaches, and I watched it for weeks. One night, we had a really bad storm, and I jumped out of bed, and ran through the rain to the beach. I sat there watching from a distance, and the lightening came down six times, and every time it hit the spike and ran into the floor. Oaken, it came down to touch the metal, they say lightening will never hit the same place twice, but that night, it hit the pole six times, what if the steps do the same thing?"

Oaken was lost for words, he stared at the smiling Ria, as his mind reeled. It took a few moments to gather his thoughts. He thought for a moment, and then took a breath.

"The book of fire, which is the fourth book, says that Bahalaran stood at the top of the steps and preached to the masses of his meeting with Bharl. He told them, that he would bring rain to the land which was suffering in a drought, and he would show that this was the gift of Bharl, and mark the steps with white light, and boom out his voice to them all." Ria smiled.

"He knew Oaken, somehow, he knew that the lightening was attracted to the steps, and he used it to convince all of the people that Bharl was real. The light and his voice, were just the thunder, nothing more, but he convinced a whole race that Bharl was real." Oaken nodded.

"He did, and my father also knew, he worked it out from the book, there is no god Bharl, only the land and natural way." Ria swigged from her cup.

"What I have never understood, is why? Think about it, Bahalaran was already the leader, it was known his son would rule after him, and his son after that, so why create a god to follow, he had no need, he already ruled with great authority?" Oaken gave a long sigh.

"I really have no idea; to be honest nothing makes sense when it comes to the Summanu. All I know is that they want complete control of everything, and they will not stop until they get it, and they use this fake named god Bharl to do it."

Ria leaned back on the tree trunk cupping her drink in her hands, and looked at him, she could almost feel the turmoil of trying to work it all out, and it reminded her of many times in her own life.

"Think about it, he was called Bahalaran, take out some A's, and removed the n, and all you are left with is Bharl. Like I use Ria, he named his fake god after himself, and ruled for many years, before his son Balatharan, took over."

It felt like an almighty revelation to him, and to a degree, he felt a little pressure lift off his shoulders, because in knowing that Bharl was fake, as he realised, he voiced his words without thinking.

"My fight is with a man, not a god, although, what about Nuada?" Ria giggled.

"I think it is safe to say your god is real. Oaken, Balathral may be a man, but he is a very heavily protected one, you may never get close to facing him." He looked up at her.

"I know, but I think I have to try in order to save everyone. How do you know Nuada is real, you share a different belief than others?" She gave a shrug.

"I watched as you closed your eyes and asked for the help of Nuada, and when you pushed out your hand, men flew into the air and were scattered to the winds. No mortal can do that Oaken, that was not the work of a man, that was something much bigger. To be honest, I had my doubts before I saw that, but not now, after seeing that, I know there is something, I am just not sure what." In a way it felt like a relief to hear her say that, for a moment he had doubted himself.

"Eliaston has always told me that all of us are connected through Nuada, even the Undine." She nodded.

"That does make sense." He frowned at her.

"How, they believe in the land, they call it the power of Elohim." She gave a smile.

"Well of course, that makes complete sense, the people of my land believe there is something, call it a power or force that drives life, for us it is the El and Elah. El drives the power of the land, and brings bounty, and Elah drives the water and the waves that we sail on. They are joined in the sky, and look down on us, it is not unsimilar to the Undine belief, the names may be different, but their meaning is the same, maybe Nuada is something similar. I have never seen a statue to Nuada, so I am presuming it is a force or spirit that drives life." She made a great deal of sense to him.

"Nuada is within all things, and it is through Nuada, gifts are placed on us through life. I believe Nuada is within all of us, and I mean all, the Undine, Summanu, and even you."

"So, what you are saying is same god, different name, is that right?" He gave chuckle, to a degree she was right.

"Yes, I suppose so." Shade came walking through the trees with an arm filled with long herbal stalks, she stopped and looked at Ria and Oaken.

"God broke, need fix, Yan tee better, need god of Yan tee, fix all." She nodded, and walked over to the pool to wash off the plants, and Ria giggled.

Shade washed off the long stems and lay them on a rock to dry. With her dagger she cut off the large leaves, rolled them up inside a cloth, and then lifted the sticks, as Elden grunted and sat up. She walked over and handed him a white stick.

"Eat, make happy." Elden frowned.

"What is this Shade, I have never seen it before?" She shrugged.

"Happy stick, me like." She bit into one and chewed with a big smile.

"Good, make strong." She walked over to Oaken and handed one to him, and one to Ria, then sat on the grass chewing with a big smile.

"Me like." Oaken looked at it, Ria nibbled a little bit off the end.

"It tastes sweet." Shade nodded.

"Sweet stick, me like." Oaken bit into it and chewed and he felt the sweet juice build in his mouth, and was surprised at how wonderful it felt, he took another big bite as he swallowed.

"This is nice, I really like them." Shade nodded with a smile; she was on her third. Ria took a bigger bite and chewed it, she gave a huge smile, it did taste wonderful, Shade was not wrong.

"I like these." Shade continued to chew.

"Water full, we make strong." Oaken looked her, she was pointing down the stream than ran from the pool.

"What do you mean, the water is full?" Shade swallowed, and smacked her lips.

"Big water, big boats, water full." Oaken turned, and looked down the stream.

"Who has boats, I thought this river was rarely travelled?" Ria stood up holding her half eaten stick, and looked through the trees, she knew the river was not far off, but she could not really see anything.

"With gates on the bridge back there, no one should be on the river, so who is it?"

It was a really good question, and one at some point they would need the answer to, Oaken just hoped they were friendly, their boat was fast, but how big were the other boats?

"I think we should wake everyone up and then go take a look, I was hoping for a fast sail out of sight, the last thing I want is people seeing us on the river." Ria looked down at him looking concerned.

"I hope it is not the Summanu, because if they have boats, that could spell big problems for Animatre. Oaken, he has been after boats for a long time, the only reason he has none, is because we will not build them for him. If he is building boats, I think that explains why he wants the Undine wiped out, with them gone, the whole coastline is clear." Oaken felt a cold shiver run down his spine.

"We need to get moving, and find out who it is, and I already know, I really do not want them to be anything to do with Millerdale or Belthaz."

Chapter Twenty

Wind and Water

The group packed up as quickly as possible, the day was moving forward, and the clouds were starting to darken. Ria made her way ahead of the others with Vesta, to the riverbank, which was not that far away, and took up a point to watch.

Carrying the boat above their heads, with Shade leading, they walked along the track at the side of the fast flowing stream, towards the river. It was not that hard a walk, and they arrived to find Ria stood on a fallen tree, that stretched into the water, using her scope to see both ways. She looked back as they put the boat down.

"I see three boats, they are shallow with a mast, so I am assuming they have a sail of some form, and possibly oarsmen." Ham gave a wide look up and down the river, he could not see the boats.

"Where are they?" Ria pointed up stream, back towards what they knew was the bridge building that housed the Order of Apostles, Elden gave a sigh.

"That is not good, I suppose the question is, can we go faster?" Ria folded her scope, and walked along the wide trunk back towards them.

"I am not sure, I am used to greater ships, but I can say, the ships of my father are not slow, they can outpace our small boat in a good wind. I did not get the best view of them, as they moved into the bank, but from what I could see, they are long, shallow and sleek. It depends on what they carry, they could be for trade, or they are for transporting the order, I am not completely sure, but I think they could have oars, it was hard to see." Oaken understood.

"Oars will make them faster." Ria nodded at him.

"It will, but they will have to be strict in their timing, I think they have a sail, so they could just be using that on the downward current, but up stream, the wind will work against them." Ham pushed the boat into the water alongside the trunk.

"We are heading downstream, so if they do come our way, they will have the wind behind them. What I need to know, is can we outrun them?" Ria jumped off the trunk onto the grass.

"Our boat is light and very fast, with all of us paddling we should have good speed. As to can we outrun them, we will not know until we try." Shade lifter her bag, and looked at everyone.

"Talk no move boat." She had a point; the boats were up stream and they were wasting time. Ria organised and placed everyone where she felt they would be best served in the boat.

"Ham, you go up front, Caleb, can you paddle?" He gave a nod.

"Alright, you go next. Vesta, I know you hate water, so sit with Caleb and Meda, then Elden, Shade, Oaken, and I will take the tiller. If things get bad, I will drive us onto the bank, one thing I know, is those vessels will not do well in the shallows, and that is our advantage."

Everyone busied themselves grabbing their belongings and taking their seats, Caleb lifted a paddle and waited. Vesta curled up as a cat under the seat, as everyone else took their place. With Elden and Ham shoving off against the fallen trunk, the boat swung out into the deeper water, and all of them began to paddle.

Ham set a good pace, and the boat soon picked up speed, the last few days had been good for them, as they could feel the power in their arms as they stroked into the water. Ria sat at the back and watched in front and behind, as they moved into the centre of the wide river, where the current was at its fastest, and the boat, which was light, picked up yet more speed.

They were gliding along at speed, and had been for a while, when they passed a wide channel to their left, Ria spotted the mast immediately, as a horn sounded up the channel. They had been spotted, and she watched as the oars came out of the side of the long boat, she leaned forward.

"They have been waiting for us, and they have spotted us and are coming."

The group understood, and pulled harder as they lifted the paddles to match the stroke of Ham, and followed his lead. They were going fast, and as the larger boat came out of the river to the side, they shot past, and had moved a good distance ahead of them.

Behind them, a drum pounded in rhythm on the boat, the oarsmen were keeping pace using it, as their long oars dipped into the water in unison. Ria glanced back, they had twelve down each side, and the boat behind them was picking up speed, she turned to look down the long river, it went on for a great distance and was open water. She felt nervous and lifted her voice.

"Faster, we need to use this current to gain as much speed as possible." Shade looked back looking anxious.

"Too small, need more."

She pulled hard in the water, as Ham increased the best he could, they were faster than they had ever been, but would it be fast enough, none of them were sure? Behind them, the drum beat began to increase, it appeared the boat was set on catching them up, and it was now travelling at a great speed. Ria looked back, they were raising a sail, and it was huge.

"Oh no... THEY HAVE SAIL!"

Oaken twisted in his seat and glanced back, it was really big, and had caught the wind, and it was a deep blood red. He pushed harder on his paddle, and tried to increase his pace, but there was only so much they could do.

"They are closing in." Ria looked back.

"Just do not stop, we have to try and outrun them."

The air around all of them was starting to fill with the tension, they were giving their all, but with the wind in their sails, the speed of the boat behind them had greatly increased. He twisted around.

"Ria, they are catching us up."

She looked back, Oaken was right, the boat was very streamlined, and she could see how it was cutting through the water. The low sides of the vessel meant it was light, so did not drag like some of the bigger boats she had seen. Whoever had designed it, knew a great deal about boats, and at this rate, it would not be long before they caught up. Ham strained on his paddle.

"We cannot keep up this pace all day, we need to do something." Shade looked back, and saw the huge red sail.

"Me no get kilt." She pulled in her paddle, Oaken stared at her.

"Shade, what are you doing, keep paddling, we need everyone?"

Arrows whizzed down not that far behind them; the large boat had archers.

Ria tied the tiller to her leg, and lifted her paddle, bringing fresh arms to the paddling. Shade pulled up her bag, and pulled out a small metal plate, which she put on the seat as she dug through her bag, Oaken heaved on his paddle.

"Shade, get hold of your paddle and stop messing around." She shook her head.

"No kilt me!" She lifted out a small bundle of fibres and her flints, Oaken frowned at her.

"Shade you cannot light a fire; this is a thin skinned wooden boat." Grabbing one of her arrows, she ripped some of the cloth from her sheet, and bound it quickly around the end of her arrow tip.

"If sail kilt, we no kilt."

Oaken had no idea what she was doing and looked back, they were getting very close and the drum beat was getting louder. Arrows landed in the water getting closer to them, and he could feel the panic inside him growing. Oaken could see a figure stood on the front of the boat smiling wearing a sling. He gasped, not believing his eyes.

"Jenmar!" The fat apostle was stood right at the front, watching with a satisfied smirk, Ria hearing Oaken turned back and saw the sick smile on his face.

"How did he get here so fast?"

There really was no answer, but he was there, and he was right on their trail. Oaken pulled harder, as he watched Shade strike her flint on the plate, he realised he was gasping for air as they shot along at a great speed. The flint did not catch and she struck again, Oaken understood.

"Shade, not on the seat it is too windy, use the bottom of the boat."

She looked up, nodded, and lifted the plate, Oaken dropped his paddle in the water and heaved it back, there was smoke, and Shade bent down to blow, as she reached for her bow. The odds of pulling this off for her was slim, but he understood she had to try, and in a way, he trusted her. So far, her instincts had been good, and to a degree she had kept them safe. He heaved on his paddle, and watched hoping she could accomplish her goal.

Shade snatched her arrow off the seat, and pushed it onto the burning fibres, and Oaken held his breath as it caught. A quick as flash, she jumped up onto the seat, spreading her legs across the width of the boat seat to balance, loaded the flaming arrow and took aim.

For a moment Oaken lost his rhythm as he watched the arrow shoot over his head, and fly at speed towards the boat, which was about twenty of their boat lengths behind them, and gaining on them. He looked back as Ria did, and he watched the arrow hit the centre of the large sail, and Ria understood, the fabric was painted, and it burned fast. Shade's arrow hit the sail, and as it did, the sheet ignited, and burned, burning a huge hole through the fabric, which fanned by the breeze grew quickly in size. With no tension, the sail flapped loose flaring up, and as it did, it was engulphed by the flames.

The oars lost their rhythm, as burning fabric fell into the boat, and Shade dropped down into her seat, grabbed the small plate, and tipped the burning contents into the water muttering.

"Me no kilt yet."

She grabbed her oar, looked back, and then joined in paddling, and behind them the drum beat had stopped. There were loud shouts and screams, Ria looked behind, they were moving away a little more, the large boat of the Apostles, was still moving fast with its momentum, but their pace had dropped a little, and that gave them the chance they needed to pick up their own speed. She looked down the river, the lake was still far off in the distance, they still had a long way to go, and it would not be long before order was restored, and then Jenmar and his boat would begin to pick up speed again.

It was an important moment for them, a second chance to get away, and all of them were grateful to Shade, but it was not over yet as they shot along at great speed. In truth, Oaken knew they had to get as far as possible, because when they reorganised, it would not be long before they were behind them again. Their pace continued, but it was taking its toll, and Ria could see that, she leaned forward in her seat.

"The river is deep here Oaken, but as we approach the lake, it drops a little and the current picks up speed, if we do not make that before they catch up, we are lost, and they will catch us. We have to keep this pace at all costs." He understood that.

"I know, but our arms grow weak, this is taking its toll on all of us." He was red faced, and sweating, all of them were, somewhere behind them, the drum beat picked up, Oaken gave a gasp.

"Here they come again." Ria looked back, as she pulled hard on the paddle, she was starting to grow frightened.

"If they catch us, we die, and Yandalla will be lost also, don't give up on us Oaken, keep paddling, your sister needs us. If only we had a sail, your winds would help about now."

Behind them, the drum beat was increasing, Oaken looked back, there was smoke coming off the boat, but the mast was empty, and the paddles were back in the water, and stroking fast. He had to do something, but what? They were going as fast as they could, but it was clearly taking its toll, and he knew they could not keep this up. The banks looked high, and he could not see anywhere they could pull the boat out of the water, and he knew, they could not abandon the boat just yet, because to do so would slow them down a great deal, and they still had a distance to go to get to Yandalla.

The beat of the drum pounded louder in his brain, and it was not helping him think, he looked to back of Shade.

"Shade, is there anything else we can do?" She gasped, as she pulled back on the paddle.

"Need wind, need sheet."

He knew that, but they did not have one, the drum was getting louder, they were catching up again, after all they had twenty four people rowing to their six. He looked back and could see Ria, she was sweating and paddling, and she was also afraid, he could see it in her eyes, and then he looked to the water as they shot down the river.

"The river.... Ria, how deep is it?" She gave gasp, as she lifted her paddle out.

"I am not completely sure, why?" He could see the boat behind them, and it was gaining on them.

"Is it deeper than the sides of their boat?" She frowned at him.

"Well yes, it must be at least three times as deep, why?" He smiled.

"I have an idea." Elden looked back.

"Praise Nuada, because I cannot keep this up much longer."

Oaken pulled in his paddle, grabbed his pack, and pulled out his rolled up blanket containing the sword, Elden watched him.

"Oh dear, you are aware if you pull that, you will die of shame long before the Summanu get you?" Oaken smiled, as he slipped it over his head.

"Have some faith, Eliaston looks like a wrinkled old dried fruit, and yet his spirit is stronger than all of ours, his radiance is within." Elden pulled back on his oar.

"I cannot deny, I love your optimism, I have seen it remember, and it is thin, there is little depth to hide radiance, admit it, the thing is an embarrassment."

Oaken swung around in his seat, and then stood and wobbled, he stepped onto Ria's seat, his leg either side of hers, and wobbled again. She looked up at him from his crotch.

"I know we kissed and cuddled, but this is moving things forward faster than expected." He looked down at her, as he tried to remain stable.

"Hold my legs and help me stabilise, I need you to keep me level." She pulled in her paddle, and grabbed his legs, they were strong and muscular, and she actually liked how they felt, and giggled, as she looked up.

Oaken stood with his eyes closed as he tried to calm down, his mind drifting as he tried to clear his head of the drum growing louder in his ears. He took a deep breath in, and felt for the sense of calm within him, his right arm came up and back, and he felt the cold metal of the hilt in his hand, he breathed in again, as he tried to focus, his voice soft and almost a whisper.

"I must save Ria, my friends, and Yandalla."

Ria smiled as she watched him, holding his legs tight, as the boat shot at speed through the water. She could feel a strong almost electric power building around him. She swallowed hard as she watched feeling the calm growing inside of him, there was no denying, for her, this was the most attractive a man had ever been to her.

The boat shot along the water with Oaken stood at the stern, forty lengths behind them, the large boat of the order of Apostles was catching up, and gaining on them. Oaken found his place of calm, and felt his hand grip tighter, he reached out his left arm, and felt the power build. Ria felt the soft breeze swirling around him, as it lifted her hair, and she could feel the power flowing into her. Shade looked back, and saw him standing on Ria's seat, she smiled and nodded.

"We no kilt today."

As Oaken stretched out his arm, Shade watched the water behind them. In the wake of their boat, there appeared to be a sort of swirling of the water, she watched as Oaken breathed, and then suddenly, he pulled the sword and opened his eyes, and the sword shot forward with pace, and pointed down at the water behind them.

It was hard to describe what happened, Shade knew of no words, except that the water divided, and parted creating a large V shape, as the water rolled back, and a wide opening appeared. As it moved from behind their boat it grew wider, and Shade leaned over the side of their boat to watch, and she could see the bottom of the river behind them, littered with rocks and sand, she was finding it hard to believe.

The gap widened, and Jenmar watched with horror, his joy and elation turning rapidly to fear, as the waters parted and came towards them, he turned and screamed at the top of his voice.

"BANK TO THE SIDE, TURN THE BOAT!"

Ria pulled his legs close and tried to look around, and she could not believe what she was seeing, as Shade squealed in delight. The large boat of the Apostles shot into the void and dropped like a stone down to the surface of the riverbed. As the boat went down, there was a loud grinding and splintering, as the boat crunched on the rocky bottom of the river, Oaken flicked back the sword, and the water rolled back into the gap. It was almost as if the wind had formed a wall to divide the water, and then lifted up out of the way. Then at the command of Oaken, it rushed back in.

Water poured in on both sides, and the men of the boat screamed as they let go of their oars, and were swept up by the current. Oaken slid the sword back behind him and stepped back, Ria turned fully around, to see men and debris litter the surface of the river. All that remained was the top of the tall mast, which stuck up above the fast flowing water, and many men swam to the tall sides of the river.

All of them had stopped paddling to watch, as the small boat still glided at speed away from the sunken boat, and down the river, and finally they had a chance to slow the pace and rest their arms. As Oaken sat down in his seat, Shade smiled.

"Yan fors ae Oaken." He smiled, and winked.

"We are no kilt, not yet." She giggled.

"Jenmar wet again." Meda and Caleb giggled with her, under their seat, Vesta coward, afraid of the water, and nervous, as her dark eyes looked up at them.

Ria put down her paddle and climbed over to his side on his seat, she leaned in and pulled him close.

"That is the most impressive thing I have ever seen, Oaken, I am feeling feelings I have never felt before, strange things I am not used to, but they feel wonderful."

He was not quite sure what she meant, she leaned forward, and pulled him into a passionate kiss, Shade smiled at Meda and Caleb.

"Mmm Yan tee!" Elden stared at Oaken kissing Ria.

"She kissed him after seeing a rusty old thing like that, love truly is blind." Ham gave a roaring laugh, as he sat back and relaxed.

"Stranger things have happened, trust me on that." Ria pulled out of the kiss; her cheeks were flushed, her eyes sparkling with life, as she smiled a shy smile.

"You saved me, you saved us, I was really scared, but you came through for us. I have no idea how you do that, but I felt it through your legs, and it was mind blowing. Nuada is very strong in you Oaken, you truly are the son of your father. I cannot deny, I doubted it when I met you, but Oaken, I felt it, I really felt it flow through you, and I felt joy." He smiled.

"Nuada is strong in all of us, and because of that, we will defeat the Summanu." She put her hand on her chest, and took a deep breath.

"Maybe you are right."

Behind them, men clung to the rocks of the fast flowing sides of the river, but as their little boat continued in the fast current, their yells and screams were slowly fading into the distance. Jenmar clung to a rock with one arm, his face twisted and contorted with pain and anger, as he stared down the river, watching once again as they raced away from him.

"You will all die by the hand of Bharl, I will ensure it."

By night fall, as the moon rose, and the clouds parted, they entered the large lake, and Ria moved back to her seat. The lake was huge and calm like a mirror that reflected the night sky, as they all paddled slowly across the large open space. Ham turned in his seat, he was tired, they all were, he smiled and nodded at Oaken.

"We should move to land and rest, there is a chill in the air, and soon the mists will come, it would be better to be under the trees with a fire. In the mists we may lose track of things, it is better we wait for dawn."

Ria gave a nod and turned the tiller, where she saw the bank of the lake with trees in the distance, so she plotted a course to land. The night was calm and quiet, broken only by the slow gentle noises of the ripples created by the paddles, Shade pulled in her paddle and pulled out a fishing line, and as they moved slowly along, she watched her line in hope of catching some food.

Ria sat back, holding the tiller, her mind filled with the images of Oaken, and the deeply stirred feelings she had felt flowing from his body. Never in her life had she known anything like this, in so many ways it made no sense at all, and yet she had felt it, seen it, and watched as he commanded the winds. The words of her father as they sailed to the plight of Undine came back into her thoughts.

"Ria, all I know is, somewhere in the centre of all of those poor souls suffering, there walks a man who is the son of Andalyn, and if he anything like his father, the Undine will have a mighty hand to help them." She smiled to herself, as in her thoughts she saw Oaken holding up the sword, her father's voice continued to bounce around her mind.

"Andalyn was a mighty man, not because he carried the sword of the winds, for it was always at his side, but because deep in his heart, he felt great love for his people, and the winds responded to that. I believe he never asked it to help him, for that was a mark of the man that he was, if I am honest, I believe the winds wanted to help him help them. I cannot explain what the

Andalan's call Nuada, all I know is I saw it, I saw Andalyn pull that gleaming blade and things I still cannot explain happened. I know it was real, for I felt every hair on my head respond, and move with the flow of it. I have studied the lands of all peoples, and I know this Bharl is not real, for there were ancients before the Summanu came, and they sort the wisdom of the Andalan's who were around long before they arrived. If this son, has those gifts of the ancients, then guide him well, for he will be saviour of everyone."

She smiled to herself, as she softly stroked her paddle through the water, lost in her thoughts and remembering how twice he had saved her, and somehow, she was really happy about that. All her life she had wondered if she would ever meet anyone who would appeal to her as a woman, most of the men she knew were good sailors, and certainly good men, but she had never been able to separate herself as a leader and a woman. Here in this boat, travelling slowly in the moonlight as she looked at his broad shoulders, she knew, if he was to ask, she would accept his proposition.

He was a man she could give herself to, but it was not his power of the winds, it was the man that he was, a man with a big heart, a man who took a hostile half Undine and befriend her, and took her in, and protected her. A man who saw the injustice of an Apostle, who had enslaved a young girl for his own sick pleasure, and Oaken had freed her, and a man who was devoted to his family, in ways no man she knew was, and it surprised her greatly.

Shade gave a happy squeal and pulled on her line, Elden leaned over the side of the boat to help, as she landed a big fish with a smile. they lifted it into the boat, and Shade looked back wearing a huge grin, as Oaken nodded at her.

"That is a good catch, well done."

Ria smiled, she could see the loyalty Shade had for him, and it thrilled her to know, because it was clear, for a long time she had trusted no one and lived a life of solitude. Here she was, smiling, happy to be in a company of friends, and showing the truth of who she really was, and that was because of the kindness of Oaken.

The boat cruised quietly up onto the soft bank of sand, and

Ham stood up, and before anyone could move, Vesta appeared, and sprang out of the boat, clearly glad to be out of the water and back on dry land. Ham giggled as he stepped out and grabbed the rope for the boat, all of them stood up, their legs were stiff from sitting most of the day. Ria lifted her bag, and shouldered it, and then stepped out of the boat onto dry land, and smelt the rich sweet scent of the plants and the flowers, and walked with smile behind them all. Oaken turned, and looked back in the moonlight, and held out his hand.

"Are you alright, that was quite scary for all of us?" She took his hand, and felt the warmness on hers, and she smiled.

"I am fine, I will not deny I was scared Oaken, especially when I saw Jenmar with them, I think it is clear, had he stayed with us, he would have betrayed us." Oaken nodded as they reached the edge of the trees.

"I always knew he would, but I still stand that it would have been wrong to leave him stranded. I knew we would part ways at some point; I could not leave him in the town when we picked up Ham, he would have had the Summanu on us much quicker. When Shade acted, I was not sure that was right, but there was a part of me that knew, we would be safer after that, and so I said little." She understood that, she too had felt the same way. They walked into the trees, up ahead Ham was stood looking at a clearing.

"We are safer now Oaken; he is with his own kind and we are fee of him." Oaken stopped and looked at the camp site.

"Are we though? We have the gold of Belthaz, I fear he will hunt us until the end to get it back. I am not ruling out his reappearance, somehow, I think our paths are tied, and we will see him again." Shade looked up from the floor, where she had her flints out and was starting a fire.

"Jenmar come back, me kilt him."

Somehow, he felt that was out of his hands, Shade was a force unto herself, and he did not think for a moment, if Jenmar returned, she would not instantly attack him. He felt it was best he left things to fate, after all, if Shade wanted Jenmar dead, he was quite sure, even the four winds would not have the power to stop her.

Chapter Twenty One

The Gathering of Forces

From the moment that Tanquilla had dropped off her daughter and Oaken in Shodalt, she headed back to her home of Animatre, and loaded her ship with food and weapons to aid the Undine. When she arrived back on the north eastern coast of Undinalashka, her crew began the long process of unloading the supplies onto the beach. She walked up the sand towards the Undine warriors who were busy sorting out the supplies.

Shaylil accompanied by thirty other Undine, organised the goods to be sent onto the supply lines, that would ship food and more arrows to Pallum in the desert. Shaylil took a break as Tanquilla approached him, he looked exhausted.

"How are things Shaylil, you look worn out?" It was clear he was trying to be as brave as possible, but his eyes gave him away, Tanquilla took his arm, and gently squeezed it. He took a long deep breath.

"I have seen things no Undine should see, and it lives in my mind." Tanquilla nodded at him, understanding the horrors that had taken place, as she saw he was trying to hold back the tears. He bit his lip, and swallowed hard.

"My people have been treated in ways we have no words for. My home is littered with our women, who lie dead and cut, and we cannot take them to the place they will become one with all things. Tanquilla, their legs are covered in the blood that has come from their flowers, the Summanu have done unspeakable things no man should to them, and then killed them. I want this pain gone from my thoughts." His tears ran onto his face, and his voice wavered.

"My sister is one of them."

Tanquilla pulled him into her shoulder and he broke down, all around him the men of the Undine watched, and one gave a nod to Tranquilla. All of them knew of his bravery for one so young, and just as he did, they all carried the pictures of their slaughtered people in their minds. Tranquilla looked at them all, standing and silently watching her, as she held Shaylil, and spoke to him.

"They will pay for the pain they have inflicted on your people. The lands of Animatre walk with you, and already we are preparing our other ships. Help will come in the shape of strong men, and we will raise our swords with the Undine, and follow the lead of Oaken of the four winds, and we will see revenge. My husband sails to Keytan with your warlord Shengara, as his anger boils, and all of you must follow his lead, and get as angry as you can, because then you will find, you have the power to defeat the likes of Balathral."

When the Summanu invaded Keytan, unlike Shodalt, which they cleared, they preserved much of lands. Keytan was a prosperous land of farms, orchards, woodlands, and a bountiful trade from the sea.

The people, known as the Ketonia, had generations of information on the seasons and how to grow food, something those of the Summanu needed, to keep the food growing and the sea food coming. Rather than take over and kill everything, they used their power and might to rule over them, and so life continued with a high presence of Summanu soldiers.

Those who stepped out of line were herded together and placed in prison camps, which were large areas with high walls of wooden posts hammered into the floor. There were platforms, on which the Summanu walked and watched over them from. Below them in the open empty spaces, the prisoners built their own homes and lived a captive life contained and unable to leave. The freer people called them the Dark Towns, for many of the camps were as big, if not bigger than most of the rural towns of the land.

The wide river that flowed from the sea into a bay, was a hive of activity, filled with small fishing boats, which each morning before dawn, would sail down the river out to the sea, and return to the port in mid afternoon, filled with fish and sea goods to be sold at the market, on the edge of the port of Pangela. The largest population of towns and villages were mainly located in this area, which was where many flocked to trade from all of the country.

With Balathral ruling the Undine as a none race, Evander and

Shengara were well aware of the dangers of sailing into the port. The ship lay at anchor at the start of the estuary, as the crew organised on the boat, of which there were copious amounts of weapons on view, Evander was prepared should any trouble be started.

On the shore, down a small path, through a dense and difficult jungle like forest, there were two long wooden huts, surrounded by a tall wall of wooden trunks. It was here that Ria and her mother, did deals with a group of smugglers, out of sight from the Summanu. Their contact was a man named Valken, or Valk. He had previously been one of the leaders at the port, but when the soldiers arrived, he took his closest allies underground and set up a network of resistance, to run smuggling operations, and bring aid to his people.

Four of the crew made contact and talked with him, and Valk came to the ship to talk with Evander. He sat in the meeting room below decks, with Shengara, and they talked of all that was happening. Valk sipped wine that he had brought with him, as he looked at Evander.

"Your daughter has always been a great supporter of my people, and her boats have been a lifeline, I cannot deny on this side of the sacred mountain, she is highly respected, and she will find friends wherever she goes. Evander, on the other side of the mountain, things are not good, the life all of us knew of is very different now. Here the filth that have invaded us need us, and so to a degree are lenient, from what we have heard from those who have manged to flee here, the filth over there have butchered everything, she may find the land far more hostile that she is used to." Evander gave a smile.

"My daughter was determined to do this, she has a strong will, and if I am honest, knowing her party, I feel that any Summanu she encounters, I feel should be more wary of her." Shengara gave a chuckle.

"My dear friend, I feel you should know that she is guarded better than all of us, for the sword of the winds walks beside her." Valk frowned, and turned to Shengara.

"What are you saying, Andalyn died, it was a massive loss to all of us, how can his sword be with her?" Shengara smiled at him.

"His son is of age, and he has claimed the sword of his father, and walks beside young Ria towards a place where they plan to save my granddaughter." Valk could not believe what he was hearing.

"How is that possible, I did not even know his son lived?" Evander lifted his glass.

"The son of Andalyn, is the biggest secret of the Undine, for they sheltered his wife and child, and he has grown very like his father, so much so, he is able to wield the sword." Valk looked at both the men, shocked, and yet feeling hope for the first time in a long time.

"Will he help us?" Shengara smiled at him.

"The wind is coming my friend, and soon the son of Adalyn will walk on his homeland again. It is not about whether he will help us my friend, this is about, will you follow him when he gets here?" Evander sat with Shengara smiling, as Valk sat stunned, and yet there was a joy in his eyes he did not have when he arrived.

Shade stood in the trees, and frowned, Ria looked at her.

"So, can we get some?" Shade was staring at the large comb covered with thousands of crawling bodies.

"Me like sting paste bugs house, no want kilt!" Ria nodded at her, and then looked at the nest.

"So, these are deadly if you get stung?" Shade nodded a reassuring nod.

"Big sting, then kilt." Ria felt disappointed.

"That is a shame, because that would really help all of us, can we not get it at all?" Shade wrinkled her face, and then licked her lips.

"Make smoke, Summanu see it." Ria sighed, and stepped back.

"Yes, you are right, we should leave it, this place has a lot more Summanu than we have seen so far, and we need to be careful, we know they are here somewhere." Shade licked her lips.

"Me get." Ria frowned, and looked at her.

"But you said they were deadly." Shade nodded at her, and then smiled.

"Get big leg fish." Ria frowned at her and shuddered.

"What is a leg fish, I don't think I know of them?" Shade's eyes opened wide, and she held her arms apart.

"Big... Leg fish eat bugs, then me eat leg fish and bug house, no smoke." Ria smirked.

"You know Shade, at times, you are quite brilliant, but scary." Shade giggled and turned.

"Me get leg fish." She walked off into the trees, and Ria stood looking at the large honey comb hanging in the tree, and licked her lips.

"I trust her, and I really would love some honey, but honestly, she worries me a lot at times."

Yesterday had been a hard tough day, and as much as no one had said anything, all of them had been worried, and this morning having had a good sleep, all of them were feeling glad to be safe. Ria came back into the camp, and smiled as she sat down at Oaken's side, he was sipping a hot tea which Meda had brewed, Vesta had gone having a look around, and had not returned yet. Ria leaned back and gave a sigh, Oaken glanced at her.

"Are you alright?" She gave a slight nod.

"I am alright, I find Shade confusing, she is looking for leg fish, and I have no idea what that is." Oaken gave a chuckle.

"I cannot deny, she does see the world in ways we never will, but I have come to like that."

"I am not sure about how she sees the world; I just know I find her fascinating, hostile, and dangerous at the same time." He could understand that, but he could not see her as dangerous, well, not to them at least.

"Ria, you have to understand, she has been alone since she was just seven summers. Her mother taught her the ways of an Undine, and she learned some amazing skills. She is an extraordinary fighter, but that is all she learned. Since that time, she has been alone in the world, and so she applies simple logic to all she encounters. I am not sure what a leg fish is, but she had a good point over meat rocks. Think about it, she knows birds come from eggs, birds are meat, and eggs are as hard as rocks, so meat rock makes sense. Whatever she wants, has legs and looks like a fish, let's see."

It took Shade a while, but when she walked back into the camp, she was carrying a very large dead lizard, and had a huge chunk of honeycomb wrapped in big leaves, Ria was stunned, Oaken smiled.

"It sort of looks like a fish, and has legs, that makes complete sense." Ria looked across at Shade.

"How did you get the honey comb?" Shade looked back at the woodland, and then back to Ria.

"Put leg fish on long pole, lift up. Leg fish make bugs try kilt it. Put leg fish on floor, bugs attack, me put knife on pole, cut bug house, now eat."

She knelt down and lifted the lizard over the fire, as Ria sat stunned, Ham giggled, and licked his lips, he was hungry. Shade unwrapped the leaves, and handed large pieces of honey comb to Caleb and Meda and smiled.

"Eat, good, make child's strong."

Their first meal of the day was possibly their strangest so far, as they feasted on cooked lizard and honey comb. As they ate, Vesta returned, pulled on her robe, and lifted some raw meat left her by Shade.

"We need to be careful; I fear the landscape is changing, there are great walls behind which I smelt people in bad health, and there are a lot of Summanu all over the place." Ham scratched his chin.

"What about the water, do they have anything that may stop us?" Vesta shook her head.

"They have a lot of people in the towns close to the water, and they have a lot of goods that they are talking up river to where they are building." Ria considered it all.

"If they are trade boats, they will not want to chase us, because they will be fully loaded, and they have a sunken vessel already obstructing their path. They may not attempt another one, I say the boat is safer, we can get wide of the banks and follow the lake down to the river opening to the falls." Vesta looked at the lake.

"I will stay on land, I will keep you in sight, and run along the banks. I want to know more of what is happening in these parts, it may aid us."

As the group prepared, Oaken walked to the river bank and stood next to the tied up boat, and looked out across the lake. In the distance he could see the mountain range rising closer and higher, and once again he felt the pull of his home, and his inner need to walk on Andalan once more. He sensed movement at his side, and then felt a hand on his shoulder, he turned to see Elden watching across the lake.

"We shall walk there again, in my heart, I know this." Oaken gave a soft smile, knowing he was not the only one feeling this way.

"I remember it Elden, I was so young, and yet I can recall all of it." Elden gave a soft nod.

"Me too, I was fifteen summers when we walked into the sand, our hearts broken at leaving, it is a walk I will never forget. Too many died on that trail, good people, who deserved better from this life. My father was bitten by a large snake, Yanark was fast to act, by my father suffered in the heat, he lay him on a sheet, and helped me pull him over the sand to the new lands." Oaken gave a nod.

"I remember, you were a little way behind us." Elden smiled.

"Yes, I had you in my sights at all times, each day my father would tell me, watch over him son, and one day our people will follow him back to our lands, and here we are moving closer each day. Once we reached the new lands, he died within a week, after making me promise to stand at your side. I want to walk there again, Oaken, I want to kneel in the temple, light herbs and talk to my father, I want to tell him how much I loved him, and how I found my way home again, and I was true to my pledge." Oaken turned to face him.

"We will, I too want to walk in the footsteps of my father. We will do it together, for you have been true to your word, and you have been a good friend to me Elden, I have always appreciated having you close by." Elden gave a slight nod, and patted his shoulder again.

"We should prepare, each stroke of the paddle will bring us closer to home, and then we can push the Summanu out, and lead our people home again." Oaken smiled, and felt a faint burst of joy deep down inside.

"Come, let us load up the boat, and then head for home."

As Oaken and his party loaded up, and then set out onto the lake under the warm day, in Keytan, Evander lifted his anchor and turned the ship around in the wide channel, moving closer to the opposite bank, facing the seaward end of the river. Below decks, Shengara prepared, as two thousand Undine warriors lifted their weapons, and filled their packs with all they would need.

The far northern bank of the river was free of Summanu, once they had taken the port and many of the cities. The land beyond the river was of no interest to them, as it was dense forest that led to the edges of the wide Heliospan Dessert, and there was little there they could use. Shengara intended to use it to travel fast, and head for the northern boarders of Andalan, where he would follow the paths that would take him along the sides of the mountain south, and down into Leyarken, and the lands that were once home to his people.

As Evander dropped anchor and readied the boats, long lines of black hooded Undine waited for their chance to be taken the short distance to land. All of them felt the tension around them, because they all knew that this was their chance to finally fight back, and pay Balathral for the destruction of their homeland.

It took most of the evening and well past dark, before all of the Undine were ready and sat in the thick forest, Valk grabbed Shengara warmly by the hand.

"Good luck my friend, I will ensure that the people of Keytan create enough of a distraction to keep all eyes away from your path, travel with speed, and we will meet on the southern boarders of my lands, and unite as we face the Summanu together." Shengara smiled as he held Valk firmly by the hand, his white eyes burning with life in his older scarred face.

"Travel with speed, and next we meet, we will be larger in size and ready for the fight. Now is the time to free your people, for the wind is coming, and we will be ready for it." Valk smiled, and released his grip on Shengara.

"Stay low and walk fast, until we meet my friend." Shengara nodded, and turned for the ladder, he smiled as he looked at Evander.

"My people owe you a great debt, it will not be forgotten." Evander gave a smile, and nodded.

"Stay safe, there is nothing to pay, it is time all of us worked to free all of these lands. Go with great speed Shengara of the

Undine, and may your battles be fierce, and filled with the heart of the land."

Shengara disappeared into the darkness, and once on the bank of the river, he looked back to see the sails of the boat unrolling, as Evander prepared to leave, and make his way back to Undinalashka where he could be of more service to the Undine. The Undine slipped through the trees behind Shengara, their eyes keen in the darkness, as they slipped like ghosts over the landscape, moving with great agility and speed.

The Summanu with their caravan of captives were days away from the end of the desert, on what had felt for the soldiers like a journey through hell. Each day was a torment of searing heat, each night as the darkness fell, was a time of great fear, as the Undine appeared and disappeared with an onslaught of chaos and death. The whole trail leading back to Undinalashka was littered with dead Summanu, left where they fell to rot and decay, half eaten by large birds, and the many animals that lived in the sands.

The soldiers who followed, were forced to walk past each contorted and disembowelled body, as they trudged on through the sands far behind the caravan of captives. All of them with eyes and minds filled with the horrors they saw on a daily basis, and all of them wishing they had never left their own lands.

Yandalla sat in her cage, surrounded by flies, all of the women were weary and worn down from the lack of food. Her face was dirty, her hair a ruffled and tangled mess, as she stared through the gap in the sheet, awaiting another attack from her people in the midst of the darkness. Behind the buzz of the flies from the bucket that served as a toilet, were a constant loud buzz in her ears. In order to save arrows, as he waited for more to arrive, Pallum had taken to catching scorpions, spiders and lethal snakes, which his men tossed down onto the soldiers in the darkness.

In the early days of their long walk, the Summanu soldiers had at first raced into the dunes to fight the Undine, but they had never found any, and soon they had stopped trying, as the final few who had tried, never returned, and all of them heard the screams of terror from soldiers they knew they would never see again.

As the days dragged on in the endless heat, their bravery and confidence diminished, no more girls were dragged from their cages and raped, as the will of the men died with their souls, in the endless misery of a desert filled with traps, delays, and Undine attacks. Yandalla stared into the darkness, her mind wandering, when suddenly she noticed something move, and she blinked.

Just in front of her, between the sheet and bars, she saw something slithering slowly, and her hand slipped to the belt of her pants, it was a snake, and it was a big one. Her eyes glanced slowly to her side, as she pulled the dagger out.

"My sisters, we have food, but be wary."

Sintalla looked up, and noticed where Yandalla was watching, the snake slithered slowly along the edge of the bars, and she moved up onto her knees, her voice the softest of whispers.

"Be wary, it feels your heat, do not move fast, or it will strike."

Yandalla understood, she has seen her mother catch many snakes, and she was more than aware of how dangerous it was. Her right arm twitched, as she lifted it very slowly, the snake was tasting the air, and she tried not to breath towards it.

Slowly she rose up, and prepared as the snake came closer, her green eyes fixed on the head, which was low to the floor of the cart. Her arm came forward, her eyes locked on it, as it passed along the bars, and then as fast as she could, she snatched through the bars and grabbed it behind its head.

"Got it!"

Sintalla lunged at the snake as it tried to coil up, grabbing the fat body, and tried to hold it down, as Yandalla stuck with speed, stabbing it behind its head with the dull pointed blade of the dagger, landing blow after blow. Her attack was merciless, driven by her empty stomach, knowing the meat of the snake would save all of their lives.

The snake flopped limp, and she took a deep breath, as she had been holding it so long, she thought she would suffocate. Sintalla smiled, as she pulled the fat dead snake into the cage, and looked at Yandalla as she drew in deep breaths of hot stale dessert air.

"Give me the blade."

The air of excitement rose within the cage, as they watched

through the dim light, as Sintalla used the blade with great skill, slicing open the belly and pulling off the skin like it was one long sock. Even in the darkness, the meat was white and glistened, and the Undine felt moisture in their mouths for the first time in days, as they licked their dry lips. Sintalla handed a large chunk of raw meat to Yandalla, as the others watched on with their growing excitement.

"This is good, our bodies need this, here, eat and feel the life of this snake grow inside you." Yandalla took the meat, she could see all of them watching with desire in their eyes, she smiled.

"My sisters, we will live, we will grow strong, and we will survive this and see our revenge on the Summanu." She bit down deep into the meat, and felt the juice of the soft meat fill her mouth, and closed her eyes, as she tore the piece off and chewed.

The meat was raw, and even though she had never eaten raw snake before, it had always been cooked, her hunger was so strong, she knew the food would end the pangs in her stomach that had haunted her last few days. She took a huge bite and chewed, as Sintalla handed out chunks of meat to the others. Shellena sat with her knees up chewing like she had not eaten in weeks, taking every second of flavour in her mouth as she chewed for no other reason, than it had felt like forever since she had chewed anything.

Flies crawled on their faces, hands and clothes, and in the corner, they swarmed around the bucket, but they did not really care as the meat was passed around to all of them, and they chewed with joy just to be eating something that they knew their bodies needed to stave off death. They were dirty, smelly, and half starved, but they were alive, and as she chewed, she knew that she was doing all she could to make sure when Oaken got here, she would be ready.

Feeling food in her stomach for the first time in days, she sucked on her fingers as she leant back against the bars of the cage, watching her sisters eat with smiles on their faces.

"Your families would be proud if they could see you, for we are living each day looking to the land to aid us, and we have been rewarded. The true Undine knows we are one with all things, and in that we know, we will continue, and our race will never die, no matter how hard the Summanu try. Bharl will never take the spirit of the Undine for his own, we will make sure of it, for we too are warriors, and we will fight to our last."

She had lost her fire in the last few days, but with food in her stomach she felt some of it returning, and she knew, as the granddaughter of Shengara, she had to keep all of them fierce in their hearts, for if just one of them gave up, they would die, and she could not allow that. Yandalla knew, many men lay dead in the lands of Undinalashka, and as she sat in her cage for days lost to her thoughts, she remembered her mother when she younger."

"Yandalla, all life is important, the lines of Summanu put all of their faith in their men, but it is folly. Men are strong and will fight to the death, but as women, we have to be stronger. There is no difference between men and women, they are both parts of the wheel of life, alone they are nothing, but together, a man and women in harmony, can lift a tribe by bringing new life. The women of the Andalan are now more important than ever, because it is from their bellies, this race will endure and grow again, my husband knew that, which is why he made sure every woman and child came out of our land first. At that moment, the future of our people, the women held the future of our race in their hands, and from their bodies, life has been blown back into the race of Andalan."

Yandalla knew, these girls and women had to survive, because they would become the future of the Undine. Outside the cage there was a terrified scream, and she smiled, her father was out there somewhere, and doing his best to take as many Summanu as possible, to lighten the load for Oaken when he arrived. She pulled up her knees and relaxed, her voice was soft, quiet, and spoken only to herself.

"Yan fors ae Cumten."

She closed her eyes and could see his face, and it made her happy knowing her road would end with him waiting for her.

Chapter Twenty Two
Journey into Understanding

For most of the day, Belthaz had rested in his cabin, as a little further down the river, two other large ships were at anchor, as the men of the ships dived into the water with axes, and chopped at the wide wooden pole of the sunken boat mast.

It was hard going, as they held their breath for as long as they could, but could only chop three or four times before they had to surface. The sunken boat was in the middle of the channel, and blocking the way for the three larger ships owned by the Order of Apostles. Out on the lake, unaware of the three ships, Oaken and the group paddled at a distance from the coast, keeping it always in sight. Ria sat at his side with the map, as both of them looked down at it. They were taking it in turns to paddle in order to save their strength, and the boat was swift on the calm lake without a great need to paddle hard.

Oaken pointed to the map, and pointed towards the end of the lake, where two rivers both led out of the lake and wove through the trees towards the falls of Andalan.

"I think the question is, which river will be safest for us?" Ria looked up at him.

"Both will get us there with days to spare, the problem is we do not know what is down either of them. I am hoping Vesta has made it to at least one of them, she said she would do her best to try and find out where all the Summanu were." Shade turned in her seat and looked down at the map, she pointed at it.

"There no deep, but filled with mouth logs." Ria frowned and looked at the map.

"Mouth logs, are they dangerous?" Shade nodded.

"Big mouth, kilt boat, then kilt us. Mouth logs bad, bad." Ria looked at Oaken who was looking equally as confused as her.

"It has mouth logs, maybe we should go the other way." Ria smirked, as Ham behind them gave a giggle, and Shade gave a reassured nod.

Across the water on the bank of the river, Vesta in the form of a leopard, crouched low in the grass, her yellow eyes fixed on the water. Across the wide river on the far side was a large wooden dock, and behind it was a new town, built from all of the trees that had been cut and cleared. The mouth of the river had become some form of trading post, from which a wide road had been cut, and there were thousands of Summanu camped along the side of it.

It appeared that they were building their numbers for something, but she was unsure as to what, but she knew, for Oaken and Ria to come this way would be suicide. She slid back in the tall grass and slunk away until she was out of sight, and then ran as fast as she could to the shore to try and work out where they were on the water, she had to stop them before dark, because if she did not, they would paddle straight into a trap.

As the day progressed at an easy pace, behind them, the clouds rolled in, and the wind started to pick up. What had been a calm lake, rippled as small waves formed, by the wind as it rushed across the water's surface, Ham looked back and felt his heart lurch.

"We need to head inland and quick."

Ria turned, and saw the dark clouds, but that was not what Ham was watching, as in the distance there were three large ships, with large black sails, and they were heading their way. Ria reached into her bag, and pulled out her telescope, and put it to her eye as all of the others had stopped and were watching her. She focused, and gave a sigh.

"They are much bigger than the one we sank, they have black sails, and even though they are too far to really make out all of the detail, if you ask me, they are part of the Order of Apostles. To be honest, I am not happy being out on the water with them behind us, Ham, turn us to shore, anything we meet on land will be better than facing them out on the water."

He gave a nod and turned the rudder, and everyone pushed their oars into the water and paddled faster, as the boat turned, and made a direct line for the shore. Vesta morphed into her human form as she looked out across the water, and gave a sigh of relief.

"Good, they are heading inland, and just in the nick of time."

In Undinalashka, the day was quiet, for now the Summanu walked around on guard or sat in groups and ate of the bountiful food supply that grew in every corner of the land. In many parts where the there were no soldiers, the bodies of the old and the young lay where they fell, many of whom had been raped and mutilated. In quiet corners of the land, cloaked in green, Undine warriors slipped out of the dense undergrowth, and with muffled sobs, that fuelled their rage, they lifted their dead and arranged them together, as they would for their fallen warriors of battle.

Every person who was laid and covered in palm leaves, had their name taken and noted on a slice of bark with red stone, so there would be a full record of everyone who died in the massacre. Once the bodies were laid out, and the songs of their dead sung in almost silent voices, as quick as they appeared, they melted away into the trees.

For the Undine, this was the saddest time of their long history, in the first big war, all of those who died, had been praised highly for their brave deeds. Already, the few who remained in their new land to show respect to their fallen, were rewriting their history, and these brave lost people would see a greater reverence than any in the future, for they fought with few weapons, on their greatest day of celebration, and the large pyres of the Summanu fallen, had burned for days.

High above them, on the only safe place in the whole land, Saraka watched as Bettle distributed food to the people of the Undine, a gift from the land of Animatre. She watched as Tranquilla and twenty women of her land, explained the foods and how to prepare them, for some of the gifts were things never seen in this land. Eliaston came up to her side with a soft smile.

"I thought I would find you here." Sarka nodded.

"I need to keep busy, if I stop, my mind fills with thoughts that I do not want to have, it helps to help others, and eases my thoughts for a little time." He could understand that.

"There is much to do, you brought us through the desert and here, you can do the same for all of those who helped us, you have the same power in your heart as Andalyn." She gave a long sigh.

"He would have handled all of this much better, as would Pallum, I fear my worries are such it clouds my judgement at the moment. I do try, but I cannot stop myself thinking of them and pleading with Nuada to bring them all back safe to me." Eliaston gave a chuckle.

"Had he been here, the Summanu never would have invaded, Balathral believes all of you were slaughtered, he has no idea that you and your son lived. I fear he has underestimated things, for he believes the books and the sword lie in the temple here alone." Sarka turned to him and frowned.

"How do you mean? Master Eliaston, they do, or at least the books do now Oatin has taken the sword, how would he even know?" Eliaston's eyes gave a twinkle.

"The four books never left the temple, what we have here are copies made in an ancient time, Andalyn saw them only once, and he laid his hand on each of them and swore to Nuada to protect them. That day after he left, four of us replaced them and placed the true books in a place only he who carries the sword can find, for within that is the power of the Sword of the Four Winds. Your son is not aware, but this path he has chosen, is guided by the hand and light of Nuada." Sarka was unsure, she did not fully understand.

"Did Andalyn know this?" Eliaston smiled.

"He held the sword, and he knew one day his son would lift it, he read the books more than any Sarka. If he knew of this time, he mentioned nothing to me, I just know that he was aware that one day his son would lift the sword and finish the work started by his father. Oaken of the four winds will bring change, that I know." Sarka gave a slight nod of understanding.

"As to whether it is good or bad, no one really knows, I understand now, this was destined for him by his own father, Andalyn always regretted not killing Balathral as he stood at the side of Shengara. My husband felt it was wrong to take the life of a child, even if he was as corrupted as his father, and so he spared the life of his son, knowing the people of the Summanu had seen that Bharl was a false god." Eliaston smiled.

"You can show some the full truth, and they will still say it is a lie, and that is how Balathral has ruled Sumanula. In that land, the truth has become the lie, and the lie has become the truth, and the people have simply accepted it because they were too afraid to challenge it. Oaken of the four winds will challenge everything in his life, and with Nuada to guide him, the full truth will be revealed." Sarka stared across the wide flat plain filled with people as they sat and ate the new food.

"Eliaston, I trust you." She turned to face him.

"If my son does this... Will he live?" Eliaston took a deep breath.

"I really do not know, I suppose, what is in Oaken's heart will be his strongest power, and if I may say so, it may be the love of his sister that guides him to his true potential. Those two have a bond of such power, I can only believe it was given by Nuada to guide and protect them." Sarka gave a slight nod of her head and her voice was soft.

"The beauty of Yandalla has always touched deeply, she reached within him in his loss and loneliness when no other could, and in that, I have the greatest of hope for both of them."

The group moved quickly as the clouds rolled in and a fine rain began, peppering the lake around them as they paddled quickly. Ahead of them was the narrow opening of a small river that flowed into the lake, Ria was looking behind with her scope, as Ham steered the boat, she pulled down the scope and smiled.

"I do not think they have seen us, although, this river ahead of us will be far too shallow for those size of ships, I think for now we are safe."

Up ahead, Ham could see the opening to the river and adjusted the rudder to guide the boat towards it. As they drew closer, up on the top of the bank, Vesta appeared in her cat form, Elden smiled and waved to her, and she shook her head and snarled at him. He frowned and turned to look back at Oaken.

"What did I do, I have always been really nice to her?" Ria leaned forward in her seat.

"Something must be wrong; Vesta would never snarl like that. Everyone, pull in your paddles, we need to go slowly and see what is up front."

They all pulled up their paddles, and glided slowly towards the opening of the river, up on the bank, Vesta watched as they came slowly into the opening of what looked like a narrow river.

It was misleading, as the trees on the banks grew out over the edges of the water, covering most of the width of the river. Ham moved slowly under a large overhanging tree to keep them as covered and as out of sight as possible, Shade turned, and stared up at the bank, filled with a thatch of exposed roots, Oaken looked through the dense green above him, his voice quiet as he sat next to Ria, the rain dripping onto his face.

"What is the problem, this place looks deserted?" Ria had no idea; she crouched low staring out from under the dripping trees.

"I am not sure, but if Vesta is wary of here, I am going to keep a careful watch, the Leyarken sense things long before we do." Somewhere above and behind them, there was a loud snarl, and the sound of breaking branches, Oaken's head whipped around.

"Vesta is in trouble."

A wild roar screamed out, followed by the yells and screams of a man, it was clear Vesta had attacked. He could feel the tension rising, something was not right, and he strained his ears as he heard more faint snarls somewhere above. It was clear they had passed the point that Vesta was fighting, as the boat moved forward, and he stared above at the trees.

Behind them, there was a squeal, the boat rocked, and then there was a loud splash, both Oaken and Ria snapped their heads around to look forward, where Shade was stood in the boat, and Elden looked alarmed as he held Meda close to him on the opposite side of the boat. His eyes were wide as he turned to Oaken.

"Did you see that, what in the name of Nuda is that?" Oaken shrugged, he had no idea, he had not seen it. Shade took a breath still staring into the water, her paddle held high as if waiting for something to return.

"Mouth Log. Big, leave or get kilt." Oaken was not sure, and leaned over the boat to look down into the water.

"I have no idea what a mouth log is."

He looked down into the crystal clear water, and his heart gave a jolt, as a huge long, green roughly barked skinned like beast, swam below the boat. He leaned back quickly and looked up at Shade, his voice more than a little alarmed.

"Those things are huge; they are bigger than the boat." Shade nodded at him.

"Big, big, mouth logs, kilt us." He looked at Ria.

"What in Nuada's name do we do?" Ria looked panicked.

"I don't know, I have heard of Crocadillia, I have just never seen or had to deal with one, we do not have them on our islands." Elden was watching.

"I say we paddle like the Summanu are after us, and get as far away from those things as possible." Oaken frowned.

"Those, I only see one?"

Elden pointed out from under the dripping trees towards the opposite bank, where Oaken saw there was a long line of the green beasts all lay in the sun on the bank. Oaken lifted his paddle.

"We need to move and move fast whilst we can see them all." Shade shook her head.

"Mouth log eat; we no get kilt." Ria frowned.

"What do they eat, we have nothing to feed them with Shade?" Shade held her paddle ready to strike out.

"Eat men, we feed, we go." Ria looked at Oaken.

"Is she suggesting we feed one of us to it, because I am not at all prepared for that?" Shade laughed, dropped her paddle inside the boat. She jumped up and grabbed the branch of the tree, swung her legs up, and rose into the branches.

"Me get."

With that, she jumped up, and disappeared onto the bank, where it appeared Vesta was still snarling at whoever she was fighting. Oaken had no idea what to do, he had never been in a situation anything at all like this, and he felt his panic heighten.

"What does she mean, she will get, do we paddle or wait for her?" They were still moving slowly along; Ham watched the water.

"I say we keep all paddles out of the water and not stir them up; they look peaceful at the moment. Looking at the size of the last one, I am not sure we could fend off his friends over there." Ria agreed, looking panicked.

"That makes sense, I have no wish for one of those things to come over here, I am with Ham on that."

Above them there were more squeals, and as they all sat watching the beasts across the river, suddenly through the trees, came the crashing figure of a Summanu warrior. He screamed as he snatched out, and all they could do was watch, as he powered down through the branches, managing to grab one and stop his descent with a jerk. The soldier was two boat lengths behind them, desperately holding on with one arm, as his legs dangled, his feet skimming the surface of the water. All they could do was watch, as he looked at them with fear filled eyes, just hanging there as they sat watching him unsure of what to do.

Without warning the water surface broke, and the huge beast came straight up, its massive mouth open, and almost swallowed him whole, the jaws snapped closed with a crunch. Ria screamed, and pushed her head into Oaken, as he watched shocked, as the beast dropped into the water with a huge splash, and all that remined was a severed arm, the hand still holding onto the branch. Ham lifted his paddle.

"Oh no, no no, I am not doing any of that." He plunged his paddle into the water and gave an almighty heave, and the boat shot forward.

It was instant motivation, as all of them followed suit, grabbing their paddles and plunging them into the water, behind them was another loud scream, but this time no one looked. The splash was loud and across the bank, the other beasts slithered into the water. Everyone, instantly knew what they had to do, and they paddled for their lives, speeding the boat as fast as they could away from them. There was splashing behind them and a terrified scream, and Oaken looked back to see the host of what Shade called Mouth Logs, thrashing about in the water, and he knew without realising, they were tearing the Summanu soldier apart.

It was horrible to see and fully understand those last moments of the soldier's life, and he could not deny, it had to be the most terrifying way to die he had ever encountered, and was glad it was not any of them.

Vesta morphed back into a human form, as Shade cleaned her sword, twelve men lay dead, five with their throats ripped open. Vesta wiped her mouth with the back of her hand, and she faced Shade.

"Thanks for that, I was fine at first but the screams brought more." Shade nodded.

"You no kilt, is good." She smiled at Vesta and she nodded.
"Are the others safe." Shade looked back to the bank.
"We feed mouth logs, they sleep, all safe."
Shade slid back her sword, bent down, and grabbed a leg of
one soldier, and the leg of another, she gave a tug and walked off
towards the river bank. Understanding, Vesta grabbed two more,
and between the two of them, they lifted the dead soldiers and
threw them into the river, where the Crocadillia attacked with a
frenzy tearing the bodies apart.

It took a while before the soldiers were disposed of, and
together Shade and Vesta walked along the river looking for the
rest of their party. Oaken and the group had paddled a long way
down the river, and had moved into shallower waters, and pulled
up on a stone and pebbled filled beach. Everyone was relieved
to see Shade and Vesta intact, as they gathered close to the large
rocks and trees out of the rain, which was getting harder as the
sky darkened.
It was pointless moving on, as night was approaching, and with
the heavy dark clouds approaching visibility was getting bad.
Ham tipped the boat on its side, and with some long branches
cut from a dead tree, they spread Shade's canvass sheet over
it to create a shelter. Huddled together with a small fire, and
three large fat rodent looking animals Vesta had caught over the
flames cooking, Vesta filled them in on all she had seen, as Shade
hammered long sticks into the beach along the water line, to keep
the mouth logs from coming on land.
"They have cleared large areas of woodland, and the town on
the next river, appears to be a place where it all gets shipped
up the river. I think they are supplying Belthaz with everything
he needs to build his new centre of worship. The word is, that
Balathral has given this whole region to the Order of the Apostles,
and he is withdrawing a lot of the soldiers back to Sumanula. It
is hard to get information, but I crept up on two officers talking
outside their huts, and it appears Bharl sent a vision to Balathral,
showing all the spirits of the Undine attacking the large steps,
and so he has ordered a great deal of his forces back to the
homeland." Ria thought about it as the others looked at her.
"It makes sense, he knows many Undine lived, I do not think

it is that big a leap to work out they will attack him, after all, Shengara has already done it once with his father." Elden gave a sigh.

"It will make it harder for the Undine, no one would be mad enough to walk into that land and challenge Balathral with all those soldiers guarding him." Ria's eyes fixed on Oaken, he was staring into the fire.

"If the army is big enough, he will come out from his city, my father knew that, which is why he united all the lines. Balathral will make the same mistakes as his father, because he thinks he is a god who cannot be defeated. Stand before his walls, and his gates will open." Vesta watched all of them.

"That is not your task, that is the role of Shengara, if you want my advice, save Yandalla, I sense something in her that you need Oaken, I think you two have a role, but it will not be at the side of Shengara." Oaken looked up at her, and her orange eyes met his.

"Do not throw your life away Oaken, I sense your feelings, you have time, think things through carefully. Yandalla is the priority here, not Balathral." He gave a soft smile, and nodded at her, Ria watched them both carefully.

"Alright, if we aim to get Yandalla, we need to get a move on, what are our chances of getting to her location quickly?" Vesta lifted a piece of raw meat and sat back, she took a bite and chewed as Elden watched the cooking meat drip into the fire with a hiss.

"This land is emptying, but there are a lot of soldiers. The bad news they are heading in the same direction as you, the river will only get you so far, it has been blocked and diverted lower down. You will be back on foot soon, but your journey will not be long, if Pallum is successful, you will be there in plenty of time to reach the falls before they do, but if you want my advice, strike them before they touch the falls. If what I have heard is true, the wide pool at the falls is filled with troop camps moving back to guard the borders of Leyarken, Zeron will talk with Aisie, and with luck they will be ready to fight for their lands." Oaken understood.

"What of Andalan, are they leaving there too?" Vesta shook her head as she chewed.

"I am not sure, your home is a large region and not the easiest to guard, I am not sure they will leave easily, that is one place that is a prize for Balathral. I know he spent a lot of time there; it is one of a very short list of places he has visited. From what our scouts heard, he really took great joy out of possessing it, I doubt he will let it go easily." Shade reached across the fire, and lifted the pole with the cooked rodent on it.

"Many holes and path, can go without seen." Ham frowned.

"Holes, in what way?" Shade pulled a large chunk of meat off the rodent and handed it to Elden, he took it and bit down hard into it, Shade's bright blue eyes glanced to Oaken and then back to Ham.

"Me knows way in, easy, not seen." She handed Ham the other large chunk of meat.

Ria sat beside him as he ate, his mind drifting as he thought of his home, in many ways she understood him better than the others, and she knew that for him, it was important he found a way to free up his land for his people. Ria glanced at him staring at his food.

"You should eat, no matter what you plan, you will be useless if you have not the strength to fight." He blinked, and took a deep breath, and then lifted the meat to his mouth. He chewed for a few moments and then looked at her.

"You confuse me, do you know that?" Ria smirked.

"Sadly, many have said that, but I am interested, because I really do not think I am that complicated, so, why do I confuse you Oaken?" He swallowed the meat.

"You do not want me to go after Balathral, you are supportive, but I see it in your face, you fear I will throw my life away, and yet you have not tried to stop me. I find that confusing, because if I knew my mother or Yandalla was risking their lives, I would try to stop them." Ria gave a small chuckle, and she leaned back and sighed.

"I want to stop you, I really do not want see you harmed, but as much as I have not known you long, and I have grown to care for you, I am also aware, I do not have the power to stop you. Tell me I am wrong, but if I tried, you would still go, but you would walk away resenting me, and I do not want that Oaken, if anything, I want you to care about what I think." He nodded at her; she made good sense.

"I do care what you think, I actually think deeply about everything you say, because out here, I really know little, I have lived with my people isolated for a long time. I trust you Ria, as I do Shade, because both of you have lived and learned much of the lands around us, but I will say this one thing to you. I may have lived a sheltered life, but you do not understand that life, isolation means you have only yourself, and so you understand that knowing who you are and what your inner strength is in itself a strength. Ria, the power of the winds means nothing, if the man who wields it is a stranger to who he is, in your time you leaned all this about people, in my time, I learned all about me. They are the same and yet different, which is why I know I can defeat him, and you have doubts, you do not know who you really are, you have much to learn in that sense, just as I have little understanding of the people around me." She blinked, and sat back as she was for a moment lost for words, Shade giggled, and Ria looked at her, Shade gave a slight shrug.

"Me know me and nuthers, me know big, like when seen." Ria took a deep breath, and gave a slight sigh at Oaken.

"I do not deny, I have learned a lot about me on this trip, and yes, I have come to care about you Oaken, is it wrong to want to keep you safe? I see dangers you are not aware of and try to warn you, and I admit it is to protect you. I have also been to Sumanula, I have stood at the base of the tall steps and seen the blood that runs down them. I know of the walls and the gated streets, and I have seen the power of his army, and I do not believe one man can walk into that city and kill Balathral alone. You would need a huge army to defeat him, and after his cleansing of all the lands, there are no longer enough to defeat him." Ham gave off a loud sigh.

"If that is the case, what do we do, build a wall around Undinalaska and move everyone behind it, because the desert is the only real protection of that land?" Oaken put down his empty plate.

"You all make a lot of sense, but all of you miss the obvious, one man can make a huge difference, we have all seen it already." Ria frowned.

"We have, when?" Oaken lifted his cup and took a swig.

"Shengara was one man, who with my father's aid, walked into

Sumanula, and he alone killed Balalaran, and in doing so, the war was ended. It does not matter how big the army is, that is not the issue, it is the man that drives them that is the problem, and if I can solve that problem, then there will be no need for war or further deaths, that is my aim, and that will be my plan." Ria shook her head slowly.

"It is folly, let us say you can do this, and you kill him, do you honestly think a whole city of people devoted to Bharl will let you live?" Oaken smiled.

"They think Balathral is a god, so I will be a god killer, tell me, would you knowingly pick a fight with a god killer?" Shade smirked and gave a nod.

"Anna Ma says no god, people Shen tey." Oaken smiled.

"Your Anna Ma was a wise woman, Shade." She gave a smile.

"Anna Ma mean all, she made me, she good." Ria just sat back trying to really understand all of it.

"I think you make some sort of twisted sense, but again, even if you are right, and if you do use the sword to kill him, you still have not considered how you will get in to begin with. You will find there are a lot of people who are interested in protecting him, and you will have to get past all of them." Oaken nodded.

"I know, and I am thinking about that, but Ria, I will not kill him with the sword, there has never been blood on that blade for that is not its purpose." She looked at him and narrowed her eyes.

"Then why do you have the sword if not to use it to bring peace by killing him?" Oaken smiled at her.

"The sword has its place, but its purpose is very different from what people perceive, I have learned that from using it. The sword of the winds has a part to play, as do all of us, and everyone who sees the injustice of Balathral, and in that we will win."

It was a strange moment as everyone watched him and listened, and somehow, he held their minds and they all believed in him. Oaken had no real idea how like his father he was, he had set off feeling out of his depth, and yet somewhere in the hot barren lands of Shodalt, he had changed, and his faith and authority had grown a little. Sat behind the boat under the canvass sheet as the rain lashed down into the darkness, all of them could see him as the man of power he was truly becoming, they had trusted him and followed him, and as they sat in the light of the flickering flames of the fire, all of them had grown to admire and respect him.

He was Oaken of the four winds, son of Andalyn, taught by Sarka and Eliaston, and it was really starting to show.

Chapter Twenty Three
The Wind of Change

As the group sat huddled under the canvass in the rain, as they ate and talked, just over an hours walk away, on the banks of the wide river that wove out of Shodalt, the large ship of Belthaz tied up at the jetty in front of the new wooden town of Lembrath.

Belthaz flanked by the bandaged Jenmar walked off the ship, down to the apostles who awaited him as they bent low, a sign of the power that Belthaz carried with him. One apostle lifted his head and gave a slight smile, he was the head of the new apostle run town, named Melack.

"Your eminence, we are blessed by your presence, everything is ready for you and done to your satisfaction, in your apartments. We are overjoyed that you will join us in praise at dawn tomorrow." Belthaz gave a stern nod of his head, his face unmoved and set like stone.

"Good, what news have you of the half Undine?" They began to walk along the path that led into the town.

"The one they name the spirit was last seen on the water with the group she has taken up with. We have watchers on the water and the other river, and all the paths through this area are being monitored, they will not pass us, and we have soldiers armed and ready on all tracks." Belthaz gave a nod as he looked towards the new large wooden residence.

"Good, I want her, and will show great favour to any who can bring her to me, but I want her alive, she is no good to me dead."

Jenmar was quiet as he walked behind the two apostles, Belthaz was impatient, he had lost his gold and the best chance to date of capturing Shade. They arrived at the apartments, and were shown to their rooms, which were at opposite ends of a long corridor, Jemar still had the door open, and as he turned, he saw the two young girls, who looked terrified being held firmly by the hand, taken towards Belthaz's room. It was no secret Belthaz preferred the company of the young, and it was also known, that when he was finished, the girls would not be alive.

That would have been the fate of Meda, but Shade had deprived him, and as a result, Jenmar had the scars on his back that were the expression of his master's disapproval. He was hungry, and felt he needed to find food, as he turned back to the door, he saw Melack approaching, and stopped as Melack smiled.

"I hope the room is to your satisfaction, Apostle Jenmar?" He gave a nod.

"It is more than satisfactory, thank you." Melack closed the door, and walked into the room.

"Can we talk?" Jenmar looked at him.

"What about?" Melack sat on the bed.

"There are murmurings and concerns about our leader, and I would like to know your thoughts on the matter. Obviously, you need not say anything, but considering you were high on the list for the order leadership, we feel you will see things in a more appropriate expression of our lord Bharl." Jenmar smiled, and lowered his tone.

"I see; indeed, you were right to approach me, tell me, what are these concerns, that have unsettled our loyal brothers?" Melack gave a slight smile, and lowered his voice.

"They are concerned by his public behaviour with the children, his rants of late have become an embarrassment, and his copulation with that animal whore of Leyarken, disgusts many. Many are displeased that he flaunts her in public."

Jenmar walked across the room to where there was a large earthen jug of wine, he considered all of this as he poured out two glasses. Turning, Jenmar looked at Melack.

"I cannot deny, I find his behaviour with that cat disgusting and offensive, his taste for young virgins is not unsimilar to our own tastes." Melack gave an agreeable nod as he lifted his hand to receive the glass.

"Yes, but we do not make it publicly obvious, we are servants of Bharl and deserve our rewards of pleasure, but it is kept away from all other aspects of our service. We feel he has become too big an embarrassment to all of us, and he is tarnishing the order." Jenmar sipped his drink, he felt a slight tingle of pleasure hearing this.

"So, Melack, what do the order feel would be an appropriate

response?" Melack gave a smile, and raised his glass.

"I knew talking to you would be illuminating, the truth is, we feel, once the order has completed the building of the temple, he has to go, and that feline bitch with him." Jenmar gave a satisfied nod, and his face broke into a wide a smile.

Shade sat on an old tree stump at the edge of the water, and stared out into the trees lost in thought. Deep inside, she felt unsettled, and flustered, as in her mind, she relived the memories of that awful night from her past. An ice cold shiver ran down her spine, and she shuddered, she blinked as Ham appeared just below her on the stones at the edge of the water. She looked down at him and he smiled.

"Sorry, I did not want to disturb you, looking at your face, I see there is still unpleasantness in your thoughts." Shade took a breath and gave a nod.

"Bad days come back." Ham nodded at her.

"I certainly know those well, I see Oaken and Ria together, and it reminds me greatly of when I met my wife, and recently I have been feeling the loss of that."

"Wife good, and child's, me remember." He smiled at her.

"I know she gave you food that day, she told me when she got home." Shade nodded at him.

"She good, made happy." Ham gave a deep sigh, and leaned back on a large rock.

"Life has changed so much Shade, I knew such happiness, and then the Summanu came, and everything died. I miss those days, and I have felt I was losing my will to fight. I have been impressed; you have grown since those times. You are small and slender, and yet you fight with great heart." She gave a slight chuckle.

"Anna Ma fight better, she kilt before show me all." Ham gave a long sigh.

"I am sorry, if you do not mind, how did she die?" Shade looked out to the trees, almost as if she was remembering the moment, Ham could see a sadness in her eyes.

"Death juice on arrow, Anna Ma say me go, go hide, then kilt." Ham closed his eyes.

"I am sorry to hear that, I know the pain inflicted with their poisons, it must have been hard for you?" Shade nodded, and took a deep breath.

"Many tears, still some, me miss." Ham nodded, and lifted his arm and patted her knee.

"She raised a good daughter, you survived in a world that killed many, I am sure she would be proud of the daughter she raised." Shade put her head down.

"Me want be good for Anna Ma." Ham could see the impact on her, and he leaned back and breathed out a long breath.

"You need sleep, go and lie down, I will watch for a while, I find my head is filled with thoughts, I will not sleep for a while." She took a deep breath and nodded, and as he looked up, he saw the tears on her cheeks, he gave a soft smile.

"Go on, go sleep."

Shade turned, and headed back towards the upturned boat, she slid into the corner out of sight, and pulled her cover over her. Vesta sat silent her eyes closed, she breathed softly as Shade snuggled down, and her eyes opened as she saw Shade settle, and then looked to the river where Ham stood staring into the water. Vesta gave a soft nod and closed her eyes, all was well for now, but her guard was up and her senses at full power, these people were special, and she knew she had to watch over them.

For Vesta it was clear, the story of all the lands and the people who inhabited them, was one of loss and suffering. Shodalt had been a land of great beauty which as a cub she had roamed, with its woodland and plains of tall grass, broken only by farm lands and fields filled with food. She had been scalded many times for straying too far by her mother, but this had always been a land she loved to play in.

The land of Shodalt was once ruled by Serrel, a man who was very honourable and worked hard to help all of the communities grow. When given the ultimatum to surrender and worship Bharl, Serrel refused, and shortly after, Summanu troops arrived at his home, and took him away in the night. It is rumoured he still hangs in the cellars of Balathral, but no one really knows. After his disappearance, the Summanu moved in and the slaughter and prisoner taking started. The pattern was the same for Undinalashka, and Keytan, although a great many were held captive as slave workers, and Vesta knew, that if things did not change, her own land was next.

She felt insecure tonight, and her mind moved to Zeron, she missed him, and wanted to get home as soon as possible to be with him. Sat with her eyes closed she smiled, as his face appeared in her thoughts, and she remembered their time together, and all those special and precious moments, a calmness washed over her, and she drifted into dreams of home.

The land around the Andarla high up on their rock land separated from the rest of the continent was peaceful. The community had expanded greatly since their arrival, and with the addition of the hundreds of Undine, that now resided there with them, the place had changed. This was a land filled with the memories of a long distant past, the soft stone carved into cave like dwellings and the designs and patterns cut into the walls, all showed that this was also once an important Andalan place of the worship of Nuada.

Since their arrival, new dwellings had been cut into the rock, and others had been built on the many terraced levels that housed plants and trees, where food and fruit grew side by side. Water collection pools had been carved into the soft rocky floor creating water catchment areas, and also places that sang to the happiness of young children, but tonight in the darkness, there was a different feeling, almost as if something was hanging in the air waiting to be revealed.

As the rain faded, a warm breeze rose up across the land and swept up the rocks to where Sarka stood, high above her own home, leaning on the door of a stone and wooden structure. She leant on the frame of the doorway, watching, as over a hundred Undine children were lay on thick woven mats, and slept peacefully.

She was quiet, her thoughts drifting as moments from the lives of her own children played through her thoughts, and her mind returning to those fateful moments when she was separated from Andalyn in the desert. His face smiling had stayed with her always, as she heard his words echo around her mind.

"Sarka, you must protect Oatin, this is his tenth summer, soon we will know if he is marked with the signs of our ancestors." She took a deep breath inwards, her voice so soft it was almost silent.

"How Andalyn, how did you know, we all thought we would live, and yet you didn't? How did you know that was the end for you?"

"I would imagine Nuada told him."

Sarka gave a slight jump, and turned to see the old figure of Bettle watching her, and smiling from the low stone wall. Sarka turned, and stepped away from the door, her green eyes glinting in the night light.

"He cannot have known, he would have told me, we shared everything." Bettle stood up, took a pace towards her, and she smiled.

"You are an intelligent woman Sarka, you are the saviour of our people, but be honest, if you were to learn you would die here before your husband, son and daughter returned, would you have told them?" Sarka felt a little shocked, and looked at the floor as her true feeling betrayed her, Bettle gave a soft nod.

"You know you would not. Sarka, he loved you deeply, he did not want to be parted from you, but in the final days he knew it would be the only way. Andalyn knew that you had to be the one to lead your people out of your land and through the desert. I know, he told me." Sarka felt her breath catch in her throat and looked up, as tears filled her eyes.

"He did?" Bettle smiled, and walked towards her.

"He knew Sarka, he had to be the last one out because he was the one chosen by Nuada, and he had to finish what he started in order to protect his family, there really was no other way." Bettle pulled her close, and held her in her arms.

"Andalyn wanted you to live, he wanted you and his son to be free, and the Undine assured it by bringing you here. This place, this land of rock shelves filled with trees and plants is the same stone as Andalan, and it was carved by the ancients who were the ancestors of our people. Here you have blossomed and lived a second life, one that was blessed with a special and sacred child, for Yandalla is special, and she is the reason Oatin lifted the sword and walked into his destiny. Without Yandalla, Andalyn's dream would have died." Sarka bit her lip and stepped out of Bettle's embrace, she kept her head down as she wiped her eyes.

"I cannot deny, even though I took Pallum in a new union, I still have great love in my heart of Andalyn, and at times like this,

I miss him so much." Bettle took her hand in hers.

"It is late, but this night feels different, walk with me."

Bettle led the way along the path, that wound its way down past the temple to the row of houses where she lived, just short of the path to Sarka's home. As they walked Bettle glanced at Sarka.

"Every night you go to see the children, I take it, you draw great strength from it?" Sarka gave a smile as she thought of the children.

"I care about them, most of them have no parents, and I suppose I would like them to know they have someone to look over them at night. There are over two hundred children left alone, I guess I want to know they see me as there if they need me."

They walked a little further down the path as the edge of the cliff came into view, and sound of the sea rolling up the beach rose up from below. The air felt warm and softly blew past them, and as the moon came out from behind the clouds, Sarka could see the glint off the sea on the horizon, and she breathed in deeply.

Bettle had a calmness around her, and it appeared to wash into Sarka, as she breathed softly and felt a deep easing within her after feeling her insides stir. There had been many nights when she had sat alone on her bed, her insides swirling, as she worried without news from her husband and children. She looked at Bettle, who was a great age, and yet she had a vitality about her that that appeared to flow from within her.

"Can I ask... You know, there has been a great deal happen in your life, and a lot of that has not been easy for you. I know you lost all of your family in the last days, so I guess, well, I wondered, how do you manage to stay so at ease with everything?" Bettle gave a chuckle.

"I talk to Nuada, I watch over all of you, and all the people of the Undine, I think for me, I have made all I see my family, for that is what we are, a family of life. Sarka, I know the Summanu destroy all in their path, but like us, they are all a part of the life that flows from this land. Nuada teaches us that we should embrace all, I do, and I feel a mother to everyone." Sarka scoffed.

"I admire you, because I am not sure I could feel the same. I have heard the stories of what happened down there, I was in the fight, I know of the butchery, rape and murder of all. I feel a lot of things, but as for motherly, I do not feel that for the Summanu. They took my child; I can feel no sympathy for those Summanu who suffer as a result." Bettle nodded her head and chuckled.

"You are still very young in the ways of life, although, watching you tonight, I could see that how being a mother is reflected in the care you show to children. Tell me Sarka, if a Summanu child was suffering, would you reach out to the child and protect it?" Sarka stopped and turned to her.

"How could you ask such a thing?" Bettle shrugged.

"Would you?" Sarka could not believe what she was asking.

"You know I would never harm a child." Bettle looked at her and smiled.

"Yes, I do. Sarka, all of those Summanu soldiers were once innocent children, there is a place in their hearts that was once that child, and Nuada says it is possible to reach in and bring forth that goodness once again. I have to believe we can do that, and I trust Nuada to help us." Sarka gave a big sigh.

"You ask a big thing Bettle, I am sure for the Undine that is no easy thing."

"So, what is the answer Sarka, do we remain enemies at war forever? If we cannot find that part that lives in the Summanu, we have no hope for a life of peace." Sarka really was unsure, she did not even understand why Bettle would even ask her that.

"Bettle, the Summanu have massacred the Undine without any feelings of compassion at all, I am not sure those soldiers feel anything but hate. Those animals have my daughter captive, there is no forgiveness in me for the butchery of my friends, and the way in which they have taken not just my daughter, but all the other young women. I want to believe there is a way to find peace, but to be honest, I cannot see a way." Bettle reached out and took her hand.

"Sarka, trust in Nuada, things change." It completely surprised her.

"How?" Bettle gave another chuckle, her eyes so bright in her old lined face.

"Read the third book, it talks of the moment of transmogrification, and at the moment that is the only thing that makes sense." Sarka had no understanding of any of this.

"What does that even mean, for I do not understand it?"

"The third book of Nuada talks of a moment of flux, a moment of uncertainty, remembrance, and a questioning of faith. It is one that will lead to a great awakening, and Sarka, I believe that moment is here, I believe it is this day, for there is a new breeze blowing and I feel it brings hope. Read the book, and trust it."

As Sarka watched her, she did not understand why, but she felt some hope flow out of Bettle with her words and it embraced her.

"I want to believe that change will come, I desperately want my family safe again, but it is not easy Bettle, you ask a lot for us to think all of this will change." Bettle wore a big smile and nodded at her.

"I know, that is the wonder of Nuada, without knowing why, we have to place all of our faith in the truth we hold for the teachings of our ancestors and their beliefs. Go home Sarka, and read, you will see." Bettle let go of her hand with a chuckle, turned, and walked to the row of small cabins.

"Sleep well Sarka, read and learn." Sarka watched her walk to her door and enter her small home, and she gave a long sigh.

"I wish at this moment I had your faith my good friend, I really do, because I really want to believe my family will return safe, but at the moment, I am struggling to believe in anything."

Sarka had always had the answer, she had lived with the vision of how to rebuild the lines of the Andalan, and they had flourished, but in recent times she had seen it all fall apart. As much as she wanted to believe that people's feelings and minds could change, she doubted any Summanu would, and for the first time since walking into the sand, she had no idea what the future would hold for all of them. She turned back to look out over the sea, and alone in the dark, surrounded by the sound of the soft crashing waves below, she felt more afraid that she ever had, because she felt she was on the edge of losing everything she loved in this world. Her long blond hair lifted on her shoulder and blew into her face, she lifted her hand almost as a reflex to stroke it back, and she felt the warmth of the wind on her cheek.

"Transmogrification, I have no recollection of ever reading that in the book, does she mean a wind of change, because Andalyn often spoke of that?"

She turned on the path as Bettle's words echoed in her ears, and walked slowly down the sandy path towards her home, her mind lost completely in thought. She did not even realise she had walked back into her home, where Eliaston sat on his bed with the door open reading in the candle light, he looked up as he saw her.

"Your mind fights with a problem?"

Sarka blinked, and then suddenly understood where she was, as she looked at the old master. For a moment she tried to find the right words, the problem was, she did not understand completely what Bettle was talking of. Sarka looked at him, and chose her words carefully.

"Did Andalyn ever talk of transmogrification?" Eliaston gave a big smile.

"You feel it too? To be honest I was not sure at first, but I do believe there is a wind of change this night. I feel the moment is upon us, I am thrilled you have come to the same conclusion." Sarka felt her frustration inside.

"I didn't think of it, Bettle just told me of it, what does it all mean?" His eyes illuminated, and he appeared suddenly very excited.

"She does... Oh how wonderful? I was sure I was right but did not want to say anything, come, let us fill a pan and sit with tea, we have a lot to talk about."

With that, he jumped up off his bed and lifted the four books of the winds off his blanket. Eliaston was very excited as he scuttled out of his room, and headed for the table, where he placed his books down. Lifting a pan he filled it with water, threw a log on the fire and then swung the metal bracket holding the pot over it, and then looked back.

"Come on, we have much to discuss, I have been dying to talk to others of this, it will be most illuminating."

Sarka was feeling a complete loss for words, she simply did as she was told and crossed the room and took a seat at his side. Eliaston was most excited, and lifted his book and then quickly flipped through the pages.

"Let me see now, oh yes, here it is, the tale of how one night all will consider their thoughts and their true inner feelings, and as a result there will be great changes. Here it is, the moment of transmogrification." Sarka nodded, but she had no clue at all of what he was about to speak of.

The cart lolled from side to side, as the mats below the wheels shifted around on the soft baked sand. All of the Undine women were sleeping leaning on each other, rocking with the motion of the cart. The normal weeping and tears that could be heard all down the line of cages were absent from the usual misery of the night time journeys, and all felt calmer than normal.

Yandalla stirred in her sleep and a gave a quite moan, her eyes moving rapidly below her closed eyes lids, she jerked occasionally, as she leant on the shoulder of Shellena, and as she gave another quite moan in her sleep, Sintalla opened her eyes in the darkness. Her voice was soft and caring as she watched Yandalla.

"Be quiet little one, the Nyen Diran stalk you this night, calm your spirit." Yandalla muttered quietly in her sleep.

"Yan fors ae Cumten." She jerked, and Sintalla jumped with her, and gasped out as she saw the faint illumination glow around her. Yandalla appeared to shake and then suddenly her eyes snapped open, and she looked right at Sintalla.

"Elohim."

Light pulsed out of her eyes, and she jerked, and then to Sintalla's horror, Yandalla lifted off the floor and rose towards the top of the cage. Sintalla brought up her knees and pushed her feet into the floor as she pushed herself hard against the bars, looking up as Yandalla lay sprawled in the air across the top of the bars and the light around her intensified.

All along the row of carts containing the women, the cages began to vibrate, and those who were sleeping woke with a start of panic. Yandalla was pressed against the bars as her cage shook violently, below her all of the Undine women and girls covered their ears and cried out in fear. Sintalla stood up her eyes still fixed on Yandalla, and her hands gripping the bars hard to keep herself upright. She looked down at all the terrified women.

"Stop your screaming, she spoke Elohim, she is responding to the undying earth below our feet." Sintalla looked back up.

"I know not what is happening, but I know no harm will come to us from Yandalla."

The cart was rocking violently as the cages vibrated, and below the women, the planking of the carts started to moved and rattle. Shellena jumped up against the bars and stared down at the floor, when the board which they had cut into with the arrow, were bouncing up and down, and each time they bounced, they pulled at the long metal shafts, lifting them up out of the beams of the cart. Shellena looked at Sintalla as she clung to the side of the cage.

"How is this possible, how can she command Elohim?" Sintalla shook her head.

"I do not think she is; I think Elohim is working through her, the land of our spirits is coming to our aid. The desert is ours; it is a part of Undinalashka, and I think through Yandalla, it is trying to save us."

As Yandalla shook, at the side of the cage which was covered with the sheet, there was a commotion, as Sintalla turned to look, the sheet was dragged quickly off the cage and fell to the sand, as a group of soldiers looked into the cage. Shellena could see all of the other cages, which also had their sheets off, and she gasped at the sight of the half starved and weak looking girls. Two of the soldiers saw Yandalla and stepped back shaking their heads, the taller one looked utterly panicked.

"Oh no... No, this is not real, I told you they were demons, one minute they are there, and the next they vanish. These people are undeads, they live after they have died, I told you I did not lie, look at her, she is like the other one, they are unnatural."

He grabbed his mate by the arm, and pulled at it, as he took another two steps back, moving away from the cage on the cart.

"Leave them, I mean it, if you do anything, they will curse you and kill you in very horrible ways, you saw Jehiar, he cut his own arm off and did not even blink, leave them, just do nothing or death will come to you."

The cart was shaking so much, the wheels kept lifting off the sand, and the soldiers could do nothing but stare with horror at what they were seeing. Yandalla turned her head as she was pinned to the top of the cage, the light around her intense and bright, her arm twitched and then slowly slid across to the side of cage. She grabbed at the bars and pulled, and her body slid across the top of the cage, and as she got closer, she pushed her face against the gap in the bars and stared at the soldiers who moved away even more, her voice was eerie, deep and powerful.

"YAN FORS AE CUMTEN!" It sounded like death, and one of the soldiers whimpered. Her eyes glowed with yellow light.

"NYEN DIRAN CUMTEN!"

That was all it took, the soldiers bravery failed and they turned and ran for their lives. Yandalla drew a deep breath, and suddenly, the light around went out, and she fell to the floor with a crash, and everything stopped shaking. Sintalla gasped in a deep breath and dropped to her knees at the side of Yandalla who was face down on the floor, and she carefully rolled her over.

"Yandalla, are you alright."

Her cheek was cut from a metal spike that stood proud of the floor, her eyes were closed but she was breathing, Shellena was at Sintalla side and helped lift her, and cradled her on her lap as Sintalla looked her over.

"I have no idea what just happened, but I am not sure she knows either, I think she is unharmed apart from her cheek. Help me, we need to take care of her." Shellena gave a nod, she looked frightened.

"What did she mean, the wind is coming and night terrors are coming?" Sintalla shook her head.

"I really do not know, all I know is she called to Elohim, and if you want my thoughts, Elohim answered, and I do not even want to know how that is possible." Shellena nodded and swallowed hard, she had seen it, and if she was honest, she did not want to admit it. Sintalla smiled at her.

"Do not be scared, she loves all of us, she would never hurt us, if anything, she is trying to save us." Sintalla looked at all of them as they silently watched and stared, their faces filled with fear.

"Yandalla is special, I think one day, she will be the one to rule our land as our leader, after Shengara leaves us."

Chapter Twenty Four

Safe Haven

It had been a long night of disturbed sleep, and bad dreams, all of the group woke up early not feeling their best. All of them looked tired and carried the strain of their inner feelings of loss and pain on their faces.

After a hurried meal, and feeling weary, they set off in the boat and made their way down the river. It was a long slow day, as they carefully made their way down the river, knowing that just a few moments' walk away level with them, was the larger river on which were all of the forces of the Summanu protecting the order. There were a few occasions when they moved in close to the bank as they heard the sounds of troops moving, and hid under the low branches of the overhanging trees.

It was like a game of cat and mouse, until they were well out of sight and reach of the order. As the evening arrived, they moved onto the bank, as Shade led the way, they carried the boat across the land to the bank of the wide river. Shade looked through the darkness up the river, back towards where far behind them, the order were based in the new town. Her half Undine eyes were far better in the dark, and she could see without any loss of vision.

As she watched, Elden with Oaken and Ham lowered the boat into the water, Shade looked back as everyone climbed in to the boat, they were ready, and she hurriedly jumped in.

"We good."

They pulled out their paddles and stroked quickly into the water, this was a dangerous moment, they had to cross quickly and stay out of sight. Ria sat at the back, her senses alert, as Vesta who hated boats sat at the front, her keen eyes watching the bank. Ham stroked fast, and the others followed his lead, the river was much wider than they had realised, and the journey was longer than they had wished for.

There was a lot of relief when they finally made it, and pulled up the boat, and dragged it into the trees, where they turned

it upside down and covered it with leaves and branches to
hide it. They would now be on foot, and walking into what was
considered hostile territory. Shade led them on a path she knew
well, and pointed to areas along the way.

"Bad place... Soldier lives there... Bad men, no good." It did
little to instil confidence in them, Ria looked around feeling
nervous.

"I am not liking this, we are but a few, if we encounter a unit,
we will be grossly out numbered." Ham gave a chuckle.

"We are safe enough, the Summanu tend to only move in
daylight, few walk out in the dark, do not forget, the animals are
far more hostile than the people around here." Ria looked back.

"How hostile?" Ham shrugged.

"Some bite, some snarl, and some will rip your leg off, it
depends on what you meet."

Oaken smiled in the dark, as he walked along the trail, his ears
aware of every sound, Shade appeared unaffected, she walked as
well in the dark as she did in the daylight. Ria took a breath, she
was tired.

"We need to make it through to the grass lands, I do not think
it can be much further, I hope so, I am exhausted and my legs
are sore, I did not sleep well last night." Oaken nodded in the
darkness, his eyes fixed on Shade, who looked like a glowing
apparition.

"Once we make it into the grass, we should be safer and harder
to see, we can rest there as we prepare." He watched as Shade
slowed down and raised her hand behind her, she gave it a short
wave, and Oaken put out his arm to Ria.

"Wait." Vesta appeared out of the darkness and morphed into
her naked form.

"There is a long line of people coming, some of them are
soldiers, you need to get off the road." Shade pointed, and
everyone followed into the trees, and headed in far enough to be
out of sight, but close enough to get an idea of who was on the
road in the dark.

Oaken pulled Meda close and held her down on the mossy floor
covering her, he could feel her shaking as he lay beside her, and
looked through the leaves and branches. Ria was at his side with
Caleb, as all of the others watched on from cover.

It took a little time, but men with bright burning torches came down the road, behind them a long treble line of Summanu soldiers. They trudged past, their feet pounding on the floor, and all of them watched set back in the darkness, unable to move or make a sound.

Row upon row of soldiers passed, and then came an equally long line of apostles, with their long robes like Jenmar, which were followed by the carriages. Oaken shuddered when he saw them, as they were the same as the one that Jenmar had been in when he found him with Shade that first day. He lay watching and counting as they passed him, and he counted nine carriages, all pulled with four white horses. Behind them came more soldiers, and Oaken estimated there were at least two hundred of them.

For Oaken, this was a new experience, he had been high above Undinalashka when the Summanu attacked, so he had not seen the soldiers up close, and there was a part of him that wished he had not. He glanced to his side where Ria was lay down watching, and he whispered quietly.

"There is a lot of them, why do you think that is?" Her eyes did not move off the road.

"I am not sure, but I am beginning to wonder about Jenmar. Looking at those carriages, I do wonder if he has some sort of status." It made some sense.

"Well, we know he had gold for Belthaz, and he did acquire Meda for him, so maybe he has some higher position than we realised. I counted nine, and with Belthaz that would be ten, do you think there is some sort of group of rulers?" Ria turned and looked at him.

"I am beginning to, which means that this order of apostles, knows about us, I think it is clear, Jenmar would have told them everything."

Oaken nodded, his mind was moving that way, and so he felt it was obvious that Balathral would be aware that he has some sort of power. It was clear, if he did not know yet, he probably soon would.

The party moved past and carried on down the road, Shade made her way forward slowly as she checked it was safe, Oaken looked down, and smiled, Meda was fast asleep curled next to him. Ria smiled as she saw her.

"She feels safe with you." She knelt up as Shade waved from the road, all was clear, Oaken looked at Ria.

"It feels wrong to wake her up." Ria shrugged at him.

"Well, it is up to you, wake her, or carry her, either way, it is safer if we get as far away from here as possible."

Oaken carefully lifted the sleeping body of Meda, and he held her close as he followed the others back onto the road. The darkness was deepening, and after the rain there was a chill in the air, as they trudged along following Shade, not really knowing where exactly they were going.

They walked for well over an hour in silence, until Shade turned, her face almost glowing white in the complete darkness. She pointed with a white hand.

"Soon there, then rest."

All of them gave a sigh of relief, as she turned from the road and walked under the trees following a narrow pathway. Ria looked at Oaken who was at her side, with the still sleeping Meda in his arms.

"I have been thinking, when we get where we are going to, how will we be able to sneak up on them? I know that Ham can open these locks, but how will we get him close enough to do it unseen?"

Oaken was watching his footing, with Meda he really did not want to fall. He thought about it, she had made a good point, but up until now he hadn't really given it as much consideration as maybe he should have.

"I am not sure at the moment, but you are right, it is something that we will need to plan out before we do it. To be honest, I thought that once I see the place to strike, I will know what to do." Ria gave a nod in the darkness; she supposed it made sense.

"I did wonder if it would be worthwhile to try and get some uniforms. If we are dressed like their soldiers, we would at least blend in a little, because we are not exactly dressed for the part at the moment."

After a little while, the trees started to thin out and they walked out onto the grass land that stretched out across a wide plain.

There were signs of fences that once enclosed the land, but under what little moonlight there was, the old broken stumps and planks, were silhouetted as the ground rose up to what looked like an old building. Shade turned and looked back.

"Rest there."

Oaken breathed a sigh of relief, Meda was small, and she did not weigh a great deal, but after walking for what felt like most of the night, his arms were aching.

They walked across what were large fields of long wild grass, he assumed at some point this was a farmland, but as with most of Shodalt, it had since the Summanu invaded turned back to nature, and the natural plants of the area moved in and took over. They walked up towards the dark house, and up the old steps onto a small deck, which creaked and groaned under their weight.

Shade turned at the door, which was boarded up, it appeared the whole house was, even the windows had planks across them, so it appeared whoever lived here, left after securing the house, and the Summanu had left it alone.

Ham leaned over and took out a tool from his bag, he pushed it behind the board, and pulled hard and the board gave way slightly. The wood was old and it had not been put up particularly well, although to Oaken, it appeared they were in a hurry to leave. The board gave way, and Ham pulled it off with a splintering crash, and Ham heaved the large board out of the way, and leaned it against the post that held up a small wooden roof above the decking.

To Oaken's surprise, the door was not locked, and Shade lifted the latch and walked in, all the others followed inside and stopped in the middle of what was a pitch black room. There was a stone fireplace, and Shade wandered over to it and pulled out her flints, she looked back at Elden.

"Need wood, find outside." Ria frowned as she watched Elden walk towards the door.

"Shade, have you been here before, do you know this house?" It was hard to see her face as she had her back to them, as she worked in the dark to arrange some fabric shreds to catch a flint.

"Anna Pa was child's here." Ria gave a slight gasp.

"This was your father's house?" Her voice came through the

darkness.

"When Anna Ma hurt, Anna Pa come here."

Things suddenly made sense, this was the place where Shade nursed her mother as she was dying, it had belonged to her father, Oaken understanding blurted out his thoughts.

"This was your home?" Elden came in through the door holding some old split logs covered in moss, Shade stood up and took one, she looked at Oaken in the dark.

"Many homes, me told once."

Once the fire was lit, the room came into view, they could finally see where they were. The room was larger than they expected, and had a few chairs, a table and some shelves, most of which were still intact, if not covered in dust and dirt. Ria was relieved to find a water pump with a large metal bucket, which was stiff and rusty, but with some heaving from Elden and Ham, it came loose and began to work, so they could pump water from a well.

Shade lit some tallows, and guided them up the old creaking stairs, where there were four rooms, all with rough beds, they were dirty but beds. Ria helped spread out one of the blankets and Oaken lay the sleeping Meda down and Caleb thanked him. There was little food to eat, and so they sat together in front of the fire, all of them were tired, especially after the previous nights unsettled feelings. It was soon time to organise, rooms were sorted out, and again the beds were old, but it had been so long since they had been in one, it did not matter. Blankets were spread out and a watch was set, and as the night progressed Oaken finally headed up to the room with his blanket for the bed.

He entered the room and spread out his blanket, dropped his bag and bow and lay back with a sigh, and closed his eyes, he so desperately needed rest, last night his mind had been filled with dreams of Yandalla, and he had not slept well. The door creaked, as he lay back breathing softly verging on the edge of sleep, and then he felt the soft touch of another blanket flow over him, and opened his eyes.

Ria stood in the tallow light, wrapped in another blanket, she smiled and then pulled at the blanket that was around her and she stood naked lit by the tallow. She lifted the blanket and slid underneath, and her warm skin pressed up against him, her voice was soft in his ear as she snuggled up.

"Hold me Oaken, I really need to be as close as possible to you tonight."

She leaned over and stared to kiss him, and his arms came up around her feeling her warm soft skin as he pulled her closer to him. Outside Shade sat on the steps watching the empty grassland, her eyes moved up, and she smiled.

"Mmm, Yan tee." She gave a quiet giggle.

The following morning Oaken awoke to see Ria fast asleep, her head on his chest, and her arm lay across him. He had not expected her to come into his room, and had less expected the result, but somehow inside, he felt happy, actually, happier than he had ever felt before. It was strange and he really did not fully understand it, but it felt right for him. He slid his arms slowly away from her, she looked so peaceful, he did not want to wake her, Ria gave a soft happy moan and opened her eyes. Understanding what had happened, and where she was, she smiled, he smiled back.

"Good morning." Ria stretched a little and breathed out a happy sigh.

"Morning... I don't want to get up, can we stay here a little longer?" He was not sure, the shafts of light on the wall showed it was morning, but he had to admit he was not in a rush to move.

"If you want, I suppose we could stay here a little while longer." She smiled.

"Yes, I am warm and cosy, and I have wanted this to happen." He frowned.

"You did?" Her head moved as if nodding.

"Yes, is it shameful that me of all people wanted this?" He was not sure really how to put it.

"I do not think so, I am happy to be here with you, Yandalla will be delighted when she finds out, she has told me often I need a woman." Ria gave a giggle.

"Your sister is wise, although, I assume Shade knows, I fear there will be some giggles today." He agreed.

"Good point, but I am not worried, let all of them laugh, I cannot talk for you, but for me, this feels right. I slept better last night than I have since I left my home." Her smile was fixed to her face.

"Me too."

It took a while, and once they both came down to see what was happening, they found that there were smirks, but it was not that bad, although Ham gave him a good slap on the back, and he staggered two steps forward as Ham winked.

"Good man." Shade gave a loud laugh as she sat in a chair by the open door.

Once everything settled down, Shade took Oaken around the back of the house, where he saw miles of grassland, which ran into the golden sands which he instantly recognised as the start of the Heliospan Dessert. As he stood looking out at the vastness of sand behind the grass, Ria came up at his side and lifted her scope to her eye. Shade pointed.

"Road from big sand there." Ria moved and focused on it.

"I see it, I see soldiers, they are marching out of the sand."

She handed the scope to Oaken, and he lifted it up to his eye. The images were not large or clear, but there was no doubt that there were lines of men. As he watched, he tried to work out what they were doing, it appeared they would walk into the sand, and then turn around and come back.

"What are they doing?" Ria shrugged.

"Not sure, I think they are guarding the way, but it does look like they are getting ready for the arrival of the wagons." Shade nodded.

"They come there." She moved her arm across to the right of Oaken.

"Then go to water."

He moved the scope slowly following the direction of her hand, and he felt his heart skip a beat, as she saw the start of the rock that led up high into Andalan. That was home, the place of his birth, and he could not resist moving up the wall of crumbled rocks that formed the stepping shelves that ran up to the high plateaux, which was where he had spent the first ten years of his life.

Andalan looked much bigger than he remembered, as its very top was hidden under the low cloud, he felt a surge swirl inside him as he viewed the place that he knew contained the old carved temple of his people, and was the location where the first four books of the wind resided. It was a moment he had dreamed of as a child, a chance to look upon the land of his father and his people, and the power of the moment held him captive.

"We need to plan Shade, and I need to get closer so I will know where we strike." She gave a soft nod.

"Me show, get sister." Ria smiled as she watched, she could almost feel the power of the impact it was having on him.

"We are closer Oaken, and soon we will get her, your sister will be free, we will make sure of it." Shade nodded.

"Need rest, need food." Oaken nodded, and pulled the scope from his eye.

"If we calculated right, we have a few days, so we need to really watch this place, and make sure we are ready when she comes."

They needed food, Ria knew of the edible plants that were surrounding them, and set off with Meda and Caleb to collect some. Shade knew the area well, so Oaken and Elden joined her with their bows, and headed off into the grassland in the direction of the Summanu.

The grass was almost up to their shoulders; it did not look as tall from the house that was built on a small hill. Once down in the grass, he realised it was much taller, and that was a bit of a problem, because the visibility was low, and it made him nervous to not know who was around. Shade appeared unconcerned as she walked at his side, he glanced at her as they walked, she appeared to be alert and listening carefully.

"What are we are looking for Shade?" Her eyes moved to his.

"Kanis."

"We are looking for dogs?" She nodded.

"Big, long teeth, bad." Elden smirked.

"Is everything you hunt bad Shade?" She turned and looked at him, and smiled.

"Me hunt what eats all, get meat good." Oaken admired her bravery.

"So, you hunt what eats everything else, because that makes for a tastier animal?" It made a strange sort of sense.

"Animal that eat good, make meat good." Elden nodded; it was a reasonable point.

Shade slowed and Oaken noted it and slowed his pace, he could see little and she was much smaller than he was, but he saw how suddenly her alert level went up. She slid an arrow out of the woven sleeve hanging on her belt, he felt it best to follow suit and lowered his voice.

"What is it?" She was staring forward and slowly moving her head from side to side. Her voice was quiet, as her senses were on full alert.

"Bad scent, not good." He nodded, and slid the arrow on to his string.

"Is it a dog?" She shook her head.

"Summanu, bad scent, not good." Elden loaded his arrow, he too was on full alert, especially if there were soldiers around. Were they hunting like they were, or had they been spotted?

Oaken stood at the side of Shade and listened, there was something that was moving, and they were not quiet, but it was hard to pinpoint them. Oaken was not keen on moving, but he also did not want to be surrounded. Shade patted his shoulder, and he turned to look at her, her eyes sparkled blue in her white face, she smiled and pushed his shoulder. He understood, he was taller and could be seen, she wanted him to lower down, and he had no problems getting out of sight of any soldiers.

Oaken lowered down and watched Shade, he could feel the sweat on his hands, as he held the bow, his right arm was tense on the string, the noise was coming closer, Elden was just to the side of Shade, and he was staring forward straining to hear what were voices. Shade turned and whispered.

"They come, we shoot, shoot fast." He nodded.

"I know it sounds odd, but try not to damage their uniforms, Ria thinks we need some." Shade frowned, then shrugged.

"Always in head, kilt good." It made sense.

Oaken leaned back and watched, he was ready, and decided it was better to take his lead from Shade, as she was far better at this than him, she had the experience and he was happy to learn from her. Shade tensed, and heard something, his head moved around as just in front to the left, there was a loud snarl, and then a scream followed by more snarls, and the screams of a man. Shade smiled.

"Kanis found Summanu." Oaken was a little panicked, how big

was this dog if it was ripping a man apart? Shade slowly lifted up and looked, she looked down and smiled.

"Kanis not know Ria want clothes."

She giggled, as the ferocious snarls and screams came from only a few feet away, he could not believe she was laughing, as what he perceived to be a monster dog tore a Summanu to pieces. She lifted her bow, sighted and fired, there was a grunt, but the snarls continued, Shade took a step forward, reloaded and sighted her bow, she fired another, and he felt he should do something to help.

Oaken slowly rose up, and could just make out where the grass was moving as something ran through the grass, and low rumbling and a slight snarl came from a little ahead. He held his bow ready as Shade took a step forward, slowly moving in the direction of what he knew was a large dog.

He followed, his insides a little flustered, as he really did not know what was happening, she had fired two arrows, but the dog was obviously still alive. He was just behind Shade, as she stepped out into a huge area of flattened grass, and his heart leapt in his chest as he saw the beast in question.

It was huge, and had its mouth inside the stomach of a Summanu guard, which up until Shade stepped into view, it was eating. Its head alone was as big as his torso, and it had a long pointed snout, above which was two dark and menacing eyes that were currently fixed on Shade. It watched her and growled, it was obvious it had no intention of giving up its meal, of which the scene alone was stomach churning, as Oaken had never seen anything as horrifying in his life.

The dog started to snarl louder, Shade was cool and calm, she lifted her bow as the dogs back legs tensed, Oaken felt it was about to pounce and brought up his bow, with his loaded arrow, the snarls grew louder, and Shade smiled and pulled on the string.

"Kanis big, meat good."

Her arrow shot at speed, as the dog jerked ready to pounce, as it pulled its head out of the soldier, the arrow hit it square between the eyes, and as it jerked forward, its front legs buckled, and flopped onto the dead soldier. Shade gave a satisfied nod.

"Kilt, me get meat, you get clothes." Oaken turned.

"What clothes?" She pointed behind her.

"Summanu kilt." His eyes moved to the spot, where through the grass he could just make out the colour of a uniform, Elden gave a chuckle as Shade slipped out her knife.

"We fast, others come." He was not sure of whether she meant Summanu or other large dogs, so he moved quickly towards where he saw the uniform, as Shade crouched over the dead dog.

Not far from the dead soldier was another one, Shade had shot both in the eye, although there was a little blood on the tunic. Oaken knelt down, and did his best to un-button the dead soldier's jacket, his hand brushed the soldiers face, and his skin was still warm, almost as if he was just sleeping. He rolled the man over and pulled at the jacket to pull the arms out of the sleeve, it came away and he pulled the jacket clear, it was not the most pleasant of tasks. Looking back, he could see Elden had the other man's jacket, he spotted the hat and reached out and took it.

By the time they returned to Shade, she had skilfully skinned the dog, removed its head, and gutted it. The pile of red ooze mixed with that of the soldier was a little disturbing to him. She stood up her arms covered in blood, and nodded as she saw the jackets.

"We move fast."

With that, she lifted the carcass, and threw it over her shoulders, and walked off back towards the house. Oaken and Elden followed her feeling useless, she was much smaller than they were, and yet Oaken felt she was far stronger than both of them. The Undine were an amazing race, and it appeared Shade had many of their physical qualities. Both of them walked through the tall grass, and Elden leaned in as they walked.

"You know, for a tiny woman, she is a little intimidating, I can really understand how she has survived alone out here for so long." He made a good point, Oaken had thought the same, but in a way, it saddened him.

"I think she had no choice, if you think about it, what other options did she have, her mother died and her father sold her? Shade has found ways to live in this hostile land that few others have, in a sense, she has become one with everything, she can be a person like us, or when needed, act like an animal. Think about it, she has been alone since she was seven summers of age, she has faced more alone than any of us will ever know."

Elden nodded quietly as he watched her walk up the hill towards the house, and he knew, Oaken was not wrong. Shade was a completely unique person, half Undine, and half Shodalt, and it was clear, there would never be another like her.

When they arrived at the house, Ria had gathered a lot of root vegetables, and was preparing them with Meda, Ham and Caleb were on watch. Shade lay down the carcass and then filled a bucket with water, which she carried outside, stripped, and washed her entire body. Caleb turned his back out of respect which made her giggle, after all, they had all bathed together in the pools. She washed her clothes and hung them on the rail, and then wrapped in a blanket she tipped the bucket out, and sat on the step to clean her knife. Calab watched as she used a small stone on the blade, she smiled at him.

"See... Stroke blade, make sharp."

He came over and sat at her side, and Shade happily showed him how to take care of weapons, he had no idea of how lucky he was, for she was teaching him a skill, that would one day maybe save his life. Elden sliced up the meat as Oaken built up the fire, and together they helped Ria prepare the meal, it had been a few days since their bellies were full, and their mouths watered as the meat hung to cook. Ria smiled as she slipped at his side and leaned on him.

"We are close, we have uniforms, now we must plan exactly what we need to do to get your sister free." Oaken gave a nod.

"I have been thinking about that, after we have eaten, I want to talk to Ham and get things ready, she cannot be much further away. I sense her and the feeling is growing stronger, I need to be ready Ria, her life depends on it." She gave a smile.

"We will get her, look, we have a safe haven here with a clear view of all around us. We can rest and prepare, we have a lot of food, so we can get ourselves in good condition ready, and then we can go and free Yandalla.

Chapter Twenty Five

Planning with Doubt

The night and day in their place of safety passed by quietly, each of them taking their turn to watch out across the wide expanse of long grass. For all of the time, they sat as a group and talked, each taking their turn to voice their ideas and concerns, over the task at hand.

The final plan had been to wait until night fall, and strike in the dark, Ham made it clear, he could undo the locks in the dark, and Elden asked what was possibly the most important question.

"What if you get killed?" Oaken frowned at him.

"He won't, we need his skills, so you all better be on your top behaviour, and watch his back." Ham gave a little chuckle.

"I can teach you the technique, but without an actual lock to practice on, it could be risky on the day." Shade nodded at him.

"You do; we watch."

Having spent the whole day resting, sorting through their bags, sharpening and cleaning their weapons, the afternoon wore on, and the group set off across the grassland, in the direction of Andalan. They calculated that when the convoy of cages finally made it out of the desert, and headed for the tall falls, there would be a line, as the soldiers would be first in the water. Oaken was hoping that if that was the case, the cages would have less men watching, and that would create an opening to sneak in, so as he walked through the grass, his apprehension began to rise.

Ria was in high spirits, since spending time together at the house, she had smiled a lot and been very easy to giggle, and she was excited that their task was heading to its final conclusion. Her eyes sparkled in the darkness, as she looked at him whilst they walked.

"This is the place you were born, are you excited to be able to walk on your homeland again?" He gave a sigh.

"I know it is my home, but I have not had time to think about it,

I want to walk there again, but for now, I need to know Yandalla is safe, after that, I will think about it."

There was the sound of voices up ahead and all of them slowed down, and lowered in the grass. They came together as a group, and Ham nodded to them in the dark.

"The road is but a few minutes' walk, and soldiers patrol it, we will need to be very careful now." Shade rose up and her haunches.

"We sit, wait."

Ham and Elden had on uniforms, both of them spoke Summanu, were dirty and unshaven, so looked perfect for fitting in with the other soldiers. Closer to the time, they would lead the group and help them sneak across the road to where they needed to be. For a long time, they just sat and listened, Elden translated what he heard.

"They were held up, some strange incident, they say there were devils and spirits."

Oaken thought about it, he knew Vesta had created a stir, but from what he understood, it had not been for that long, what else could have caused problems, did they mean Pallum, was he still out here? He looked at Ria.

"On the boat you said Pallum had gone after her, what else do you know about his plans?"

"Well, he intended to track her, I am not sure for how long, because my mother arranged to take the boat back to our home for supplies to bolster him. He must have had to return to get them, but considering the time and the conditions he would have had to face, I doubt he would have returned in time." Oaken thought about.

"I would not leave her, so neither would he. If he found her and could not free her, he will follow her and stay with her." Ria nodded in the darkness.

"It makes sense, do you think he is out there watching?" Oaken took a breath in ward.

"If he is, then has no idea we are here yet, if he has seen your mother, then he will know. We have two men in uniform, that is a little worrying, I do not want him mistaking them." Elden gave a nod in the darkness.

"Me too, I have seen him when he is angry, I do not want him on me, if I blink, it will all be over." Shade turned.

"Who Pallum?"

"He is Yandalla's father." She understood.

"Then no kilt him." Oaken smirked.

"No, he is not to be kilt, you focus on the Summanu and kilt as many as you want." She gave a small giggle, and her eyes sparkled in the darkness.

"Kilt big already, now kilt more."

The air changed and it was noticed, Sintalla sat up and breathed in. Under the canvass it was not easy, all of them smelt foul after their long journey through the desert. She stretched out her foot to Yandalla's, and gave it a tap. Yandalla opened her eyes, she felt weak, and exhausted, Sintalla smiled.

"The desert is coming to an end; can you smell the dampness of the air?"

Yandalla blinked, and turned to the canvass covered bars, where there was a long rip in the sheet. She leaned over to get closer and breathed slowly in. Sintalla was right, it felt cooler and different. As she breathed it in, she could smell the sweet scent of grass. It felt like a big relief, she knew that soon they would get water, her mouth was so dry, and her cracked lips were painful as she tried to lick them. She leaned back against the bars and looked at Sintalla, her voice was strained and dry.

"When we stop, we pull up the boards. The gap is not wide, but looking at us, we are so thin we will get through." Sintalla gave a smile.

"We will be alright, Elohim is with us, we will find a way."

"We need food, we need water, all of us are weak."

It was true, and yet they had been better fed on the journey out of all of them, due to Yandalla's fast actions with the berries and catching the snake. Pallum had tried several times to get more food to them, but after the first assaults, the guards had taken to sleeping under or next to the cages, making it harder to get to them.

In the other cages, the women were thinner and weaker, the last half of the journey through the dessert had been hard, as they were given less food and water, and most of them lay motionless on the floor of the cages sick or too weak to move.

Shade ducked down and looked at them all, her eyes almost glowed in the darkness.

"See trees, we go there."

She pointed, and Oaken lifted his head above the grass slowly, he could see the dark outline of what looked like a wide stretch of trees and shrubs.

"I suppose if they do not get here before sun up, that would give us good cover. Alright Shade, we will move out slowly." She gave a nod.

"Good."

In single file, and keeping low, they followed the path of flattened grass made by Shade, and slowly crept silently towards them. Shade took a wide circle bringing them to the back of the trees, to make sure there was no one else there. After what felt like an age, they crept in through two thin bushy trees and found a small open circle surrounded by low growing bushes and shrubs under the much taller trees.

It actually felt good to be able to stand, and Oaken stretched his legs, it was a good spot with a good view of the road up close. Ria pulled out her scope and looked towards the falls, she panned the whole area, it was still a distance to where the river crossed the paths. As she panned, she stopped and stared down the scope.

"We have a problem." Oaken turned and looked at her.

"What do you mean?" She took the scope away from her eye.

"It looks like there is a large camp on the other side of the river, I see tents and lights, lots of them." Ham looked up from the floor.

"That is probably the Summanu withdrawing from Shodalt, Vesta said they are pulling back. Over the river is the long road past Leyarken to Sumanula, it is the fastest route back, and has many new bridges over all of the rivers. They will have rest posts all along it." Ria gave a sigh.

"It is never easy, is it?" Ham gave a chuckle.

"Well, you know, six of us, and ten thousand of them, I say we wait until they get more men to make the fight fairer." Elden gave a chuckle; Shade gave a grin.

"Me no like fair, me kilt, is easy."

Ria smiled, somehow, she felt Ham was not wrong, Shade would kill most of them before they caught up with her. Oaken sat down, the odds to start with were impossible, he had no idea how he would get to Yandalla now.

"I do not even know which cart she is on, this is becoming impossible, we have to find her, then free her, and do all of that with thousands of soldiers on watch." He looked up at Ria.

"How do we even do that?" Shade gave a shrug.

"Need Caltha." She had point, Vesta was supposed to be back by now, and he was worried, she was the key to everything.

"I do not know where she is, she was supposed to be back before we left." Shade patted his shoulder.

"Trust Caltha, she come." He wanted to, but with thousands of soldiers around, he knew she too was at risk. Ria sat down at his side and took his hand.

"Oaken, have some faith, Vesta is the best, I have known her a long time, and I know what she has done in her life, trust her, she will not let us down."

He wanted to, but his doubts were growing, the truth was, he needed more time, he needed more men than they had, and he had not had enough time watching to fully understand what numbers they faced. He closed his eyes and put his head down, he needed to think, he needed another plan. Shade patted his shoulder, he lifted his head and looked at her, she smiled.

"Me fix, you wait." He frowned, but as quick as a flash, she twisted, and shot off back through the trees. Oaken turned to look back, his voice low.

"No... Shade, wait!" It was too late; she had been swallowed by the darkness, and was gone.

Shade moved silently and quickly through the grass, heading in the direction of the desert. She knew Vesta was looking for the carts, and so she knew at some point she would find her, and her senses were at their highest. She took a moment to gain her baring's, and gripped her sword hilt, something felt off, she looked back, the trees with the group in were quite far behind her. Shade crouched low, and peered through the tall stems of the grass, she could sense something, but it moved in ways like no other soldier she had ever known. She waited, knowing she had made no sound, and had not been detected.

Up ahead there was movement, and her blue eyes narrowed as she zeroed in on the sound. Moving almost like a stalking cat, Shade tensed ready, moved her hand off her sword, and slid her hand behand her to grip the hilt of her dagger. The grass up ahead moved again, she saw it and turned slightly to face whatever it was moving slowly towards her. Her legs went taught as she leaned back ready to strike, more grass moved, and she saw the hint of a black hood, and she was ready.

The movement stopped, and then rose slightly in the grass, and Shade saw the dark shape. As quick as lightening, she launched herself forward, and as her leg came up, she hit the target as it rose in the chest, and like a pouncing cat, she grabbed with one hand, and as her whole body twisted. Shade was moving at high speed, her legs went around the back of the man and came up and she wrapped around their shoulders, as she pulled up one of her legs under their face, and she lifted her dagger to strike.

To her left, a black shadow moved fast, and came up into the air towards her and morphed into a woman.

"SHADE NO!"

Vesta hit her head on and both of them went sprawling backwards, crashing back into the grass covered floor, and she gasped out in shock as she saw Vesta's panicked face close to hers. She hit the floor hard still gripping her target firmly as Vesta landed hard on top of her with a grunt. Still holding her dagger in her hand, Shade relaxed slightly and allowed the person trapped in her hold to move. Vesta lifted her head and took a deep breath, and closed her eyes for a second.

"That was too close, Shade, let him go, he is with me."

Shade lay back and moved her legs, the hooded figure sat up, and took several deep breaths, as Vesta sat up and looked down at Shade.

"This is Pallum, he is the leader of the Undine who have been trying to protect Yandalla." Shade frowned at her.

"All Undine kilt." Vesta shook her head.

"Not all, some lived." Pallum slid down his hood, revealing his long sleek black hair, and looked at her, she stared at him.

"Shen tey." He frowned at her, and looked angry.

"Yun Shen tey, yen ae Yun?" She sat up and slid back in the

grass, and slid her dagger back in her sheath on her belt, she looked at Vesta.

"Late, need Caltha, help Oaken." Pallum looked at Vesta.

"Is this the half bred Undine who has been helping him?" Shade scoffed.

"Me more Undine, you nearly kilt." She stood up in the grass and looked around, she pointed.

"Need Caltha, find sister." Vesta looked at Pallum, and looked apologetic.

"Shade has unconventional ways of fighting, but here, that is a requirement. I am sure had she known who you were, she would have held back. Pallum, I am late back, and I am needed." She turned back to Shade.

"Where is Oaken?" Shade looked at Pallum, and lifted her arm to point.

"He there, big tree." Vesta nodded and looked at him.

"Can you and your men head over to him; he will be needing help." Shade smirked.

"Shen tey, no help." Shade turned.

"Me go." Pallum was not happy as Shade walked off through the grass, he watched her looking angry.

"She is as disrespectful as the rest of her Shodalt kind, she needs to know her place." Across in the grass, her voice came back.

"HA! Shen tey." Vesta smirked, Pallum had his pride hurt and it showed. Vesta looked at him, she felt bad for him, his pride had been severely dented.

"Shade needs my help, go to Oaken and Ria and they will fill you in on their plans." He gave a nod, and brushed the dust off his cloak.

As Pallum headed towards Oaken, Vesta morphed back into her black cat form, and bounded through the grass towards Shade. Shade was bent low and moving fast through the grass, as Vesta came up at her side, Shade looked down at her.

"Undine make noise, me caught. If no Caltha, me kilt him, he Shen tey."

She walked on watching the road, and taking note of everything, Shade needed to find a way to spot Oaken's sister so that he could get to her and save her. Vesta walked quietly at her side.

"Need other side, need high rock for look."

In the trees, Pallum arrived to a warm and happy welcome as Oaken hugged him hard, and then introduced Ria and the others. After a few minutes of catch up, where Pallum outlined what the full truth of what the Summanu had done in Undinalashka, they settled to talk quietly. Pallum looked tired, as he explained that knowing Oaken was drawing closer, he had left his men, and come on ahead to try and meet up. The rest of his men were level with the cages and doing all they could to cause problems. Pallum let out a long sigh.

"Things are not good for Yandalla, the conditions they are in are hard for one so young. They have been left in their own filth, and food and water has been limited as the soldiers get most of it. I cannot deny, I am worried, we cannot get near the cages as the Summanu sleep under them, making it harder." Oaken could see the strain behind his eyes.

"No matter what, I will get her, I have good people with me, and all of us are focused on freeing her and as many of the others as possible." Pallum nodded.

"The Shodalt, I have met, she is unstable and undisciplined, I was surprised to see one such as her with you." Oaken frowned at him.

"The only Shodalt we have is Ham, the rest are other tribes." Pallum nodded.

"She speaks Undine, but she has short hair, no self respecting Undine would cut their hair such, I see the Shodalt only in her." Oaken understood, he meant Shade.

"You met Shade, when?" His eyes looked fierce.

"I ran into her with Vesta; she was rude and disrespectful." Ria gave a little giggle.

"That sounds like Shade, but do not judge her Pallum, she has been true to us and has shown great loyalty. Shade is a little hostile at times, but in a tight situation, she has proven her value many times." Oaken nodded.

"Her mother was Undine and trained her in the ways of an Undine, sadly her mother died when she was only seven summers, since that time she has fended for herself, which even you must admit is a great feat." Pallum was unconvinced.

"One Undine parent does not make an Undine; her lack of a discipline is the Shodalt within her." Oaken shrugged.

"It matters not to me, I have a great trust in her, and she has not let me down, and that is what I need here, people I can trust. Shade will be the one who makes it possible for us to get Yandalla, and I need her for that reason."

"I must admit, that concerns me, she is unpredictable, and you will need to act with precision if you plan to get Yandalla before the water." Ria shook her head.

"You are wrong about Shade, and to be honest, your daughter will be saved because she is with us. I have absolute faith in her loyalty, and she has not let us down yet. She is a fierce fighter, and worth ten men, I trust her." Pallum gave another sigh.

"So, how do you intend to free her?"

Oaken sat with Pallum and Ria, and together they began to look at all the elements of the situation they were presented with. As the day faded into the evening, they looked at what was possible, after all, they would only be able to use the six of them, as Pallum and the Undine would have to stay hidden, and only appear if needed.

The Heliospan Desert was vast, the central core was a land of baked sand, where the sun beat down relentlessly. As it came towards the edge of the Shodalt lands, the large dunes dissipated into a hard packed earth filled with rocks, as it met the edge of the two lands of Shodalt and Andalan. Where the three lands met, the mountain range of Andalan started, with large areas of scattered rocks that grew out of the soil ten full sized trees high.

Taking advantage of a break in the Summanu soldiers retreating to the river, Shade made her way out of the grassland, and onto the steep side of the Andalan mountain range. Moving quickly, she wove her way up the side through the rocks, keeping an eye of the road below. As dawn rose, and the day wore on, she worked out the route the Summanu were taking through the rocks. There were two high walls of rock, set apart about two carts width, through which was the sandy track, it was a perfect point from which to watch, and so she settled down and viewed the desert.

In the distance, she could see the dust from the long row of carts, as they moved slowly towards her. Vesta stuck to the grass land, moving quickly through the rocky terrain towards the dunes, where the carts were still moving in the scorching early evening sun.

As the evening began, and after a rest period, the carts jerked and began to roll, and Yandalla opened her eyes. She got up off the floor where she had been curled up in a tight ball, and sat up with her back to bars. Shellena sat at her side and leaned her head back on the bars.

"Being dead is better than this. I smell, and I itch, my hair is so matted when I try to pull out the knots, lumps of it come out." Yandalla gave a soft nod, she understood her, she felt the same.

"We are almost out of the dessert lands, soon Oaken will come." Shellena turned to her.

"Yandalla, as much as I want to get out of this cage, I am not sure I walk well. I feel so weak, I have never felt this weakened in my life. How can we escape if we cannot run far, they will come after us, and then catch us or kill us." Yandalla shook her head.

"Oaken will not let that happen, we must not give up, we are Undine, and we need to fight and keep fighting."

She looked to Sintalla, who was sleeping, she knew Shellena was right, she had been feeling weaker for a few days now. She had no energy at all, which she had thought was her hunger, but Shellena was right, she knew there was no way she could run.

As the cart rocked onto the bumpy stones and hard surface, the canvass sheet at the side of her moved, and her eyes glanced sideways. The large black cat slipped under and walked towards her along the bars, Yandalla felt her heart beat quicken, as she recognised Vesta. Vesta morphed into her female form and smiled, she crouched low and whispered.

"How are you Yandalla?" She licked her dry lips.

"We are weak, we have not eaten for more than day, and we need water." Vesta smiled.

"Your father has found it harder as the soldiers are sleeping at the sides of the carts as well as underneath them. Yandalla, Oaken is waiting at the edge of the dessert, and your father is with him, they are planning a way to get you free." Yandalla felt the air catch in her throat.

"I have missed them, but I am not sure I can do anything if they get me out. I cannot go alone, these are my sisters, I cannot leave them, but we are too weak to do anything." Vesta smiled at her.

"Then we will have to do something about that, and Oaken will find a way." Yandalla tried to smile.

"He has always been there for me." Vesta reached into the cage and took hold of her hand, and gave it a soft squeeze.

"Do not worry, but prepare yourself, try moving around to get your body working, and I will see you get what you need. I have to go, the darkness will soon be here and I need to return to Oaken, but fear not Yandalla, and your sisters, we will get all of you free."

Vesta smiled as she let go of her hand and morphed back into a black cat, Yandalla watched as she walked to the end of the sheet and watched outside, with a soft growl, she jumped from the cart, and sped off away from the convoy.

Yandalla gripped the bars and lifted herself up to her feet, she was unstable, but she knew, she had to prepare, and that meant moving more. She looked at all the others who had been watching and listening to Vesta.

"You heard her, we have to do everything we can to be ready."

All of them nodded and shakily got to their feet, they were dirty and smelt, and yet, even though their bodies hurt, they gritted their teeth, and slowly began to walk around the cage.

Shade sat weaving the tall grass that grew up the rocky slope and all around her. She sat back against the rock wall on a ledge slightly hidden by a low spiky bush, and worked the grasses together making a long pouch. On the floor in front of her was a large pile of milk berries she had gathered, and she needed a bag to carry them in. She had eaten many berries, and was now chewing on a stick of dried meat, when Vesta arrived and walked into her space. She sat back against the rock at her side, and morphed back into her human form.

"I expected you lower down." Shade nodded.

"Need food, it here." Shade lifted a strip of dried meat and handed it her; Vesta took it and bit a large chunk off and chewed.

"They are weak and hungry, I fear if we get them out, they

will not be able to travel far, and with the large numbers of Summanu, it will be hard for all of us." Shade nodded.

"Me know places Summanu find hard follow us." Vesta nodded.

"Yes, but those are close to the falls, Oaken wants them before that."

"Me know." She smiled as she glanced at Vesta.

"I take food, then make strong." Vesta looked at the milk berries, she knew the potency of them.

"All the carts are covered in large sheets, Yandalla's has a long cut on the top down the centre. Each cart has two drivers, so we will have to be careful, because the cart drivers behind could see us." Shade twisted the grasses in her hand.

"You go Oaken and Ria, talk, me get food to them." Vesta shook her head.

"We should stick together; I am not sure being alone is wise." Shade shrugged.

"Me like Caltha, better on own."

"Shade, it is dangerous, I would be happier if it was both of us." Shade smiled.

"Oaken need word of sister, you go." Vesta sat back, she knew Shade was right, but she felt very uncomfortable about the idea, Shade noticed her unease and gave a chuckle.

"Caltha not carry bag, me will. You go Oaken, me better on own."

They sat and ate together, as the time slipped past, and Shade continued to weave as the light faded. When it was dark enough, Vesta turned to Shade.

"Be careful, do not take risks you do not need to. I admire you Shade, you have been loyal to Oaken and served him well, so please, take great care, and I will see you soon my friend." Shade smiled in the darkness.

"Me friend Caltha. You good." Vesta pulled her into a hug, and Shade lifted her hand and patted Vesta on the back, Vesta parted with a smile.

"As soon as Oaken knows I will head straight back, stay low and stay safe." Shade nodded.

"Me will."

She stood and watched with her keen eyes, as Vesta morphed into her cat form again, and then turned and ran at high speed down the rough path, back towards where she knew the others were waiting. Shade turned on her rock and looked out across the desert where a long line of small lamps burned in the darkness, it would not be long before they passed by, and so she needed to get ready.

322

Chapter Twenty Six

Night Raid

Hidden deep with the valleys, covered in trees, there was a large open space, which was an amphitheatre, carved from the rock, in front of which, was a large semi circular flat area. In the centre of flat stage like area, there were five chairs of heavily carved wood, all of which were a great age. Aisie sat in the centre, to her left sat Zeron, with his brother Lexan, and to her right Almae and then Shengara.

The people of Leyarken were all gathered, and listened as Aisie told the story of the Undine people, and how the men of Andalan had survived, which came as a big relief to many of the Leyarken. The story of Oatin of Andalyn, was told by Shengara, who filled in the details of Oatin's life, his sister, and how through her, he took the sword and became Oaken of the four winds. The people of Leyarken sat astounded, and yet happy, they had been great friends with the Andalan's who had helped them many times.

The Summanu had spread the rumour that every life of Andalan had been taken and the race wiped away forever, and Balathral had even boasted that he was now the owner of the sword and the four books of the winds, which the Leyarken now understood to be a lie. As Shengara finished, Aisie rose from her chair, and walked forward to the very centre of the stage where she could be seen by all.

"My people, we have all sat today and listened carefully to Lord Shengara, and feel his pain at seeing the destruction of his land and his people. The Undine under the command of Lord Shengara once saved our people from the Summanu, and we swore a union with the Undine to be forever linked. I am your leader, and Lord Shengara is my life mate, such is the power of the bonds we have forged." The whole of the circle was absolutely silent; she smiled as she looked around.

"We have reached a turning point in the history of our people. The Summanu aims to rule all of this land, including the jungles of Leyarken, which Balathral has threatened to burn down to ensure no Leyarken lives. My people, the Andalan, the Shodalt, the Keytan, and now the Undine, soon it will be Leyarken unless we act." One man at back stood up, and looked down on Aisie.

"Leader Aisie, Balathral has been threatening to burn us out for years, and yet he has not done so, how can we be sure that he will?" Aisie gave a gentle nod.

"It is a fair question Fallat, but look at his behaviour. After the death of his father, he swore the Andalan would fall, and cursed the lands of the Undine. Andalan lies empty this day apart from a company of guards, Shodalt, a land we did good trade with for foods of the earth, is now a barren wasteland, and most of Keytan is filled with slave camps. Now Undinalashka is filled with the dead of their people. My people, we are the only ones left who are free to live as we choose, you can sit in denial all you wish, but I am telling you, it will not be long before the flames of the Summanu rage through our lands." Fallat sat down as others turned to look at him, Shengara got up out of his seat.

"People of Leyarken, I once lived amongst you with my people, and like my people, we shared many common bonds, especially in the way we hold family above all other things. What you do not know, is that Sarka, who was the saviour of the Andalan, her daughter Yandalla is now a prisoner on her way to Salanula, where she will stand at the top of the steps of blood and be sacrificed with all of the other Undine women to Bharl. People of Leyarken, know this, Sarka was joined in a union to my grandson Pallum, Yandalla is half Undine, she is my great granddaughter and I need your help to join with Oaken of the four winds, her brother, and save her."

The whole place was silent, and Shengara took a deep breath, as thousands of pairs of eyes looked at him. Aisie felt his deep worry, and her hand slid out and found his. She took it and gave it a squeeze, and he put down his head, he felt that he had failed. Aisie turned to him and saw him with his head lowered, she took a deep breath.

"It would be my honour to fight at your side my husband." Shengara lifted his head and turned to her, and she smiled.

"It is time for the white panther to show her allegiance, and honour the pact we made many years ago." Behind her, their daughter stood up.

"I too will fight with you." Zeron stood up.

"I am already fighting and my life mate Vesta is already out there at the side of Oaken fighting. My teeth will taste the blood of the Summanu." Lexan stood up.

"Mine too." Shengara turned to see them, and bowed to them, and behind him other voices rang out, as members of Leyarken stood up from their seats.

"We will fight at the side of our lord of high honour."

It began as a wave, as others stood and shouted out their commitment, men and women alike, and Shengara stood lost for words as he saw most of the Leyarken stand with shouts of support. Aisie squeezed his hand, as she smiled.

"I believe you have what you came for, and if you can command them, you will have an army of great power." Shengara gave a nod.

"We need one, what I ask of everyone from every race is great, for many will fall with the hope that all of the peoples of Pangela survive in their hearts."

As the Leyarken rose to stand with Shengara, on the far side of Andalan, Shade looked down as carts slowly came through the gap in the rocks. She watched carefully in the darkness, and when she saw the cart with the ripped canvass top, as light as a cat, she dropped quietly wrapped in her black cloak, on to it.

The soft thud alerted the women below, and they sat up, Yandalla looked up at the hole, where on previous nights she had watched the stars, and she saw two eyes looking down on her. A voice whispered in Undine.

"Ca Baska." She rose to her legs, and stood below the torn canvass in the darkness.

"Ca Baska, Yen ae Yun?"

"Ae yan, Dar len eah ae lune." Yandalla took a deep breath, and smiled.

"Ae yan, Yandalla." A woven bag came through the hole, and lowered down to her, and Shade spoke Undine.

"Yandalla, I am with your brother, I bring food and water, he is here, and will soon come for you."

Yandalla bit her lip as she took the bag, she felt the feelings, but no tears came to her eyes. Holding the bag, she handed it to Shellena, as a large water sink came next, and she felt utterly lost for words, because in truth, her need for water was like a torture. She took it and pulled out the cork and took several greedy gulps, and gasped as she handed it to Sintalla. The two eyes watched her.

"Be brave, and be strong, you have milk berries, eat them, and you will feel the power of life in you once more. Be ready, we will come fast." The eyes moved, and Yandalla spoke out quickly.

"Please wait... Mentee, we are in your debt." The eyes looked like they smiled.

"I was once a captive of a Summanu, you will not suffer my fate, I will make sure of it."

Around Yandalla, Shellena was handing berries, and dried strips of meat, as the water skin was passed around, Yandalla stood looking up as the eyes moved away and she stared at the hundreds of stars high above her, through the tear in the canvass. Lost for a moment as hope washed through her for the first time in many days.

After a few moments she turned and saw how happy everyone was, she sat in her corner and Shellena handed her, her share of the food. Yandalla looked at it and felt the pain in her stomach. She lifted a milk berry and placed it on her tongue, and felt the moisture rush to her mouth, and closing her eyes she bit down, and the berry popped, spraying its juice into her throat. Yandalla gave a soft moan, as she chewed and swallowed, and there was a slight giggle, she opened her eyes to see Sintalla smiling.

"Wonderful, isn't it? All my life I have seen these berries, and yet never bothered to pick them. Here in this cage, it has become a sacred berry, and if I live, I will eat one every day for the rest of my life." She smiled, and Yandalla swallowed.

"Every time I eat one for the rest of my life, I will think of my brother. The wind is coming my sisters, eat and grow strong, he will need us."

Sat in the darkness, Ria watched through her scope as the carts came closer. They rolled down the road in a long line, the first carts were half empty and filled with what was left of their supplies. Oaken stood in the trees and watched them as they rolled past, and then looked down towards the river, where he could see people unloading them. It made little sense to him, as once they unloaded, they turned around and then headed back up the road past them, and headed back towards the edge of the desert. He turned and looked at Ham.

"That makes no sense, why do they unload on the edge of the river, and then head back and stop on this side of the road?" Ham was watching them with equal interest.

"I cannot say for sure, but I am starting to wonder if the river is not becoming some sort of camp. They have tents and things on the other side, and I think this side will be another camp for those returning from the desert." It made some sort of sense, after all, it appeared that withdrawing soldiers from Shodalt and the desert, would need some place to rest and prepare for the long road to Salanula.

The time appeared to drag, as eventually the carts loaded with cages came down the road and pulled in close to the mountain side of the road. Oaken looked at the line of carts with canvass covered cages, and he could not believe how long the line was. Ria came up at his side as he looked at the line with each cart holding a blazing torch in a holder, at the side of the front seat. The horses were given bags filled with straw, and then the men who drove the carts walked down the road towards what was fast becoming a camp.

"Do they leave them unattended?" Oaken gave a shrug.

"I am not sure, I hope so, it will make our job easier."

By the time Pallum returned, it was almost midnight, and a large force of soldiers had marched wearily out of the dessert and down towards the river, where they all stripped and walked into the water and bathed. Oaken was ready to move, and came out of the trees and made his way quietly through the grass, to where two hundred Undine lay in wait. Pallum pointed at the carts, which still had canvass covers on them, a guard had been set, which was around forty soldiers who sauntered around not really paying that much attention. Pallum pointed at two of the guards, who wore unforms that were a little different.

"Vesta tells us that those two are the men who can open the cages." Ham looked at him.

"They have keys?" Pallum gave a smile.

"I know not what keys are, but if it is the metal that opens the doors, then yes, they have them."

Ham gave a nod and smiled, that would greatly help his cause. The one thing that everyone noticed, was the smell, it was stomach churning as the gentle breeze blew across from the carts towards them. Ham eyed the two men carefully.

"Shoot those two first, we need their keys, it will make the job faster." Ria was at Oaken's side, she touched his arm, and whispered.

"Are you nervous?" His eyes were fixed on the long row of carts.

"I am not sure if it is nerves or fear, if I do not get her out, she will be lost forever. I have to get her Ria; I cannot let my mother down." She understood.

"Shade is out there somewhere, and she will be with us, trust in us Oaken, tonight Yandalla will be freed from the cage." He nodded, and took a really deep breath.

"I will be fine once we start, I hate this waiting around."

When the cart stopped, Yandalla looked around the cage, she could hear the drivers talking, they were leaving. She pulled out the dagger and with all her might thrust it down into the wooden plank at her feet.

"My sisters, let us prepare, if we want freedom, now is the time to act." She heaved on the knife, and the board lifted, Sintalla was at her side to try and help her lift it. Both of them heaved, as the others watched, and the board lifted up. Shellena tried to get her fingers under it.

"Yandalla, the metal spikes are long, it has to come up more to lift out." Yandalla strained as she pulled with all her might, the boards of the floor were much thicker than they realised, and they needed it to be a lot higher before it would lift free. Sintalla shook her head.

"It is useless, we need something longer to prize it out, and we have nothing." Yandalla gave a desperate sigh, and the board slid back.

The wait was hard, as Oaken fixed his eyes on the three carts in front, of which he knew somewhere inside the middle one, was his sister. The guard with the yellow feather on his hat walked slowly along the line checking on each of the guards. Pallum was ready with a long line of archers, the guard passed the gap in front of the cage containing Yandalla, and suddenly, he was dragged back out of view, as Shade struck hard killing him.

That was the signal they were waiting for, as the long line of Undine archers lifted out of the grass and fired with pin point accuracy, and all the guards fell dead. Before they hit the floor the team was crossing the road heading at speed for the carts. Shade came into view as Oaken got closer, she smiled and threw him the key on a ring of steel, then jumped up onto the back of the cart, and pulled up the sheet.

Yandalla was alert, as she heard strange grunts and the soft patter of feet. The canvass got pulled up, and she jerked. The dark cloaked figure of Shade climbed the bars and tugged the cover higher, and then her heart almost broke as she saw him, and her voice almost died in her throat.

"Oaken!"

Ham was at his side as both of them climbed up, Ham took hold of the lock and inserted the key, as all of the other women began to get up, but Yandalla was frozen, her eyes filling with tears as Oaken smiled, and the door opened. He came into the cage and snatched into his arms, and she could hardly breathe as her tears flowed onto her face.

"Yandalla, I am here."

Her arms came up and she felt him, and just folded around him, her emotions flowing up through her, as he squeezed the life out of her. Behind them Ham tossed the key to Elden.

"Get the others out."

Ria was busy helping the women with stiff legs out of the cage and down onto the floor, where Undine warriors, quickly moved them over the road and into the grass. Half the Undine kept watch with their bows loaded, as Pallum sent others with Ham to open the cage and free all of their people. He arrived at the cage as Oaken hugged Shellena, Oaken turned as Pallum stood on the floor and dragged Yandalla out of the cage and into his arms, he held her so tight as tears filled his eyes, and spoke the quiet words of the love of a father. Shellena wiped her eyes and looked at Oaken.

"She never doubted you; she believed from the moment they

took us; you would come for her." Oaken gave a smile.

"We are not free yet, we still have to get away, and there are a lot of soldiers to avoid." He held her as she stepped down and Pallum released Yandalla.

"Stay with Oaken, I have to free the others, do not leave his side." She nodded with a smile.

"I will Anna Pa." He nodded, pulled up his black hood, and turned to head back to the others, Shade tapped Ria on the shoulder.

"We go, no time." Ria nodded at her, and reached out for Oaken's hand.

"We have to go Oaken; we need to get further up the road."

Along the line Ham and Elden, were freeing up the others, who were not in a good way, many of them were far too weak to walk, Elden turned to an Undine Warrior.

"They will not make it unless they have transport, use the empty carts, get everyone on them, and then go."

It made sense, and soon the warriors were carrying their weak and exhausted women quickly over to the carts in the darkness, and lifting them on. Those who had enough strength to walk helped them, and as each cart was filled, a warrior took the seat, and the carts rolled into the grass and headed away from the road.

The alarm was raised when a group of Summanu soldiers came out of the desert, and screamed out the battle call. Down by the river, the Summanu realised what was happening, and came up the road towards them, and the Undine warriors let fly their arrows.

Oaken was between the carts and the rocks with Shade and Ria, as he moved quickly holding Yandalla by the hand. Behind them, Shellena and Sintalla held the hands of Meda and Caleb, who were helping them. Shade looked back as Elden appeared with Ham.

Two Summanu came through the gap between two carts, and Shade, pulled out her sword and swept it through the darkness, and there was a resounding ring as the blades met. Oaken pulled his sword, behind him Elden and Ham both battled as he looked back. Yandalla looked scared, Summanu were coming up behind them, in front of him Shade sliced with aggression, taking out one of the guards and lunged at the other. Sintalla snatched a sword from the floor, that had been discarded by a dead soldier, she looked back, and pushed Yandalla and Shellena on.

It was getting chaotic, fighting in the total darkness was not easy, guards came out of nowhere, and it was impossible to move out onto the road. Elden yelled to keep going straight from the back, as he fought another soldier who had appeared from behind the carts. Holding his sword with Ria at his side, and pulling Yandalla behind him, as Shade slashed her way forward just in front, she glanced back.

"Road not safe, bad, we move on rocks." She turned slightly, and pointed.

"Know path, we go."

There was no time for debate, as Summanu soldiers were everywhere, fighting with the Undine, the roadway across to the tall grass land was out of the question. One more Summanu stepped out and Oaken lunged at him, catching him off guard. He let go of Yandalla's hand, as he clashed with another appearing soldier. Sintalla slashed wildly, hacking into another behind them. Oaken looked back.

"Ria, get her out of here."

He gritted his teeth and swung his blade around taking out another one. Ria took Yandalla's hand, and pulled her. Shade stood at the start of the path that headed up into the rocks, and slid up her bow as Ria came forward with Yandalla, she loaded the bow and held it up marking her targets, as the small group moved swiftly onto the path.

"Go, go quick!"

Ria had no need to be told, she pulled at Yandalla who was looking back and watching her brother fight beside Elden and Ham. Ria had her bow loaded, as she walked backwards in the darkness, she gave a soft smile at Yandalla.

"He is fine I am watching him, now move, and get up in front to safety."

Meda and Caleb pulled the other two up with them, and Oaken with Elden moved back onto the path. Across the road in the small light in the flickering cart torches, the Undine fired volleys of arrows into the Summanu. Oaken caught up, as Shade shot passed them, and took hold of Yandalla's hand.

"Come, move, need get far." She nodded, her face filled with fear, and together with Ria they turned, and moved quickly up the track, and were swallowed into the darkness.

Pallum was pushing the walking captives in the direction of a place they had prepared, the carts were rolling quickly and were packed with the weakened members, and were moving quickly ahead. A large group of Undine warriors took up the rear and with bows and swords they fought off the Summanu, as they retreated as quickly as they could. The darkness hampered the Summanu, who were at the mercy of the sharp night vision of the Undine, who were shooting with precise strikes. They retreated quickly.

Oaken had no time to think, he rushed up the slope, almost dragging Yandalla and Ria with him. His mind was filled with nothing more than getting all of them away as fast as he could, and they had come quite far up the path. High above the road, the rock moved backwards onto a wide shelf, and Yandalla staggered and stumbled.

"Oaken, wait, I am struggling."

His heart was pounding in his chest, as the adrenaline pumped inside him, he slowed his pace, and realised he was gasping for air. He looked back into what was a vast darkness, and could see the pale face of Yandalla, and behind her Shellena and Sintalla.

"Shade, we need a moment." She stopped and looked back at them all gasping for air, she gave a nod towards him.

"We rest, short time." Oaken stopped as Yandalla was there in front of him, breathing hard and gasping in air. Ria came close and slipped her arm round him as she breathed hard.

"Well, you did it, what now?" He took a huge gulp of air in.

"Shade, where are we; I cannot see a thing?"

"Andalan." He turned to her, and frowned.

"What?" He could just about see her face, under her hood.

"Up there Andalan, round big rock, Ranblate, down Shodalt, and soldiers."

"Where are Pallum and the others, I thought we were all together?"

"We cut off, no choice. Undine down there, we no safe, so here." Oaken looked at Ria.

"The plan was to stay together."

"How Oaken, they came at us from both ends, if we had run onto the road, we would all be dead? I don't think we had much choice. Oaken, Yandalla is free, that was our goal, and we did it, be honest, it was never going to be easy." He was not sure, he had planned to take her straight home, and then set off back to Andalan.

"This is not what I wanted, we are now between the eastern and western forces of the Summanu, and to add to that they hold Andalan. Ria we are a small group cut off from everyone, what do we do now?"

"Pallum told us Shengara is heading to Leyarken, why don't we catch him up, he will have supplies and soldiers?" Oaken felt a soft warm hand slide into his.

"Oaken, you are on Andalan, this is your home, this is where you were born. Oaken, you should be here." He turned to her, and she smiled in the darkness.

"This right place for you Oaken." He gave a sigh.

"But I promised to take you home, mother is hurting, she needs to see you." Yandalla gave a smile.

"I want to see Anna Ma, but that will come later, this is home in your heart, you need to walk here. The wind says walk here." Shade shuffled feet.

"Rest over, we walk now."

The three freed captives were tired, even though they had eaten, they were not as strong as they would normally be. Most of their strength had been borne out of fear, which helped motivate them. Guided by Shade, they walked on into the darkness away from Pallum and the Undine, as they retreated across the grassland of the western edge of Shodalt. The Undine were heading back towards the edges of the Heliospan Desert, and the outer reaches of Undinalashka.

In the darkness it was impossible to see the black cloaked Undine, and the order was given for the Summanu to stop and wait. The officers of the Summanu knew they had some of their carts, and so they were leaving a clear trail, so they held back their army. and prepared their equipment to start the search as soon as the sun rose.

Predicting that, Pallum left one hundred of his men at the rear, and led the other one hundred with the carts and the captives towards the desert in the direction of home. He was going to go via a vast lake on the edge of Shodalt, to take up water and organise better. Out of the two thousand, he had just over eight hundred captives freed, but they were nowhere near prepared enough for the long harsh desert, and so he needed time to work out, how he would get his people home safe.

It felt like they had been walking all night when Vesta appeared, she had been with Pallum helping him, and had returned to the carts, then tracked them up the mountain pass and caught them up. They stopped beneath a large overhang, and Yandalla and her friends collapsed onto the floor absolutely exhausted. Ria passed out dried bread and meat strips, and they all drank from the water skins.

Oaken sat at Yandalla's side, placed his pack against the wall, and leaned back on it. He covered Yandalla with his cloak.

"Try to sleep and get your energy back, we have some tough days ahead of us. I have clean clothes for you if you want them." She shook her head.

"Oaken, I am dirty, I need to wash, then I will change my clothes." He gave a smirk.

"Yes, I was not thinking, we will find water tomorrow, and you can get clean."

In the darkness, Shade sat above them all on the rocks, eating berries and chewing on a meat leather, Vesta walked up and sat beside her. Shade lifted a meat strip and handed it to her.

"Eat, need strong." Vesta gave a chuckle and took it.

"Pallum asked me to thank you, he told me he was sorry that he angered you. Yandalla is his daughter and he is very grateful to you for helping Oaken get her free." Shade nodded.

"He Shen tey, but me thinks good man." Vesta gave a chuckle.

"He was a little surprised at the speed you took him down, he was very impressed with your abilities." Shade gave a shrug, and bit into her dried meat.

"Life danger, Anna Ma knew, taught good."

"Shade, how did your mother end up in Shodalt, you know, it is clear she was a skilled Undine warrior by what she taught you, why did she leave her people?" It was an understandable question, and one she had been asked before.

"Anna Ma told when was young, she wanted help people. They sick, she make better." Vesta nodded, it was understandable, Shade sat back.

"Anna Ma say, no want life Undine give, she say, she want see all lands, learn people."

In a strange way it made sense to Vesta, to a degree she had been the same, which was why her and Zeron had travelled often to meet with Ria and see the other lands. Vesta gave a soft sigh, she could feel the powerful emotions inside Shade, her voice was soft.

"You must miss her Shade, it cannot of have been easy growing up alone." Shade gave a gentle nod.

"Me miss big, big hurt inside, is why help Oaken, he miss big too."

Shade and Vesta sat side by side as in the east the Sun started to rise, as the first light came over the horizon on the far side of Shodalt. Below them, Ria was curled around Oaken fast asleep, next to Yandalla and her two Undine warriors, Meda was snuggled into Sintalla. Far below them, the Summanu emptied the cages of those Undine who had not been freed, and they were chained together, then marched down to the river, where the men jeered and whistled, as they were stripped naked, and pushed into the water to wash.

Teams of Shodalt prisoners, were ordered to fill buckets, and then scrub the cages free of all the filth. The terrified and weakened Undine, cowered as they washed, as all the men looked down upon them, and they were then taken onto the bank and handed new clean robes of red. They were fed a good meal, and then loaded into the clean wet cages, ready to be taken to Salanula to be sacrificed to the glory of Bharl.

The Undine walked all night and by dawn they were far ahead of any Summanu. They reached the edge of a small lake, where the freed Undine got to wash, and Undine warriors collected food from the wilds to feed them. Pallum stood alone and looked back to the mountains of Andalan.

"Take care of each other my children, I have sent word to your mother that you live. Walk with the winds and return to me safely, it is time the winds returned to Andalan."

Chapter Twenty Seven
A Needed Friend

Yandalla woke up, and turned over to see Oaken fast asleep, his arms around Ria, and she was snuggled into his chest. She lay for a few moments simply watching, for so long he had been lonely, and to see him with Ria gave her great joy.

Eventually she noticed movement and turned, Ham was up and had made a circle of stones that he had built up, in which was a fire, over which he was cooking something. She saw the meat drip into the flames, and her mouth watered, as she licked the inside of her mouth. She sat up and he noticed her, and gave a smile.

"Good morning." Yandalla sat, pulled off the cloak and rose to her feet slowly, she was stiff and ached, she gave a small bow.

"Ca Baska." He gave another smile as she walked over to the fire.

"I am Yandalla, I do not know you... Sorry." Ham gave a little chuckle.

"They call me Ham, I take it you are hungry, would you like some, Vesta has provided more than we will eat today?" Yandalla nodded with a smile.

"Mentee." He cut off a large slice, and plopped it onto a wooden plate, and held it up to her, she took it gratefully.

"Tac yeat." She gave a little bow, which was the Undine custom, and a token of thanks.

Yandalla stood and looked out at the land below her, and in the distance across what looked like miles of soft white sand, she could just about see a faint outline of what was the mountain that had been her home for all of her life. She stared at it as she bit off a chunk of the freshly cooked meat and began to chew. It was a place for a while she had thought she would never see again, and she felt a deep stirring inside her, her soft whispered words in Undine unheard by the others.

"Home, where my Anna ma waits for me."

As she chewed from somewhere above her, Shade appeared.

She came down the rocks and walked up to Yandalla. Shade stood and watched her with great curiosity. Yandalla turned and smiled, Shade gave a gasp as she saw her deep green eyes, and she smiled a wide smile, and patted her chest.

"Like me." Yandalla frowned, and Shade nodded looking excited.

"Me thought only one, you like me." Understanding she smiled, and spoke in her Undine tongue.

"Anna Ma Andalan, Anna Pa Undine." Shade gave a broad smile, and tapped her chest again.

"Anna Ma Undine, Anna Pa Shodalt. Me more Undine." Shade lifted her hand and softly touched Yandalla on the cheek, where she had been cut, and Yandalla could see the curiosity in her, as Shade's eyes filled with tears.

"I am Yandalla, flower of meadow, daughter of Pallum and Sarka, Sister of Oaken. My spirit is blessed to be before you." Shade gave a sniffle, and took a deep breath, and nodded.

"Ae yan, Dar len eah ae lune." She took a deep breath, and then stood tall and proud, and spoke in the common tongue, as she patted her chest.

"Daughter of Yendee, of Shodalt, and Ae Lune yan, of Undine." Yandalla gave a soft bow.

"Tac yeat, you saved me, I owe my life to yours, we are sisters." Shade gave a serious nod and bowed back, and both of them smiled. Yandalla looked down at her top, splattered with food, mud, and blood.

"I am dirty and unclean." Shade nodded.

"Me know good place, can clean." Ham gave a giggle, as he sat chewing, he had never seen Shade act in the remotest bit female, and yet around Yandalla, she suddenly appeared quite girlie.

It had been a long hard night, and most of them slept well past dawn and into the morning. Ham took up a watch on the trail back down to the road, but nothing appeared to be following them. In the darkness they had been lucky to get away unseen behind the carts.

Once they were all awake and fed, which gave them all renewed energy, Shade led the way, and after a longish walk in the heating day as the sun burned onto the rocks, they arrived at a series of pools on the eastern side of the rock, that looked out over Ranblate far below them.

Shade took over almost as if she was mothering the Undine, and soon, Yandalla, Shellena, Sintalla and the two children sat up to their necks in the warmish water and washed themselves thoroughly. Shade even helped them wash their hair with a bar of waxy soap she had in her bag. Ria sat back soaking with Oaken in a pool not far away, and she smiled.

"Shade appears to be taking her role of caring for our new charges seriously, she is quite motherly in the way she is helping them." Oaken smiled.

"She has been alone for a long time; I suppose for her; this must feel like belonging to something she was raised to be. She is far more Undine than Shodalt." He watched as Yandalla leaned her head back, and Shade helped wash her hair.

"Yandalla is quiet, I have never known her to be this silent, she has always been loud and happy, there is a sadness to her I have never seen, it worries me." Ria looked over.

"She has been through a bad time Oaken, and she and her friends have suffered. She is thin and very pale, she needs to rest, give her time, she will not recover from this quickly, she will need to find her feet again." He gave a slight nod, he understood that.

"She looks so thin, well, they all do, I need to find a place where she can rest and eat again to put back what she has lost."

"We will, and I am sure in Shade's care, she will recover quickly."

Caleb and Meda helped wash the soiled clothes of the three Undine, and spread them out on the rocks to dry in the hot sun, The two Undine borrowed the cloaks of Ria and Oaken, and sat warm in the sunshine, as Yandalla dressed in new clean clothes of pants and a new long top. Ria handed her a brush to do her hair and helped do the back, Yandalla' hair was long and fell right down her back, as was customary in Undine culture, she was interested in Ria.

"You are with Oaken; you are his women?" Ria gave a nod.

"I am with your brother, yes." Yandalla gave a smile.

"It is good he has you; he has been alone too long. You know good yan tee to make him happy?" Ria stumbled on her words, and gasped, as her cheeks went red.

"I have joined with him, yes." Yandalla gave an approving nod.

"He not have any before, I hope he made your yan tee happy?"

Ria looked down going redder, the Undine were very natural in their approaches to life, and she did not know what to say. Shade giggled, as she helped dry Sintalla's hair.

"Me heard them, both good, both happy yan tee." Ria looked shocked.

"You listened?" Shade nodded.

"Good yan tee, noisy, was good." Ria did not know where to look, Yandalla gave a soft chuckle.

"I am pleased Ria and Oaken are happy, I want that for him." Ria took a breath, and tried to smile to hide her deep embarrassment.

"I have come to care for him deeply, I want him to be happy Yandalla, and I want that to be with me." Yandalla turned, and looked across to him where he sat with Elden and Ham looking at the map.

"He helps everyone, but never himself, my brother is Shen tey at times, and forgets he has to live as well." Shade nodded.

"Big shen tey, me thought he never yan tee with Ria. Me glad he did."

Ria gave a soft smile, and would much rather they talk about something else, but she was also glad that Yandalla accepted her, she had worried she would not, after all, both of them were very close.

Oaken sat with Elden and Ham, as he looked at the map and traced his finger along the eastern fork, and a mountainous region that was a large wide land mass with two long forks on either side. He pointed to the area between the forks.

"Ranblate was created by those fleeing the other lands, my mother has spoken often of the times my father tried to convince them to leave with him. My mother told me, they refused, and after that time the area became lawless and wild." Ham gave a nod of understanding.

"I have heard many things about this place, not many of them good, from what I have heard it has become a den of exploitation, where everything is for sale. The Apostles are hated, but it is well known that they send in traders to buy children for them to misuse. To be honest, we have their money, so we can get anything we need, and we need supplies, but my concern is this proclamation from Balathral. He has named all Undine as not human, and he has offered to pay a lot of money for them, and we have four with us." Elden scratched his head.

"The problem is Andalan is a big place, and it has been unoccupied for a long time, there will be no supplies, and without the growing plateaus, I doubt we will find many plants to eat. There are plenty of rock goats and wild sheep, or at least there used to be before the Summanu took over the place."

It was a difficult situation, there was no real hope of taking Yandalla back home, but Oaken was afraid to move on to Andalan and risk her life again. The second problem was they needed supplies, but the only place he could get those was Ranblate, but again, that would risk the lives of Yandalla and her two friends. He felt caught in a trap, because deep down inside he had this powerful feeling that something was calling him back to the temple. He sat back and looked at them both.

"It feels like whatever we do, we walk into some form of trap. Ranblate is as dangerous, as is Andalan. We cannot get back to Undinalashka, as the only two paths through the dessert are filled with Summanu, and even if we do, Undinalashka is now also full of Summanu. We have nowhere to go, we are here and we are surrounded with Summanu, and I do not know which way to go, what do I do?" Elden shook his head.

"You are not seeing this right, Oaken, I understand your concerns, we have just freed Yandalla, which is how we got here, but I do not believe this is the end. Oaken, you are the holder of the sword, even unpolished, which to be honest, you really need to do at some point. Look, we are on the edge of the place we were born, a place our parents fought for, and I know it might be dangerous, but Oaken, we owe it to every Andalan to walk in our home once again." Oaken gave a sigh.

"Elden, I know that, but what if it is crawling with soldiers, I owe it to Yandalla to keep her safe." Ham took a deep breath inward.

"Oaken, we understand that, but answer me one question, how?" Oaken frowned and shook his head.

"What do you mean how?" Ham looked him right in the eyes.

"How are you going to keep her safe? Oaken, every land apart from Leyarken is swarming with soldiers. Leyarken will not last long unless defended, there is no place on Pangela that is safe, and it won't be until the Summanu are defeated." Oaken, felt caught out, and voiced his thoughts without really realising.

"How can I risk her; I just got her back, and I need her to return home with me?"

"What choice do you have?" He turned, and saw Ria stood just behind him, she smiled.

"Oaken, you cannot walk away from your destiny because you fear for your sister. The truth is, we have all been in danger since we left the safety of the boat. Our parents and families are in danger in their own homes, that is what Balathral wants, which is to rule all of Pangela with fear. You are the owner of the sword, it is up to you to know as to what you will do with it, for that is your task, but if you want my thoughts, I will give them. I think you need to go to the temple and return the spirit of Nuada to it, I love you, and even though it could mean death for both of us, I aim to walk at your side as you do it."

He felt the pressure mounting on him, and he wished he could talk to his mother or Eliaston, he knew they would be able to advise him well. He stood up and looked at the group.

"I need to think." They all understood, and watched him as he walked away.

Oaken walked to the edge of the rock and looked out over the desert, and the miles of high dunes of sand, he took a deep breath and tried to clear his mind of his thoughts, inside he was in turmoil. He closed his eyes and tried to focus and clear his mind, he had so many doubts, and he knew his father would know the answer, but he was long gone, and he felt alone, lost, and unable to move forward.

He took deep breaths, and simply breathed in the world around him, as he tried to remember every conversation, he had with Eliaston. Behind him, the gravel on the rock crunched, and he heard her soft quiet voice.

"Oaken." He turned, and Yandalla stood looking sad.

"Oaken you are sad, why are you sad because I am feeling better and happy to be here?" He gave a sigh.

"I have a lot on my mind; I was thinking of home." She came forward, and like she always had, she put her arms around him and snuggled into him.

"I do not want you sad, you have Ria, and she is nice, you should not be sad Oaken." He looked down at the top of her head, and she looked up at him, and she gave a soft smile.

"I missed you Oaken." He nodded, and slid his arms around her holding her tight.

"I missed you too, I am sorry it took so long to get you, I wanted to be there for you sooner." She smiled.

"I knew you would come; I could feel it."

"I would not let you or mother down, and I promised her I would bring you home." She gave a happy sigh, and snuggled more into him.

"Anna Ma will be happy to know you helped us all get free." He breathed in.

"I do not think we got everyone, Pallum released a lot, but many were sick, and could not walk away. Vesta told me there are still others who got left behind, and are still captive. Yandalla, a lot of our people were captured, and many at home were killed, the Undine have suffered a massacre, but we did our best to try and save as many as possible." She understood and nodded.

"Will we be able to help them Oaken? If they go to the Summanu land, they will die or become slaves, can we do nothing to help them?" He could see the concern in her eyes.

"I do not know, and I have no one who can advise me. Your great grandfather is going to go to Leyarken for help. I have thought about going there to meet him, because the way things are, we cannot get back home at the moment." She nodded.

"To go to Leyarken, won't we have to go through Andalan?"

"Yes." She smiled.

"This is where you were birthed, this is your true home, we should go, I want to see it." He frowned.

"Yandalla, it might be full of soldiers, it might not be possible." She gave a light frown at him.

"Oaken, we should try, you have to, you have to try and go to your home again, Anna Ma would be proud to know you did it. Oaken, you must talk to Nuada in the temple, Master Eliaston would want you to." He smiled, she had been quiet, but just for a moment there was that part of her he had always seen.

"I need to talk to everyone and work out what to do, Ria understands a great deal of all of the this, I know she will be helpful." Yandalla nodded, and turned to look across the camp.

"I am happy you have Ria; she was calm last night when I was afraid, I think she is like you, and that is good. Oaken, I want your bow, if we meet soldiers, I want something to defend myself, last time I only had a knife, and it was not enough. I do not want to be a burden, and I have always been better with a bow, you have two swords. Sintalla is a warrior, she fought hard when they took her, we need to find weapons for her too." He gave a nod.

"Alright, I will look into it and see what we can do." She gave a smile, but her face was so pale with the thin red line on her cut cheek, and he could see how much the strain had been on her.

It took a while to prepare, Yandalla got one bow, and Ria handed hers to Sintalla, Shellena was given a long knife, but Oaken promised he would get more weapons for everyone to ensure all of them could protect themselves.

Finally, after a long talk with Ria and Shade, and dressing the Undine women in hooded cloaks, the group set off following Shade along the edge of the ridge that looked down on Ranblate. It was not long before all of them could see the vast canyon that housed all of those who had escaped the persecution of the Summanu, and turned the region into a mixed race refugee territory. Oaken looked down as he walked with Shade.

"I know we need supplies, but it concerns me how hostile Ranblate has become, one wrong step and all of us could be killed." Shade glanced at him as she walked.

"We all get kilt one day." He frowned as he turned her.

"What do you mean, we will all get killed?" She gave a shrug.

"Age kilt, sickness kilt, soldier kilt, we all get kilt."

"Do you mean death is inevitable?" She nodded.

"We birth, live, get kilt." It surprised him to hear say that.

"Shade, you have survived all of the attacks of the Summanu, to be honest, I find you to be an incredible survivor of what I see as really hostile conditions, and yet you think death is inevitable." She gave a smile.

"Me like live, like sun, food, hoss, and yan tee, but one day, get kilt."

Oaken was not sure what to say, he looked at the floor to watch where he walked as he thought about it, it made no sense to him. Shade was the best survivor he had met, she had defied all of the odds and survived as a small girl in a world that had killed and destroyed men. She gave a little giggle at his side.

"Me live good, when old, will get kilt, life can kilt, me like life." He gave a nod of understanding.

"So, you are not looking for death, you actually like being alive?" She gave another giggle.

"Me like big." He smiled; in a strange way it pleased him to know that.

They walked on along the path, to his right the steep bank rose up to what were start of the flat plains of Andalan, to his left, the land fell away down a steep drop into Ranblate. Far ahead in the distance, which was a tiny speck, Oaken could just about make out a waterfall, which as a child his father had taken him to. The water fell a from a great height, down into the valley of Ranblate, where it formed a huge lake, that flowed into a river that snaked its way through the country below, and around the tip of Andalan, flowing at the side of the dessert towards Keytan and the sea.

It stirred his thoughts, as he remembered his father and his younger days of his first years of life. He had never forgotten his first few years living here, if anything, the memories he had of his father were even more precious to him now. After a long period of walking, they came to where the path forked, one path rose up the side of rock face, and one went down towards the territory of Ranblate.

They took a break and shared what little food they had left, they had filled their water skins at the pools, so for now had plenty to drink, but their main problem now, was to choose to head up in Andalan and possibly confront Summanu, or head down into Ranblate and trade for extra goods to keep them going for a long period.

Sintalla was interested in everything, she had never left Undinalashka, but knew all of the history of her people, she looked down the steep path.

"These people all ran away from the fight, and yet they fight each other, this makes no sense to me. If they can fight, why did they not defend their land?" She turned, her long hair hanging around her white face, her eyes the purest of white. Ria understood.

"They feel the need to protect what little they have, and so fights break out for ground and possessions." Sintalla, looked confused, and turned to look down the slope.

"That still makes no sense, they do know that the Summanu will not ignore them forever, they will come one day and wipe them all out?" She made sense, and Ria answered the only way she could.

"Sintalla, once you leave your lands, nothing makes any sense. The Summanu have destroyed everything, all of the rules that existed at one time have gone. In these lands now, the only thing that matters is survival, and that is what is happening in Ranblate, people are doing their best to survive." Sintalla shook her head.

"By killing each other, they do know that by killing each other it leaves less to defend against the Summanu, because they will come at some point?" Oaken took a drink of his water.

"My mother told me of how my father did everything he could to convince them to leave, but they refused and decided to stay where they are. It does not matter what makes sense, the truth is, they left their homes once, and do not want to leave again."

"Then they will die." Shade nodded.

"No care, think Summanu no come, they shen tey."

They sat and talked and it was agreed, the only real way to continue was to head into Ranblate to restock, once again Shade had a contact there, and so it was decided that it would be worth taking a risk, as long as the Undine stayed hidden under their cloaks. Shade estimated they would make it down just after night fall, and so they set off doing their best to keep at a fast speed, to quicken their journey.

Sintalla walked with Elden and talked of weapons and home, Ria took point with Shade, and Yandalla with Shellena walked just behind Oaken, with Meda and Caleb, who were followed by Ham. Yandalla looked at the back of Oaken.

"Oaken, why do we have to stay under the cloaks, do the people of Ranblate hate us?" He looked back as walked.

"It is not hate, Balathral has decreed that all Undine are a lower species that do not deserve to be treated as proper people, and they must be rounded up and taken to him to sacrifice to Bharl. Ranblate is a place where everything is for sale, if they see Undine, they will want to take you and sell you to Balathral. Keeping covered will protect you, as will we." She wished she had not asked as she looked at Shellena's frightened face.

Yandalla tried to smile and took her hand and held it, but she could feel the feelings of her own fear. Being in a cage was bad, but she was to a degree protected by the bars, out here in this vast open land, she knew, if someone tried, they would have to fight to the death, or be taken again.

By late evening they reached the bottom, which was still semi lit by the sun, and the day was warm. They walked on rich grass land, which was a big bonus of the large lake which seeped into all of the lands around, creating fertile pastures for crops and animals. Shade took a direct route across the land avoiding any of the small settlements, as she headed for a thick forest of broadleaved trees. Somewhere inside was a homestead, which was run by people she called friends, Bellot and Tannet.

Bellot and Tannet lived in a large wooden house deep inside the woodland. They had a large plot and took care of the trees which they worked for trade. Bellot was also a blacksmith, and he made a lot of tools for those who needed them. The rock walls of the cliffs of Andalan had many ores, which his brother Kellem mined, and sold to Bellot.

The woodland was far larger than Oaken realised, and it was almost dark when finally, they arrived at the long fence that surrounded the property. Shade led the way, but walked slowly, and Oaken remembered the careful way they had approached Ham's house back in Shodalt. It appeared these days, you simply did not walk up quickly and knock, as he would at home, out here, people shot first and asked questions later.

The group hung back a little as Shade walked slowly, and inside the house a dog started to bark, she stopped and waited. A few moments later, the door opened. and out walked a huge man with a long brown bushy beard holding up a bow, with an arrow fitted.

Shade gave a nod.

"Ca Baska Bellot." The man leaned forward his voice gruff but soft.

"Lune, is that you girl?" She smiled and gave a nod.

"Yan... Ca yan." Bellot lowered his bow, and broke into a huge smile.

"Well knock me down, I thought they would have got you by now, come here Lune, it has been way too long." Shade broke into a huge smile and ran to him, and he wrapped his huge arms around her gave her a bear like hug.

"I am so glad they did not get you; we worried about you."

With fast introductions, everyone was ushered inside quickly, it was getting dark, and Ranblate in the darkness was not safe. Bellot introduced his wife Tannet, and she flustered and wept at the same time. She put on a pan to boil, and everyone sat around what was a very large and sturdy house, and each side told their story of what had and was happening, as Tannet wiped her eyes and smiled at Shade.

Bellot and Tannet were delighted to see Lune, which was what she had been called as a child, and Tannet told the group of how they had found Lune, or Shade hiding in the woodland aged only nine summers. It was the middle of winter and she was freezing to death, she was badly beaten, as she had escaped from the apostle and thought she could hide like the others in Ranblate.

The Apostles came after her with slave hunters, and they almost had her, but she had managed to fight them off and escape through a fence, and had run for her life up to the lake and then hidden when it started to snow. When Bellot found her, she was cut and bruised and had a fever, and so he had brought her home, and Tannet nursed her back to health.

When the Apostles arrived, they hid her in a secret root cellar, and they left having found no trace of her. Shade stayed with them for two years, but the word got out that she was hiding in the woodland, and so one night she had packed her things and left to make sure Bellot and Tannet were kept safe. She slipped out of Ranblate and returned to Shodalt.

After that she joined and ran with a bandit gang for a few years, where she discovered the secret of her stone house up near the hot springs. The bandits did a big raid on a Summanu store, of which she did not take part, and all of them were killed by the Summanu. Since that time, she had lived alone, practiced her skills and devoted her life to the teachings of her mother, which was Undine, until the day she attacked the bandits who wanted to take Caleb and Meda, and as she finished, Arak appeared and attacked her, Shade smiled as she looked at Tannet.

"Oaken came, thought he want to kilt me, he not. He want save sister, and me help." Tannet smiled, and looked at Oaken.

"You watched out for her, she means a lot to us, and we are grateful. Knowing who your father was, we know now she is in safe hands." Oaken gave a small chuckle.

"To be honest, she has sort of been our protector, Shade has been true and loyal, it is us who owe her our gratitude, she has guided us faithfully and fought by our side." Ballot gave a stern nod.

"The Undine in my house are always welcome, we did a lot of trade with them in the days of our lands in Keytan. They are a good people, and we knew Lune was when we found her, you will be safe here. Be aware, there are some in these parts that would want to take you for Balathral has put a high purse on the heads of every Undine." Ria gave him a big smile.

"We are more than aware of the situation, and to be honest, we need supplies and weapons, as we are heading up to Andalan, we have gold so we can pay, we are asking for nothing we cannot buy."

Bellot looked at Tannet, and she gave a nod at him, and he turned to face the group, and gave a smile.

"We can help, there is plenty of room in the upper workshop, there is a log fired tub to wash, and we have furs and blankets, it gets cold here at night. If you hear the dog, be on your guard, and we will talk tomorrow about what supplies you need." Oaken stood up and held out his hand.

"I am grateful, we will try to stay out of sight, we do not want to cause you trouble, and once we have stores for our journey, we will be on our way." Bellot took his hand and gave it a firm shake.

"Your care of Lune means much to me, I will show my gratitude, because if truth be told, we see her as the daughter we could not have."

Chapter Twenty Eight
Lake Side

The workshop was a long, tall, wide building of wood, filled
with tools and piles of timber. At the back was a staircase that led
up to a large storage room filled with kegs of salt that contained
preserved meats. There were long shelves of glass jars filled with
preserved foods, all labelled and dated. At the far end, which was
above the front of the workshop, there was a small window, a
long work table, and a large empty space.

There was a large store of blankets and furs, so Bellot lit two
lamps that burned oil extracted from meats, and left them to
organise. Beds were laid out and Tannet provided bread and
cheese to eat, and the group settled down. Shade stayed over
at the house for a while longer, Tannet and Bellot spoke fluent
Undine, and there were words that needed to be said between
them. It was clear there was a great fondness for her, she meant a
great deal to them and it showed.

The group settled down, and Oaken took the first watch
through the small window, Ria sat beside him and snuggled up
as they quietly talked, they had spent little time together, and so
as the others drifted into sleep, they chatted and chuckled, their
bond deepening, which for a while, Yandalla watched with a
smile, as she drifted into sleep.

Morning arrived after a long sleep, and as Oaken woke up,
Bellot had already been up hours and had lit a fire under the large
metal container behind the workshop. Ria with Yandalla, Sintalla
and Shellena were all soaking in the steaming water, when
Oaken came outside to find everyone. Shade sat rubbing her wet
hair wrapped in a blanket with Meda and Caleb, wearing happy
smiles, and Elden and Ham chopped more wood.

Being washed and clean felt good, Oaken changed into clean
clothes, and felt much better, as Bellot arrived with food and
opened a large box filled with weapons.

"They were collected from those who strayed into places they should not, I have no use for them, but kept them just in case, take what you need, and I will help you get supplies."

Oaken appreciated his help, and sorted through them, handing out weapons to ensure everyone had something. Meda was given two long knives on a sheath belt, which with some adjustment and trimming fitted her. Sintalla was happier with a sword and dagger added to her personal weapons, although she still wanted the bow. There was a good stock of arrows, which delighted Shade, and she filled a wider pouch with her extras, as well as the woven one on her belt. Sintalla helped herself to a good stock of extra arrows, as an Undine, it was the one weapon she had great skill with, and happily shared her love of the weapons with Elden, who spent most of the day talking battle strategies with her.

Meda's clothing was worn and filled with holes, Tannet took control and sorted out some of her older clothing of her younger sister who had died of a virus. They were a little bit on the large size for her, but with some sewing and adjustments, she had a good pair of pants and a new top. She was thrilled and gave Tannet a huge hug. Bellot took Oaken and Ria to one side, and spoke quietly.

"Look, I know the path you travel, and it is no place for children. Do you have to take them with you, we could offer them a place of safety here?" Ria gave a sigh, as she looked at his face.

"Bellot, if they were any other children we would, but these are not normal children, and if we leave them in your care, it could place you in incredible danger." He did not understand, as he looked at her.

"But why, what danger would we be in?"

"Shade rescued those two children, who we found out had been purchased by Belthaz. Bellot, those children are his property and he wants them back, if he finds out they are with you, he will bring an army and tear this place down looking for them. At the moment, Shade is the one person who can protect them better than any other, I know you know of what his father did to her?" Bellot looked shocked, and nodded.

"Yes, I do, she understands better than any the evil of that family, I see your point, but fear not, no one will ever know they were here." Oaken patted his shoulder.

"It is a difficult thing we face with four Undine and two wanted children, but for now they are safer with us. Trust me, Shade has made them her biggest priority and we have seen them change from terrified children to happier and more contented with her. She is good for them, and will always protect them." He understood, but Oaken looked him in the eyes.

"If we survive this, they will need a home, so with your consent, if things go well, we will get Shade to return here with them, and if you can give them a normal happy home and they would wish that, I will make sure they come back here."

For the rest of the afternoon, the group sorted out their bags and provisions. Shade with Shellena wove new back packs from the long reeds that grew near the lake, so the three new Undine could help carry provisions. They were given furs and Oaken handed them a bag of gold coins, Bellot objected that it was too much, but to Oaken it was not enough, because their help was so important to them.

Their stay was only a day, but leaving felt hard, and all of them gave Tannet and Bellot hugs and their thanks, and with that, they left the homestead, and headed through the trees to the side of the lake. They walked along the lakes edge heading towards the huge falls, which filled the clear lake with fresh water. Shade held a letter for Kellem, who would watch over them over night, and then first thing in the morning they would set off up the rock face and head for the top of Andalan, which for Oaken, meant going home to his roots and the place of his birth.

Bellot walked a little of the way with them, and made sure they were on the right track, and then turned to Shade, as he prepared to leave, and smiled as he stood before her.

"This is not goodbye Lune; I will never say that. I want you to know how very proud I am of the woman you have become. I remember our talks of your mother, and the pain you had at that time, if I am honest, I am not sure how you overcame it. I remember how you told me you wanted to be like her, and be everything she wanted you to be, and I have to say, today as I stand before you, I feel you have done her proud. That fact you have survived from such an early age alone is a tribute to you, and you should hold your head up and be proud of the fact you are the daughter of Ae lune yan. You know, I see you as I would a daughter of my own, and so I will tell you now, you will always have a home here, there will always be a place you can come to. Now go, and live as a true Undine warrior and protect your friends." Shade stepped forward with tears in her eyes, and he pulled her close and held her tight, as she sniffled.

"Ca feya... Tac yeat." She looked up at him and smiled.

"Me, big care for you, be safe." He gave a nod, and looked to Oaken.

"Good luck, and watch her back for me." Oaken gave a smile as he saw the love between them, and he understood the power of this man who had saved her.

"I will, we will all take care of each other." Bellot released her and stood back.

"Go Dar len eah ae lune, be the warrior daughter you were raised to be." Shade gave a sniffle and picked up her bag, then wiped her cheek on her hand.

"Ca feya, Anna Pa." He smiled, and all of them could see the impact that had on him, and with a gentle nod, he turned and walked back down the path leaving them. Shade swallowed hard and began to walk towards the front of the line.

"We go, need move." Ria wiped her eyes, and lifted her bag, and at Oaken's side, they began to walk. He looked at Ria and her eyes moved to him.

"What?"

"If I am honest, I do not understand why two people of such care would want to live here, they both know at some point the Summanu will come. My father tried so hard to get all of them to flee with him, and yet, they chose to stay in the one place that if the Summanu come, will be a trap. It makes no sense to me Ria." She looked down the track watching Shade up ahead talk with Yandalla.

"All I know is, that I once asked my father something similar, and he looked me right in the eyes and he told me, Ria, most people do not really understand the true depth of what evil is. They know that it is evil, but they cannot really see the full potential of that. He then said something that really surprised me, he told me, evil is not dark Ria, because people can look into the darkness. True evil is brighter than the sun, and because of that, no one can look into it and see its full depth, and so people underestimate evil and think they can overcome it, but they cannot. Oaken, it really made so much sense to me at that time, and I have never forgotten it." Oaken took a moment to really think about it.

"So, what he is saying is that because they are good, they are blinded to the real truth of the evil that dwells in this land with the Summanu?" She gave a nod as they walked along.

"Bellot and Tannet are good people, they are too good, because they are blinded by the darkness and are unable to really see the truth of it. Bellot believes the Summanu have forgotten them, and it is foolish, because they will come Oaken, and when they do, Ranblate will be wiped from the world completely, and all of it will burn." It was a chilling thought, and he felt a cold tingle run down his spine.

"We have to stop that, Ria; we cannot allow the likes of Bellot and Tannet from being wiped away." She gave a nod as she walked.

"I know, and Shengara is hoping to get the numbers it will take. You know Oaken, when you first told me you wanted to destroy Balathral, it really frightened me, because I did not want you to walk to your death needlessly. Since then, which is not that long ago, and after seeing Shade's reaction to Bellot, I want to save this land. Corrupt as it is, I do not want it destroyed, I want Shade to always have a place of safety. If the sword of the winds in your hand will save this, then you must do it, and I will stand beside you as you do." He took a deep breath as he looked at her bright eyes, she held such belief in him, and yet he doubted himself.

"It is a big task, Ria; it will not be easy." She gave a smile and nodded.

"You said the same thing on the ship about saving Yandalla, and yet, there she walks up in front with Shade talking. I think if it can be done, you are the one to do it, and you should consider that."

He looked up the path and could see her up ahead, dressed in all black with a pack on her back, a sword and knife on her belt and carrying her bow, as she walked side by side with Shade, two Undine warriors walking and talking.

"I do not want to put her in harm's way Ria, she means too much to me, I lost my father, I do not want to lose her too." Ria smiled.

"Look at her Oaken, she is not the girl you knew at home, Yandalla has changed, we all have. I really do not think you have a say any longer, and I have thought about that a great deal of late." He turned to her.

"You have?" She gave a slight nod, as she watched Yandalla.

"Yes... Oaken, she came to you in a dream, and she handed you the wind, how did she do that? I am starting to think Yandalla has a part to play in all of this, I am not sure what, but somehow, I think both of your destiny's are linked together, and the winds wanted you both side by side to accomplish this task that Nuada has set for you. This is no longer about our small group, this is just a part of a wider game, and I think somehow your father knew that." He stared at her.

"How could he, that was years ago?" She gave a shrug.

"I am not sure, just call it a gut feeling, but I am sure that there are forces moving closer and they all have one aim, which is to take the fight to Balathral."

Ria's point, filled his mind with a thousand questions, which he really could not answer. He walked lost in thought not really paying that much attention, as his mind tried to work through all of the possibilities. It was true, Yandalla had come to him in his dream, she told him to wake up. In a bright white light, which surrounded her, she handed him the wind to overcome the soldiers which were trying to take them captive. His eyes were fixed on the floor, as he asked the question over and over, how did she do that, does she have another kind of power from Nuada? He turned to Ria and went to speak and then noticed she had stopped walking, and was looking forward. She looked scared, he frowned, and turned to look where she was looking, which was up ahead, and his insides twisted.

There was a tall man stood slightly ahead of a large group of unshaven and rough looking men. The tall man stepped forward; he gave a smirk, as his eyes wandered over the group.

"Well, what have we got here, did you honestly think you could sneak into our territory and not be noticed? Four very highly priced, and may I say, tasty looking young Undine, who will fetch us a very good price indeed. Although, I cannot deny, me and the lads here will have a bit of a play first, after all, we have three times the number you do. Now, this is what I will do, turn around and walk away but leave the girls, and no one needs to get hurt." Shade glared at him, her hand on the hilt of her sword.

"Brighem, Stenghem!"

She slid out her sword, and pushed her feet into the floor, in a stance of defiance. Yandalla stood at her side and lifted her bow, she had one arrow on the string and held two in her hand gripping the bow, she stared down the arrow, and gritted her teeth.

"I am Undine, I am warrior, I will take three myself, name yourselves, so I know who to hit."

Behind her, Sintalla held up her bow, and Shellena, who looked terrified, held her sword in the stance of a warrior. Oaken walked between the rank as the tall man laughed.

"You hear that boys, these little ladies, want to know who is going to take them?" One large man took a step forward and winked at Yandalla.

"I am looking forward to tasting your sweet skin." Yandalla gave a nod.

"Ca feya."

Her arrow fired at a fast pace, and before any could move, it hit the man in the forehead and he went sprawling back dead. Yandalla had another arrow on her bow.

"Next!" Shade smirked, Oaken was shocked, but why, how many hours had Pallum stood with her shooting? Ria gave a small chuckle.

"Wow, never saw that coming, although, neither did he." The tall man looked unsure, as he looked back at his man dead on the floor.

"Nice shot, but you still have two left, do you honestly think after that, you are quick enough?" An arrow whizzed past Yandalla's shoulder, and hit one of the other men in the chest, he buckled, and fell to the floor.

"No, but I am." Sintalla stared at the man.

"I will take you next."

Her eyes were white but bright, and her face was stern, she was a seasoned warrior much older than her sisters, and she had no intention of being taken again. Ria stepped up between the two Undine with her sword in her hand, she was ready and knew what was coming, and she was right.

There was a scream, and the men rushed forward, arrows unleashed, and Shade sprang into the air with her sword and dagger out. Oaken moved swiftly, backed by Ham and Elden. Oaken gripped Yandalla with her bow by the shoulder and pulled her back as he stepped past her, she loaded and fired as he ran towards the group, the tall man dodged the arrows of Sintalla which hit a man behind him. As his sword came up, Shade clashed with him with a loud snarl, and she sliced at great speed, cursing in Undine.

He stumbled and hit the floor and she was already moving on, as Oaken and Elden clashed side by side with two others. Ham holding a sword and hammer battered his way through, killing men on both sides, as he roared out in anger. Ria cut up in front of the Undine women, as she sliced into one man, and another at his side took an arrow to the forehead. She grunted as she cut up, and her arm whiplashed back, swiping across the face of another man, who screamed out, as his blood sprayed out of the side of his face.

There was a lot of them, and it was not easy, Oaken looked back, as he swiped and cut the hand off the man he was fighting, Ria was facing two, he had to get to her. He twisted and punched out at the man in front, and then moved quickly, and grabbed at the back of one of the men and yanked him backwards away from her, an arrow hit the man and he coughed and fell. Oaken's head snapped around as another group of men arrived with bows, he saw them come up, and felt panicked, there was too many.

The arrows unleashed taking out eight of the men attacking them, and for a moment he was a little caught off guard, they were helping. The few remaining saw the new group and turned, then ran for the trees, Ria was breathing hard as she came up to him.

"Thanks, I was panicked." He nodded as the new group came forward, the man in front was tall, and clean shaven, although his eyes looked familiar, he smiled at Oaken.

"Are you alright?" Oaken nodded, momentarily lost for words.

"Yes... Thanks, it was getting a little frantic." The man gave a nod.

"Been watching this scum for a while, I warned them to stay off my land, they should have listened." He came forward and lifted a hand.

"I am Kellem, as soon as I saw Lune, I knew you were safe." Shade turned and gave a smile as she cleaned her sword.

"Ca baska, Tac yeat, Kellem." He turned to her and smiled.

"It has been too long little Lune, where have you been, my brother has missed you?" She walked over the sheathed her sword, he pulled her into a hug.

"Me grow strong, no small, still Lune." He giggled as he held her.

"I am pleased to see you." She giggled as he let go, across the way, Sintalla looked down on the tall man who Shade had attacked first. He lay back covered in blood and breathing hard. He stared at her, as she simply stood over him, and spoke Undine.

"You see a woman, and that was your mistake, we are proud warriors and we have no fear of combat. My Anna Pa trained me when I was but five summers, because he knew there are men like you in this world." She turned and walked away, as he turned his head, and gasped for air.

"Don't leave me like this, kill me." Yandalla turned, and looked at him.

"I am only a woman, if you want death, ask a man, your blood is not good enough to mark my weapons." Ria walked over to him, and stared down on him with no mercy.

"Now do you understand how proud the women of the Undine are?" He gasped in air and swallowed the blood in his throat as he shook on the floor.

"Yes… Yes, I do." She nodded, and then swiped her sword fast across him, and his face flopped to the side, he was dead, she turned and looked at Sintalla and Yandalla.

"He understood before he died, and that is what counts my warriors." Yandalla smiled.

"Tac yeat, Ria."

Once the group understood that the man who had arrived with friends was the brother of Bellot, they relaxed. Oaken introduced himself and gave him the letter from his brother. He read it and understood the situation, and with his arm around Shade's shoulder he led the way. They all walked to the rock face, where there was a large opening carved out of the rock, creating a man made cave.

There was a fire over which hung a huge animal cooking, and he waved his hand, pointing out how the hunting was good, and allowed everyone to help themselves. Everyone settled down and ate, as Kellem sat with Ria and Oaken, as they talked of their aim to return to the temple on Andalan. His other men busied themselves helping the group of Undine, and ensuring their comfort. Kellem sat back and looked at them.

"The problem around here is that there are a lot of rumours, so I have no idea what is correct. It is said that Balathral left his chief apostle up at the temple from Lembrath, which is a large religious section of Sumanula. Apparently, he is very devout and a bit of a crazy person, who kills his own guards if they do not pray hard enough to Bharl. At first there was a huge presence, but over the years it has dwindled. The thing is, I have no idea what you will be walking into, but I will say this, if you aim to take that temple back, you will have a fight on your hands, because that will be the most defended." Oaken understood that.

"I have an item of my father's which will help me enter." Kellem gave a chuckle.

"I knew your father; I met him often when we were in Keytan. His sword is famous and not forgotten easily, I take it he passed it on to you?" Oaken gave a nod.

"Yes, and I feel I have to finish what he started, which is why I am going back." Kellem sat back in his seat.

"I wish you well, I do, but you have a big task ahead of you, and if the word is out there are Undine with you, I fear you may find there will be others looking to catch you. Those four will fetch a very big purse, we hate what Balathral has done, the Undine are a kind race, none of this makes sense, apart from the fact he is a mad man. The best advice I can give you, is leave in the dark, the start upward is a ladder bolted to the wall many years ago, and it is high, you do not want to be caught out in the day light on that wall. Once you hit the path, you will find caves on route, so you will have shelter."

It was good advice, and something Oaken had not considered,

which worried him. Kellem went to get food, and Ria snuggled up and cuddled into him.

"Feel better?" Oaken gave a long sigh.

"There is so much I need to learn still, I feel out of my depth, I was never prepared for this. Pallum showed me the ways of the Undine, Eliaston has taught me all I need to know of Nuada, but how will I learn how to follow my father? He knew it all Ria, and he guided his people well. Ria, I have no idea how to do that, look at me, I walked us all into a trap today, and it risked Yandalla." She squeezed him tight.

"You are too hard on yourself, look Oaken, as much as you want to, you can never fully protect any of us, and at times, we will need to stand together and protect each other. Oaken, Yandalla stood her own ground, she is very well trained and can look after herself, she defended herself and her friends, and she did a great job."

"She should not have to Ria." Ria sat back and looked at him.

"Seriously, okay, answer me this. The other night, what if you had been killed and she escaped with Shade and me?"

"That is irrelevant, I didn't." She rolled her eyes at him.

"Humour me, what if you had?" He gave sigh.

"It is a stupid question." She shook her head.

"No, it's not Oaken, I know she is your younger sister and you feel responsible, hell I am just your female companion, and even I feel a sense of responsibility towards her. Oaken, if you had died, she would have had no choice but to fend for herself, she would have been forced to step up to the plate like she did today. You forget who she is, her father is one of the leaders of the Undine, and her great grandfather is the leader. She has been trained from a young age for a role within the Undine hierarchy, that is her destiny, and today it showed. She may be quieter than she was, that is not surprising, but I can tell you now, Yandalla has what it takes to survive, after all, she walked from her cage, which is more than a lot of the others did." Oaken shook his head.

"I cannot win, no matter what I say you will find a way to weave it against me. Ria, she is my little sister, and she has always been there for me, is it so wrong to want to protect her? If you want to know, I do not see you as just a female companion, you mean more to me than that." Ria gave a big smile, and then bit her lip to try and hide it.

"Thank you, that actually is nice to hear, look Oaken, I understand, I really do, I want her safe too. I really like her, she is sweet and kind and she really cares, but she is also a very proud warrior. You cannot take that away from her, because whether you like it or not, that was the future written for her the day she was born. Oaken, look at her name, only Undine of high rank get a flower or plant names, all of the others have names that mean other things, she will rule one day." Oaken frowned as he looked at her.

"What do you mean, high rank and flowers?" She shrugged.

"It is common knowledge; I thought you knew that? Only an Undine of high rank is named after plants. Yandalla is a mixture of words that translates into flower of the meadow, or meadow flower." He nodded.

"So, using that logic, what position would an Undine have if they were called Moon Flower?"

"That is a powerful name, it would only be given to a very high ranking Undine, why do you ask?" Oaken looked across the cave.

"Ae lune yan, it means moon flower." Ria nodded.

"Alright, so who is that?" Oaken turned to her.

"That is the name of Shade's mother, but it makes no sense, why would someone of high rank be in Shodalt, joined to a farmer?" Ria turned and looked behind her, to where Shade sat with the other Undine and Elden eating.

"Really, honestly, I have no idea, although in a strange way, it does make some sense, after all she is called Night Shade, maybe that refers to her living in the shadow of her mother." She turned back to him.

"Maybe you should talk to Shengara, out of all the Undine, he would know." Oaken looked at her, and then back at all of his group.

"Why do I feel that there are unknown forces at work, and they are bringing powers I know nothing of to surround me?" She gave a shrug and smiled.

"You are the four winds, who holds the sword that controls them, and if you ask me, other forces are being drawn towards you. In a way, considering the evil of Balathral, it is not such a bad thing if all of you are together in one place to fight him." She had a good point, and it was one he had not considered.

"I think we need to get ready, if we have to climb in the dark, we should move as the sun sets to give us as much time as possible."

Ria gave a nod and stood up, she was starting to realise there was far more at stake than when they first set off from the boat. This was no longer about saving a sister, there was something much bigger to all of this, and it was revealing itself slowly to them. It was clear something big was coming, and strangely enough, Oaken appeared to be walking straight towards it, or was he? Ria looked across the cave as a new thought entered her mind, and she spoke softly more to herself than anyone else.

"Is he walking towards it, or is something drawing him towards it all?"

Chapter Twenty Nine

Understanding the Gods

Pallum looked up as the sun slipped downward in the sky, as three horses rode towards him, one of which was an Undine. Pallum watched, as Twendala turned his horse and rode towards him, he came riding up and slipped off the horse, and Pallum was happy to see him.

"Ca Baska my friend." Twendala gripped his arm tight, and smiled.

"Ca Baska." Pallum patted his arm.

"Tell me we have good news." Twendala gave a chuckle and smiled.

"I met Mondate, he has a horse, and is rushing back to Sarka, he told me you had changed the route, and the sick and exhausted you guide need help. Tanquilla has landed more supplies, and there are five thousand men of Animatre to aid us, I have two hundred behind me on route to help you." Pallum looked behind him at the long rows of slow moving carts.

"We have tried to go as fast as we can, but those on foot are exhausted, they need food and healing plants to cure their spirits, we need the help." Twendala gave a big smile.

"Fear not, help is close, within the hour you will have far more men than you need."

"I need to get back to my warriors, I have four units back there holding back the Summanu." Twendala understood Pallum better than most, he patted his shoulder.

"Go, I know how much you need to be with them, when the men of Animatre get here, gather your men and go back, and take some of Tanquilla's men with you. Kill as many Summanu as you can, even the numbers of our people, for we have much to repay the Summanu for." Pallum gritted his teeth.

"They do not have enough blood to quell my anger, the only good thing that has happened, is my daughter is free and with her brother. She is a warrior, and will aid him greatly."

Pallum prepared his men as he waited, and when the men of Animatre arrived, Pallum gave the care of his people to Twendala, and with new supplies and arrows, he turned back, and headed towards his men, who were keeping the rear guard, and holding off any Summanu who tried to catch up.

Kellem walked them to the ladder which was not that far away from the high waterfall. Meda was afraid as she looked up turning white, the light was fading, but it was clear how high the ladder went. Kellem explained it had been made by him and his brother, and had taken two years to fit it to the wall, it did not help quell Meda's fear. Ham solved the problem, he was big and strong, and so offered to take her up on his back, it did not help calm Meda down. Eventually, with a harness made of rope, Meda was attached firmly to his shoulders, and he headed up behind Shade, followed by Shellena, and then Yandalla, Caleb and Oaken. Ria followed with no fear at all, although she had climbed the tall masts of the ships of her lands many times. Sintalla and then Elden followed. Vesta was still absent, she had wandered off when they stayed at the workshop, which was normal, and Oaken knew she would find them again easily.

The ladder was easy enough to climb, it was the height that was worrisome, as the higher they got, the stronger the breeze felt, and the light had faded into a blackness, which would have been aided more by the moon. The breeze blew the fine mist off the waterfall that thundered down at their side, which wet the hand and foot holds, so it was slow going. It took most of the night, and their arms ached and were painful as they slowly reached the top, and slipped with gratitude on the wide path.

They were half way up the mountain, but at least they would be on foot from here on. Ria sat back against the wall, and gave a long sigh as she rubbed the tops of her arms.

"That was awful, I am so glad there was no one waiting for us, there is no way I could lift a sword at the moment." Oaken looked around trying to make out the details of the path and the high wall.

"We need to find shelter, there are caves all along this pathway." Ria sighed and stood up; her legs were aching.

"As long as it is not too far, I am fine with that."

With Meda released from the harness of Ham, she walked close to the wall, Shellena took her hand to give her more confidence. They all set off with Shade and the other Undine being able to see far better than they could leading the way and guiding them in the darkness. There was a small ravine cut through the rock in which water thundered down, passed under large wide pieces of stone that had been used to bridge it. It was not long before Shade pointed out an opening in the rock, although most of them could not really see it that well in the darkness.

They were guided in, and Elden unpacked some of the wood that had been tied to his pack, and at the back of what was a deep cave, he built a fire. Flickering flames and the small amount of light it gave out, somehow gave them a sense of relief, as they could actually see something. It had been a long day, and they all bedded down for what was left of the night. As the fire flickered the opening of the cave could be seen, with the heavy darkness outside, Oaken lay back with Ria curled into him, and stared into the darkness.

He drifted off into his thoughts as he tried to work out what was really going on. In his mind, he wanted to know how he could snuff out the candles in the temple with Eliaston, or throw the soldiers back down the mountain pass? How did Yandalla reach inside him when she was trapped in a cage, and how did she hand him the wind? It rolled around within his thoughts, as he tried to figure out why him. Was Ria right, did his father know, and if he did, how did he see so far ahead into the future? Nothing was making sense and he felt a really strong feeling to talk to his mother. He wanted to simply drift off into the darkness and gain the understanding he needed to continue, he relaxed and tried to see inside himself, and let his mind drift, and his thoughts drifted away.

Through the darkness he walked alone, the sound of his soft leather shoes tapped on the floor, and a mist of grey swirled in front of him. He could hear the voice of a man as he chanted, and it echoed off the walls.

"Bharl, oh great and mighty master of darkness and light, hear me as I offer up the souls of the undying race."

Oaken looked around, but all he could see was the swirling

mist. He took another step, and felt the step, he looked down and realised it was familiar, he knew it, and lifted foot onto it and realised, it was the temple steps. The voice was echoing somewhere praising Bharl, he looked up, he felt it was inside the temple, and he wanted to know why. This was a temple of Nuada, no one had the right to praise Bharl here, he took a step forward and felt a soft hand slide into his, his voice rang out in the mist.

"Who is there, this is a sacred place, you are not welcome here?" A laughing sound echoed through the mist.

"Be gone, this is now the land of Bharl, he will strike you down, as he will all of your weak gods." Oaken shook his head.

"You are wrong, Nuada is more powerful, and Bharl will never defeat the power of goodness and enlightenment." The laugh echoed through the mists.

"So why are we here, tell me that son of Andalyn? Do you really think if your god was so powerful your father would have died? Bharl had no problems claiming this land, there is no one who can defeat him, go hide in your caves with the rest of that dying breed you aliened yourself with." Oaken could feel his anger rising as he stared into the thick swirling mists, he wanted to take his sword and kill them for their insults. The voice echoed through the mist.

"Praise thee my noble and merciful master of the darkness and light, guide me, light my path so that I take more spirits of the undead, and feed them to your power."

Oaken felt the hand squeeze his, and he turned and looked down, and Yandalla stood at his side, her face as white as snow surrounded by her black hair, and yet light was radiating out of her. She smiled and shook her head, her voice was almost ethereal, as if she was talking from some great distance.

"Now is not the time, come, we need to prepare."

The lightening came down through the sky, hit the floor with a deafening crack, and he jumped and breathed in in shock, gasping loudly as he jerked.

He opened his eyes, and Yandalla smiled, she was kneeling in the cave in front of him, and holding his hand. He blinked his eyes as he looked at her, not really understanding what was happening and could not understand why he was back in the cave. He sat up slowly and saw Ria holding a cloth, she looked worried.

"How are you?" He took a deep breath.

"How do you mean, I am fine?" Ria stared at him, and he could see the concern in her eyes.

"Oaken, you had a really bad dream, you were shouting out all sorts of things, and you were burning hot, and water was running down your face."

She handed him the cloth, as he lifted his hand to his face and felt the heat and moisture. Taking the cloth, he wiped his face as he tried to breathe better, and regulate his breathing. Yandalla released his hand, and he looked at her.

"You saw it, please tell me you saw it, Yandalla?" She gave a soft smile and a slight nod.

"I know what you saw, but it will not happen Oaken, they have no power there, they just think they do." He took a deep breath, his heart had been racing, but he was calming down, he looked at Ria.

"How bad was it?" She lifted her eye brows, as she looked at him.

"You scared the children, screaming out the name of Kabazan, but apart from that we coped with it. The hot face and jerking was pretty alarming. Once Yandalla took hold of your hand, you calmed down. I will add, when your sister glows white, that sort of terrified some of the others, Elden was really panicked, but apart from that we are fine." Oaken put his head down.

"I am sorry, I have no idea what is happening to me, all of this is so confusing, nothing makes sense at the moment." Yandalla gave a nod and she smiled at him.

"Oaken, we are family, we will work all this out, and we will do it together."

He was not sure, as each day had passed as he drew closer to Andalan, he had found himself becoming more uncertain. He had so many questions with no one who could help him get the answers. He pulled up his legs and stood up, he felt shaky, but he managed to stand properly.

"I need air, I feel I cannot breathe in here." Ria gave a nod and watched as he walked towards the entrance of the cave, where he stood alone breathing in the fresh air in the sunlight. Ria looked at Yandalla.

"Do you know what is happening to him?" She gave a nod.

"I feel what he feels at times, and I think Nuada is reaching into him and showing him what needs to be done, and I think he does not understand that." Ria nodded at her.

"I hope you do not mind, but you appear to be far more Undine than Andalan, how can you feel the power of Nuada inside him? Yandalla gave a slight chuckle.

"You ask what you already know Ria, you have felt it also, I know that you felt the power, I felt you." Ria sat back on the floor.

"You felt that, the boat, you were with him?" Yandalla smiled at her.

"Your feelings for Oaken, came to me, and it made me happy to feel it, I did not know who you were, I just knew what you felt like. On the mountain as we ran up the path, I could feel your worries for him, and I knew then who you were. Ria, I feel things, and I do not know why, but I think it is a gift given me by my mother. I am proud to be Undine, but Andalan is also inside me."

In a strange way, it made some sort of sense to her, after all, she was of two races, so she did have the gifts of both lines. Ria had talked often to her father about the power of the faith in Nuada, but this was her first time actually seeing it in real life.

It took a while for everything to settle, but the sun was up and they were wasting daylight, so they all packed ready. Once organised, Elden and Sintalla led the group as they followed the wide path and headed upwards towards the top, and the first level of what was the territory of Andalan. This was a place which was once the home of thousands of scholars and philosophers.

As Oaken and his group walked slowly up the steep path, on the beachhead to the north of Undinalashka, a rider dismounted from a white horse, and hurried up the ladder which would take him to the top and the settlement of safety that was the second home of the Andalan's.

Sarka was busy, the whole of the grass square was lined with boxes and cloth bags as she inspected the contents and then looked at the soldiers.

"This one has food for the stores." He gave a nod, grabbed the bag and headed off, as she turned to where two men were opening a crate, she looked inside as the lid came off.

"Oh good, medical supplies, we desperately need them. Take these to the temple, and hand them out to the women nursing." The two men gave a slight bow, lifted the box and disappeared. Tanquilla turned with a smile.

"You have everything very well organised, I am sure everyone here appreciates it, but you do look tired, how much sleep have you been having?" She looked washed out.

"I will sleep when I know my family is safe. I know it sounds stupid, but the house is so quiet without Yandalla, and I am finding it hard to deal with it."

Tanquilla understood, she was missing Ria. She noticed an Undine Warrior walking quickly towards her, and she was about to answer, but something about the urgency of the man paused her thought. He came quickly towards them, looked at Sarka and gave a small bow.

"Lady Sarka, a messenger has arrived and wishes to see you as soon as possible." She looked at Tanquilla with hope in her eyes, Tanquilla gave a smile.

"Go... It sounds important, I will keep things moving here."

Sarka hurried, and followed behind the warrior, as he led her up the path towards her home, where there was an Undine waiting for her, he turned as she approached, and gave a bow.

"Lady Sarka, I have important news about your children." She stopped, almost holding her breath.

"Are they safe?" He gave a smile.

"Your daughter is free; her brother was able to release her, and she is now at his side. We raided the carts two nights ago, and we have many of our women free, but they are in bad condition, and they are heading this way." Sarka took a deep breath and closed her eyes.

"Oh, praise Nuada, she is free again. Where is she?" The tall Undine nodded.

"We raided in the night, and it was very dark, and some of us were separated. Leader Pallum told me to tell you that they headed up towards Andalan with their group." Sarka swallowed hard.

"Pallum is safe?" He gave a smile and nodded at her.

"Yes Lady Sarka, he told me to tell you, he misses you, and he thinks of you every day." Her eyes filled with tears as she smiled.

"Thank you, you have no idea how much it means to know all of them are safe." The Undine warrior gave a nod.

"I am glad I can bring this good news for you, and it is a good omen to know that your children are safe, and they are together. Leader Pallum hopes to return once we get all of the injured to this land, and he aims to go after your children to join them and help them. He told me, you should prepare, many weak women are heading your way, they freed a lot, but they need great care."

Her emotions were all over the place, as she felt them surge inside her, the Undine stepped back and gave a bow. He turned and started to walk away, and she suddenly realised and called out to him.

"Warrior, what is your name?" He turned and looked at her.

"I am Mondate." She gave a nod of recognition.

"I owe you a debt Mondate, and I am so grateful to you, you have my thanks for bringing me this news." He gave a slight bow.

"It was my honour, and I am pleased the news I brought was good to you."

As Mondate walked away, Sarka sat on the wall, as the tears streamed down her cheeks. The sheer relief seemed to strip her of energy from her legs, and she simply sat and leaned forward breathing in and feeling the emotional relief flood through her as she cried.

Up ahead, the path came to its end in what looked like a grassland full of trees. Shade was on her guard and pointed to both sides of the path, where Yandalla and Sintalla took up a defence pose, crouching down with their bows ready and loaded with arrows. Oaken gave a smirk.

"I think Shade is training the next generation of rebel warriors." Ria gave a chuckle.

"For someone who says all the Undine will die, she does appear to be doing her best to keep a few alive." They both laughed as they held back, and watched as Shade moved slowly forward into the first line of trees.

As Shade advanced into the trees followed by Yandalla and Sintalla, the others slowly followed. Oaken looked around what he knew as a child as an area that was once an area in which food was grown. It was hard to take it in, as he looked around.

"Why let this land go, it was really fertile, what is the point of taking a land off people if you do not intend to use it?" Ria looked around at the wild growth.

"The fruit trees did well, we are not short of food, but I can see your point. Oaken, I am not sure you understand, his taking of this land was never about occupying it, it was to show his power over everyone else. Look at Shodalt, it was once beautiful, green and lush, you saw it, you walked through it, now it is a dead wasteland of dust, debris and stones." He shook his head.

"It makes no sense Ria, and I do not understand why he would do this." She gave sigh and looked at him, her voice softened.

"You have never been to Sumanula, I have, and so maybe that is why I understand this. Oaken I was there ten years ago with my father, as I said, Balathral wanted to acquire boats, I saw how people live there. The centre of Sumanula is stunning, it was built many ages ago by the Jandarian's, and the buildings are beautiful and ornate. The whole of the central city of Salanula is one huge circle surrounded by a large wall, and it is filled with the cream of all the privileged, which are those of means and power that bow down to Balathral and treat him like a god. Outside the circle is a different story, that is the true home of the Summanu, and it is filthy and filled with the poor, who scavenge for a living off the waste of the rich. Salanula is what the elites of the Summanu live within, because all of the wealth of the Summanu is there. Beyond the towns of filth and poverty there are fields filled with foods, and there are mountains and lakes of great beauty, and all of them are patrolled by soldiers, and the poor are never allowed to visit them." He could not believe what he was hearing.

"But if that is so, why do his people fight for him?" She smiled.

"They want to live in Salanula with the rest of the privileged. Loyal soldiers who excel, are given rewards, and if they are lucky, they can become a district leader. It is the first step out of poverty, and if they prove to be loyal to Balathral, their promotion is a boost in pay and a small dwelling in Salanula. It is the only way, which is to snuggle up to the political class and do their bidding, and if you can flatter the officials enough, and find a way to corrupt others for profit, they let you in to the good life. His farms and orchards, of which there are many, are all run by his rich fat governors, who have a workforce of slaves to toil all day for little, many of which are female children. Balathral has no shortage of space in his land, it is all his to use as he pleases, and that is what he wants with the whole of this continent. He wants it to use as he feels fit. His fight with your people was never about taking this land and using it, he wanted it to show he is a god, and more powerful than Nuada."

"But he is not, he is just a man." She shrugged.

"In your eyes he is no god, but to those who killed the Shodalt, Ketonia, and the Undine wearing his uniforms, he is not a man, he is a god, or at least the voice of one. Think about it, to them, he appears, more powerful than any other god on this continent. The question is Oaken, if you really know him to be a man, then why does he rule?"

"Fear!" Ria turned to see Caleb looking at her, she smiled, and gave a soft nod.

"Yes Caleb, it is fear, for no one since Shengara has challenged the rule of Bharl. Balathral revived the beliefs of Bharl after his father's death, by telling the Summanu, that he had been bestowed with greater powers, which is why the mighty Shengara had not returned, and his people believed him." Oaken gave a frown and shook his head.

"That is not true, Shengara feared for his people, and so with my father's help, he led his people through the Heliospan Desert to new lands." Ria gave a nod.

"Which Balathral used by telling his people Shengara had run away in fear to hide. Think about it, at that point, all he had to do was take out the only other man who had ever opposed him, and when the illness struck down your father's people, Balathral moved fast and removed him. There is no one left to confront him, all his enemies have been vanquished, and the Undine have been slaughtered. Ask yourself this Oaken, if you lived in Sumanula cut off from the rest of the continent, who would you believe?"

It made a strange sort of logic, but Oaken still found it hard to believe, was all of this simply for no other reason than one man wanted to look God like to his people? It was hard for him to accept.

"Ria, Nuada has proven to be more powerful, his people must know that?" She gave a smirk.

"Oaken, his people do not even know what the lakes of their land look like, they are not like you, they have not been educated all their lives in a temple by a scholar and mystic. His people are uneducated, all they are fit for is searching for food in the garbage heaps, and living in one room houses made from the scraps of whatever the rich throw away. If you control the food, and the materials, and only tell the people your version of events, then they know no different. The rich and powerful control the narrative, and they make sure no one knows the real truth of life in their country. If the poor speak out or complain, they are punished and executed. He controls everything backed by his elites, his people most likely have never heard of Nuada, or Elohim. They know nothing that would give them a chance to rebel, and they bow and scrape and praise Bharl for no other reason than they hope one day it will be noticed, and they are lifted out of the poverty they live in." Ria walked up to a tree and pulled off a fat plump fruit, she looked at it, and then lifted it to her mouth and bit into it.

"Grab some, we can eat as we walk." Oaken pulled a fruit from the tree and lifted it to his mouth, and paused as he looked at Ria.

"If what you tell me is the truth, then by those standards, we are all privileged too." She dropped three fruits in her bag, and gave slight nod of agreement.

"You are right, we are... We are free, and we know it. That Oaken, is the biggest privilege of all." Ham wandered up to them, up ahead Shade was relaxing with the two Undine and eating. Ham looked at Ria.

"It appears to me everything is based on just one man, so what I want to know, is if we kill this one man, what will all those who back him do?" Ria shrugged as her blue eyes twinkled.

"Considering their lifestyle, and how they pander to Balathral, because they know nothing different, I would imagine, they would fall to their knees and worship their new god." Ham nodded at her.

"I could play god for a while, give me the space to swing a sword, and I could end one god and create another." Elden chuckled.

"You would need a golden hammer." Ham considered the point, and nodded as he thought.

"I can smelt gold if needs be." Ria smiled at them both.

"You are forgetting one small thing." Ham furrowed his brow as he looked at her and she smiled.

"It matters not if they are rich or poor, if they believe he really is a god, they will fight to their last to protect him. No matter which way you look at this, what we face is a holy war, one god's side against another. When you fight for a god, you do not give up easily, Balathral is out of reach to all." Oaken started to walk towards Shade.

"Not all, Nuada can reach him." Ria gave a big smile and nodded.

"Yes indeed, only a god can kill a god." Ham looked at the back of Oaken, and then back to Ria, and he smiled, he understood her perfectly. Oaken looked back as he walked.

"If I am right, there used to be a large pool up here and some storage sheds, if they are not occupied, we may have shelter. Look at the clouds, there is a storm coming, and it could be a bad one." Ria turned on the path and looked up, and spoke quietly to herself.

"There has been a storm a coming since you left Undinalaska, you have just not realised yet Oaken."

She walked on, following the back of Oaken, as he took the lead with Shade, and led the way towards what he remembered as a boy as being the centre for the storage of all the grain. Shade walked at his side with her bow in her hand, and Ria watched, behind her Yandalla and Sintalla spoke quietly as the group made their way under the trees, and out of sight towards shelter.

Ria's mind was lost in thought, as she pondered if Oaken really understood what was happening. The closer they got to the temple, the more she realised that the temple had some sort of task for him, which she felt must have something to do with the power of Nuada, and the writings of his father. She was not sure what, but since meeting Oaken she had felt a strong sense that there was some sort of task that would define his destiny. It was true, he had much to learn, but as she walked and considered the many conversations she had with her parents, she was starting to wonder if his blind belief in Nuada was the key.

It is true, no other knew more of the old beliefs than his father, but his father had fallen, and so knowledge was not the key to the fall of Bharl, it had to be something else, although Oaken had talked on the trail of how his mother had told him of how his father was reluctant to use the sword. Was that the answer, was there some task or some role that the sword had to play a part in? It was an interesting question, of which she was unsure as to what the answer was, and yet in some strange way, it made complete sense, although, what was Yandalla's part in all this?

It was clear there some role destined for her, and Ria was convinced it would be at the side of Oaken. She was raised an Undine and had many of their qualities, but she could not rule out that Yandalla was also the daughter of a very well educated Andalan, Sarka. Her parents had been important figures in the past history of the Andalan, and maybe she had some gift also to pass on to her daughter. Was the answer between the two of them, was it all part of the plan, it would take two to defeat Balathral, or was there far more to this than she realised?

It felt frustrating to her not really knowing the answer, for all of her life she had figured things out, and yet she felt she was close to understanding something the others did not. She was missing something, and she did not know what. In her head, she knew she was right about this being a holy war, one faith pitted against another to prove they were the only true faith, but Yandalla had been raised to the beliefs of the Undine, who did not really have a god, they believed they were a part of all things born of the land that was nurtured by the sun and moon, so it was not all about Gods, so what was she missing? She knew she was close, but could not figure it out, and she found that annoying.

They all walked in silence, all of them lost in thought, as the trees passed them, and followed the lead of Oaken. Behind them the skies rumbled as black clouds rolled in, and it was clear that the storm that had been brewing was about to start. The group came slowly out of the trees and were faced with a large pool, cut from the white stone of the rocks of Andalan. Across the water was a wide band of green, lined with a white roadway, and after that was a tall white wall, into which were carved several large cave like buildings, all of which had heavy wooden doors.

These were the grain houses of Andalan, and had been the main source of food for not just those who lived here, but for others who suffered at the hands of the Summanu, and the strange thing was, they were all still full. Locked for years they lay untouched, lost in a land cleared of its people, for the sake of one man's greed to own all of it, with no care for what was there. To a man who knew its value, it was a powerful tool, for those who controlled the food, had sway over the people, and as Ria looked upon them, she realised, she was finally starting to understand that this truly was a war for the love of a powerful god. She smiled as she heard Oaken's soft words in her ear from that day and night alone in bed together.

"Ria, Nuada protects all who believe, and in doing so, none shall go without."

Chapter Thirty

The Road to the Temple

Oaken was surprised to find the store houses were still full, one huge room was stacked with thousands of bags of grain, and also filled with barrels of salt that contained preserved meats. It was a little drier than they liked, so Meda joined Ria and boiled it, and made a meaty broth, which whilst a little salty, was warm and good. They all gathered inside the store, as the clouds broke and the rain hammered down, so they decided to sit put for the night.

The following day, they rose with the sun, and set off on what was to be another long walk up hill, and onto the next flat level of Andalan. The weather was a mixture of rain and cloud, and even though they were on a quite rocky area, in some places they trudged through what was a thick sandy mud. As night fell, they huddled under the trees in the rain, and slept as well as they could, but it was not easy, and Oaken rose aching to start what he hoped would be the last day.

His mind was filled with conflicting thoughts, as they began to walk. In the distance, he could see the large area of land that formed the heart of what had once been the land of philosophers, and warriors, who had carved intricate homes into the soft rock. As the day progressed, he began to see the empty places along the side of the rock that rose to the high paths, which marked the edge of the territory, and his mind drifted to the place he once lived with his mother and father. Ria was excited, she had never seen Andalan, so for her, this was a new and wonderful experience. She looked around in awe, at all of the colours of the carved rock.

"I never knew that this land was made of such beautiful rock, why are there so many colours." Oaken smiled at her side.

"Andalan has many different minerals, which we used to mine, it is why there are so many tunnels, not all of Andalan life was about prayer, we dug many things, such as lime, salts and ores for metal, this is a vast and rich land for the people who live here, or at least it was." She gave him as soft smile as she saw the pride in his eyes.

"It will be again Oaken; of that I am certain."

Elden came up at side of Oaken, as he walked, Oaken could see in his eyes that they both shared the same excitement and apprehension. Elden glanced at him as they walked.

"Oaken, where is everyone, this placed was sacked by the Summanu, so where are they?" He had been thinking the same.

"I am not sure, and it is bothering me, because this is supposed to be Balathral's prize, and yet there are no soldiers here. I considered them living here, and did expect a fight, but it has not happened." Elden looked around.

"I must admit, I am on edge, I think I would be happier cutting my way through, it is what I expected." Oaken understood that, he had been feeling the same.

"I think being alert is wise Elden, we are walking towards the unknown, and I feel that as we approach the temple, we will find them there."

After several short breaks, where Oaken stood and gazed into the distance, they continued on towards the evening, and as the day crept slowly towards a close, they made for the shelter, in what was once the home of one his people, cut into the side of the rock. Elden sat talking with Ham, and the Undine women, sat with the children, as Elden spoke about his life growing up on the other side of Andalan. Oaken felt restless and stood in the doorway watching across what was the centre of the large horseshoe shape of Andalan, and where he knew the large temple of Nuada was carved from the rock at the end of a long ravine.

Yandalla came up at his side and gave him a smile, as she looked up at him, with her bright green eyes. He knew she sensed his feelings as she always had, and so it was pointless to even argue if she mentioned it. She looked out across the vast stretch of rock, her eyes bright, and able to see more than he could

"I feel it too Oaken." He glanced at her.

"Feel what?" She smirked; he knew what she meant.

"I feel them, they are over there, just like the dream." He gave a soft nod as he understood.

"They are, I do not know how I know, I just do. I expected to meet a lot up here, but I think all Balathral wants is to hold the temple, which is why they will be there."

"I can sense them over there, Oaken, you do know it might not be possible to walk in the temple?" His eyes were locked on the where the temple stood in the distance.

"I do not care what they think, that is the temple of my people, and I aim to walk there and talk with Nuada as my father did." She gave a smile as she watched him.

"You are my brother, and I will walk with you and watch with you, and it will make me happy Oaken, because it will honour your father, and I want to see that." He gave a little chuckle, and lifted his arm to her shoulder, and pulled her close.

"I missed you, and I am glad you are here."

As the light began to fade, he saw the light in the distance, the torches were lit around the temple. It was clear that there was a presence there, but as Oaken looked across all of the rest of territory, there was no light anywhere else. He was right, the Summanu had left, and were only interested in guarding the temple, which was where he knew he had to focus his attempts to take it back. Ria came outside, pulling her cloak tight, it was getting cool.

"How long will you watch; Oaken you should rest?" She slid her arm around his waist, and leaned onto his shoulder. He took a deep breath, and breathed it out slowly.

"I was right Ria, this is nothing to do with the land, all of what we have seen is about destroying people's hearts and beliefs. In a way, this has become a sort of holy war, as they pit their god against ours." She gave a soft nod.

"I know, he invented his own god Oaken, what else can he do? I told you, if his people for just one moment, realise he is a fake, they will rebel, and could overthrow him. He cannot let that happen Oaken, he has too much at stake." He felt her squeeze his waist a little tighter, he glanced at her, and she was watching him carefully.

"So, what do we do?" She shook her head.

"I am not sure, we are all here, but if all of this is true, what do we do?" He smiled as his eyes watched the horizon.

"This is a task only I can do, and it starts with taking back the temple of my people." Ria gave a shudder, and pulled her cloak tighter.

"We may be out numbered Oaken, that might not be possible." He gave a slight nod.

"I think that is why Nuada gave me the sword, it has a purpose, and it has something to do with here. I have felt it since I first lifted it, and I think in some strange way, it brought me here for that purpose. I aim to learn that and then use it, for that is the only way my people can return home."

For Ria, it was a chilling moment, because she knew he was right, this was something to do with the sword, but for her that was the worry. She had really come to care for him, and as she watched him, and could see his eyes taking in every detail of the landscape in the dim light, she knew he could be walking to his death, and she would lose him, and she was afraid.

It was late when he came back in, she was lay under the blankets waiting. He slipped in at her side and his hand came around her, she put her hand on his and pulled it close, and just for a moment she felt a little of the insecurities subside. Ria closed her eyes, and breathed in, listening to him breathe beside her, in her mind, she wondered if this would be the last time she ever held him close.

When she opened her eyes, the place was a hive of activity, Ham was going over things with everyone. It was clear, they were less than a day's walk away from the centre of Andalan, and Ham and Elden were getting prepared. The only one who needed no guidance was Shade, she was always prepared, and her weapons were kept sharp and in immaculate condition.

The upper level of Andalan, was exposed to the elements, and so trees had been planted in wide groves to shelter from the sun, and grow fruit. Elden led the party, he was on home turf, and kept them under the trees and out of sight. It was a long walk, but the skies were cloudy and there was the occasional light rain shower, which helped keep them cool. Andalan could have days of extreme heat, and in the past, people would sit under the trees to read, pray or talk. In the winter there was deep snow fall, and the trees protected the houses from the worst of the biting winds.

As they walked, Oaken became more and more alert, and pointed areas he could see with guards, in what looked like Summanu unforms, up ahead. Shade was hyper alert, walking with her bow and flanked by Yandalla and Sintalla, as they walked a little behind Elden. Ham at the back, watched the rear, and had the children holding Shellena's hands just in front. The tension was growing, and Ria could feel it building in Oaken, there was a fight coming, and she was a little afraid, but she knew, there was no going back. Her concern was, there was only ten of them, and they had no idea of what number they faced, and she was beginning to think they were all walking towards their deaths.

On one side of the trees, there was a steep drop to a lower level, and the wide plain began, filled with trees and paving, between which, tall grasses grew up. Oaken remembered how when he was a child, they were all cut low and well tended. There were ornate arches and statues, all rising up out of the weeds and grass, all of them faded memories of what felt like a life he lived before. He recognised areas that had once contained pools, skilfully cut from the rock with ornate designs around them, which were now filled with dust and debris and covered in weed. It felt such a shame to see this place, which was once a shining example of the care his people put into the place they lived, fall into ruin, and left to the wilds.

Elden slowed his pace, as Shade came up to his side and peered out through the trees. Across the wide central circle of Andalan, which had always been a place to gather and meet, Summanu soldiers walked up and down, and some stood idle by the walls of what were once the dwellings of those who attended to the temple. They wore black uniforms, unlike the sand coloured of other forces, but there was no doubt they were Summanu. Shade's blue eyes were fixed on their movements as Oaken came to her side, she felt his presence.

"Summanu, watch road into rock."

He understood, in the centre of Andalan, a wide gorge had been carved out of the rock. It formed a wide road that led through to a huge open rectangle of smooth stone walls, in front of which were the steps that led up to the sacred temple, built on the highest part of Andalan. All of the walls of the large carved area, were filled with homes cut from the rock, one of which was the home he was born in.

"That is the temple pass Shade, that is where I need to go, it will hold most of the soldiers we face." She turned, and glanced at him.

"Many Summanu, we no enough."

"This is my task Shade, I ask no other to risk their life, I have faith in the sword, and Nuada to guide me." She gave a soft nod.

"Your god, good yes, no bad like Bharl?" Oaken nodded.

"Nuada is merciful, and all loving." Shade shrugged, and then gave a slight nod.

"Me fight for good god. Kilt Summanu." She smiled, and he understood, no matter what, they had stuck together from the moment they had met, and her loyalty to him had been total.

"Be careful Shade, I would hate to lose you." She gave a little chuckle.

"Me scare lose me too."

They took a break, as they watched, logging the movements of the soldiers down Ria' scope. When they felt better rested, they headed off with a plan in mind, which was basically, Oaken went down the centre with Ria, whilst the children with Shellena, and the others worked the flanks under the supervision of Shade, to provide cover should it be required.

It was a longer walk than expected, but as they got closer, and the large rock face of the rear of Andalan loomed up, Ria found her breath taken away.

"Oaken, your home is stunning, was all of this carved out by the Andalan?" He gave a smile, as his eyes fixed on his route.

"My people had a lot of time, and we are well known for our ability to focus. It made sense, if we were going to cut away at the rock, we should make it as decorative as possible."

Oaken worked his way around through the trees, until he faced the pass through to the temple head on. He walked slowly into the full view, and stepped on the long path that went straight through what were decorative gardens in his youth, filled with pools, statues and grassed lawns under trees. As he walked, he could see up close how much things had gone to waste, most of the statues were vandalised and smashed, heads were removed, and lay on the floor and arms and legs were smashed off.

He hated seeing it, and it just added to his anger, as he now knew that the Summanu had not even wanted to live here. They just wanted to occupy the temple, and destroy as much as they could, and because of that, they killed his father and slaughtered his people. Ria could not believe her eyes as she saw the destruction, it was hard to look forward, as she saw what were beautiful statues butchered and broken, on each side of the wide path.

"This feels so wrong Oaken, I can understand wanting to live here, I just do not understand why anyone would want to simply violate and destroy it then leave."

"That is all they do Ria, and if they win, Animatre will be next. They will not stop until everything is smashed down to rubble, so that only the signs and symbols of the Summanu and Bharl remain." It was a chilling thought, and one she did not want to contemplate, as they came closer to the pass it had a row of guards standing either side of it.

"Oaken, we need to defeat them." He gave a nod.

"That is not as easy as it seems, here there are not many compared to what attacked Undinalashka, but there are still many more of them, than us."

She nodded, as she looked around, there was no sign of the others, and Shellena and the two children were holding back and staying a good distance behind them. There was no sign of Shade or the others, but she knew they were there, but not having a visual worried her, and she felt her heart start to beat, her voice was soft.

"Is it alright to tell you, I am afraid?" Oaken understood.

"Only fools would be unafraid in this situation, but I am here with you, and I will stay at your side, and we are not alone, the others are here somewhere watching over us." She took a breath, and tried to calm down a little.

"I know, I am actually glad to know Shade is somewhere, she is fast and fierce, I just hope it is enough."

"We are about to find out, so relax a little and be ready, they will watch us until we are close enough, and when they think they have the advantage, they will rush at us." Ria took a deep breath, she had been in some pretty close situations in the past, but this was the most dangerous thing she had ever done.

"I wish I still had my bow." He smirked.

"I am sure Yandalla has her arrows trained on them to protect you. She told me she highly approves of you." Ria gave a small gasp.

"She did?" He gave a smile.

"Yandalla has taunted me for years to find a wife, and so her approval is a big thing Ria, she will make sure you survive, just so she can prove her point." He gave a chuckle as he walked, as he saw her surprised looking face.

"So, it is true, she really wants you to find a wife?" Somehow, he knew she would pick up on that.

"She does, I have always told her I am very particular about who I associate with, and that in time I would seek the right person for me." Ria smiled at his side.

"So, what have you told her about us, did you tell her we have a future?"

Up ahead, the guards had been watching, and a group who were armed with long spears with trident fork like ends, appeared to feel they were close enough and easy to take. They thrust the long forks forward, and with deathly screams, they started to charge at them down the long road. Oaken was swift, and pulled out his sword from his belt, as he went into preparation for the attack. Ria saw them, and pulled out her sword, cursing under her breath, as her anger exploded out of her.

"You could not wait another minute, he was about to tell me the most important sentence of my life, and now you decide to attack?" Her eyes narrowed, as they came at her, she was really angry, and could feel her temper rising.

Eight of them ran straight at them, with a few others lagging behind. The first four were hit with arrows from nowhere, and smashed into the floor, the four behind came towards them. The first met Oaken, who weaved out of the way of the spear, knocking it upward with his free hand, and lunged at the soldier, slicing deeply into him with his sword.

Ria bobbed and weaved, her anger showing, as she side stepped the spear and struck deep and aggressively with her sword, and grabbed the spear with her free hand. As the soldier stumbled, he let go of the spear, so she twisted, swinging the spear around at speed, and she lifted it up and rammed it into one of the other moving towards Oaken. She pushed the spear into him, with all her might, her temper roaring out of her.

"All I wanted was one more minute, just a sentence, and you ruined all of it!"

The soldier looked shocked, and had no idea what she was talking about, but he knew his time was done. Oaken headed on to the next one, as arrows flew out of the trees, and more of the Summanu fell. Ham came thundering out of the trees lower down the road, and ploughed into a second group, with Elden joining him from the other side of the road. They clashed hard with their swords, as around them, others fell to the floor impaled with arrows.

Oaken and Ria, side by side ran towards them, and joined in the clash. Somewhere a bell started to ring, and more soldiers came running out of some of the side buildings, pulling on their jackets.

Seeing the fight, and unprepared, they tried to organise, and run to the aid of their men, a good few of them fell before they could even take ten paces, as Yandalla and Sintalla targeted them with deadly accuracy, following Shade's command to shoot for the eyes. It was chaos, as none of the soldiers fully understood what was happening, their officer lay dead, hit by Shade's arrow, as she picked off the leaders, or anyone shouting out orders.

The soldiers with their black tunics opened, pulled out their swords, and ran towards Oaken and the others. Shade burst out of the trees, she was down to her last arrow, and as she ran towards the others, she dropped her bow and pulled out her sword. Shade clashed with brutality, cutting two down in one savage blow, Yandalla and Sintalla, were still firing, when three of the soldiers veered from their path, and ran towards them.

Oaken grunted, as he shouldered his way onto another soldier, twisting his sword and ramming backwards into the soldier, pulling it back out as he rolled around him, and moved swiftly onto another heading for Ria. Yandalla turned and fired, hitting the first man to enter the trees, and reloaded, as Sintalla dropped her bow, and pulled out her sword, he was no match for her, and she knew it.

Oaken looked across at Shade beside Ria, as they cut up together taking down another two.

"There are more coming down the pass, we are going to be outnumbered."

Ria sliced hard, and plunged her sword deep into a soldier, she had picked up a second sword, and struck out hard, at another one.

"Oaken, we need to retreat, it is too many."

He looked back to where Shellena was fighting off one man to protect the kids, Calab had his sword in his hand and was trying to help. Shade saw him, and then seeing the kids in trouble, she lunged into one man, then pulled her dagger out of the back of her belt. She lifted the dagger, and threw it straight down the centre of the road. It spun through the air glinting, and hit the man attacking Shellena in the back of his neck, and he fell back, as Shade twisted into another soldier, and Shellena stood looking relieved, with Caleb at her side defending Meda.

More were approaching, and Oaken was starting to worry, he reached out and grabbed Ria's arm, and pulled her back. He was about to speak, when from nowhere there came a hail of arrows, and the soldiers before him fell, his head snapped around to see a swarm of black hooded figures spilling out onto the road behind them, they were Undine, but he did not understand. Why were they here, and where did they come from?

They walked in a rank down the road, loading and shooting, as arrows whipped past them, and hit the soldiers that were approaching, and then fell to the floor. Nothing made sense, where had they come from? Ria gripped his arm and pulled him back.

"Looks like we have back up." He turned to her, not really understanding.

"How?" She shrugged.

"I don't care, I am exhausted, and we needed the help."

The Undine warriors walked past them, and kept firing, and then Oaken fully understood, as two more groups came out from the trees, and Yandalla hung from the neck of her father, and he held her in his arms. Pallum smiled as he saw Oaken, who gave a long sigh of relief, and smiled back. Yandalla let go and smiled as

Pallum came towards him.

"We wanted to be here sooner, but it has been a busy few days." In the trees he heard the familiar roar and snarl of Vesta, and understood, she was finishing off for them. Oaken gave a big smile.

"I am grateful, they were starting to worry me." Pallum looked back where his men had formed a line across the pass, and were holding out against all of the Summanu.

"Once Vesta understood your plan and where you would be, she returned to me. I was already heading back when we met, my people are safe, and they are on route to be helped and healed in their own land." Oaken was relieved.

"I owe you my thanks, it was starting to get a little overwhelming." Pallum looked around at the dead on the floor.

"Oaken, what we see here dead is but a few, the temple will have many more guards, but for now, we are safe." Oaken took a deep breath as Ria leaned on him.

"I think so too, but we have time, that is the only way in or out, we can take our time, until I know what I am going to do." Yandalla looked back at the pass, being guarded by the Undine.

"See Oaken, I told you we would find a way." She linked her father's arm, and gave a big smile, somehow, he felt she was far more aware of things than he was.

Chapter Thirty One

Earth, Air, Water, Spirit, Fire

Shade walked around pulling arrows from the dead, and wiping the tips to put back in her grass woven pouch. She had collected many arrows, a few of which were Undine, so she had more in her pouch than ever before. Sintalla joined her, and collected up replacements for her and Yandalla, as she watched Shade carefully. Shade noticed, and Sintalla gave a nod.

"You feel ill at ease with my people?" Shade turned her head, and looked back to where all of the Undine stood guard watching the pass.

"Me no same." Sintalla lifted an arrow, and walked towards her.

"You have some Shodalt, but when I look at you, all I see is a true Undine warrior, and I have great respect for her." Shade gave a smile.

"Anna Ma, teach good."

"It was your mother who was Undine?" Shade gave a gentle nod.

"Anna Ma better warrior." Sintalla smiled.

"I want to be as good as my mother's sister, Holis, she is a noble and true warrior." Shade stood holding an arrow in her hand, behind her the sun shone, casting her small thin shadow on the floor in front of her. Shade watched her carefully.

"Me tired, want quiet, sit in pools, walk in tree, live peace, no kilt." Sintalla understood, no one had wanted this war, it had come out of nowhere, and turned everyone's life upside down.

"We are fighting, and if we all come together, we can defeat Balathral." Shade shook her head, and walked towards the trees.

"He have lot son's, who next?" Sintalla stood, as Shade walked away, she had no idea Balathral had children, although how did Shade know that?

The day was moving on as the sun lowered in the sky, and

Oaken was becoming restless. His chest felt tight, and his stomach churned, and he felt a burning desire to move. Ria frowned as she looked at him.

"Are you alright?"

"I am not sure, I felt something, like I have to do something, and I have to do it soon. I do not know what to do." Ria looked at Pallum talking with the others.

"Oaken, it will soon be dark, you are not thinking of walking into that place in the dark, are you?" She could see his discomfort; he was clearly feeling something strong.

"Ria, something is reaching out to me, I know this makes no sense, but it is like I felt at home in the temple. I know none of this makes sense, but I feel Nuada wants me to do something."

This was her greatest fear, and somewhere deep inside she knew it would come down to this, he would do this alone. All her life she had doubted Bharl and Nuada, and yet, in recent days she had seen things that left her lost for words. In a strange way she had a faith in Oaken she had never possessed before, and she was not sure why. Was it love, or was it something else, because as odd as it was to her, she believed in him? Ria looked him in the eyes and lowered her voice.

"What do you want to do?" He took a deep breath.

"I need to go to the temple, and soon." Ria gave a nod and smiled.

"Alright Oaken, I have no idea why, but I trust your instincts, and I will be right at your side no matter what happens. Get your sword, and we will see what becomes of all of us."

It was dark when they walked up to the two carts that had been pushed across the road. Undine warriors stood on guard, their eyes which could see better in the dark watching down the long cut out gorge, to where a hundred torches burned around the huge temple of Nuada. Oaken stopped with Ria at his side, and gave a nod to the Undine warriors.

"Ca Baska, Ae Yan Oaken." One of the Undine stepped forward, and spoke in the common tongue.

"We know who you are, and Ca Baska son of Sarka." Oaken was a little relieved, it made things simpler.

"I am the son of Andalyn, and his heir, that temple is the most sacred place of my people. Only I can claim it, I wish no other be harmed, and so I wish to pass." The Undine understood.

"We see the sword and remember the past, we owe you our lives." Oaken gave another respectful nod.

"If you owe me your lives, then I wish them unharmed, let me pass and they will be." The Undine gave a bow, and then stepped back, Ria looked at Oaken.

"Is that it, you just ask and they say yes?" Oaken smirked as he walked forward.

"There is a code between their people and mine, that is built on honour and truth. They know the power of Nuada and the strength of our connection to it, they would never prevent a servant of Nuada from doing his work." Ria looked back as they passed the cart, all of them had returned to their posts.

It was much darker once they passed the cart, the torches behind them were set to the sides, so their light did not penetrate much of the long road. Ahead they could see the wide green, which was cut low, and the ten hand cut steps that led up to the temple of Nuada, and when Ria saw it, her breath caught in her chest.

"Oh my, Oaken, it is magnificent."

The steps led up to a wall of stone, out of which were carved pillars that held up huge arches, above which was a lintel. As Ria stared at it, looking above the huge lintel, there were more arches, which contained statues of people from an age long past, all of them stood in a pose of welcome, their arms reaching out. In the centre above the central door arch, there was a larger statue, set in an elaborately carved archway, it was a figure who was holding a sword aloft, pointing it to the heavens, above which were two round windows cut from the stone, which had in the centre, a sun and a moon. It towered up high into the sky, carved from the largest rock face on the whole of Andalan, its rock a dusty red, and weathered with great age.

Oaken walked slowly, his heart filled with the love he felt for this place, he felt emotional, because he had at times never thought he would look upon it again, lit by the flickering flames of a hundred torches burning brightly in the darkness. This was a road he had walked many times with his father as a child, and now after years of exile, he felt the responsibility of walking in his father's footsteps.

Oaken's eyes were fixed on the temple and the hand cut steps, worn in many parts where for times long past, members of his race had walked. He was transfixed, reacquainting his eyes once more on a site he had honestly thought he would never see again. He was so absorbed he did not notice Ria as she turned to look behind them.

"What are you doing here?"

Behind them in the darkness, Ria looked at a line of faces, as Shade, Yandalla, Sintalla, and Elden stood watching. She jerked on Oaken's arm and he snapped out of his thoughts and turned, and saw them, and his eyes narrowed.

"Why are you here, this is not your fight?" Elden stared at him.

"That there is my temple, my homeland, and my sacred place to talk to my father. I told you Oaken, I will walk with you when you enter, it is my right as a man of Andalan." Oaken took a breath and nodded at Elden.

"This will be dangerous, I want no other harmed, but I understand your need to walk there, I too am feeling it." Elden gave a smile.

"Don't forget, I am the only one here who will not be disappointed when you pull out that rusty old blade, I am sure the Summanu will die of embarrassment when they see it and realise, they actually feared it." He smiled and Yandalla gave a little giggle. She came forward and took his hand.

"Oaken, I feel Nuada with you, but you must not walk alone, we are here because all of us want to walk with you and protect you. I will not let you go alone; we belong side by side in this moment, and I know Nuada will want this." He gave a long sigh.

"Yandalla, there are a lot of soldiers here. You may not see them, but they are here watching, and they will not us let us walk up the steps without confrontation." Shade gave a reassured nod.

"Good, me kilt them." Sintalla looked down the road.

"It is quiet now, but if they appear, do what you mean to, and we will keep you covered. No matter what you think, you need us here Oaken." It was clear he was not going to win, he gave a slight nod, and looked at them all.

"If you come, stay back, and follow my lead, all I want is to get the Summanu out of my temple without harming it." They all nodded, and Ria smiled as he turned. She linked his arm, and gave it a squeeze.

"Lead on Oaken of the four winds." He glanced at her smile, and tried to ignore it, as he began to walk forward again. The group hung back allowing him ten paces, and then began to walk at his pace in a long row.

They walked at a slow pace down the dark road, all of them with their senses at high alert, as they watched every aspect of the what was the temple plaza. Their pace was slow, Oaken was nervous as there were no other soldiers, he had expected the place to be filled with them.

As they came closer to the end of the long road, more of the huge site came into view, and Ria could see the whole place had been carved out of what was once thick rock. She marvelled, as more of the site came into view, and she could see how from either side of the temple, all of the walls had been elaborately carved into what she already knew were the dwellings of the Andalan, one of which used to be the home of Oaken.

They reached the end of the road, and stepped out into the light, Oaken placed his hand on his sword hilt, he was very wary, deep inside, his feelings were building and his apprehension was growing. Something was not right, he felt it, and it was a powerful thing, as he felt himself more on his guard than he had ever been before. He took a breath as Eliaston had taught him many times, and tried to relax himself a little.

Ria noticed, she was feeling the same, she could feel cold prickles running down her back, she noticed his hand and slid hers over to her sword, and looked slowly around to make sure there was nothing waiting down either side of what was a wide smooth stone area, broken up with wide lawns of short green grass, she had expected trees, but there were none.

"Oaken, this is wrong, we know this place is full of soldiers, where are they?" He stared at the temple doorway.

"They are here; I feel them." Ria glanced back at Yandalla.

"You do?" She nodded.

"There are many souls here Ria, and some of them are dark."

Ria swallowed hard.

"You feel souls, even dark ones?" Yandalla nodded, her green eyes appeared to be bright in her white face, that somehow made her face quite scary.

"There is one here who frightens me, his soul is the darkest." Elden glanced at her.

"You may be small and very womanly, but I have to say, Yandalla, I wish you had not said that." Ria nodded.

"Yeah, me too." Oaken took a step forward.

"They will appear when they are needed."

Oaken walked out into the light, and stepped onto the grass, and walked straight towards the temple steps. It was useless waiting; he was sure they were aware of their presence. With his feelings of caution and apprehension growing, it made more sense to simply head towards the temple and confront his fate.

Oaken began to walk, and as soon as he did, there was noise inside the temple, he looked up to see Summanu soldiers dressed in black. They flooded out and lined the whole of the top five steps, and drew out their swords, Oaken slowed to a stop, and Ria grabbed his arm.

"I am not sure we should do this Oaken, there is far more than we can handle." Oaken looked back and the others were stood still, right behind him. He turned to Ria.

"Do not show fear, that is what they want, if you show it, they will attack sooner." She nodded.

"That is not an easy ask Oaken, there is a lot, if we anger them, we will surely die. I will not deny, looking at them, is pretty terrifying." He softly patted her hand.

"Stand with the others and follow my lead." She frowned as he gently removed her arm from his and took a step forward, Ria went to move, but Yandalla reached out and took hold of her arm.

"Ria, let him do this, it is important he does."

Ria watched feeling terrified as he walked slowly towards the temple steps. As he moved closer, the soldiers tensed, and he sensed that they were nervous, but they were holding back, which was strange, because he was one against all of them. It was now or never so he took another step forward, and took a deep breath and shouted.

"KABAZAN!"

Ria jumped, as his voice echoed all around the carved out area of the temple, and it sounded powerful. She stood holding Yandalla's hand and trembling, her voice so quiet it was barely audible.

"Please be careful, I don't want to lose you." Oaken looked at the temple.

"Your god has no place here Kabazan, he cannot and will never rule here, this is the house of Nuada, built by our ancestors, and Bharl has no place here."

The soldiers did not appreciate that, they stared with hatred, and then took two paces forward coming lower down the steps. Shade did not like that, she moved forward and walked past Yandalla and Ria, and came right up to the side of Oaken. She stared at the guards; her hatred was obvious.

"Stay, you move, me kilt you." Her hand slid to her sword hilt, and Oaken stretched out his arm, and put his hand on hers.

"The time to die is not now Shade, I am safe enough here." She turned and saw him look at her, and smile, she nodded and relaxed her arm, Oaken turned back to the soldiers.

"Tell your worshiper of Bharl to stop hiding behind your swords and come forth, it is showing his cowardice. Tell him to show me his bravery, I am but one man, no one here will harm him."

It was clear that the soldiers did not like his words, and they looked uncomfortable. Oaken stared at them all as the others moved to his side, and he heard a familiar growl, and looked down to see a large black cat walk up and sit beside Sintalla. Oaken turned back and noticed movement at the back of the line of soldiers. The back line moved slightly, then parted, and as they separated, Oaken saw Kabazan stood watching, he came forward onto the top step. Elden gave a slight gasp.

"Son's of Andalan, he is a big one!"

Elden was right, Kabazan was huge. He stood tall, and wide, his thick arms bulging from his long black sleeveless tunic trimmed with gold. His arms were decorated with an array of black tattooed symbols, and around his thick waste was a wide golden belt, off which hung a large and long golden sword scabbard. His head was dark skinned like his arms, and was round, with a long snow white beard, his hair long and swept back across his head. He had a hard cruel face, which scowled, as he watched the group with small dark evil looking eyes. He stepped down and gave a grunt of a laugh, and his voice was coarse and deep.

"Well look at all of you, a collection of nations, here to unseat the mighty and powerful lord of thunder and fire, Bharl. Go away, you irritating bugs of the ground, or I will slice you and feed you to the birds." Shade growled like an animal.

"Me want kilt him." Kabazan gave a smirk.

"Little girls with swords die fast, yet, I will spare you, and hand you as my prize to Belthaz, he has a need to talk with you as he peels your skin slowly away for his pleasure." Shade scowled at him.

"Ha!" Kabazan looked at Ria, and smirked.

"Nutriana, daughter of that thief, and smuggler, Evander of the land of thieves and deception of Animatre, Bharl will enjoy watching you burn before me, you are fish out of water, powerless against the flames of my master." She was scared, but she was not going to show it, and no one insulted her father in front of her, she gritted her teeth, her blue eyes defiant as they looked at him.

"Bring Bharl swimming, and see how long his fire lasts, there is great power in shallow water, do not underestimate its power, pretender of a fake god." He growled at her, and noticed the black cat.

"Well, well, one of the spirits breeds, and a bitch I believe? I hope your new master feeds you better than Belthaz does his bitch?" Vesta growled a loud and intense growl, her eyes growing orange, Kabazan smirked, and his eyes moved to Oaken.

"Son of Andalan, I hear my arrow was on target, and your father wore it well. Look at you, the last lord of a line of air, and worshiper of your failed master Nuada. His home is now mine, and even though you stand before me, a voice bigger than your stature, with you companions of water, earth, spirt and air, you lack the fire to face me and win, now use what little air you have left in your line, and blow away like a fallen leaf." Oaken smiled.

"Big words from an empty man. You creep from behind the skirts of your fake prophet Balathral, and dare to stand on the steps of the power that is Nuada. Come down and face me, and before the dawn rises, this place will be free of Summanu puppets, and host the only god that belongs here once again." Kabazan snarled, his teeth clenched tight, and lifted his arm to point.

"Kill them!"

The Summanu soldiers moved to the sound of drawing steel, as Oaken, and the others drew their swords as Yandalla and Sintalla lifted their bows. The soldiers surged forward and Shade gave a war cry, and launched herself at them, and from behind them came a volley of arrows, and the first row of soldiers crumpled under the hail of arrows sent out of the darkness by Pallum and the Undine.

Pallum had realised that Oaken was gone, and it had not taken more than a moment to realise what he was doing. The Undine came quickly down the dark passage, hidden under their cloaks, and formed a long line out of eyesight in the shadows.

The clash came as Oaken lifted his sword and struck hard into a Summanu soldier, Ria at his side fought with increased anger, as did Elden, who sliced with hate, as he remembered the bravery of his father. Shade was in the thick, slashing and snarling with an anger greater than any of them had ever seen, and Vesta snarled as she lunged at the throats of the soldiers tearing them out with a vicious and horrifying bite.

Kabazan stood back and watched, his face filled with a conceited smirk, as he saw his troops fall, overwhelmed by the hail of arrows. He watched Oaken, twist and swing, fending off crashing blows from soldiers far bigger than Oaken was. He was impressed, this boy of Andalan fought with great heart, but even so, he knew he would die tonight, and he licked his lips as he tasted the oncoming of victory.

The fight was brutal, and the bodies began to pile up, as Ham smashed and slashed his way towards the steps, Oaken grabbed Ria by the back of the shirt and dragged her back as a soldier lunged at her. He moved in swiftly and slashed with his sword cutting the man who was aiming to kill her. His sleeve was cut, and his dirty white shirt stained red, but he fought with an anger and determination, his eyes fixed on Kabazan, as he cut his way towards him.

All around the steps of the temple, the stone ran red with blood, as the Summanu fell to the anger of a people whose lands had been devasted, and even though they knew that Balathral had a thousand times more than any army they could muster, here in this sacred place, all of them were determined to restore the one thing everyone could look to, they would restore peace, and the power of love and compassion that was Nuada.

Andalan, a place of peace, a place of study and wisdom that had helped and advised many over the years, on this night would rise again. Oaken would not let any who stood in his path stop him. In his head all he could see was the love of his father's eyes, and those final words he had spoken to his mother.

"Take my son, for in him is the love I hold in my heart, protect him Sarka, he is our future." In his thoughts as he cut and slashed, he spoke the words he always wanted to tell his father.

"I will never let you down, and I will take back our lands and Nuada will rise again in honour of you father."

He brought round a crashing blow, and his sword sliced through bone, and the face before him flipped into the air as the body flopped. Before him all was clear, and all he could see were the steps to the temple, and two large feet stood at the top. Oaken lifted his eyes, and they met the dark unfeeling eyes of Kabazan, all around him was silent, and he glanced back to see his comrades, standing in between the mass of dead that was the Summanu. He turned back and looked up to face Kabazan as he panted, sweat dripping off his hair, as tried to refill his lungs, as his arm fell limp holding his chipped and worn sword.

Behind him, the others stepped back and came together, Ria looked panicked, Sintalla was cut on her leg and limped, helped by Yandalla who had a face covered in blood. Ham held his arm, which was bleeding badly, Elden had slashes across his shirt, and it hung loose as he inspected his chest and stomach that bore cuts. Shade stood proud between them and Oaken, she was covered in blood, but smiled from her blood covered face, as she looked up at the steps, and the blood dripped from her slightly longer hair.

"Need more soldiers, me kilt these." She gave a smirk, and it angered Kabazan, which pleased her.

Oaken stood panting but gave a chuckle, Shade's ability to

annoy members of the apostles, was one of the things he loved most about her. He looked up at Kabazan, and took a deep intake of breath.

"It appears earth, air, water and spirit have little use of fire, we appear to be doing fine without out it. Tell me apostle of a fake god, where is he, where is all the fire that was supposed to burn us? If you need a spark, my friend Shade has flints."

"Ha!" Shade smiled with white teeth, but to be honest, with her blood covered face and body, and her bright eyes, she actually looked very scary.

Kabazan looked more than angry, his face contorted, and he gave a loud snarl, as he drew out his long sword, and stepped down to the next step.

"They are men to be wasted nothing more, they are no match for the skills of my arm filled with the power of Bharl, the lord of power and God of thunder. Now you will feel the rumble of a true god, and see the flash of steel so bright it will blind you in the last moment of your life." Ria took a deep breath and grabbed Ham by the arm, and he flinched in pain, she realised and looked down to see she was clutching at his wound. She let go quickly and looked apologetic, as she looked at him.

"I am so sorry, did that hurt?" He smiled through gritted teeth, and gave a slight nod, as he swallowed hard trying not to release the scream he had stifled.

Kabazan took another step forward onto the next step, and Shade flinched ready, Oaken threw out his arm.

"No Shade! If I fall, he is yours, but for now, this is my task." She stepped back, and nodded at him. Her voice was ice cold and devoid of life.

"Kilt him!" Oaken nodded and stepped back, he needed room.

Pallum understood the moment, he had two hundred Undine all with their bows loaded with arrows pointing at Kabazan. He walked forward slowly onto the grass and lifted out his arms to his sides, and then with his palms facing down and his eyes locked on Oaken, he lowered his palms slowly, and the bows of the Undine tipped to the floor, their arrows still loaded, pointing at the stone. Pallum spoke softly.

"Oaken needs room, Ria, Yandalla, Elden, Ham, Vesta, and Night Shade, withdraw, give Oaken the space to finish this, for tonight it is his task to lift back the Andalan to their rightful place. Only then can he rise as the new high lord of his people, as Oaken of the four winds. Do not interfere, this is his fate, and his fate alone." Ria turned with tears in his eyes.

"Can he really do this; I am afraid for him?" Pallum smiled at her.

"Is your heart filled with the love of this young Andalan?" She nodded, and wiped the tears from her eyes.

"Yes, it is, even more than he realises." Pallum gave a gentle nod as Yandalla took her hand.

"Then believe in him, and trust that he is destined to do this, for Nuada picked him for this very moment." Ria gave a sniffle and nodded, but she could not help feeling such fear, for never in her life had she felt anything like it before.

Oaken took several paces back, stepping over the bodies until he was stood in a clear space, on green grass, as Kabazan came down the steps, his tall thick frame, clumping on the stone, as he swung his sword from side to side. His voice was deep, loud and contained an element of amusement.

"This blade has never tasted blood, I look forward to bathing it in the blood of an Andalan, and letting it taste the true power of its master." Oaken gave a smirk.

"The blood of the Andalan does not run so freely, but when it does, it purifies all it touches."

Kabazan stepped off the last step, and lifted his thick leg over the bodies of his fallen men. He took a few giant paces, and was stood on the grass facing Oaken. He ran his tongue around the inside of his mouth as if tasting the fight, and he smiled an evil smile.

"Prepare to meet with your father young Andalan."

Yandalla stood in front of her father, and watched feeling afraid as she saw Kabazan raise his sword, Oaken breathed in and tried to focus as Master Eliaston had taught him, his words were soft and quietly spoken.

"Be with me father, lend me your strength, for tonight I will need the power of Nuada within me, as it was within you." He breathed out letting the air flow past his lips, and raised his sword ready.

Yandalla jerked, her arms shot out at her sides, and her bright green eyes rolled into the back of her head, and turned a bright snow white, as she went ridged, and her head flopped back looking up to the sky. Her voice was eerie and ethereal, as it flowed out of her.

"Yan fors ae Cumten." Ria turned to see her, and as she did, Yandalla exploded with light as Oaken's sword clashed into Kabazan's with the loud chiming ring.

Sarka turned in the darkness, Eliaston had risen from his bed and walked out into the night. She felt the urgency in the air all around them, as she rushed through the door to see the old master walk to the edge of the rock and face Andalan. She froze on the spot as the old master's arms shot out to the sides and his head fell back, and fear flowed into her as she watched his eyes roll into the back of his head turning them white. Eliaston stood held like stone and jerking, his mouth opened, and he drew in a long haunting sounding breath. His voice came up from between his lips, and it sounded, ancient, deathly, and terrifying.

"THE WIND IS COMING!"

Chapter Thirty Two
Power of the Wind

Kabazan lifted his sword with both hands, and swung it with all of his might, as Oaken locked his arms and held up his blade. The two swords collided with a deafening chime, and sparks flew from the blade's edges. Oaken was lifted into the air as Ria screamed, and pulled her hands to her mouth. Oaken crashed into the floor, and rolled backwards to get back to his feet as quickly as he could. He could feel the pain running up his arm from the clash, and it felt like it had shaken the bones under his skin. Kabazan did not stop, he roared out in anger, as yet again Oaken had blocked his sword and defended well.

Pallum gave a nod, he had taught Oaken most of what he knew, and he could see how advanced he had become in his combat. Oaken took a deep breath, as around the whole of the temple, the light that flowed from Yandalla illuminated everything. She stood frozen, lost in a trance, and connecting to other worlds, as she sought the power of Nuada to help her beloved brother.

Oaken planted his feet, trying to keep his mind focused, as he held his sword up once again, and felt the pain in his arms. Kabazan's blade came around like lightening, as Oaken lifted his and locked his elbow, ready to fend off yet another mighty blow, to add to the pounding of this large Summanu warrior. The blade thundered into his, and he felt the intense pain as he tried to hold it off him, Shade's arms twitched, and Ria screamed again, as this time, she saw Oaken's sword sheer clean in half, and Oaken was yet again lifted and tossed backwards, smashing into the floor, his body screaming inside his head with pain.

Kabazan roared out with laughter and Shade gritted her teeth, the huge frame of the Summanu Apostle walked slowly towards him laughing.

"It appears your words were much bigger than your sword, now I will end the line of Andalyn forever."

Kabazan lifted his massive sword with both hands, as Oaken

lay back on the floor, riddled with pain, and Ria's heart broke, as she felt the final moment of Oaken approaching. Oaken breathed in and tried to move, he was still holding half a sword, he threw it aside as Kabazan approached, and reached his arm up to his shoulder, and inside his head, Yandalla screamed.

"YUN AE FORS AE!"

He blinked, and understood, he was the wind, and she was there with him, for she was his guide in moments of doubt. He pulled hard, and felt the old sword slip, and then without understanding how, he felt a huge burst of energy, and pulled the sword free, and swept it up in front of him. It sounded like a thunder ball had exploded from the sky, as both swords met with a mighty flash.

Ria felt a slight breeze lift her hair, dropped her hands to see Oaken lay on the grass, and aura of white light surrounding him, the old sword held tightly in his hand, and up in front of him. Kabazan leaned over him, a look off bewilderment on his face, Oaken's sword had stopped his, and as the Summanu Apostle had leaned over, such was the power of the Sword of the Winds, it had jolted up, and sliced into Kabazan' scalp. The giant Summanu stepped back, filled with surprise as he saw his own blood drip onto Oaken's white shirt.

He lifted his hand and felt the warm moisture, and lowered his hand to see it covered in blood, he could not believe it, and stepped back trying to understand what had happened. Oaken got up off the floor and faced his enemy, a surge of energy flowing into his aching limbs, his voice soft as he swallowed.

"Tac Yeat, Yandalla." Her soft words echoed around his head.

"You are the wind, use the wisdom and power of Nuada, it is with you, as is your father. I feel him Oaken, and he is all around you, believe in him, and use the wind he gave you."

All around the temple, and dust stirred on the old stone, and lifted swirling in a gentle breeze that softly stroked through the grass, swirling to the base of Oaken's feet. Oaken took a deep breath, gripped his sword hard, his mind shifting and flowing in rhythm with the soft breeze, he lifted his arm, and dust swirled around his feet, as Ria saw the changes within his stance, and she breathed a sigh of relief.

"The wind has come."

Oaken looked at the wounded apostle, gritted his teeth, as his eyes narrowed, and lifted and swung the sword, and from nowhere, and gust of wind blasted into the air from the floor, and swirled around him.

Oaken wasted no time, he saw Kabazan, and launched himself at him, his teeth gritted and anger at the Summanu flowing with his focus. His sword served a crashing blow onto Kabazan, as the large Summanu panicked, and quickly raised his own weapon. Oaken hit it hard with a deafening chime, and then twisted his wrist and brought the sword back with great speed, and whipped it back with fury. The blades rang out as everyone watched, as Oaken moved forward, and crashed blow after blow onto Kabazan, who staggered back under the renewed power of his opponent, not really understanding how it was happening. Oaken yelled out, as he brought another pounding blow around at him, and it echoed all around the temple.

"WHERE IS YOUR GOD NOW, WHERE IS THE FIRE YOU TALKED OF, SHOW ME, SO THAT I CAN SNUFF IT OUT WITH THE WIND OF A TRUE GOD?"

Kabazan staggered under the power, as the sword swung back into him, and all he could do was counter the blow by clenching the blade with both hands, and locking his wrist, as the sheer power of Oaken blasted into him down the blade. Oaken swung back, his focus now complete, and his blade swung with determination, and all of his power, as the wind around swirled faster stirring everything, and bending the short blades of grass around flat.

"Show me apostle, show me the power of your weak god."

Oaken's sword hit harder than any of the previous blows, and the pain in Kabazan's arms was so intense, he wailed out in fear. Oaken's sword swept once again through the air, collided with the long large sword, and this time it swept right through it, sheering the golden blade completely in half. Ria gasped out in shock, and Kabazan gave out a cry, as Oaken swept his blade back with gritted teeth, and lunged straight into the midriff of Kabazan, and his blade went straight through to the hilt, and he held it there, his eyes almost level with Kabazan's as he sagged with a gasp.

Kabazan looked down and saw the hilt of the rusty old sword

sticking out of him, and the shock hit him, he lifted his head to look at Oaken, and dropped his sheered in half sword.

"How?" Oaken stared into his shocked eyes, as he breathed in more air between gasps.

"Nuada is real, Balathral lied to you, as did his father." Kabazan looked shocked and afraid, as he shook his head, and his voice sounded weak.

"No!" Oaken nodded, holding his sword fast.

"Yes Kabazan."

Oaken gripped the hilt and pulled hard, and Kabazan jerked as the sword came out, and he fell back, as Oaken stepped away. The wind flowing around him softened, and fell back to the floor as a soft and gentle breeze, stoking the blades of grass and stirring the dust on the stones.

Kabazan hit the floor and stared up into the sky, it was clear and free of clouds, there was no thunder or lightening, Bharl had deserted him. His breathing was laboured, as he lay there, he could not believe after a life of service, his god would desert him. He had given him everything, and yet when he needed him most, Bharl had deserted him. It was getting harder to breathe, and he swallowed hard tasting his own blood, Oaken stepped back away from him, and stood trembling and weakened, as Ria ran across the grass crying, and dragged him into her arms, where he hung weak, and exhausted. Behind him, Kabazan sat bolt upright.

"YOU LIE!"

There was a flash of silver, and the head of Kabazan flew into the air, it landed with a thud, as the torso flopped back to the ground, and Shade stood covered in blood, with her sword in her hand. She looked up from his body at Ria, and smiled.

"He kilt now!" Her blue eyes glinted in her reddened bloody face, her teeth as white as snow, in her smile.

Across the grass, Yandalla flopped back into her father's arms, and he pulled her close, she looked up with green eyes and smiled.

"Anna Pa, Oaken safe now." She closed her eyes and felt weak. Pallum smiled as he looked down on her, and then looked to Oaken held tight in Ria's embrace.

"He is, your brother did good, and he has saved his home and freed it from the Summanu. This is a good thing my sweet flower of the meadow, for it brings light into the lives of all of us." She smiled, but was simply too tired to talk.

Ria loosened her grip, and he slid back a little as she looked into his eyes and smiled.

"You really scared me; I thought I would lose you. Oaken, never do that again, never make me stand back and watch you fight, I love you, I would rather die at your side, than stand helpless and watch on."

She leaned in and kissed him, and was glad that she still had him to hold close. Never in her life had she been as frightened, as she was watching him fight. He pulled out of the kiss and smiled.

"Ria, I have one more thing to do." He slid back out of her arms, and smiled at her.

"Do not worry, it is nothing dangerous." She nodded with relief.

Oaken turned, and still holding the sword he walked slowly back towards the steps, he stopped at the bottom of the step and looked up to the sky.

"I am here father, I kept my promise, your land is returned unto you, walk with Nuada and rest now."

Oaken walked slowly up the steps, and on the top step, he turned and faced out into the wide plaza. He saw Elden watching him and smiled, then lifted the sword up to point to the sky. His voice was loud and filled with the pride of his ancestors, as a huge wind rose up again and blasted around him at high speed, and funnelled upward into the sky.

"I, Oaken of the four winds, bearer of the sword to the sky, claim back my heritage in the name of all the free people of Andalan. Hear me, my most merciful Nuada, and bless this land and this sacred place, so that Andalan can thrive again, as it once did."

Ria watched as out of the sky, a bright flash shot down and hit the sword, the whole place lit up with bright white light that was impossible to look at. Ria shielded her eyes, as a crack of thunder boomed into the air, and when she looked up, Oaken stood proud, holding aloft a bright golden sword, as the wind swirled down and blew through the lands of Andalan, as white light streamed from his sword up into the sky. She smiled; her voice was soft.

"Oaken of the four winds, filled with the power of Nuada, and a free man of his people." Behind her Shade giggled, and she turned and looked at her, Shade gave her a smile as she saw Ria watching, she lifted her eyebrows.

"Mmm, Yan tee!"

Ria started to laugh, she had no idea how Shade always knew, but yes, she was right, because in that one moment watching him hold up his sword, she knew, she would never see anything more attractive in her life.

Sarka stood and watched as the winds howled up from the coast and swept across the land, clouds swirled in wide circles, and in their centre above Andalan, white light funnelled into the sky. Eliaston came out of his trance and smiled a huge smile, the old man scuttled across the stone floor.

"I must tell the leaders and muster the warriors, we have a lot to do, if we are to return." Sarka took her eyes off the light, and looked at the old man.

"What do you mean?" He gave another huge smile.

"Andalan is free, Oaken has won it back, the sword is connected and rising to meet Nuada, the four winds blow through Andalan again. We must prepare and send warriors; he will need others to help guard our land." Sarka was almost lost for words, and she blinked as she tried to understand.

"Eliaston, are you serious, is that Oatin, are you saying he is in Andalan with Yandalla?" Eliaston nodded quickly.

"Yes, my dear Sarka, he has defeated the enemy, and is stood on the temple steps with the sword, as I told him to do. The four winds blow around him and have returned to our homeland, no Summanu walk there this night."

It was hard to believe, hard to even understand, how could her son who was so quiet and good natured have taken back what his father lost? She could not fully understand it all. She felt the warmth of Eliaston as he took her hand in his.

"Sarka, he stands with his father and in his father's place. Our people are free and can return to our ancestral home land, Andalyn would be very proud of his son this night."

She gave a slight nod, still trying to fully comprehend that it was her son who did this, she watched as the light in the distance, dropped back to the land and deep down inside, she felt her heartbreak.

"That land took his father; how do I know it will not take his son?" Eliaston understood, and he smiled.

"He wanted this Sarka, Oaken wanted to take back the land to honour the man that gave up his life for his people. You should pack and go with them, go and reunite with your family, and walk in the land of our people once more. Sarka, you more than any should walk into that temple and give thanks on behalf of all of us. You have earned the right, for without you, there would be no people of Andalan left to stand by Oaken." Sarka gave a sigh, and looked to the mountains in the distance.

"No, that is no longer my home or my place, my life is here with the Undine, and my husband. I left a lot of pain in that desert, and it can remain there, I have no wish to return Eliaston, those demons are buried, I shall not dig them up." He gave gentle nod, and released her hand.

"I think you are right; you have done what was needed, rest now, and live a happy life with your husband and these wonderful people. Sarka, actually live for you, and let others take care of everything, you have earned that too."

He gave a little giggle, and shuffled off to alert the others. Sarka took a deep breath and walked slowly back to her new home, as she approached the door, she stopped and looked back.

"Forgive me Andalyn, I had to let you go, for to hold onto you was too much pain for one soul to bear. Live now in your son, and finally let me go, I need to live my life now free of the pain of those days, so you should watch over him now, not me."

Ria walked up the steps and looked at him, he looked exhausted.

"Are you alright?" He took a deep breath, and gave her a slight nod.

"I did it, I am not sure I believe it." She slid her arms around his waist, and stared into his eyes.

"It probably sounds strange, but from the moment I met you, I think I knew you would. It makes little sense to me, I just accepted that you would." Elden walked slowly onto the steps, and gave a smile as he saw the gleaming blade in Oaken's hand.

"I must say, now that is a vast improvement." Oaken looked down at the sword and then back to Elden.

"See, I told you it had an inner beauty, I also said I would clean it, I have just been busy." Elden gave a chuckle.

"It is less embarrassing now it has a point again." Ria gave a giggle, as Elden walked up the steps and gripped Oaken by the shoulder, he looked emotional but very sincere.

"Thank you Oaken, my father will rejoice knowing we stand at the door of our temple. It broke his heart to leave here, I have his ashes in my bag, with your say, I would like to return him to his rightful place." Oaken gave a nod.

"Yes, it would be my honour to see him return home." Elden gave a smile and nodded, he was clearly lost for words, as his eyes glistened and he looked to the large wooden door, that housed the most sacred space to all of his people.

The Undine warriors brought the carts to the temple, and stacked the bodies of the dead Summanu into them, which were then carted off to the edges of the territory, and burned lighting the sky for all around to see.

As they worked, Oaken walked into the large temple lit by a hundred burning oil lamps with Ria and Elden. The walls, which had alcoves filled with the stone carved statues of the men of the past, the great scholars, philosophers, and temple leaders, had been covered with wall hangings of a red faced, brutal and evil looking being, who Oaken assumed was Bharl. He tore them down, revealing the statues.

"I want this vile filth burning, and every trace of him gone, this is a place of purity, not death, decay and destruction."

With the assistance of Ria and Elden, the three of them pulled at them, and tore them from the walls, and heaped them in a large pile at the doors to be dragged out and burned. Caleb arrived with their bags, and Oaken knelt before the place of prayer and lifted his sword, and laid it down into the two remaining golden brackets. Ria watched as he carefully placed it down, and then took out his book of winds, and placed it on a small raised stone block, beside the three other empty ones.

Removing a hollowed out bamboo tube, he slipped out one of his incense sticks and lit it, then knelt back on his heels and closed his eyes. In his mind her heard the voice of his father from that day aged only three, where his father guided him.

"Close your eyes Oatin, breathe slowly and think of Nuada. In your mind talk to him, and then sit and think of the words that you used, and wait for your answer." Oaken breathed in deeply, his thoughts swirling inside his head.

"I miss you father; I grew up wanting you to see me become a true man of Andalan. I want you to have peace knowing I am here to continue what you began. Father, be proud of me, for that is all I have ever wanted."

He breathed in and slowly released the air out of his lungs, and his mind drifted, as all of the memories of his life before being with the Undine flowed through his thoughts. In his mind he heard his father, and his heart filled with warmth.

"I am with you Oatin, I always have been, be the man you were meant to be. I have always been proud of my son, and that will never change as I walk with Nuada." He took a deep breath, and felt the warmth of his father all around him, and for several long moments, he basked in the love of his father.

Later that night, Oaken walked out of the temple holding Ria by the hand, and crossed the grass towards what was once his home. It had not changed much, it was empty, looted by the soldiers, but as he looked around, so many memories flowed through his thoughts. This was his place of birth, the home his mother made for him and his father, it was the place that has stayed in his thoughts for every day since leaving, and he was finally back where he knew he belonged.

His bed was tiny, which made Ria giggle, so he walked her through to where his parents had slept. The bed was bigger, and just an ordinary wooden frame, that lacked a soft place to lie on. Ria cleaned the wound on his arm, and bound it, and then snuggling under their blankets, he blew out the oil lamp, and relaxed. His body ached and he was tired, and soon drifted into a sleep filled with the memories of life in Andalan.

The following day, was a hive of activity when he woke up, all of the group had taken homes in the large open space surrounding the temple. The Undine warriors had been posted by Pallum and walked on the high rocks as look outs, and those not on duty, helped with the cleaning of the site. The temple was brushed clean by Sintalla with Elden, the children gathered stores and shared them out around each of the houses, and Ham sat at the door of one of the houses and smiled.

Pallum lead him up the stone steps that led up behind the temple, and there set on the edge of the huge rock that towered over the lush green lands of Leyarken below, was a giant golden statue of the disfigured and evil Bharl. Pallum turned to him.

"What do we do this, it is stone, but it is covered in the shiny metal of the Summanu?" Oaken looked at it and it revolted him.

"Take it down, Elden knows where the smithy is, take it there and get Ham to chip off the metal and melt it down, then crush that monstrosity into dust. I want Balathral to see his god has no power here." Pallum smiled.

"You sound like your father." Oaken breathed in, and looked out over Leyarken.

"Which one, I have two, and both of them have educated me well?" It was a nice compliment, and Pallum was touched as it showed him great honour.

"I played my part Oaken, but in truth, you really are the son of Andalyn." Oaken smiled, he liked the idea of that.

Together they walked back down the steps as Oaken talked of what was to come, he knew Eliaston would bring aid, they had talked of it often, and so for now, he felt his place was to get the temple ready for its people. They reached the bottom talking quietly as Oaken looked across the grass, where Shade knelt on the grass in front of the two children and Meda cried.

Shade tried to smile, as she looked at both of the children she had saved, and put her hand on her heart.

"In here, you child's of me." Meda sniffled.

"I don't want you to go, I love you, and it is not safe for you out there." Shade took a breath.

"Me, big love too. My body spoilt, no have child's, to me, you mine." Caleb nodded with tears forming in his eyes.

"I don't understand why you have to leave us; we will come with you." Shade gave a big smile, but shook her head.

"Not safe, bad man where I go." Meda wept, and Shade stood up.

"Child's safe with Oaken, he good man, good lady Ria." Oaken walked up with Pallum and frowned.

"What is going on?" Shade stood with her bag over her shoulder and holding her bow, Caleb turned wiping his eyes.

"She says she has to leave, Oaken stop her, we do not want her to go."

He did not understand as he looked at her, she had been such a powerful protector, and she had become such a good friend.

"Shade, you belong here, why would you want to leave, I have houses, you can pick anyone and have a real home here?" Shade nodded and stepped back, she turned and looked back at him.

"No belong, only me, no nuther like me, me go." Oaken shook his head, as she started to walk, he walked after her.

"Shade, please listen, you do not have to be alone any more, you have friends here who care for you." Shade stopped and turned around; she wore a happy smile.

"Me know." It made no sense at all.

"Then why leave here?"

He walked closer to her; he could see in her eyes how hard this was for her. Shade took a deep breath and looked at the floor for a moment, then she looked up and she turned slightly and faced him, and spoke Undine.

"Me lived long time alone with heart only filled with Anna Ma. Me do not belong anywhere, Anna Ma Undine warrior, me like that, Anna Pa bad Shodalt. Yandalla understand, she two also. Me have home, place for me, is where belong, not here. Heart now have friends, me like that, good feelings, but me have to fix things, old things, is thing only Dar len eah ae lune can. Oaken, big fear lives inside, time now me get it out. Me go now."

Nothing made sense to him at all, he looked at her, and felt a pain inside him growing.

"Shade, I don't want you alone anymore, I care about you, stay with us, you are one of us." She gave a beautiful smile, and her eyes filled my tears.

"Me know, me like big. Me no belong, Dar len eah ae lune,

belong nowhere, me no fit, me go." Oaken looked back where Pallum stood watching just in front the weeping children.

"Pallum, tell her, she is an Undine and has a place with us." Pallum gave a nod, and looked at her.

"You are a valiant warrior, and have impressive skills, my people could learn much from you." Shade gave a slight chuckle.

"Me like Pallum now, but talk like Summanu. Me good ears, me hear. No Undine, Shodalt, me go, have task." Oaken shook his head.

"Shade, it does not have to be this way, you can stay here." Shade gave a nod.

"Sister saved, me help, make good feeling. Oaken good man, me care, but me go now."

Shade turned, hitched her bag on her shoulder, and holding her bow, walked towards the pass, as Oaken stood lost for words watching her walk away, and feeling heartbroken. He knew, he never would have made it without her, she was the reason he survived, and he wanted her to stay and be safe at his side. She had been alone for so long and it had been his hope that she would stay and never be lonely again, and yet he knew deep down inside she was right. Yandalla had talked often with him about being made of two tribes and the confusion she felt, but he had hoped that with Shade it would be different. He did not really know what to do, and just instinctively pulled out his sword in salute, and it shone in the sun, as he shouted at the top of his voice.

"DAH, LEN, EAH, AE LUNE... TAC YEAT!" She turned and saw him, smiled, and raised her bow.

Oaken watched as she turned, and walked slowly into the passage that led back to Andalan and her world. She was small, with tufted scruffy black hair, a small tight top of black, blood stained fabric, and her short skirt. On her feet were her foot bags and soft shoes, across her thin back was her woven bag made from grasses that contained the only real things she owned, and from her waist swung her sword, and her thin woven pouch filled with arrows.

She was small, but fierce, with a heart more powerful than any man he had ever known, and he felt a deep honour knowing she was his friend. Watching her walk away tore at him, but he knew she was right, she was not a full anything, she was simply Night Shade, a girl who had lived from her seventh summer alone in the wildest of lands, and somehow, she had survived. He deeply admired her, and was honoured to know her, and he knew without doubt, he was going to really miss her. He stared, as she slowly shrunk up the pass, her pace steady and never looking back, and deep inside he knew she was walking towards danger. His voice was low, as he breathed out his thoughts.

"You are my sister, no matter what you think, in my heart, you are to me as Yandalla, and I will always care for you. Take care my warrior, and live well and free always."

Oaken turned and walked back towards the two children, and looked at them as they offered them his hands.

"Like you, I do not want her to go, but she has other things to take care of, they are important. For now, you are as you have been in the care of Ria and myself, and all of us must do our best, and ask Nuada to watch over her, and then return her safely back to us." Caleb gave a nod, and Meda took his hand, and together they turned with Pallum, and walked towards the temple. Ria stood at the top of the steps with a sad smile.

"I had hoped not, but somehow, I always thought she would leave. Belthaz will hunt her down, and that will bring him on to our heels, and she knows that. I hope, and I feel, we have not seen the last of her, but who knows, after all, out of everyone I have ever met, she is more at one with land than any other. I know you care for her, but letting her walk free, is the kindest act, she belongs out there Oaken, that is her place, like the winds, she breezes across the plains, that is who her mother made her to be."

Four days later, Shengara arrived with his warriors and a large group of Leyarken fighters. Oaken was busy organising and Shengara wanted to know his thoughts as they sat at a table and broke bread together.

"The winds have changed Oaken. Men of Andalan are on route home, the warriors of my people have cleared the dead and watched the Summanu withdrawing. Your mother has healed many good warriors, and below in Keytan, there have been raids on the prisons and a lot of men are free. Shodalt is clearing as the Summanu leave, and the roads to Salanula are filled with his men retreating home, Balathral is said to be rebuilding his fortifications. The rise again of Andalan has frightened him, as he now knows there is another who wields the sword of the winds, you have the advantage, will you take it?" Oaken sat back as he chewed, and thought for a moment.

"I am waiting for the return of Eliaston, he knew my father better than any, and I will listen to his wisdom before I decide anything. If Eliaston feels we can defeat Balathral, I will march against him, but I will never leave Andalan unguarded again, that is my first priority." Shengara gave a nod.

"Your people have grown in number, far more will return than left here, it is a good start for your people, we have much to rebuild in Undinalashka, but you will have extra guards here until such time as you have greater numbers."

Over the weeks that came, Pallum returned home to Sarka, taking Yandalla with him. It was a tearful reunion as Yandalla held her mother tight and wept. Many of the young women that had been caged with her, came to visit and were happily reunited as sisters once more. Sintalla remained on Andalan at the side of Elden they had much in common, and had found a mutual attraction in talking weapons and tactics.

Eliaston finally arrived, brought in by ship to Keytan, where the port had been overrun with wild gangs of escapees, forming a resistance movement, under the command of Valk. The Summanu did not have large forces in Keytan, and had appointed leaders and a security force, which had proven to be Balathral's weakness. Over the weeks following Oaken's return to Andalan, Valk led his rebellion and soon overpowered the Summanu in the north of the lands, and an army of Ketonian forces was growing bigger, armed and supplied by Evander who brought in more supplies and weapons.

Eliaston returned to the temple in tears and prayed for days, as members of his order took over and cleared the temple of any final traces of the Summanu and Bharl. They brought with them many sacred items and placed them back in the spots where they had stood for an age. Oaken housed returning families keeping everyone close to the temple, and in the houses at the end of the cut passage to Andalan. The rest of the country was wild, but for now, the whole of the area was cut and cleared of weeds, and all of the wild fruits were harvested.

His home improved as Ria and Meda helped weave new bed matts which were softer to lie on, and Caleb with the help of Ham, who lived next door, repaired beds from other dwellings and he and Meda got a room each in Oaken's home, where they settled. The rest of Andalan was wild and barren, but Oaken knew in time, his people would increase again, and he hoped that all of the land would one day fill, and all of the homes would be cleared and rebuilt, back into the glorious place it had been under his father's rule. His days were spent busy with running affairs of the territory, his evenings spent walking with Ria as he gave her small tours of the places where he had grown up, and they grew closer and closer, as their life together blossomed.

He sat in the temple most days, and prayed for Shade, asking Nuada to watch over her, as he worried about her and had heard nothing at all about her, or even any rumours of a spirit, and it bothered him. In a strange way, almost like a spirit she had entered his life, and now she was gone, it was like she was a spirit that had faded away forever, and he missed her.

In Shodalt, Jenmar plotted with Melack, and Belthaz grew colder and more brutal, he too thought of Shade on a daily basis, and his hate for her intensified. He became more sadistic in his treatment of Lithana, who had taken to staying a little further from him than she had in the past, just in case he lashed out. Every evening, he would stand on the bridge above the water and stare down the river, that he knew Shade had escaped from him on, and he brooded over her, Lithana sat watching five cat's length away from him.

He leaned on the rail and watched the water flow, his hard face looking eviller in the moonlight, when he heard a creak at the other end of the bridge and turned as Lithana stood up and growled.

Shade stood, her face even whiter in the moonlight, in a tight top, and Yandalla's old black pants, which she had tied with a belt made of woven reeds. She took a pace forward, her sword already in her hand, as she faced him several long paces away. Her blue eyes shone in the darkness, and she gave a soft nod as she looked at the cat, its hair stood on end, and ready to pounce.

"Me back."

Lithana gave out a long whine of fury and readied herself to pounce, when at the side of Shade, a large black cat walked onto the bridge, its orange eyes filled with hate, as it growled. Shade smiled.

"Me got Caltha, she young, kilt old Caltha." Shade lifted her sword and prepared her stance, as Belthaz turned with a smirk and pulled out a sword and a long dagger.

"I am going to enjoy this little half breed; your skin will look good as a page in my book." Shade gave a nod.

"Skin smooth, no wrinkled like yours. Me kilt you now."

Shade gave a wild scream, and launched herself forward, and at her side, Vesta pounced. A day of reckoning had come to the apostles of Shodalt.

More Author's
From
Violet Circle Publishing

Mike Beale. (Children's Book)
Crumble's Adventures.
ISBN: 978-1-910299-06-7
Digital ISBN: 978-1-910299-08-1

Colin Smith (Play)
Heaven knows I'm Miserable Now
ISBN: 978-1-910299-16-6
Digital ISBN: 978-1-910299-23-4

Ted Morgan. (Poetry and verse)
Wordsmith's Wanderings.
ISBN: 978-1-910299-04-3
Digital ISBN: 978-1-910299-09-8
Peregrinations of the Wordsmith
ISBN: 978-1-910299-18-0
Digital ISBN: 978-1-910299-21-0
Silhouette Soldiers
ISBN: 978-1-910299-19-7
Digital ISBN: 978-1-910299-22-7
A Menu of Memories
Digital ISBN: 978-1-910299-32-6
Digital ISBN: 978-1-910299-33-3

Robin John Morgan. (Fiction/Fantasy/Slice of Life)
Heirs to the Kingdom:
Book One, The Bowman of Loxley.
ISBN: 978-1-910299-00-5
Digital ISBN: 978-1-910299-10-4
Book Two, The Lost Sword of Carnac.
ISBN: 978-1-910299-01-2
Digital ISBN: 978-1-910299-11-1

Book Three, The Darkness of Dunnottar.
ISBN: 978-1-910299-02-9
Digital ISBN: 978-1-910299-12-8
Book Four, Queen of the Violet Isle.
ISBN: 978-1-910299-03-6
Digital ISBN: 978-1-910299-13-5
Book Five, Crystals of the Mirrored Waters.
ISBN: 978-1-910299-05-0
Digital ISBN: 978-1-910299-14-2
Book Six, Last Arrow of the Woodland Realm.
ISBN: 978-1-910299-07-4
Digital ISBN: 978-1-910299-15-9
Book Seven, Bridge Of Sequana.
ISBN: 978-1-910299-17-3
Digital ISBN: 978-1-910299-20-3
Book Eight, The Circle of Darkness.
ISBN: 978-1-910299-26-5
Digital ISBN: 978-1-910299-29-6

The Curio Chronicles:
Part One, Abigail's Summer.
ISBN: 978-1-910299-27-2
Digital ISBN: 978-1-910299-28-9
Part Two, Curio's Summer.
ISBN: 978-1-910299-34-0
Digital ISBN: 978-1-910299-35-7
Part Three, Curio's Christmas.
ISBN: 978-1-910299-38-8
Digital ISBN: 978-1-910299-39-5
Part Four, Abigail's Wedding
ISBN: 978-1-910299-42-5
Digital ISBN: 978-1-910299-43-2
Part Four, Curio's Carnival
ISBN: 978-1-910299-46-3
Digital ISBN: 978-1-910299-47-0

Of The Ravens of Berengar Trilogy:
Rise Of The Raven
ISBN: 978-1-910299-30-2
Digital ISBN: 978-1-910299-31-9

The Countess Of Darkness
ISBN: 978-1-910299-40-1
Digital ISBN: 978-1-910299-41-8
Violet Stone
ISBN: 978-1-910299-44-9
Digital ISBN: 978-1-910299-45-6

The Sword For The Sky:
Oaken Of The Winds.
ISBN: 978-1-910299-48-7
Digital ISBN: 978-1-910299-49-4

Other Works.

Han's Cottage.
ISBN: 978-1-910299-36-4
Digital ISBN: 978-1-910299-37-1

Find out more about our authors and their books at
www.violetcirclepublishing.co.uk